Curse

Of

The Eraser

By

C.A. Fiebiger

Cover art work by Gary Markley

DEDICATED TO WALTER AND SHARON CLARK,

Who without them and their guided tour of the Olde Palmer Home, and ·
their introduction of Harold Palmer to me, would not have piqued my
interest in my wife's family.

CONTENTS

PREFACE

The adventure you are about to take spans the generations of all American History. Based on the family of my wife, this historical novel guides the reader through a framework of historical fact and fiction; of treasure hunts and historical finds; of people dead and alive, real and made up, honorable and despicable. It is up to the reader to discern them all.

Immigration to America in the 18th century began due to many factors: religious persecution, social upheaval, famine, and tyranny. Amongst this great group of American Immigrants was a family, the Palmers, which wanted to live in peace. Upon their arrival they were thrust into war, death, and also into what seemed to be a new beginning. Sometimes, beginnings are not what they seem- a new start into what? The New World Order! Having moved to New York State in 1792, Lawtin Palmer Sr. began life again after having served his new land in the continental army.

When Larkin Palmer received an eraser from his grandfather before he died, he didn't know what it could really do. He didn't know what power it possessed. He didn't know that it was cursed! Given as a gift from its creator to the patriarch of the family, Lawtin Sr., neither of them knew what had been placed upon it by a jealous Mason. In reality, he placed a generational feud between a righteous Christian family and the evils of Freemasonry and its plan for a New World Order. It was an invisible war, this war between the Palmers and the Masons and much like the veiled war between good and evil, ever present in our lives, and only seen by the players involved.

This is a story of international interest. Wishing to expose the evil plans of persons past and present, Larkin wanted to contribute to the family Journal in a way which brought it together for all of us to see. In so doing, Larkin showed us much more than that, how Christian families really live, and revealing his loves, his personal struggles, and his faith in Christ. This work compiles the information of over 200 years of Palmer men and their struggle to maintain balance with the great burden placed upon them. It is a proclamation of good over evil and of delivery from the domination of tyranny. Each piece of the puzzle has been placed here, each entry a shadow of the horror it proclaimed, each tale a sacrificial testimony of valor. And finally, in order that men everywhere would be free, it's last use by him. This then, is the story of the curse of –

THE ERASER!

Chapter One

The Eraser

"Larkin Palmer, quit your daydreaming and pay attention," shouted the elderly Mrs. Hall. The white-haired teacher at Five Corners Elementary School had seen this kind of behavior from many students in the past, not to mention Larkin's own father, Lawtin. Larkin, a fair haired boy of 12 years, sat up straight, inching up in the wooden desk seat and said softly with more than a bit of remorse, "I'm sorry, Mrs. Hall."

The school was on the same land that John Hoxie Jr. had given to the town for the first school house in 1797. In fact, Mrs. Hall, hired by the board in 1920, was a distant kin to Asa Carrier, the very first teacher there. It was a small world. But really, people never moved too far away from Madison County, New York. It was just too- nice. Sometimes though, and in times like this, Mrs. Hall wished she had. The Palmers had never moved away- the crazy ones, that is. They still had the same Homestead. Besides, the people all knew there was *something* about the Palmer men, but they just couldn't explain it. All the town of Brookfield knew, and spoke of it much like it was a matter of fact, not gossip, even though that was what it was.

Larkin's ancestors, the Lawtin Palmer family, had sailed aboard the Fortune, suffering severely. They moved to The Homestead in 1792, like many of the early settlers moving west. Due to his Christian beliefs, much like those of the Quakers who lived around him, Lawtin Sr. had fought, somewhat reluctantly, but more than bravely in the Revolutionary War. Afterwards though, he never really became a Quaker, but he was sympathetic to their thinking, especially separatism from the world. He was a quiet, patient man, who loved the Lord and was a keeper of the Sabbath as a Seventh Day Baptist. He died on The Homestead and is

1

buried right there with many of his family. These Palmers never wanted to move away and be involved with the rest of the world, never craved the big city and all its frills, and instead, were happy and content to be isolated there in their own little world, and safe from its temptations, trappings, and titillations, as well.

Although mature for his age, Larkin was prone to such an "attention deficit" at the end of the day during Mrs. Hall's history class. It wasn't that he didn't like history. On the contrary, he loved it so much that his mind would drift to the time of his great grandparents, the patriarchs of the family, Lawtin Sr. and his wife Nancy. They had settled the farm right after the War for Independence, and he wondered what they were like. He was even named after a friend of the family, Mr. James Larkin, a Quaker who lived in the county and whom Lawtin Senior admired because of his strong beliefs and diligence in remaining a pacifist during the war.

The last time Larkin was on the farm with his Grandfather Elias was just a month before he died. Elias Palmer was a devoted father, arborist, and to Larkin, the best grandfather a kid could have. Named after his Great Grandfather Elias, who was born there as well, he ran the farm and marketed the apples from the orchard planted in the early 1800's. Now, Elias was dead. Just before Mrs. Hall woke him from his daydream, Larkin remembered how Elias had given him a gift on that last visit and he pulled the box out of the desk slot. He had never seen an eraser in its own special box before. The top inscription said, "Nairne Erasers, 20 Cornhill, London." Opening the top carefully, he pulled the fragile note he had found out of the box, cautious not to tear the crisp, obviously old paper and read once again the words written so neatly with feather pen and ink:

Dear Sons,
In the course of a lifetime are many mistakes.
To remove the mark, this is all it takes.
With malice it never take away,
For with consequences you must pay.
Use it sparingly. Strive for perfection.
If you do, you shall receive God's election.
Destroy it not for you all shall be
the object of its hostility.
Lawtin Palmer Esq. −1770 A.D.

'Pretty cryptic,' he thought, 'why did people talk like that in olden times?' He treasured it. His grandfather had explained to him how Lawtin

Palmer Senior had given his son, Lawtin Jr., this same eraser almost 200 years before. The small, almost square, opaque gum eraser looked like new and almost pristine, in fact. It bore the marks of use on but one corner, a mere rub at that. Larkin wondered about that. Why would anyone not use an eraser? It was just an eraser! Sure it may have been the first one in the country in 1770, but why pass it down from son to son, generation to generation? 'I guess it was just a keepsake and a way to connect each generation to the one before. Interesting,' he thought, 'but why to me and not Dad?' When Mrs. Hall woke him, he quickly put it all back in his desk.

"All right class, you will want to listen to this as many of our town's founding fathers fought in this battle, including Larkin's ancestors. And now that Mr. Palmer is done daydreaming, let's read all about the Battle of Lexington. Virginia, please begin reading for the class on page 47 of our book."

"Yes, Mrs. Hall," replied the young Miss Berry in her ever present singsong voice most of the boys hated. She began the task as the clock struck its first chime announcing the four o'clock hour, "Bong, bong, bong, and bong." Virginia looked forward to get instructions from her teacher and stopped after only one line.

Mrs. Hall looked up and glared at Larkin in frustration, knowing she did not complete the lesson plans of the day. "We will pick up where we left off on Monday. Class dismissed. Mr. Palmer, please see me before you leave." The class chuckled at her remarks as they put their things away, jumped out of their desks, and ran toward the door for home and the long awaited weekend. The last to go out was Bill Clarke, and his tennis shoe made an irritating squeak on the tile floor as he turned going into the hall.

"Yes, Mrs. Hall?" quizzed the boy, wondering why she had called him to the front after his apology as he approached the huge oak desk which held all of the teacher's resources of forty-nine years of teaching.

"Larkin, this is the third time this week I've had to disrupt the class due to your incessant daydreaming. The next time I have to reprimand you, I'll be forced to speak with your father."

"Yes, Mrs. Hall. It won't happen again," he said, eyes looking straight at her as if he were more than a mere teacher, but a parental figure, because they had known each other ever since he had come to school.

Looking into the boys eyes, she could tell he meant it. "That's good. You may go."

"Goodbye, Mrs. Hall. Have a good weekend."

"You too, Larkin!" she said with an ever growing smile. She just couldn't stay upset with him. Pulling on his Yankee ball cap over his full head of light brown hair, the blue-eyed boy leapt into a run and headed for the ball fields.

Unfortunately, a dark band of clouds was looming overhead, just waiting for the boys to begin their game and drop beads of liquid life on the rain parched earth. It had been a dry spring. Larkin's father would be glad to see the rain as he had planted all the crops just weeks earlier. Larkin hung his head and thought about how his father would need help with the cows and as it was raining, he should start towards home anyways. Virginia had lagged behind the rest of the girls and observed the boy's disappointment in God's sudden release of rain on his day. Smiling, she came up behind him on her Schwinn almost scaring the pants off of him by singing out, "Want to ride home together?"
"Man, Ginny, you scared me! Sure, I may as well."

Ginny, as they called her, was much taller than many of the boys, having sprouted as girls do, earlier than most. She had blond hair, blue eyes, and dimples which cut her face deeply when she smiled. "Cute as a bug", said many of her teachers.

Larkin picked up his bike with the banana seat and hopped on. They started out towards home just in time to make it to the big oak tree on Church Street before the rain came down in buckets, the first drops hitting the dust and splashing out creating mini-mud craters. They hopped off their bikes and huddled under the expanse of the majestic oak that was older than their grandparents and maybe even their great-grandparents. Suddenly, there was a loud "crack" and lightening shot across the sky seeming to disappear into the creek down the road. Then as quickly as the rain began, it stopped.

The two kids looked at each other in amazement, shrugged their shoulders and got back on their bikes. Before they peddled off however, someone yelled, "What do you think you are doing in my yard, Palmer?" It was the relentless bully, Jim Coone. Bigger than most of the boys, Jim was a sure candidate to play center on the only sports team the school had, football. He came towards them, chest pushed out like an angry rooster protecting the hen house. Using her wit and knowing that Jim thought she was pretty, Ginny replied, "Just getting out of the rain, Jim."
"That's okay, Ginny," toned down the seventh grade terrorist. "But don't let it happen again, Palmer!"

They raced toward Academy Road never looking back at the boy and laughing all the way to Ginny's door. She lived right next to the creek on Spooner Road. Larkin really liked that and came over quite often to fish when the creek was up with her little brother, Andrew. Andy, still pudgy with baby fat and somewhat shy, but a real boy, popped his head out the door when he saw them come up on their bikes and said, "Hi, Larkin! Wanna do something?"

"No, Andy. I should go help my dad with the cows. Maybe tomorrow."

"Okay. I'll see ya," Andy replied, waving as Larkin left him and Ginny.

Peddling off towards home on Hwy 99, ball glove flapping on his handle bars, he thought about Jim Coone and how he had always harassed him. Coone did it despite the fact that a couple of years ago they had fought on the playground and Larkin had beaten the tar out of him. He thought Jim wouldn't bother him again, but obviously he had a short memory and Larkin figured he'd have to whomp him again someday. He just hated fighting, that's all, but he wondered, 'Why?'

When he peddled up to his house, he heard his dad whistle for the cows. Following the bell of the lead cow, Helga, the rest of the herd followed her up to the barn for the evening milking. Throwing down his bike by the front door, he went to his room, changed his clothes into his overalls like his dad, ran out the back and made it to the barn as the last cow went into her stall. His dad smiled when he saw him come in and said, "Hello, Son! Glad to see you. How was school?"

Not mentioning the daydreaming or the altercation with Jim Coone he just said, "Fine, Dad. Want me to start with Heidi?"

Moving his stool to the lead cow Lawtin replied, "Sure. I'll meet you in the middle of the line."

Lawtin Palmer had inherited the farm on Waterman Road from Harold Button, his wife Shirley's father. In turn, Harold had inherited it from his mother-in-law, widow of Elton Morgan, who, it was rumored, had stolen it from someone in a game of chance years ago. It was with strange circumstances that Mr. Morgan had died, seemingly that he just plain-old, as they say, "up and died" for no reason at all one night in his sleep, well before his years. Lawtin was glad to have come onto the farm, as his older brothers had inherited The Homestead from Grandpa Elias when he passed last spring. He would have had nothing if not for the generosity of the elder Button, who loved his daughter dearly. Lawtin thought about his son, Larkin, and what he someday would do with the place. Would he continue in the dairy business? Would he sell the cows and just farm the acreage? Or would he move to the city and give up on the way of life his family had held for so many years?

Hopefully, thought Lawtin, he wouldn't become like the kids that had gone to Woodstock last year. For a bunch of supposed "Peace Loving Kids", they sure wrecked the Yazgur place and were selfish.

Someday they would probably wreck the country too, he reasoned, especially if they were like their fathers. Brookfield, much like Bethel before it was invaded, had always been a pleasant place to live, despite the periodic friction caused by The Eraser. A sleepy community, it never became a hub for commerce, much to the dismay of entrepreneurs, but much to the delight of those that hated anything that would destroy the status quo. They liked the town that way. And that's the way it had stayed- all of these years. The Hippies had not even managed to place the new "lingo" upon their children as yet. Lawtin could not get used to that "far out" stuff.

Just as they were finishing the milking, Shirley came out to the barn to announce that dinner was ready. "Soup's on!"

"You didn't have to come out to tell us that, Shirley," Lawtin said to her.

As he stood up from the stool at the last cow, she came up to him and gave him a hug. "Oh, I'm just checking up on you two."

"Aw, Mom," Larkin said, as he saw her give his dad a peck on the cheek.

"We'll be up in a minute to wash up," said Lawtin and he patted her on the behind as she trotted toward the door.

As Shirley walked toward the house, Sam, their blue healer, came running up to her, tail wagging as fast as a propeller. Getting to the door, Sam just sat down on an old sofa cushion that had flown off someone's truck and there beside the patio he reclined, always grateful for a place to live.   Shirley was in her mid-thirties, as was her husband, and she was still as vigorous as she was when they had met. She fit the description of "farm wife" to a tee- resilient, resourceful, and always ready to do what was necessary to get a job done. Her hands were strong, yet not hard, still soft to the touch. Lawtin, on the other hand, was a hardened example of farm life; being strong, lean and an inspiration to Larkin. The three were truly meant for the farm life.

As Lawtin went from the kitchen to the bathroom to clean up, he saw through the hall that the dining room table was filled with a mass of papers and what looked like charts. When he got back to the kitchen, he asked Shirley about it. She said, "Grandpa Elias was working on the Palmer genealogy again before he died. I thought I'd go through some of his stuff that he left and learn more about it."

"Well, that's interesting. I know a lot about it, but don't know it all. I heard he was just about done with it."

"Yes, I think he was. There are only a few names missing and most of them are from recent family names."

Laughing Lawtin said, "Well, when you get done with it, let me know." She laughed too, knowing it was a formidable job, and they sat down at the table to say grace. Larkin plopped down in his chair and they bowed their heads. Lawtin led the prayer. "Father, for these gifts which only you provide, we give thanks. Amen."

"Amen", chimed in the other two at the table and with that Larkin grabbed a roll and his butter knife.

Chapter Two

The Boxes

The Barn Box

After dinner, Larkin went out to the barn to sit in the loft as he
often did in the cool of the evening. He'd listen to the sounds of the night,
(he loved the crickets), and watch for shooting stars. From time to time
he'd see one's sudden streak of light, and even sometimes two, an
evening. City kids would make fun of a country boy like this in the
1970's, but he didn't care.

He started to think of his grandpa Elias again. He missed him.
He never knew his Grandma Mary, because she had died before he was
born. Grandpa told him all about her and how she would bake such
wonderful pies, make maple syrup, and can enough food to last longer
than the whole winter. Grandpa said that best of all was that she had
won many ribbons at the state fair for her strawberry-rhubarb pie.
Grandpa missed her, and through Grandpa Elias, Larkin missed
Grandma Mary, too. Her maiden name was Chase. Everyone knew her,
because she was said to have a special "gift" of finding things for people,
and when she fell on the ice hit her head and died, the funeral had to be
held a full week afterwards so all the people could make it in time.
Grandpa said the saddest thing was that Larkin's Uncle Ethan, Elias'
brother, was most disturbed by it saying he was at fault and should never
be forgiven. Consequently, within three years Ethan was committed to an
insane asylum in Albany and died six months later. Just then, Larkin's
thoughts were interrupted by his mother as she called out to the barn for
him. "Larkin come in, it's time for bed."
"Aw, Mom! Its' only 10 o'clock."
"Come in! You need to rest."
With disappointment he answered, "Okay."

Larkin jumped down from a stack of straw on the second level,
straw flying all over as he landed on the dirt floor of the barn, and his foot
hit something which caused a resounding, but hollow "thud". Wondering
what it was, he grabbed a shovel from the corner and probed around to
find it. The shovel hit something metallic and he stopped, getting down
on his hands and knees to shove the dirt and straw aside. Then, he
found it. It was a tin box buried in the floor of the barn! Taking the

shovel, he pried it out of its earthen cocoon and slowly lifted the lid. He hoped it was money. But then in the midst of his exciting discovery his mother yelled, "Larkin get in here or I'm going to get your father!"

He quickly closed the lid and took it inside with him. Not letting his mother see it as he passed by her he said, "Good night, Mom. I'm going up to bed."

She didn't get up from the couch where she was sewing and his dad was already sleeping in his chair. She just said, "Wash up and brush your teeth. I'll get you up at five."

"Okay, Mom."

Larkin ran up the wood stairs, his footsteps announcing his departure to bed and then, halting suddenly, slowly closed the door to his bedroom. He went and sat the box down on the bed, pushing aside the desire to open it immediately. Going over to the dresser, he took out his Pj's and made his
way to the bathroom. After washing his face and hands, he brushed his teeth and put on his Pj's. Then he went back to his room, closed the door and turned off the light. He got out his flashlight and turned it on under the covers so as not to let the light filter out around his room. He had done this so many times before in order to listen to the Yankees after bedtime. He figured his Mom knew anyway.

Slowly and with trepidation, he opened the lid of the box- papers. He had found letters and papers. No money. No treasure. He sighed. He opened the first letter. Folded in many directions and written on all the available space, he could tell it was very old. In fact, the date that he thought he could make out was 1789. Or was it 1769? No matter, he wouldn't have time to read them all tonight in the dim light. Besides, he thought, these were an important historical find! Of course he would look at them all first, but he knew he'd have to give them to his father. Therefore, he closed up the box and put it under his bed. He'd get back to them tomorrow. He was very tired and fell asleep immediately after praying, asking God to help him sort through it all.

After helping with the chores in the morning, as was his custom on Saturdays to help his dad, Larkin had a visitor. Andy had ridden his bike down to ask him if he wanted to ride over to Beaver Creek and go swimming. Andy said, "My mom won't let me go without someone else with me. Come on, Larkin." It was unseasonably hot and the temperatures were breaking records. The offer was tempting. Larkin thought about it for a minute, but remembering the box, he turned him down and told him he'd go with him next weekend. Andy wasn't too disappointed in his answer and he rode off toward Henry Fitch's house to see if he'd go with him instead. As Larkin made his way into the house his mom asked somewhat surprised, "Aren't you going with Andy?"

"No, Mom. I'm going to my room and read."

This was not unusual for him. He was an avid reader. Anything he could get his hands on and especially anything historical. He was always going to the library at school. Larkin was running out of options there though, having read almost every book, all 3,479 of them! Miss Thompson, the young librarian, apologized to him often and always let him know when new books were received. 'The contents of this box,' he thought, 'didn't even compare and was going to be interesting reading!'

Larkin pulled the barn box out from under the bed and took a closer look at it in the light. It looked to be an old cracker tin of some sorts. Not any he knew of though. Where did it come from? Why did someone bury it in the barn? How long had it been there and who put it there? Opening it again, he started to pull out each document and placed them individually on his neatly made bed. He briefly looked at each item as he did this and counted how many there were in total. By the time he was done there were fifteen documents. Larkin went over to his student desk by the window that he used for studying and got out a tablet and pencil. He began with the first item he placed on the bed and opened it. He labeled it #1 on the tablet and on the documents' bottom corner. Then, he began to read. He couldn't believe it! This letter was written to his Great Grandpa Lawtin Palmer Senior in 1769 and it was all the way from England! He had a hard time making out much of the handwriting, but he surmised that he was good friends with the man from England whose name was Colonel Wm. Edmeston. He recognized that name. Lots of places were named after him. He placed it back in the box. One by one he read and marked them all, finally coming to one dated 1770 from a Mr. Edward Nairne of London. "That name sounds familiar", he said to himself out loud. Larkin read,

"Please be advised my dear friend, that my partner and former apprentice has gone quite mad, having joined the Illuminists. We should no longer invest in any of his holdings nor endeavors. We have since parted company and he has established a business a mere two doors down from ours! He has, from reports of others to me, even gone so far as to place a curse upon me and my family and on every eraser he helped me produce. What that may accomplish is of a bit of amusement to me. What I do know is that we must not entertain nor consider joining these who wish to control us by the power of the evil one."

It went on to speak of other things and even mentioned Benjamin Franklin and his home in London. Larkin placed it with the other documents when he finished reading it. Being done with his work, he put his list with it all in the box. When he was about to go and give it to his father all of a sudden he thought, 'Eraser? *He placed a curse on every eraser he helped him produce?!'* Larkin opened the box again and removed the top letter. He read it again. Yes! That was what it said. This Mr. Nairne was the one who had made The Eraser in the box! The Eraser in the box he got from his Grandpa Elias! And it had a curse on it! He put the letter back in the box again and slammed the lid shut. He was dumbfounded. He wanted to see The Eraser- right now! But it was at school in his desk. What should he do? His dad didn't know he had The Eraser. His dad didn't know he had the box. Heck, his dad didn't know anything! What was he going to do? And the note in the Eraser Box, what did it mean? Was Great Grandpa Lawtin Senior trying to tell him something? Did he try to warn the whole family of something? Did anyone else know about this or was Grandpa Elias the last to know? Larkin had to know!

It was getting late. Larkin had spent the entire afternoon and early evening in his room with the box. He came downstairs to find his mom at the stove making homemade applesauce and it smelled good, and as he was hungry, it almost distracted him from the thought of his new discovery. His dad was out in the barn finishing up the milking. Percy Alby, the hired man, had come by to give him a hand and talk to Lawtin about the crops and first haying. It was way past time for that because it was so dry. None of that mattered to Larkin now. He asked his mom, "Mom, do you know anything that is weird or unusual about our family? I mean, in the past?"

Looking up from the pot she was stirring she answered, "Why, no Larkin, not too unusual. Why do you ask?"

"Oh, nothing. I was just wondering, that's all."

"Well, that's a funny question to ask just right out of the blue," she said.

"Well," he thought about it for a moment and then changed his mind about continuing, "I guess I was just wondering."

"Okay, but if you want to know anything just ask and we'll see if we can answer your questions."

Larkin walked out the door to go to the barn and Shirley watched him with a puzzled, yet worried look on her face. He had been acting funny lately.

As he approached his dad, Lawtin came up to him with Percy. "Say Larkin, Percy tells me your uncle would like to hire the two of you to rebuild the stone mail box over at The Homestead after you get out of school this summer. He said he'd pay two hundred fifty dollars for you to split. It will be hard work. It's stone you know and has been there for years on that old rock wall."

Larkin remembered it well. He used to hit baseballs toward that direction and the old wall worked great as an outfield fence. Always ready for an opportunity to make some money, he jumped at the chance. "Sure. I wanted to go out to see the place anyway. It's only three miles away, but we never go over there since Grandpa died." He was right.

Lawtin raised an eyebrow and looked at Percy. "Yeah, you're right, Son." He redirected his speech avoiding commenting on Larkin's statement any further. "So Percy, you'll tell my brother you'll be out there and he has a deal? Will you pick Larkin up on your way out?"

"Sure will, Lawtin. I'll be here by six o'clock and we'll work until it gets too hot or we are at a good stopping point."

Turning to leave and addressing Larkin, Percy said, "I'll see you in a couple of weeks."

On Monday morning, Larkin rode his bike to school as fast as he could, not even noticing the fact that Mr. Hobbs had just hayed the field next door and its' sweet smells of clover. He was the first one in the door and he went to his desk throwing his books and homework on the floor as he sat down with a thud and reached into his desk to get The Eraser. He opened the box again. This time when he looked at it, he looked at it with a totally different eye. He examined it as if he had it under a microscope, holding it up to the light, turning it from side to side and looking for marks and smudges. His second opinion was the same as the first time he saw it. It seemed like new, with one corner having a small rub. That's it. He read the note again. Nothing new there either and maybe in time he'd understand the verses. Nothing else was written on it and nothing else was placed in the box. He looked at the inside and outside of the box- nothing. He had no clues, except the obvious, and it wasn't clear at all!

When he got home from school that day, saying "hi" to his mom on the way through the kitchen and going up to his room, he placed The Eraser box on top of the, "Barn Box" as he now called it, under the bed. When he received it from Grandpa Elias, he had taken The Eraser to school thinking he'd use it there like normal kids used erasers, but not *this* one. He wondered if the other Palmers found out about the curse, or if their fathers or grandfathers had told them about it and how. 'Grandpa Elias sure didn't think anything about it or he would have surely told me,' thought Larkin. He wondered what the curse was or effect it had. He figured –someday- he'd find out or ask his dad all about it.

Larkin got up from the floor in his bedroom and went down the hall to the stairs. As he turned at the first step he looked out the window. He had never noticed it before, but from this spot high up on the second floor and through the trees on the hill of Waterman Road he could see the tops of the trees at the Old Homestead on Chase Road. The trees there were the oldest ones around as Great Grandpa Lawtin Sr. had saved all the trees on the perimeter of the farm for posterity. All the others, of course, had been cut for fuel and for lumber for the houses, and to clear the fields. It was a beautiful view. They used to call it "Button Hill" and there was even a falls of the same name nearby. He was grateful that he lived in such a wonderful part of the world, isolated from the hustle of the big city and the life people thought they might like there. He stood there daydreaming again about what it was like to have lived on the farm, so long ago. Then once again, his mom broke the dream apart. "Larkin, come down and set the table."

"I'll be right down, Mom."

She smiled as she heard him scamper down the stairs.

When he got down to the kitchen, his mom handed him the plates and said, "Thanks, *Honey*."

"Aw, Mom, don't call me that."

She changed the subject as he began to set the table. "You know that question you asked me last night? You know, about the family?"

"Yeah?" He sat the last plate down at his father's place.

"Well, there is something. But you can't tell your dad I told you. Okay?"

"Okay."

"I heard, and this is all I know, I heard that years ago people said that there was something weird about all of the men in the family and like they had a secret or something. Not that it was bad or anything, but as if they had something they didn't ever want to talk about or admit. It was like a feeling passed down from generation to generation."

Larkin's hair stood on end. That was it! *It was passed down from generation to generation! THE ERASER!* Larkin sat down in his chair and just stared forward and said, "Thanks." But what was it that The Eraser *did*? What was it? Was this some kind of game?

Larkin woke the next morning tired from a restless night spent thinking about what his mom had revealed. He also wondered if it had affected all the other Palmer men before him this way. Obviously, his dad was spared the knowledge of this. Why his grandpa did this, why he gave *him* the Eraser, he may never know. Maybe he felt his dad couldn't handle it. What Larkin did know, is that it placed a heavy, unexpected burden upon him.

As the days passed and spring went into summer and being the dreamer he was, he forgot about it, this eraser curse, being all wrapped up in the final days of school. He was glad to be done with the seventh grade. He had grown almost four inches this past year. He was as tall as his mother at five foot eight inches. His dad was about six feet and he figured he'd catch up to him in the next couple of years. He was lanky, but strong, using his God given health to work on the farm like a man.

Being an only child, he had no one to help him help his dad with the chores. It wasn't a burden and he enjoyed working alongside his dad and he was ready to be out for the summer.

On the last day of school, Ginny came up to him on the playground. "My sister is going to be gone for the summer visiting family in Iowa. I won't have a lot to do without her home. Can I ride my bike over to your house sometimes and hang out? I could bring Andy!"

Taken aback by this request, Larkin was actually quite pleased. He had liked Ginny, but never thought she would want to be seen with him. Playing it cool he just said, "Sure. But call first to make sure I'm around, because I have a job to do at The Homestead this summer."

"Okay. I'll be seeing you. Bye, Larkin."
"Bye, Ginny."
Larkin turned to go back to the ball fields with a big smile on his face!

The Mail Box

Percy knocked on the back door just as Larkin was putting his cereal bowl in the sink. He asked through the screen door, "Ready to go Larkin?"

"You bet, Sir!"

"You don't have to call me "Sir". Percy will do."

"Okay."

They walked out to the truck and got in. The old black man, who was in excellent shape for his age, about sixty, cranked up the rickety Studebaker half-ton and put it into gear. They started off down the road with a puff of white smoke coming out of the tailpipe. Larkin noticed, but didn't say anything. Half of the trucks in town were that way, all in need of a ring job and no one caring a bit. They passed the red barn on Five Corners and he looked forward to the corner at Chase road to see the big trees that surrounded the property of The Homestead. He loved those trees.

When they arrived at The Homestead, Percy pulled up to the mailbox on the house side of the yard. The land was flat there with no barrow-pit. They got out and let the tailgate down, exposing all the mason's tools necessary to complete the job. When Percy was younger he worked as a hod-carrier and then a mason in the big city. He didn't last too long there, just not caring for it or the people, he was sad to say, and he came home in a few years to the life to which he was accustomed . Larkin looked up to see his Uncle Tom coming from the house. He was the older brother of his dad. "Hi, you two. How are you?"

"Just fine, Mr. Tom," said Percy.

"Hi, Uncle Tom," said Larkin.

"You've got a big job here guys. Grandpa Elias did a good job on the place, and he even partially rebuilt the wall, but he let this mail box go for some reason. Larkin, your Uncle Harry and I don't have time to deal with it, so I figured you two could handle it."

"Yes, Sir, we sure can." responded Percy, "We should be done in a couple of days."

"That sounds good. Let me know if you need anything."

"Shouldn't, but thanks."

Tom walked off toward the bee hives.

"Grab a pair of gloves there, Larkin. We have to take this apart before we can put it back together," said Percy with the authority of an experienced hand.

With that, Percy grabbed a hammer and a chisel, and meandered over to the mail box. None of the stones on the fence were put together with mortar, just the ones which held the mailbox in place. He started to tear it apart ever so slowly, stone by stone. After he pried one apart, he'd direct Larkin to remove it and if it had cement on it, to chisel it off before setting it aside in a special place as Percy directed. In a couple of hours the mailbox was almost torn down to the bottom. Percy said, "This is unusual. There's never a false top piece like this a foot from the bottom." He removed it and there underneath was a box- another cracker box. Larkin looked at the box in disbelief because it was exactly like the barn box! Percy said, "Why don't you take that out of there so we can get a look at it."

Larkin took it out of its coffin of limestone and went over to the tailgate and sat it down. Percy walked over, took off his gloves and pointing to the box he said, "Seeing as you're kin, why don't you open it up?"

An excited Larkin said, "Yes, Sir!" Larkin did just like he had the month before in the barn and lifted the lid ever so carefully. Inside the tin were articles just like before; papers. No money- just papers. They looked at each other and simultaneously said, "No treasure!" They laughed.

Ready for a break, they sat on the tailgate and sipped a cup of water. Larkin looked through the box with Percy reading along over his shoulder and they saw only clippings from newspapers. What was odd is that by looking at the dates, they progressed in time each back about 40-50 years apart. What was also weird was that they each told a story of someone's passing. Most were obituaries. One was an article. In total there were seven. Larkin asked Percy, "Do you think Uncle Tom would mind if I took this home with me tonight before I gave it to him?"
"I reckon not."

They worked for a bit longer and being pretty tired, the two loaded their tools and got into the truck. Percy figured they could put the mail box back together tomorrow. But, he'd put a new metal farm style mailbox into the opening this time. It would last longer that way. Percy dropped Larkin off at his house and said, "See you same time in the morning."
"Bye, Percy." Off he drove in the Studebaker, and trailing along behind, white smoke pouring out the tail pipe.

Larkin was glad to see that his dad was still out in the fields and his mom had left him a note saying she had gone to the store. He ran upstairs to his room and repeated what he had done the last time with the barn box. He got a piece of paper off his tablet and catalogued each piece. This time he copied each document entirely, because if he had to give the Mail Box to his uncles, he wanted to be prepared. Then, as before, he read each of them in chronological order and in detail:

Sept. 11, 1807– The Pilot– Obituary
Mr. Alpheus Hitchcock– School Teacher – Today convicted felon Alpheus Hitchcock was hung by the neck and was brought to his eternal rest by order of the court for the murder of his wife after falling in love with his student Lois Andrus. –Jeremiah Whipple–Sheriff.

Jan. 12, 1813– The Pilot–Obituary
Jeremiah Button– Of Brookfield– Infant son of Mr. & Mrs. John Button died as a result of the epidemic that has taken the lives of many of the young, infirm, and aged. He was buried at the Palmer Cemetery.

Sept. 12, 1827– Madison County Eagle– Article
The abduction, disappearance, and presumed murder of Wm. Morgan has led to the closing of the Masonic Lodge in De Ruyter. There was much to do about it and all the details have not been forthcoming from the leaders thereof.

March 23, 1855– The Madison Observer– Obituary
Mr. Moses Johnson– Of Brookfield– Found murdered in his home– Laid to rest this day. May God find justice where man cannot.

February 14, 1901– Hamilton Republican– Obituary
Conagwasa– An Oneida Indian– Of Hamilton– A "Prayer Indian" of Catholic faith and of means in the community was found dead of no apparent cause. He was purportedly a relative of the famous Indian Chief Abram Antone. Laid to rest in the Catholic cemetery.

March 19, 1929– Hamilton Republican–Obituary
Elton Morgan– –Of Brookfield– Cause of death unknown. Was interred this day on the family plot. –Madison County Coroner

June 12, 1945–Oneida Dispatch–Obituary
Sgt. John Clinton– Of Oneida– Great– great– great Grandson of Gov. Wm. Clinton serving in the Pacific shot and killed at Corregidor. Buried at the family plot with military honors.

When he finished reading them all, he lowered his hands to his lap and just said, "Huh. I wonder what all of these mean?" As far as he knew, they were not related, except maybe the Morgans, nor were they even friends of the family. He picked up the clippings and placed them into the "Mail Box" as he had come to call it. He shoved it under his bed with the other two boxes as he heard his mom come in and the screen door slam shut.

"Larkin," she yelled upstairs, "will you help me put away the groceries?"

"Coming, Mom." He ran down the stairs and as he flew past the table in the dining room a piece of paper dropped to his feet. He stopped to pick it up. As he did he read, "Mr. & Mrs. John Button". He paused for a second before he sat it down, remembering the obit he had read just a minute or two before.

"Larkin?" his mom queried.

"Be right there, Mom. I knocked some of your stuff off of the table. I put it back."

"Okay, but come on now, please. I want to get this done before your dad comes in for dinner."

During dinner Larkin was very quiet. His parents noticed, but didn't say anything. Their conversation centered on the farm, the chores of the day and plans for tomorrow. The same old stuff and Larkin could only think of the Mail Box. Deeply engrossed in this thought his dad broke the dream and asked, "Larkin, how's that mail box coming over at your uncle's?"

Larkin came out of it slowly and said, "Huh?"

His dad smiled and said, "You must be tired. I asked how the mail box was coming."

"Oh, just fine, Dad. We should finish it tomorrow, Percy said."

"Good. Do a good job for your uncles."

"Oh, we will. Say Dad, when was the last time anyone did anything with that mail box?"

"If I remember right, your Great Grandpa Elias rebuilt it right after the First World War. Some drunken soldier hit it with his truck and he had to fix it."

"That's funny."

"Your Great Grandpa didn't think so, and if I remember right, I think your Grandpa Elias helped him, too."

"Really? Well, it shouldn't need fixing again for a long time. Can I be excused?"

Looking at his mother who would normally have him dry the dishes she answered, "Go ahead. I'll take care of it tonight."

"Thanks, Mom." She knew he was tired from a rather hard day and could see it in his eyes.

When he got to his room he pulled the "Mail Box" from under the bed. He now knew his Grandpa had placed it in under the mail box. He now knew that his Grandpa wanted him to find it. Not his dad, nor his uncles, but him and him alone. He wanted him to find it like it went with The Eraser box. He wanted him to find it like the Barn Box. 'Wait a minute' he thought, 'did he bury the Barn Box too?' They all went together like a piece of a puzzle. And each was critical to understanding the whole. Then, Larkin pulled The Eraser box out from under the bed. He looked at the top and ran his fingers over the edges. Then it hit him! The Mail Box had *obituaries!* The Eraser created *death*! It did evil things! But- how? That was the one part of the puzzle still missing. Where would he find the answer? Why was everything so cryptic? Why didn't his grandpa just tell him? Was he ashamed? Didn't he know? What was he going to do with the Mail Box? Give it back to his uncle or keep it? With these questions flying around in his head it was a wonder he ever got to sleep.

In the morning, Larkin watched out the window for Percy to arrive and when he did, he ran out and hopped into the pickup with him, the boy holding onto the Mail Box with both hands. "Good morning, Larkin." Percy said.

"Good morning." Larkin was in a somber mood. He didn't know what to do. Percy could tell.

"I see you brought the box."

"Yeah."

"Have you decided what to do about it?"

"Well, I know that it is legally my Uncle Tom's, but after thinking about it, I know my Grandpa Elias wanted me to have it. I found out he put it there after the First World War. And he purposely didn't fix the mail box knowing I'd be the one to find it. He knew and he *wanted* me to find it."

"So what are you going to do?"

"I think I'm going to keep it."

"I thought so."

They arrived at the wall just as the sun was starting to warm the air. The dew was rising from the grass evaporating in clouds of fog under the trees. When Larkin got out, he left the Mail Box in the truck and walked to the tailgate. The bottoms of his blue jeans got wet from the dew. The grass showed every step as he walked across it like steps in sand. When he saw this, he took his foot and wrote his name on the rich green lawn. Percy just smiled seeing the boy's demeanor change and the weight of the box lifted from him for just one moment.

They worked hard that day. By noon Percy had placed the new metal farm style mail box on its platform. Although Percy was older than his dad, he worked like a man half his age. Larkin had a new found respect for Percy. Being a hod carrier was hard work! Mixing the mortar by hand and keeping up with him as he laid the stone was not easy. Percy laughed when Larkin opened a bag of mortar and dropped it to the ground, a billow of grey mix flying up to his face. Larkin didn't even react to it and just kept going, even though it left his hair and shoulders covered in a fine layer of dust. Percy laughed and said, "It's time for a break. Let's sit."

Larkin brushed his shoulders and hair with his hand, dust flying into the air like the smoke from the Studebaker. He wiped the dust off his face with a bandana. Then, Percy and Larkin took a seat on the tailgate and watched Larkin's Uncle Tom work with the honey bees. He moved slowly and cautiously with the colony showing respect for them and they trusted him. In all the years Larkin could remember, Tom had never been stung. Tom finished what he had been doing and he saw them sitting on the tailgate and came over to check on the progress. "Looks like you're almost finished!" He took off his gloves and funny hat, exposing his graying hair and receding hairline.

"Yes, Uncle," said Larkin. "We'll have it done in a couple of hours."

"Don't be so sure," said Percy. "This is where it gets tricky. We have a lot of fitting to do from here on out and each piece has to be cut to fit. It'll take some time."

Tom smiled and said, "If you need anything to drink there's plenty of cold sodas in the ice box in the garage. Help yourselves. I have to go to town and pick up some parts for the John Deere."

"Thanks, Mr. Tom," said Percy. "Let's get back to work, Larkin."

They hopped off the tailgate and put on their gloves. Percy noticed Larkin had not mentioned the "Mail Box".

Larkin saw that they were running out of stone and that with each selection it made it more difficult to find what they needed to complete the mail box. The pile of stone on the lawn was getting smaller and smaller. Percy started to break some of the pieces in order to get them to fit the design. Larkin watched the experience of the old mason's hands show through with each cut. He was amazed by it and was in awe of Percy's skill. Percy said to Larkin, "I'd like to show you something Larkin. Come here." Percy waited for him to step next to him and said, "I left this trap door in the bottom front of the base, just in case you'd like to put the "mail box" back in here someday."

"Great idea, Percy. You never know do you?"

Percy admired this boy and his loyalty to his family saying, "No, you never know."

It all came together and by three o'clock they were done. The new Mail Box was beautiful! In fact, Larkin thought it was a work of art. In reality, it was. "Want a bottle of soda, Percy?" Larkin asked him.

"Sure. Let's take a break before we load up."

Larkin walked up to the garage and went in. He saw the refrigerator and opened the door and found- Coke and root beer. He took two Cokes. Looking for an opener, he noticed an old fashioned ice box in the corner. It had an opener attached to its side. Placing each bottle in it and lifting up he had them opened quickly. He turned and started to walk away, but then it hit him, an *ice box?* He went back and set the cokes on the top of the old wooden cabinet. He opened the door and peered in. It was empty, except for cob webs and dust. It must have been in the garage for a long time now. Seeing nothing, he picked up the Cokes and went back out to the truck. Percy asked, "What took so long?"

"Oh, there was an old ice box in the garage and I took a look at it."

"Oh yeah? They are kind of neat aren't they? Glad we don't have those any more. I hated having to drain the water out of the drawer. That was my job."

"Drawer?"

"Yeah. On the bottom."

Larkin got up and ran toward the garage, leaving Percy sitting on the tailgate alone and clueless. After his eyes adjusted from the bright sun outside to the darkness of the closed garage, he looked at the bottom of the ice box. In the shadows of the corner he had not noticed the drawer. It looked like one piece of wood trim, but as he saw it now, there was a place on the front where there used to be a handle. It was gone. He took out his pocket knife and pried it open. When he saw it, he could not believe his eyes- another box!

The Ice Box

By this time Percy was standing behind him. "I was wondering where you had disappeared to. Find something?" he asked.

"Yeah. Another box."

Larkin lifted it out of the ice box drawer. It was old, dusty, and much larger than the other two boxes, but of the same style and material. Rather than open it there, Larkin carried it out to the truck first. He sat on the tailgate and Percy did the same. They were both excited! "Think there's treasure this time?" asked Percy.

"To tell you the truth Percy, I don't think there will be." Larkin opened the box to find a journal. He lifted it out of the box and looked at the cover. On it read, "The Journal".

"My, oh my, that looks old," said Percy.

Just then, Uncle Tom's truck came down the road. Larkin looked at Percy and he quickly put the Journal in the box. Jumping down from the tailgate, he placed it in the cab with the Mail Box, covering them with his jacket. He shut the door with a slam and came to the back of the truck just as Tom pulled up beside them. "Percy, I must say that you have outdone yourself this time. It is just beautiful."

"Thank you, Mr. Tom, but half of the credit goes to my helper here."

"Aw, Percy, you did it."

"Regardless, you two earned your keep. Here's the wages I promised." Tom handed Percy the money in cash.

Percy said, "Thank you. If you ever need the wall repaired let me know."

"You never know, Percy. I'll keep that in mind."

Tom got back in his truck and drove toward the barn. Percy walked over and started to load up. Larkin gave him a hand and the two were done quickly. Before they drove away, Percy took the money out of the front pocket of his overalls and counted out half. Handing it to Larkin he said, "There's your part of the take."

"You don't have to give me half. You did the work."

"No, Larkin, you did the *hard part* of the work."

"Thanks." He took the money.

"What are you going to do about this new box?"

Slowly Larkin said, "I'll have to think on it for a bit."

"I understand." Starting up the truck, Percy headed back to drop Larkin off at his house.

When they got back to Larkin's place, his dad was out working in the barn. "Oh man, there's my dad!" Larkin exclaimed.
"Don't worry. I'll take care of that," Percy said.
"Thanks, Percy! See ya."

Running interference for him, Percy got out of the truck and went over to the barn to speak with Lawtin. Larkin picked up the boxes and ran to the house. Opening the back door slowly and taking a breath of air from his run, he noticed his mom was in the dining room working on the genealogy. 'Great,' he thought, 'how am I going to get past her with these boxes?' He went over to the pantry, took out a grocery sack and placed them in it. Setting them on a shelf, he placed some old magazines on top of it to make it look like it was supposed to be there. He walked into the dining room and pulled the money he made out of his pocket. Showing it to his mom, he said, "Look Mom! I made a hundred and twenty-five dollars!"
"What are you going to do with it?" she asked.
"I think I'll save it for a car."
"A car? You're only in the seventh grade!"
"Eighth grade Mom, eighth grade, remember? Besides, it'll take a while to save up enough." Changing the subject he remembered what he saw the other day on the table. He asked her, "Say Mom, could I help you with this somehow?"
"Why Larkin, I didn't know you had an interest in genealogy. Sure, let me show you all about it."

They spent the next hour or so pouring over it before Lawtin came in from the barn. They heard him washing his hands in the kitchen. Coming into the dining room wiping his hands with a towel he came up to Larkin and said, "What are you doing in here? Has she got you all wrapped up in this now, too?"
"Dad, this is real interesting. Mom's got almost all the names and dates all the way back to Lawtin Senior."
Walking back to the kitchen, he pronounced, "A waste of time if you ask me."
Larkin looked at his mom and she whispered waving her hand, "Don't worry about him. We'll find time to do this together."
Calling from the kitchen Lawtin asked, "What's for dinner?"
"There's a casserole in the oven. It should be about done."
"Hungry?" she asked Larkin.
"Man, am I ever!" And they went out to the kitchen to eat.

After they said grace, Lawtin took a bite and said to Shirley, "This is pretty good."

"Do you doubt me?"

"Mom, you're a real good cook," interjected Larkin.

Lawtin asked his son, "I heard from Percy that you finished the mail box and Uncle Tom paid you. What are you going to do with your portion of the money?"

Before Larkin could answer his mother said, "He said he's going to save it- for a car!"

"A car? You're only in the seventh grade!"

Laughing, Shirley said, "Eighth grade. Besides, he said it would take a while to save for the one he wants." Larkin didn't say a word, but smiled at his mom for the eighth grade comment.

"Well that sounds like a good idea to me. That way you'll have your own wheels and you won't have to take the truck when we might need it." Larkin was thrilled at his dad's response. Hopefully, nothing would get in the way of his plans like- life.

After they cleaned up the dishes, Larkin went back into the dining room to look at the chart. He recognized some of the names on it. Some of them he had never heard of, like Denton, Dalton, and Fones, and many shirt-tail relatives that had moved away, which Larkin couldn't understand. Why would anyone want to move away? His mom was still in the kitchen and he wanted her to leave so he could go retrieve the boxes. Fortunately, his dad called her from the back porch to come sit with him on the swing as was their summer time custom. Hearing this, he went back to the pantry and picked up the bag. Moving slowly so they would not hear the creaking of the old wood floor, he stealth fully made his way back to the hall and up the stairs to his room. 'Whew', he said to himself.

When he got into his room, he took the boxes out of the bag. He placed the "Mail Box" back under his bed with the "Barn Box" and the "Eraser Box". He took the "Ice Box" out and sat it on the bed. Once again, he opened it. He looked a little closer at the cover of the Journal this time. It was made of brown leather, with stitched binding about two inches wide. Someone had taken the time to stamp the leather with the words, "The Journal". It was very well done and it looked to be very old. When he opened it he was right, for there on the first page he read, "*A Journal of the men of the Family Palmer*, begun this first day of February, 1813 AD." 'That's odd,' he thought, 'why would someone begin a Journal for a family to contribute to? And who?' Opening it past the first page, his heart began to beat hard. He could almost hear it in his chest. The suspense was killing him. Not literally, but his questions may now finally begin to be answered, and he was excited. Before he read it, he thumbed through to see how many pages there were and if anything was written on them. It looked like there was about one hundred pieces of old parchment bound together and about one third were written upon.

He flipped back to the beginning and read:

"This Journal is begun with the intention to inform my beloved family, of the events and horrors of the curse of The Eraser. I contribute here my part, after becoming aware of its necessity, and as a means to convey a warning to future generations. I pray that each of you do likewise. However, to confuse or deter those that may do evil, there are five boxes to fit the puzzle and all, you must find. May God be with you."
Lawtin Palmer Sr. – 1813

Larkin was getting tired. 'Great,' he thought, '*five boxes,* and I only have four.' But he knew he didn't have time to read it all tonight. With just that much information, which made him more than a bit uneasy and nervous, he placed it back in the Ice Box and under the bed. He had so much to learn, about his family, and about- The Eraser! He didn't want the rest of the family to worry. Larkin decided to keep it to himself and bear the burden that his family- his ancestors, and the guy named Nairne, had placed upon him. He would learn all he could about it and in the meanwhile, not to use The Eraser! It was to be an adventure into the past and one he would and could not forget!

The Glory Box

The next morning Larkin got up to find his dad had already left to hay the field with Percy. "Mom, why did dad leave without me?"

"He felt sorry for you and wanted to let you sleep. Besides, he thought you and I could spend some time together and look at the genealogy today."

"Great!"

"If you want, I left a biscuit and some eggs out in the kitchen for you."

"Thanks, Mom." He went out and gobbled it down fast so he could get back into the dining room.

When he returned his mother asked him, "Will you help me move the Glory Box to the corner over there?"

"The what?"

"The chest your Grandpa Elias left me when he died. It's been in the family for years and it's too heavy for me to lift. Your dad just sat it there when we got it, but I'd like to move it by the window."

"No, I mean, what did you call it?"

"The Glory Box. This one was made by a German cabinet maker in Pennsylvania about 1810 or so. It has Sulfur inlay. I heard it is quite rare. They called them "Glory Boxes" because it was like a hope chest for women waiting to be married. This one was Denton Palmer's wife's. I think her name was Abby. Here, let me look." Going over to the chart on the table she traced it back and pointed saying, "Yes, see here. It was Abigail Palmer's, "Glory Box.""

Looking at the chart, Larkin saw what he thought to be a clue. The name, "R. Button", was circled. Why? "Mom, what's in the box?" he asked her.

"Lots of keepsakes that the family has placed in it throughout the years. For instance; birth certificates, the family Bible, medals from wars and stuff like that. It has been somewhat helpful in doing this work."

"Any treasure?"

She laughed and said, "Well not much of that, but there are a couple of silver dollars."

"Can I look?"

"Sure go ahead, but I have most of it out on the table and floor."

Larkin thought, 'This is it- the last of the five boxes!' He went over to it and looked at the intricate detail in the inlay and rubbed his hand along the cool, smooth ivory. He saw how the maker had placed a shelf and little compartments to store things in. Then he saw it! Carved on the top center of the design on the shelf was what appeared to be a *button*? 'Ironic,' he thought, 'a button and R. Button.' He pushed it. Nothing happened. It didn't even move. His mom saw what he did and said, "Looking for something?"

"I saw that button there and thought there might be a secret compartment, but when I pushed it, nothing happened."

"You're right in thinking that. Sometimes they would place secret compartments in these and desks of the period, kind of like, safes. There weren't as many banks around then, so people had to have a place to hide valuables. I don't think there's one in this box."

"Too bad, Mom."

He pushed it again and then, something popped open! There in the bottom of the trunk, was a square with a flap on the corner next to the button side of the trunk. He lifted it to open the trap door the rest of the way and under it was a small box! He recognized the material. It was the same as The Eraser Box! Even though he was excited and about to explode, he tried not to draw attention to himself and sat down on the floor by the Glory Box. He opened the box and inside was an old piece of paper. Carefully, he lifted it out. He recognized the handwriting on it- it was Nairne's! Unfolding it he began to read,

"My Dear Lawtin, It is with sadness that I must write this post to you. There have been reports to me that much has come of this "curse" placed upon us and our produce. I have since spoken with the madman, and he has told me the nature of it. Be advised it is nothing to trifle with. The curse he placed has this effect: If a man places a name on paper and erases it with malice or hate, the person whose name disappears shall also disappear. That person will die. Secondly, if any man shall destroy The Eraser he shall be destroyed. He shall die. And last of all, if The Eraser is not passed down from generation to generation, then the family, it too− shall die. The results here have been horrific. People now believe! The amusement I felt upon hearing it is no more. I, too, have lost family. I have tried my best to retain as many of the accursed things myself so fewer are affected. Heed my warning dear friend and do what must be done. There is no removal of this curse as the madman himself has also died, being disposed of by his mentor Weishaupt. Please forgive me for sending you such a terrible gift. I am most sincerely sorry. Respectfully, Edward."

So that was it! The last box! The "Glory Box". He now knew it all. He understood the note from Lawtin Senior! No, he didn't know it all- not all. He still had not read of the Journal and its horrors. He had an idea of what was in it and he didn't look forward to the task, because, he thought, that is what has happened here, to *my* ancestors. But he knew he must. 'Someday', he thought again. He stuck the "Glory Box", which was the same size as The Eraser Box, into his pants pocket. His mom didn't notice.

The day was one of historical adventure for Larkin. He saw all the generations of Palmers come to life as his mother showed him this or that item from her Glory Box that connected to a name on the family tree. Benjamin Palmer left his map to buried treasure on the farm. Hanna Palmer left a poem she wrote in the fifth grade about trees. And Samuel Palmer, well, he left a letter he received from Abraham Lincoln congratulating him on his appointment as Republican committee chair of the county. "Wow, Mom, that letter is probably worth a lot of money! This *is* a treasure chest."

"It certainly is, and in more ways than one."

He went over by her and asked, "Say Mom, can I make a copy of that treasure map of Benjamin's? He might have left something neat!"

"Do you really think so?"

"You never know."

"Okay, but before you dig anything up, you better ask your Uncles for permission first."

"Okay."

He picked up the paper from the past and placed it on the window pane. Taking a piece of tracing paper he used for art class, he traced the images exactly. He recognized the layout of The Homestead, except that the original house that Lawtin Senior had built there was still on the map and the existing house was not. All that remained of the original one was the footings, which you could still see sticking up just enough to make the grass seem higher, like ridges on the earth. The outline was very clear to the naked eye. The phone rang. He ran to the kitchen to pick it up. "Hello?"

"Is that you, Larkin?"

"Yeah, is that you Ginny?"

"Yeah. Say, can I come over?"

"As a matter of fact I have something fun to do. Want to come along?"

"Sure. What is it?"

"Treasure hunting!"

"Neat! I'll be right there." They both hung up the phone. They knew where to meet.

His mom overheard the conversation and reminded him, "Make sure you ask your uncles before you dig!"

"I will, Mom. See you in time for supper." He ran out of the room!

The Treasure Box

First, Larkin went to his room and placed the Glory Box with the others. Then, he went out to the barn to retrieve his bike. He figured he could borrow a shovel from his uncle. He put the map into his pocket and went to wait for Ginny by Stanbro Road at the end of the fence line like he had so many times before. From there, it was only about a mile to The Homestead, so it wouldn't take long to get there. However, Ginny arrived there first and she turned off toward Academy Road. Larkin waved for her to wait for him to come down by her. No sense in her riding back and forth. He got there and they started riding toward his uncle's. "Where are we going?" she asked.

"The Homestead. I found a treasure map from a dead relative of mine and I thought we'd check it out."

"Really? How exciting," she squealed. He wondered why he brought her along. By the time they got there, he was worn out from all the questions and not the riding. What was his name? When did he die? Where did he live? What did he bury? Do you think he was nice?

'Man,' he thought, 'girls are weird.'

Seeing no one around when they arrived, Larkin went to the door and knocked. He knew that his oldest uncle, Harry, would be there. He was about seventy years old and a full thirty years older than his dad. He didn't do much, because he had gotten hurt on the tractor about ten years before. Harry yelled, "Come on in."

"Hi, Uncle Harry! It's Larkin."

"Well, hello Larkin! I like the job you and Percy did on the mail box."

"Thanks. Say, would you mind if I borrowed a shovel and went and did a little exploring on the land?"

"You mean a treasure hunt? I sure wish I could go with you. Go ahead. Just show me what you find. Oh, and you had better put back all the dirt, if you don't mind?" He smiled.

"Okay. Thanks, Uncle Harry."

He ran out the door and went to the garage. Picking up a shovel, he pulled the map from his pocket. Ginny was hovering over him like a bee ready to dive-bomb a flower. "Where do we go?"

He pointed in the direction of the big tree on the left side of the yard and said, "That way."

Off they traipsed toward the tree. He showed her the map as they walked asking her, "See that fence line there?"

"Yeah," she replied.

Pointing at the map he said, "That's there. The big tree is this one, the one my family calls the "Wedding Tree," I think."

"What's this box?" she asked, pointing.

"I don't know. I don't think it exists anymore. Maybe it was a chicken coop or something. These are markings in feet and we just have to see where they all intersect."

"But how do we do that if one doesn't exist anymore?"

"Well, we use all the other directions and guess on that one."

She shrugged her shoulders and said, "Okay, we can at least try."

The two had a lot of fun stepping it off according to Ben's map and marking it here and there in the yard. Finally, they determined a spot. He said, "I guess this is it. Let's dig!" Larkin took the shovel and let fly. He dug for about a foot each direction and went down that much as well. He wasn't having any luck and the dirt was hard, so he began to get discouraged.

Ginny said, "My turn!"

Larkin handed her the shovel and got out of the hole. He didn't think a girl was going to do much good, but he thought he'd humor her. "Good luck," he told her and he folded his arms in front of him and smiled. Ginny got into the hole and began to dig.

She said, "I think it's going to be right--- here." She put in the spade and- clunk! She hit something! She did it again. It sounded metallic.

"You did it Ginny, you found it!" Excited, Larkin grabbed the shovel out of her hand and went after exposing it, trying not to damage it. Soon he had uncovered a metal box, just like the others. Now, this time, Larkin wasn't too excited, because it *was* just like the others. Prying it out of the ground, he lifted it up to Ginny. He crawled out of the hole and they sat down on the grass to open it. Before handing it back to him Ginny said, "I want to open it."

"No. Wait. If it's on The Homestead it is Palmer family property. Let *me*."

Disgusted she said, "Oh alright. But I found it," she huffed, folding her arms in front of her.

She handed the box to him and he opened it slowly. Time and the elements had taken its toll on the contents of this box. The papers inside were crumbled to dust. They held onto the remains of a rusted pocket knife, a couple of marbles made of clay, and what looked like a tooth. There was also one penny, dated 1793. Somehow, it was in excellent condition. Larkin took a look at it and said, "If this is what I think it is, we're rich!" Grabbing Ginny's hands, he jumped up and down, and up and down. Then he thought of his uncles. "We had better go show this to Uncle Harry, because rightfully it's his. We just found it."

Ginny, being disappointed said, "Yes, you're right Larkin. Let's go see what he says."

The two explorers picked up the box, filled in the hole, and made their way to the house. First, Larkin put the shovel away, putting off the inevitable release of the coin to his uncle. Then they knocked on Harry's door again. "Come in. Is that you, Larkin? I hope you found some treasure!"

"We sure did, Uncle Harry." Introducing Ginny he said, "Uncle Harry, this is Ginny my partner. Ginny, this is my Uncle Harry."

"Pleased to meet you, Miss Ginny. Your partner you say, Larkin? By the sounds of that, your find must be substantial!"

"Indeed it is, Uncle. If I'm right, this coin is worth a lot of money."

"You found a coin?"

Larkin handed the cent over to him. "It's a 1793 large wreath cent in excellent condition. If I remember my coin book right, there are no others like it. None. The last one in poor condition sold for a half a million dollars at auction."

Uncle Harry set the coin down on the table. "What else was in the box there?" He pointed at the box Ginny was holding.

"Not much, just a couple of marbles, a tooth, a pocket knife, and some rotted papers."

"I see. How did you know where to look?"

"Well, in the stuff in the Glory Box..."

Harry interrupted Larkin, "The Glory Box?"

"Yes. Grandpa Elias left Mom a hope chest when he died. In it were things that the family thought was valuable, like the family Bible, birth records, and stuff. Someone by the name of Benjamin left his treasure map. So, I copied it and came out here to look for it."

"I see," said Uncle Harry, "I think I'm going to have to speak with your Uncle Tom about this Larkin. This is a most unusual occurrence. I ask you to leave everything here with me until such time as we have had opportunity to come to an agreement on a course of action."

"Yes, Uncle. I understand." Larkin motioned for Ginny to place the box next to the coin. "Goodbye, Uncle. See you soon."

"Goodbye, Larkin. It was nice to meet you, Ginny."

"You too, Sir." They went out the door more than disappointed. Harry just smiled at them knowing how they felt. But, he wouldn't allow that to continue. Harry was a good man.

Picking up their bikes, they didn't speak a word and they rode back toward home in silence. When they arrived at the corner of Academy and Baldwin they stopped and rested. "Ginny, I guess we should keep this to ourselves until they make up their mind what they are going to do."

"I guess so. It sure would be nice to be able to have that coin though."

Starting toward his house Larkin said, "Sure would! Bye, Ginny."

"Bye, Larkin." And off she went.

When he got to his house, Larkin ran in the door to tell his mom what happened. But she wasn't there. She had left a note about his dad. He had fallen off the tractor and was taken to the hospital. She had gone to be with him and asked Larkin to go to the neighbors, the Clarkes, until she returned and picked him up. "OH NO!" he shouted out loud.

Shirley stepped into the Doctor's office to speak with him. Lawtin was resting, but he was not in good condition. "Be truthful with me, Doctor Fitch. I know he is not going to be well for a while is he?"

"You're right Mrs. Palmer. He is not. When he fell he crushed his spine in four places. If you look at the X-Ray here with me, it shows breaks that cannot be repaired, even with surgery. There are doctors in

Rochester that may be able to help by fusing them together, but it would take a great deal of resources and a lot of prayer."

Shirley was devastated. They had no insurance. As it was, they would have to pay for all of this out of savings. How did he fall? Who would work the farm? What would she do? What would *they* do?

The news of the accident went around town quickly. When Lawtin's brothers heard of it they knew what they had to do. Immediately Harry picked up the phone and called his friend Israel Waterman. He was an antique dealer and auctioneer in Hamilton. "Israel, my friend," said Harry, "I have something I need to arrange for you to sell at auction for me. It's a 1793 Wreath cent in excellent condition."

"Harry, you must be joking. As far as I know there are only a few fair examples. There is no such thing as an excellent coin."

"Oh yes, indeed, there is! I have it on my kitchen table right in front of me."

"Well, you had better get it into a safety deposit box then, because if what you say is true, when we sell it, it will bring over a million dollars!"

"Then my nephew was right. Arrange the sale Israel. I'll put it in safekeeping until you tell me when the sale will occur."

Lawtin was to be in the hospital for quite some time. His bones would need healing time even before they could be repaired. Every day Shirley and Larkin would go to visit. Their pastor, Pastor Johnson, would sometimes be there too, praying with his father and encouraging him. It was a hard sell however, and Lawtin was down in the dumps, blaming himself for the fall and worrying about the future. Pastor Johnson said, "We know that our God is in control, we can always count on Him." Lawtin wanted to believe him. In the mean while, he waited for a miracle. Larkin just prayed.

In the mean while, Percy moved the tractor into the barn from the field where Lawtin had his accident. There on the first step was a glob of-grease. Percy thought about that. Lawtin had not done any maintenance on the tractor lately. But how did the grease get there?

Israel had arranged for the sale in a month so that adequate time was available for advertising. He listed the owner and seller as anonymous, so there was no danger to Larkin's friends or family. In the mean while, he contacted Harry about his commission. When he found out the circumstances, he withdrew it and pledged the sale to the family for free. Harry was pleased. He called Larkin.

"Hello?" said the boy on his parent's phone.

"Hello, Larkin. I'm sorry to hear the news of your father."

"Thank you, Uncle."

"Considering the circumstances, your uncle and I have made a decision. We have decided to sell the coin at auction and donate the proceeds thereof to your family. It will first go to your fathers' medical expenses and then to the needs of your family until such time as it runs out. I hope you find these terms adequate, Larkin."

He began to cry right there on the phone, "Oh, Uncle Harry, thank you so much! Please tell Uncle Tom thank you, too."

"I will. And please tell your mother. We are praying for you all. Goodbye, Larkin."

"Goodbye, Uncle." Larkin put the phone down and yelled, "YAHOOO!"

Shirley had come into the room and heard Larkin's side of the conversation with his uncle. Keeping his promise to Ginny, he had not told his mother of the treasure he and Ginny had found that day. He explained it all to her, how they used the map to find the treasure box, how they had given it to his uncles, and how now they were selling it at auction to help them. Shirley sat at the table and wept. In her tears she thanked the Lord for His help. Larkin said to her, "Mom, little did Benjamin know it, but when he put that penny in the treasure box, he helped save some of his family. I think I should thank him."

Looking up from her hands that cupped her face she asked, "How are you going to do that, Honey?"

"I'm going out to the family cemetery and see if I can find his grave. It just might be there."

"Okay. Wait until your father hears this story. He's never going to believe it. You see Larkin, our God does provide!"

Larkin got on his bike and started peddling toward The Homestead. He thought about everything that had occurred since his Grandpa Elias had died. So much had changed. So much had remained the same. His death meant Larkin's life would forever be changed. It meant that the family would remain the same.

When he arrived at The Homestead, he kept riding down to where Chase road ended. That was where the cemetery lay, about one hundred yards from the house. It was always kept as neat as the rest of the yards. Grandpa Elias had seen to that. In fact, he had restored much of it in the past twenty years. It had been a labor of love for Grandpa Elias. It was good to see his uncles gave it the same priority. Even so, many of the family cemeteries in the county had fallen into disrepair over the years. Headstones overturned by cattle wandering amongst them, trees growing all around pushing headstones over, and the brush totally obscuring everything. Larkin felt sorry when he saw cemeteries like that from the road.

Uncle Tom saw him ride up to the cemetery and came out to greet him. "Hello, Larkin! How are you?"

Larkin ran over to him and gave him a big hug. Uncle Tom was not ready for this. Being a bachelor and not having any children of his own, he was not a demonstrative man. Still, he accepted it gladly and put his arms around the boy, almost a man. "Thank you for all you are doing for my dad, Uncle Tom."

"My pleasure, Larkin. Besides, *you* found the treasure box. It would have stayed there forever if you wouldn't have. It was meant to be yours."

"Uncle Tom, where is Benjamin's grave?"

"Follow me and I'll show you." The pair walked over to the headstones on the far end of the cemetery. On the way they passed Lawtin Senior, Lawtin Junior, and their wives. By the time they got to Benjamin, they were a few families away. And there he was. His headstone was small. It read:

"Benjamin Palmer"

Born Oct. 17th, 1828 - Died Oct. 17th, 1848. Aged exactly 20 years.

"That's odd isn't it, Uncle Tom? I mean, the fact he died on his birthday."

"Yes. But you'd be surprised how many people do die on or close to their birthdays."

"Is that a fact?"

"Yes, indeed it is."

"Huh. I'd like to bring some flowers out here and put them on his grave from time to time. I owe him that. Will you take them down when they wither?"

"I always take care of the cemetery, Larkin."

"Thanks. Say, Uncle Tom?"

"Yes, Larkin?"

"Could I have the treasure box?"

"Oh, I think we could arrange that."

The two went into the farm house and found Uncle Harry taking a nap on the sofa by the TV. The room was always dark, due to inadequate lighting in the house, and Larkin figured it probably made it real easy to take a nap at almost any time. When they came closer, he stirred. Larkin went up to him catching him by surprise and gave him a hug, too. "Well it's nice to see you, too, Larkin."

"Thanks for everything, Uncle Harry."

"You're most welcome. Has your Uncle Tom told you about the sale of the coin?"

"No, we haven't talked about it. I only know that it is next weekend in Hamilton."

"That's right. People from all over the country are coming to place a bid on one of the rarest coins ever offered for auction. The hotels are already all full and people are staying as far away as Albany."

"How much does Mr. Waterman think it will bring?"

"Rumors have it that some of the big wigs will bid as much as two million. But conservatively, he thinks a little over one million."

"Wow, I was right!"

"You sure were!"

Larkin looked at both of his uncles and said, "God sure knew when to have me dig this up didn't He?"

"He knows our needs even before we do, Larkin," said Uncle Tom. "Oh, by the way, before you leave make sure you take this." Looking to Uncle Harry for approval, Tom handed him the treasure box.

Harry smiled as Larkin took it and said, "You are the best uncles anyone could ever have!"

"We want you to come with us to the auction next Saturday, Larkin. Can we stop and pick you up?"

"I'd like that."

Tom led him out to his bike and he waved goodbye to Larkin as he rode away. Then Tom went back to the barn to work. When Larkin got home, Percy was in the barn working. He saw the boy walk to the door and go in. He didn't tell him what he had found on the tractor, because he knew someone had tried to kill his father. Instead, he'd keep better watch and maybe someday tell Lawtin. When Larkin went up to his room, he placed the treasure box with the others under his bed.

The Gift Box

The auction was at 9:00 a.m. that next Saturday. By the time his uncles came and picked up Larkin, his mom had already left for the hospital to keep his dad company. Lawtin was doing better and holding his own. When Shirley told him about the coin and the map provided by Benjamin, he began to sob. Lawtin was so overjoyed he raised his voice above all others in the ward and proclaimed he would never doubt the Lord again.

When the three, Harry, Tom, and Larkin, arrived at the auction in Hamilton, they found the place to be almost full. Israel had reserved them a seat toward the front, but didn't want to let them loose their anonymity, so he kept them in the second row, center. By the time the auction started, the place was packed.

There were other items to be auctioned that day, so Israel placed the coin about two thirds through the proceedings in order to make sure some of the other inventory sold, too. He did this just right, because some of the folks were getting antsy and wanted to get to it. When it finally came up the crowd cheered. He said, "Up for auction I present to you a rare 1793 Wreath Cent rated as uncirculated by a coin dealer in Albany. It is of the Strawberry leaf variety, which makes it even rarer. Who will start the bid at two hundred thousand dollars?" The bidding started to climb fast. At one point the auctioneer could not keep up with the bids. When it got to one million, the field was narrowed to three men bidding. Larkin sat on the edge of his seat rooting on the bidders as it progressed. His uncles smiled and were in awe of the proceedings. When it was all finished the final bid was 1.5 million! It was an auction record!

On the way to drop Larkin off at the hospital to see Lawtin, all they could talk about was the auction. Mr. Waterman said he would be in touch about the payment of the monies. The only thing that would be taken from the proceedings was the taxes, both state and federal. As he had promised, he waived his commission. Besides, he said it was the best auction he had ever had and he was grateful. He expected the Palmer's final check to be somewhere in the one million dollar range. It would go a long way in paying Lawtin's hospital expenses and keeping the farm alive.

His uncles let Larkin off at the door of the hospital. They wanted to get back to Brookfield, so they told Larkin to wish his dad well for them and that they would come by next week to see him. He just about ran in to tell his parents what happened, but thought he should not run, as it was a hospital and all. Lawtin was ecstatic about the news. "Shirley, this means you can hire a hand to finish the crops for the season. You can maybe even buy some cattle like we planned."

"Hold on, Lawtin. Let's not plan any more than we can handle right now. We should do like the doctors have suggested and take it one day at a time."

"You're right. You're right. I can't wait to get out of here and go home."

"Just a few more weeks and then we can see about the specialist. Maybe they can put you back together like new, or almost new." Shirley bent over the bed and gave him a hug. Larkin smiled.

The following Tuesday, Larkin rode his bike out to The Homestead. On the way, he stopped and picked anything that grew that looked pretty. It wasn't a normal bouquet by any means- in fact, many of them were weeds. But it did, from a boy's point of view, look nice! When Larkin got to the cemetery he saw Uncle Tom by the garage and he waved to him. He walked over to Benjamin's grave and placed the bouquet at his tombstone. He said out loud, "Here ya go, Ben. Is it okay if I call you Ben? You know, you were only a few years older than me when you died. I wonder why? Anyway, I'll be back and thanks again." He turned to see Uncle Tom coming out towards him and he had something in his hand. It looked like a gift box. In fact- it was!

His uncle said, "Your Uncle Harry and I wanted you to have this. We hope you'll use it wisely."

"Thanks!" Larkin quickly opened the wrapped box and moved the paper aside. In it, was a bound stack of bills; one hundred dollar bills! "How much is here?"

"There's ten thousand dollars there. We have one in the house for Ginny as well."

"You got the check! Yahoo! Thank you, Uncle!"

"Calm down, Nephew. Please come inside with me. Harry and I would like to talk with you."

They walked in and found Harry washing the dishes. Slowly and deliberately, he sat the last one down and dried his hands on the towel. "Hello, Larkin. I thought I'd like to explain the gift box to you and this one for Ginny, too. Sit down."

Larkin sat at the table and placed his box on it. Looking at his uncle and waiting for him to speak, the old man, instead, went over to a desk drawer and opened it. He pulled out a box, an ornate wooden box made of what Larkin thought was cherry wood and inlaid with pearl. It was beautiful. He came back over to the table and sat down by Larkin. "The box your Uncle Tom gave you is a small reward to you for finding Benjamin's treasure box. Ginny gets one exactly like it. You may do whatever you wish with it, but we hope that you would use it wisely." Pausing and proceeding ever so slowly he said, "Larkin, we *know*."

"Know?" the boy asked.

"We know about The Eraser."

You could have heard a pin drop. After a moment, his uncle went on. "Each of us throughout the years has been told the story by our fathers. Each of us has been groomed to take on the responsibility if we were chosen to be the one. Each of us has come to grips with the history it has and the horror of its makeup. We know what you have been struggling with. We've seen you find all of the boxes. It was exciting for us to watch, because not all of us have been lucky enough to do the "box" hunt. We don't know how you feel about the fact that your Grandpa Elias chose you. He had his reasons. We assumed it would be your father. That is why you were never told about it before and had to find out this way. But, Grandpa Elias made it easy for you and also made it an adventure of discovery. He knew you loved history. This, although it is not one of the five boxes, is the final box left to us by our family. It comes from Lawtin Senior. It is "The Gift Box". In this box was placed The Eraser Box when it was first given to Lawtin Sr. Open it." He handed it to Larkin. Indeed it was beautiful. Inside was another letter.

Again, he recognized the handwriting-Edmund Nairne. "Nairne," the boy said. He didn't remove it. Instead he asked his uncle. "What does it say?"

"It is the original gift letter he sent to Lawtin Senior. He sent The Eraser as a gift to the family because it was, at the time, something very special. He had no idea what it actually would bring."

"I know. I saw his apology letter."

"You saw what?" asked Harry surprised.

"I found what I thought was the Gift Box in a secret compartment in the bottom of the Glory Box. That's what I call it, "The Glory Box."That's where I found Nairne's apology letter."

Harry asked hypothetically, "So I wonder what the letter in the gift box says?"

"I don't want to know, Uncle. Not yet. This is a lot for me."

"Have you read the Journal?"

"Just the first page. I didn't want to get into it yet."

"Your parents will help you with that, if you wish."

"My parents? They know?"

"Yes, and they are proud of how you have handled it thus far."

"Hum," was all that the boy said.

"Larkin, we have placed the rest of the money in a trust which pays your families' bills until it runs out. Of course it gains interest as well, so it will be quite some time before it does run out. Your mother has decided to hire Percy and one of his sons to help on the farm. You will be relieved of your duties there."

"But what am *I* going to do?"

The two men smiled a big grin. "You tell him," said Tom to Harry.

"Well, we would like it if you came here after school and lived here during the summers, and helped your uncle with the orchard. He can teach you all there is about it. It will be grafted again soon. We want it to be in the family for a long time to come."

Larkin smiled. "Really? I'd like that."

"So be it then! We'll speak with your parents and make the arrangements."

Larkin was on his way home and he saw another bike rider coming toward him. It was Andy! It had been a while since he promised he'd go swimming with him. Too much had happened. Andy greeted him by saying, "Hi, Larkin!" Andy placed his feet on the ground and stopped in front of his friend.

"Hi, Andy. Sorry I haven't seen much of you this summer. A lot has been happening since my dad got hurt."

"Oh, that's okay. Is he doing better?"

"Yes. They may take him to Rochester in a couple of weeks to see if they can do something for his back."

"I heard all about the treasure you found! That was pretty cool!"

"Yeah it was. In fact, I need to see Ginny. Is she around?"

"She's at home with Mom. Wanna go with me?"

"But where were you going, Andy?"

"Aw, nowhere. I just ride around sometimes." Not an unusual thing for boys…

The boys rode the two miles or so to the Berry house. It had been a long while since Larkin had been inside as the boys played in the yard most of the time. When they got there, Andy dropped his bike and raced to the door to announce that he had Larkin with him. Andy called out, "Ginny, I have Larkin with me."

In her singsong voice she replied, "Okay, I'll be right there." In a second or two she came down the stairs and out the front door to the porch. Larkin had sat down on the front steps in the shade with his box and hers. He looked at the flowers in the planter by the window while he waited. He imagined that Ginny must have planted them, because the petunias were pink and purple. He knew that those were her favorite colors. She sat down next to him. "What do you have there?" she asked, pointing at the presents.

"This is for you," Larkin answered. He handed her the box.

"Why thank you, Larkin."

"Oh, it's not from me. It's from my uncles."

"How kind of them," she said surprised.

Her mother came out of the house to see what all of the excitement was about. Andy stood over their shoulders. "What do we have here, Larkin?" Mrs. Berry asked.

"It is a gift and reward from my uncles. I got one exactly like it."

He held up his box to show her. Just then, Ginny took the top off her box. She looked inside to see what it was. She exclaimed, "Oh my Lord!" and pulled the bundle out of the box. Her mother fainted right there on the porch! While Larkin tried to help Mrs. Berry, Ginny asked him, "How much is this, Larkin?"

"It's ten thousand dollars! All- *yours*!"

Larkin helped Mrs. Berry sit on the steps to adjust herself. "You mean this is my part of the treasure?" asked Ginny.

"That's what they mean!"

Larkin and Ginny then told her mother the entire story. She was amazed at the uncles' generosity. Larkin said, "They are fine men and they would be most offended if she didn't accept this gift. Take it. I'm going to put mine in the bank for college and a car."

Mrs. Berry said, "So be it. Please convey our thanks to them and in the mean while, Ginny will send them a proper thank you in the mail."

Andy was still standing there all wild-eyed. "Andy, I think you had better keep this to yourself. Know what I mean?" Larkin suggested to his younger friend.

"Yeah, Larkin, I do."

Mrs. Berry said, "That's a good idea, Larkin."

Before he could react, Ginny came up to Larkin and gave him a great big kiss on the lips. "Thanks for the whole wonderful treasure hunting adventure, Larkin! You're the best!"

Ginny's mom smiled and Andy just laughed. Larkin's face turned beet-red.

When Larkin arrived at home, his mom had just come back from the hospital. "Where have you been, Honey?" she asked.

"Out at The Homestead with uncles and then over to Ginny's to deliver a gift they had for her. I got one too." He shoved the gift box toward his mom and she looked inside.

"How much is that?" she asked lackadaisically.

"It's ten thousand dollars, Mom!"

"What are you going to do with it?"

"I'm going to save some for my car and most for college."

"Good. And Ginny got one too, huh? Well, your dad will be coming home by Friday. He's going to need some help getting around for a while, so I'll need you to be around. Percy and Arville will be coming every day from now on."

"I understand. Say, I think my Uncles want to talk to you and Dad about something, too. I expect they'll be calling."

"Okay."

Grabbing the gift box Shirley said, "I'll put this in the bank for you in the morning. Okay?"

"Thanks, Mom."

Larkin went up the stairs to his room. Taking the "Gift Box" out of his pocket, he placed it with the others under the bed. It was starting to get crowded under there. There was The Eraser box, the Barn Box, the Mail Box, the Ice Box, the Glory Box, and now, the Gift Box. 'Well now,' he thought, "I know the whole story. Or do I? I still haven't read The Journal. Uncles seem to take that and this whole thing about The Eraser pretty seriously. Maybe I should read it? No, I think I'll wait until Dad is around in case I have any questions.' He got up, went to the bathroom and took a shower. He was tired, dirty, and just wanted to relax. When his head did hit the pillow, he was out like a light. What an eventful day!

The next morning Larkin said to his mother, "Mom, I'd like to work on the genealogy over at Uncles. Could I take it over to their house so I could ask them some questions about the gaps we have?"

"I'd say that's a great idea," she replied.

First, Larkin placed all the information on the dining room table in a cardboard box. Then he went back upstairs and pulled the boxes from under his bed. Finally, he put it all in the cardboard box on the table. He'd ask Percy to give him a ride the next time he was passing by The Homestead and he'd drop it off there. Besides, he figured that all of this needed to be there- it all *belonged* there.

The next Friday, Percy finished his chores and saw Larkin just standing there by the barn, shoving dirt from side to side with his shoe, as if he was waiting to ask him something. Larkin knew Percy was hot and tired, and that it was also out of his way to take him to The Homestead. He didn't want to be a burden and ask. Percy sensed it, so he went over to Larkin and asked. "Larkin is there something you'd like say or ask me?"

"Yes. Percy, I don't want to be a burden or take you out of your way, but I need a ride over to Uncles house with a cardboard box I have on the table. Could you take me?"

"Oh, Larkin, sure I'll take you. You should have asked me sooner."

Larkin went in and picked it all up and headed out the door. The box was full and kind of heavy, so Percy grabbed it out of his hands and looked inside. Seeing all the papers and the boxes he said, "Let's set this inside between us."

"Good idea. I'd hate to lose any of this stuff."

They pulled up the drive at The Homestead, the gravel crunching under the tires and the truck slid as Percy stopped. Larkin opened the heavy door and got out of the Studebaker. He pulled the corner of the box toward him and Percy shoved it at him over the slick vinyl truck seat. "Thanks for driving me over, Percy."

"You can ask me anything, anytime, Larkin," said a smiling Percy.

"Thanks," said the grateful boy.

Larkin walked over to the door with the cumbersome box and Tom met him there. Opening the creaky screen door for him, Tom moved out of the way so Larkin could get the cardboard box past him and into the kitchen. Uncle Harry asked inquisitively, "What's in the box?"

"It's all of the Boxes and the Journal, also the family genealogy that Mom has been working on. She got it from Grandpa Elias. I'd like to go over it with you two to try to fill in the blanks. Would you help us?"

Looking at Tom for approval while he answered Harry said, "Sure! We'll see what we can jog from these cobweb filled minds of ours." They all laughed. Larkin closed the lid on the box and sat it under the table. Little did he know, it would be a while before he thought of it again.

Chapter Three

The Storm

When Lawtin got home from the hospital, half of the summer was almost gone. Hot August days were on the rise and when he got frustrated with his progress with rehabilitation, his temper rose as well. The family took the brunt of it, but they understood. Larkin had to be around almost all of the time, so going over to his uncles' was out of the question for a while. Larkin and his uncles understood the situation. They all prayed the doctors could do something for Lawtin.

Sitting in the kitchen sipping their coffee, Lawtin and Shirley were having devotions. Larkin went up to his bathroom. The phone rang and Shirley answered it on the second ring, "Hello?"

"Hello, this is Dr. Samuels in Rochester. Is this the Palmer residence?"

"Yes, this is Mrs. Palmer. I'm glad you've called, Doctor. What news do you have?"

"After reviewing all of the information and X-Rays, we believe we can help your husband. We have scheduled surgery for August 19th. Can you be here?"

"Yes, we can Doctor. That is great news!"

"Then I'll have my secretary call you when the day gets closer and set it all up."

"Thank you, Doctor. Thank you!"

"You're welcome, Mrs. Palmer. Good-bye."

Turning to Lawtin who could hear she asked, "Did you hear that, Lawtin? They can take you in Rochester on the 19th!"

"Thank God," Lawtin responded, "we'll have to arrange everything so Larkin can go to school, and then you can rent a place to stay in Rochester. There's going to be a lot of things to consider with this."

"We can handle it, Lawtin. It'll be fine. Don't worry. God is in control. Look at what He's done!"

"You're right. What am I thinking? It'll all work out."

Larkin came down to the kitchen. "What's going on?" he asked.

"They are going to operate on your dad in Rochester on the 19th," said Shirley excitedly.

Larkin smiled.

By the time the 19th came around the family was all prepared. Larkin was to stay with his uncles until school started in September. Percy and Arville were going to make sure the farm ran smoothly. And Shirley would stay at a family's boarding house in Rochester until Lawtin could leave the hospital and come home. The doctor arranged an ambulance to transport Lawtin to Rochester, but Shirley would have to take the truck up there for her own transportation. The doctors hoped Lawtin would recover quickly because of his health and age, but they weren't promising anything. It was all just a very delicate operation. They said if all went well, he could possibly leave in a month; sometime in September. Larkin watched his mom pull out of the drive and wave goodbye. She was smiling as she left. She always smiled and it seemed the normal thing for her to do, even in these delicate circumstances. She had faith…

Larkin hoped everything would get back to normal soon. He missed doing things with his dad and working alongside him. He missed life like it used to be. He almost wished he had lived back in history and life was simpler than this for him and his family. But had life been simpler for the Palmers back then? The Journal could answer all of his questions but, he still hadn't read the Journal…

Up until this time life had been pretty normal for Larkin. But now, life's journey for him had taken a huge turn. First, he received The Eraser. Then Grandpa Elias died. Then he found the boxes. Then he found the treasure and then, unfortunately, his dad was hurt. Now, he would be living with his uncles. Man, was he ever confused! All this, and the fact that Ginny showed she liked him as more than a friend, made every hour of the day a maze of paths for him to choose from. His life's destination, at least for him, was unknown, so that night, the first night with his uncles, he went out to the barn to think.

It wasn't the same as at his house. Sure, he had spent a lot of time out there with his Grandpa Elias, but it didn't have that peaceful feeling like at home. So, he got up off the bale of hay and went out in the yard by the big tree. Looking up at it limbs, he saw the perfect one for a swing. He thought the family had called it the "Welcome Tree." He'd ask his uncle about it. From there he could see the stars in all their glory. He pondered God's universe and His plan for him. Still, he wondered why his family was stuck with the curse. He felt so helpless. Yet in it all, he felt loved by them all, and best of all, God. And that was all he needed.

Larkin was given the downstairs back bedroom of the house. It was closest to the barn. Uncle Tom suggested a work schedule for him and how he could help out. Doing the work would take a burden off Tom and his Uncle Harry, who couldn't do much anyway. Larkin was glad to help. In fact, learning about the orchard sounded interesting to him. He actually looked forward to this new adventure!

Everything at The Homestead seemed like it was from another time. For sure, they didn't have a lot of modern conveniences at his house, but his uncles lived not only modestly, but in a style which seemed- old fashioned. They still used the livestock as much as possible instead of the tractor; two mules and even an ox. They had no modern harvesting equipment and picked everything by hand. They still had a black and white TV, which was rarely on, but sometimes the news at night and maybe Ed Sullivan from time to time. They did listen to the radio every day though, but it was never what Larkin would have enjoyed. And they were very frugal. Uncle Tom made sure you always turned off a light if you left the room. And Uncle Harry, well, he made sure you only took three squares of TP to the outhouse. No more. And that was another thing; the shower was in the barn. Summer use only and the hot water was created by solar energy in a drum on the roof. That was one thing Uncle Tom used the tractor for; he lifted a 50 gallon drum of water up there every other day with it. Actually, Larkin thought the whole system was pretty cool, but in the winter the men got really "ripe" when they only boiled water once a week for a bath. At least *his* house had a bathroom. There were two wells, one in the house which had a pump handle on it in the kitchen, so at least they didn't have to carry water. The well for the stock was electric and came into the barn.

They used to have a windmill, but it rotted totally away and the family never replaced it for some reason. Whenever he had come here to visit his Grandpa Elias, he thought these things were neat, but he never had to stay for a long period of time. Even so, he felt blessed because so many people in the world had so much less. When the rooster crowed, he knew it was going to be time to get up! Up with the sun would give him plenty of time to help on The Homestead.

That first night there, he didn't sleep much. He worried about his dad. His mom called to say they had arrived and things were all set to go, but he knew the doctors said there was a risk. Even if they did a great job on the fusion, he would never be able to do what he had done before. That in itself, would kill his dad. He wouldn't be able to work the farm. The doctors never promised him that. And he knew it, so in a couple of days, he'd be praying even harder than now-for his dad's health, his spirits, and his attitude towards life.

When the rooster crowed, it *was* time to get up! But the next morning he was waked, not by the rooster, but by a thunderstorm. The skies seemed to have opened up and all the rain of Noah's flood burst forth on the farm. It needed it. The drought of the spring had continued through the summer and it was dry, very dry. He went down to the kitchen, took three squares of TP and ran out to the outhouse. On the way he saw Uncle Tom putting one of the horses in a stall. When he went to the barn to help, he found no one there and all in order. The rain was still coming down and the sound of it hitting the roof almost made him tired again. He loved that sound. He looked back at the house in the storm induced darkness and saw his Uncles standing at the kitchen sink under its light, looking out at the downpour. Larkin took an old wooden chair that Tom had placed by the door and under the overhang; he sat down to watch it. It was so dark from the cloud cover the yard light had come back on. Larkin wondered how this rain would affect the orchard. It had to help. At least he thought so…

It took an hour for the rain to let up enough for him to run toward the house and he still got soaked. Uncle Tom met him at the door with a towel and he said, "Here you are Larkin. I was wondering when you'd try to make it in." Uncle Harry had the TV on. The newscaster was saying that a tornado had struck a farm in Hamilton. They warned people to be on watch. Just then, everything got quiet and the rain stopped. Tom said, "Finally, maybe it's going to quit." But Larkin was worried. He had heard that before a tornado comes through it did that sometimes. Suddenly, they heard a noise. It sounded like a train. The wind picked up and the cedar tree outside the window was slapping against the house. The doors rattled and the whole structure seemed to feel like it was going to flee its footings.

Larkin yelled, "I think we should take cover Uncles. This doesn't sound good!"

Tom exclaimed, "The cellar!" They hurried out the kitchen door to the porch and opened a trap door which swung up from the floor. Harry went down first with Tom following. Larkin came down last closing the door behind him. It didn't take long before they heard a rush of wind that the uncles said they had never heard before there on The Homestead. The house shook violently, windows were breaking, and they heard a horse run past. That was not good. It meant the barn was no longer intact. Then- it all just stopped.

Curious, Larkin pushed the cellar door up and ran out of the house. There before him Larkin saw that the barn was destroyed! The house and the grounds looked okay, but where the barn had stood, no more than 100 yards from the house, now stood- nothing! He didn't even see the ruble. It was all, all, just- *gone!* Tom and Harry made it out of the cellar and looked around in disbelief. Harry began to cry. Tom got on his knees and thanked God that He had protected them through the storm and asked that no others in the area be hurt. Now Tom was saddened that he had put the animals in the barn. Just then and to his great joy, one of the horses and both of the mules ran past them out toward the north pasture. But, he did not see the ox. Larkin walked over to where the barn once stood. The *only* thing remaining was the chair that he had been sitting on right before he had run to the house and some scrap lumber. It was a miracle he was alive. Harry and Tom came up to him. Tom said pointing to the chair, "I think that the Lord was trying to say something there Larkin."

In astonishment he agreed and said, "Yeah, I think so Uncle. He's always with me."

Confused, Larkin didn't know what to do and where to start. His uncles were in shock. Although the structure was basically gone, there was quite a mess to clean up. The ground was saturated and a muddy mess. Larkin started to pick up scrap lumber and place it in a pile. Tom came up to him and said, "Let's go into the house and let this go for now. It's too wet anyway. We have plenty of time to clean this up." He put his arm around the boy's shoulders and the three of them walked back into the house. When they walked through the door the phone began to ring. "Wow! How did the lines stay up?" asked Larkin.

"That's amazing!" said Uncle Harry.

Tom answered the phone to hear Shirley ask, "I heard there was bad weather out that way. Are you all okay?"

"Yes, Shirley we are, but the barn is gone."

"What do you mean "gone"?"

"That's what I mean, gone. The tornado just picked it up and took it away. There's only a small bit of scraps out there for us to pick up. It's a miracle that Larkin is alive. He was sitting in the barn no more than three minutes before it hit. It is truly a miracle."

"Thank God he's alright!"

"We have. The ox seems to be missing, but the other stock is spooked and running around the pasture land. Otherwise we haven't really checked out the farm, but when we pull ourselves together we'll do it and take a survey of the property."

"Well, I thought I'd call and see if you were okay. Everything here is fine. Lawtin will have the surgery tomorrow. I know you will be busy Tom, but don't forget to pray."

"Don't worry Shirley, it will all be fine, both here and there."

"Thanks, Tom. I'll call you after the operation and let you know how he's doing. Bye."

"Bye, Shirley." Tom hung up the phone and turned toward the other two, "Let's pray."

Harry replied, "Amen, Brother!"

They all stayed in the house and watched the reports on TV. Brookfield was hit hard by the tornado. Many trees were down and some out buildings, too.

Larkin wondered how his house had made it through the storm. Being located at the end of Chase road, they didn't hear anyone moving about. They figured they had enough of their own worries to contend with and wouldn't be coming out to The Homestead unless they asked for help. The sun began to come out. They could see out to the West that the orchard seemed okay. Larkin was antsy and wanted to go out. The uncles could sense that, so Tom got up and said, "Lets walk the property Larkin."

"Sounds good, Uncle."
Harry said, "I'll wait here for a report."
As they went out the door, Larkin's dog Sam came running up to him. "Sam! What are you doing here? Are you alright?"
Tom bent down and looked over the dog, and just saw a frightened animal. "He's okay. Just scared like everyone else. But it makes me wonder if there's anything wrong at your house. He wouldn't leave the cows or your house if there wasn't a problem." The dog seemed to convey Tom's words as he beckoned Larkin to come with him. Sam started running toward his house and stopped, and then barked. Larkin looked at his uncle. "I think you better go with him, Larkin. We'll put off walking the property until later. If you can, call me from your house and let me know how it is. I'll call Percy and see if he can come over, too."
"Okay, Uncle." He picked up his bike from the back of the house and headed toward Waterman Road.

The road seemed to be fine. There was no evidence that there was even a storm as he rode the familiar route up Baldwin Road toward his house. As he turned the corner off Highway 99 the scene changed. On Waterman Road lay all the debris from The Homestead. He could see pieces of the barn all over the place, like the tornado had picked it up and dropped it there like a thousand pixy sticks. He tried to see his house and barn, but the trees obscured his vision. Many of them were broken off half way and he could trace the tornado's path through the fields and trees. It seemed to have hopped and skipped through the countryside. He peddled as fast as he could, trying to keep up with the dog which was now a quarter mile ahead of him. Going around all the stuff on the road made the going slow, however. As he got closer, he could finally see the corner of the barn. It looked fine. So did all of the trees there. The fields looked fine too. He could even see Helga leading the cows up for the evening milking. But then he saw it. The house! The house was flattened, the front of it lying pushed over toward the road.

As Larkin arrived at the driveway, bike between his legs, Percy drove from the other direction. They both just stopped there to look. Larkin didn't say anything. Percy just said, "My Lord! Thank God no one was here." Larkin thought about that for a moment. He was devastated that the house was destroyed, but by God's grace, all his family was spared, because God had arranged that they all be somewhere else.

"It's amazing Percy," said Larkin to him, "we are never gone all at the same time, just this time."

"It's going to get dark soon, Larkin. We can come over and clean this up later. I'll take you back to The Homestead. Put your bike in the back."

Percy turned the truck around and headed toward The Homestead. Going was even slower than by bike, as he had to miss all the debris from the barn on the road. He had Larkin get out a couple times to move the bigger things so he could sneak by. When they got back to The Homestead, Tom came out of the house and went over to the truck. "I tried to call you Percy, but your line must be down."

"It is, Mr. Tom. And I hate to have to tell you this, but so is your brother's house." Tom's face turned ashen white.

Larkin said, "We need to get hold of Mom so I can tell her what I saw over there." He hopped out of the truck and Tom stayed to talk with Percy. Running into the house he said to Uncle Harry, "We need to call Mom. The house was destroyed. Everything else is fine."

"Oh, my Lord." Harry went to the phone and looked at the note with the number at the boarding house for Shirley. He dialed.

While they called Shirley, Tom and Percy came up with a plan for cleanup. Percy would get a report from the sheriff on damage in the town and surrounding areas. Then, he'd call his pastor and the local Red Cross to get volunteers out to help with the cleanup as soon as they could come. They knew there would be a priority need list. They may not even be on it for a while! In the meanwhile, Percy and Arville would go to Lawtin's place and Larkin would help there at The Homestead. Percy said goodbye to go take care of the livestock and Tom went back into the house to see what was happening. Percy thought to himself, 'Just think, if Lawtin would not have been in the hospital, they may all be dead right now. It is awesome how God turned something bad into good. If only the Palmers knew.'

Larkin was on the phone with his mother. "I'm sorry, Mom. Don't cry. Yes, the barn and the cows are fine. Sam? He's fine too. He even came to get me to tell me there was something wrong. Yes I know, he's a good dog. Mom, don't worry. Concentrate on the operation tomorrow. I wouldn't either. Dad doesn't need to know right now, I guess. Right. I love you, too, Mom. I'll be praying. Bye." He hung up the phone. His uncles waited for his reaction. He said, "She's pretty upset. She's not going to tell Dad now. She doesn't want to upset him before the operation."

"We understand," said Tom.

"I'm tired Uncles, may I go to bed?"

"No dinner?" asked Harry.

"No, I'll eat a big breakfast. Good night."

"Good night, Larkin."

Larkin went to his new, seemingly permanent bedroom. He didn't know what they were going to do now. The money they had made on the auction would pay for the operation and all, but would they have enough to rebuild the house, too? It all seemed like, too much for this fast maturing, eighth grader to handle! He thought to himself, 'What would Dad do?' Instinctively, he got down on his knees and prayed.

Chapter Four

The Change

The storm had changed everything. Not that there was much stable in Larkin's life anyway! But, his demeanor seemed to change. Called upon to do extraordinary things, the boy changed as well. His uncles could see him reach to the depths of his aptitude. Larkin seemed to suddenly have purpose. It was as if God had placed His hands upon him to use him for the good of the family. He did everything joyfully. He did it with the intention of learning it for life. He did it all as to please the Lord, not his family. His uncles saw it. They were not only pleased as they worked each day to clean up the mess, but they felt as if they were the ones learning from him, not the other way around. The most amazing thing to them was that he no longer played baseball. He loved it more than history. He had planned on being in Cooperstown someday. Now, that too, had changed.

Lawtin made it through the operation with flying colors and was able to return home sooner than expected. He had taken the news about the tornado and the house well. He had learned to finally trust the Lord to be in charge. Instead of going back to the farm, he had to come to The Homestead until the new house could be built. Larkin didn't know, but the house was insured. It would take the rest of the year to be completed however, and the old farmhouse was going to be crowded for a while! Larkin gave up the bedroom for his parents and took the couch. As a gift to his uncles, he also contacted a plumber for an estimate on putting a bathroom on the back porch. They were amazed at his generosity and resourcefulness. Indeed, he had matured. The months with his uncles at The Homestead not only brought him closer to them, but the entire family now grew closer. The three brothers renewed bonds that had been lost when they all established their own lives. Now that separation was gone. They laughed, sighed, and wept. They prayed together, relied on each other, and were now a family- The Family Palmer.

The cleanup efforts went like clockwork. As it turned out, only one other farm in the area was as adversely affected by the storm as the two Palmer farms. Townspeople came to both places and within a week the rubble was cleared, the debris hauled away or burned, and some semblance of normality returned to each farm. What was noticeable, especially to the rest of the townspeople, is that even though the Freemasons usually helped with such efforts and had at the other affected places, they were mysteriously absent from the cleanup at The Homestead.

Uncle Tom and Larkin finally had time to walk the Homestead and assess the damage together. While doing so, much more information was shared by Tom and Larkin digested it like a thirsty tree. By the time the efforts were complete however, school was to begin again. It was fall! This was unfortunate for Tom. The apples that did not get bruised or knocked from the trees during the storm would need to be harvested. As the harvest was to be diminished substantially, Tom was debating whether to pick it at all. But after reconsidering, he decided to go ahead. In fact, Larkin was pushing him to do so, pledging to help after he got out of school each day and to work until dark. The boy was a fireball!

When Larkin returned to school, he no longer was the daydreamer he was the year before. Mrs. Hall found him to be attentive and inquisitive. In fact, he was now her best student and was excelling in every subject. He was glad to see Ginny again, as the storm had not only put a damper on life on the farms, but also on his love life as well. He knew they would always be friends. His priority was now his family and his future. He excelled in history, but his new appreciation for science pleased his teacher. Working on the Homestead placed horticulture at the forefront. What he did not learn practically from his uncle, he learned technically in the classroom. Mrs. Hall knew he could succeed in that field if he did not lose the zeal he possessed at this young age.

The work on the new house progressed immediately. Percy, even though he had the duty of working the farm, was also retained to supervise the building of the home for Lawtin. The plan was of similar architecture, with the exception of it being more accessible for Lawtin with a minimal amount of stairs on the main floor and wider doors. Larkin was surprised that his parents had asked for his input into his room and his own private bath! It was something he had not expected. (He figured it was a reward for using some of his money to get his uncles the bath at The Homestead!) Percy expected the family would once again live on the farm by Christmas, because the contractor had double crews working on it six days a week. They were excited! But, they also dreaded the fact that the closeness they felt would be diminished by their move back to the farm. Larkin was determined to not let that happen by spending as much time on The Homestead as possible. It would only be possible if the money didn't run out.

When all the bills came in from the operation, it was more than expected. It always goes that way. The insurance on the house took care of most of the cost of rebuilding, but when it was all said and done, Lawtin would have about two hundred thousand dollars left. This would pay Percy and Arville for about three more years after expenses on the income from the farm. In that time, Larkin knew he'd have to make some extensive changes to both farms to make them more profitable or his dad would have to try to work again. Larkin knew he didn't want that to happen. One thing he knew for sure is that God was in control and no matter what, the Palmers stuck together!

At Christmas they moved into the new house. It sat in the same spot, looked like the old one, except it was new and modern. The old house was almost a hundred years old. Larkin figured it was God's plan of "urban renewal" in Brookfield. His family laughed about that one.

These Palmers had a Christmas tradition of one gift per person and one gift each given by them to the church for someone in need. Usually, they both were home made. Larkin was taught by Grandpa Elias how to whittle and to do wood working. If given enough time he could do quite well, so this year, he decided to make two tree ornaments- one for his parents and one for the needy. He used apple wood from the orchard and sawed it in quarters and turned it slowly. The ornaments turned out beautifully with reds, browns, and gold streaks. In some ways it looked like cherry and the final product shone bright in the light.

He was pleased and so were his parents when they opened it on Christmas Eve. They placed their one new ornament on the tree. With the lights, that was all there was. All of the ones they had collected for 30 years were destroyed by the storm. That was okay and it didn't bother them at all. They would have time to build another collection starting with this one. So, with all of them sitting by the fire his mom gave him his package. He opened it. It was a watch. "This watch used to belong to my father, Harold. He was a railroad man and this was given to him when he retired. It keeps perfect time."

"Thanks, Mom," said a grateful Larkin, "but where did you have it so that the storm didn't get it?"

"Actually, Son," replied Lawtin, "I had it in my pocket at the hospital. I never used it, but brought it along so your mother would have a way to keep time. She never wears a watch."

"Wow. God really *is* in control isn't He? I've never had a watch before. I'll take good care of it."

"We know."

"Did you give Ginny her present yet?"

"No. Wait a minute, how did you know I had something for her?"

Shirley ignored his question and just asked, "What are you going to give her?"

"I made a bracelet from some of the wood. It's all one piece and I think it turned out pretty well."

"Can I see it, Honey?"

Larkin rolled his eyes at being called "Honey" and went over by the tree to pick it up. He said, "Mom, can Ginny come over tomorrow after church? I'll make sure it's okay with her parents."

Shirley looked over at Lawtin. They had expected this and had already talked about it. "Sure. We'd like that very much."

"Thanks, Mom. But you know she's just a friend." He was in denial on that.

They smiled.

That evening, a Nor'easter came in and dumped a foot of snow. When Larkin awoke, he looked out the window and saw an incredible sight. There in the drive was a sleigh with a team of horses. The edges of the window were all frosty and looking out at it made the scene look like a post card. He didn't know who the team belonged to. Larkin heard someone knocking on the door and the new door bell chime. He liked the new door bell. It even sounded like Christmas! He went down the stairs to see who it was, but his mom beat him to the door. The door hung open with the cold winter air pumping into the room and standing there was- Ginny! "Ginny!" sounded out Larkin, "What is going on? Where did you get the sleigh?"

Ginny just came up to him and gave him a hug and said, "Merry Christmas, Larkin! I rented it from the Amish in Leornardsville. I'm taking us to church!"

"This is cool. Let me go get ready. I'll be right back."

Larkin bounded back up the stairs to his room and threw on his suit. Grabbing Ginny's gift off his dresser, he ran back down to her. She had been waiting and talking to Shirley in the hall. He asked his mom, "Did you know about this, Mom?"

She handed him his coat and hat replying, "Sure did, Son!"

"You traitor!" he said smiling and giving her a hug. Lawtin came into the hall too, and said, "We'll see you both in church. Be careful."

Going out the door they both replied, "We will!"

Ginny went around the sleigh getting in to drive. Larkin asked, "Do you want me to drive the team Ginny?"

"No, Larkin. Mr. Larkin the owner, and yes, that's his name, wanted me to drive as I am used to them. Besides, my voice seems to calm them."

Larkin went up to the horse closest to him and patted it on its nose and asked, "What are their names?"

"The one you are petting is Maurice and the one over here is Wendy."

"Well you two, I hope you don't get too tired in this snow."

Larkin hopped into his seat and Ginny grabbed the reigns. She made the sound, "nick-nick", and off the team went. They didn't say anything, instead watching everything go past them, the sun gleaming off the new snow, the birds flying from branch to branch, the squirrels dislodging the snow hanging precariously on each bough of the pines. The trip was shorter than it should have been, because it was just too much fun. They got there before many of the congregation, so they pulled the sleigh up next to the fence by the back door and tied the team there. The horses were not tired at all. Larkin asked, "When do you have to have them back?"

"We have them for the day. Seeing as it is warming up, I think we can leave them here until after service. Hopefully, the snow won't be all gone when we to back. Mr. Larkin said he'd pick them up at my house at four o'clock."

"I wonder if he is related to the family that I'm named after?"

Pastor Johnson came up to the couple and said, "Merry Christmas you two!" Commenting on the team and sleigh he asked, "This is just wonderful, where did you hire the team?"

Ginny answered, "They are Mr. Larkin's from Leornardsville. I rented them for Larkin's' gift."

"That's so romantic," replied the Pastor. Turning toward Larkin he asked, "What did you get Ginny, Larkin?"

He replied, "OH! I almost forgot!" He picked up Ginny's package from the seat of the sleigh and handed it to her. Going over to his pastor he whispered in his ear, "It's a homemade bracelet. It did it myself."

Whispering back he said to Larkin, "Nice. I hope she likes it."

"Me, too."

Ginny opened the wrapped box and pulled the lid off. When she saw what it was she recognized it immediately. "Oh, it's beautiful, Larkin." She came over and gave him a peck on the cheek.

Larkin blushed and Pastor Johnson said, "It looks like others are beginning to arrive. Let's go in."

The service was beautiful and the Palmer family all sat in their customary pew. Fortunately for Larkin and Ginny, they always sat right behind her family. This service, the Palmers made room for Ginny to sit on the end, by Larkin. The tree was lit up with thousands of white lights and it seemed like the tree top went all the way to the ceiling. The scent of pine wafted through the air and it made the sanctuary smell like outside. It all made for a distraction for the children who seemed to be paying more attention to it than Pastor Johnson's message. He ended with this: "For unto us is born this day in the city of David, a Savior, which is Christ the Lord. Amen."

The congregation replied, "Amen".

Chapter Five

The "Lost" Treasure

When spring came around, Larkin started going to The Homestead more often. His uncles made it fine through the winter, especially with the new bathroom on the porch. All that was left of the barn was a pile of scraps which Tom wanted to burn and that had been sitting there since the tornado and that the cleanup crews had not taken care of. They soaked the pile with kerosene and waited until the three of them were there to watch and contain the fire. They picked a calm afternoon with no wind. It was a Friday the 13th! The pile went up in flames quickly as the spring was again a dry one and the wood was almost a hundred years old. In three hours it was gone completely. All that was left was a pile of ash. Larkin took the hose and made sure all the embers were out before he left to go home. As he sprinkled, he heard the water hitting something more solid than the earth. It sounded out of place. He took the hose closer and directed it to the area he thought it came from and sprayed until he located the sound. It sounded hollow or *metallic!* 'No, it can't be another box?' he thought.

He took a shovel and cleared the rest of the ash and debris from the top of it. Then he soaked the area again so he could walk there. Some of the embers were still hot! Trying not to soak the box because he didn't know what was in it, he sprayed one last time over and around it to be safe. Then he took the shovel and pried it out of the earth. It was heavy. Very heavy! This one was larger than the other boxes and was made of iron. It seemed to be a *real* treasure chest. Not like Benjamin's kid's box, but a true chest for valuables. He went to open it. There was no lock on it, but it would not open due to rust. He picked up the shovel put the blade in the gap between the lid and the box and pried. He pried hard. Then with a jerk it gave way and flipped back so hard Larkin lost his balance and he fell face first toward the box into the top.

After gaining his composure, he looked inside. There in front of him was a true treasure chest. It was full of coins- hundreds of coins- old gold and silver coins. He could tell that they were not American coins. They looked Spanish and English. Larkin pushed the rusty lid shut again and picked up the heavy box. He only made it half way to the house before he had to stop to rest. Tom saw him coming and came out to see what he was carrying. "What do you have there, Larkin?"

Responding almost lackadaisically Larkin said, "Uncle Tom, you are not going to believe this, but I have found another treasure."

Tom opened the lid, took a look inside, closed the lid and said, "It seems you have, Nephew. Pick it up and let's go in."

Larkin picked it up and headed in behind his uncle. When Larkin sat the box down on the kitchen table with a thud, he wondered if it would stand up under the weight. The box had to weigh at least 200 pounds. Uncle Harry heard the noise and came out to the kitchen. Without much excitement Tom said to him, "Looks like Larkin found another treasure, Harry."

"Ah yes, I see that, Tom. What's' in it?"

Larkin said, "Looks like gold and silver coin from England and Spain."

"Anything else?"

"I don't know. I really didn't look at it much." Larkin flipped it open again. On one side was a medallion. On it were the initials, "PC".

Larkin picked it up and gave it to Uncle Harry who said, "Ah, just as I thought- Percifer Carr. But I wonder how it got here?"

"Tell me about it, Uncle."

"Well, about 1778 a man and his wife came out here to care take the Edmeston place. Because the Indians were still raiding, he buried his money. They captured him and his wife and carried them away. Everyone thought he couldn't remember where it was buried when he returned five years later, but that must not have been it. The Indians must have gotten hold of it and reburied it here on our land. Lawtin Senior didn't buy The Homestead until 1792. I think someone found some of his dishes in 1903 or so, but they never found the *real treasure*. Not until now!"

"Uncle, I don't know why God is providing all this for us, but He must have a plan for it."

"Yes, you thought the last treasure was worth a lot for you, this one is worth a great deal more. Pray He gives you the wisdom to use it wisely." Larkin closed the lid and sat down in silence. Harry said, "I suspect Larkin has inherited his Grandma Mary's gift. Do you agree, Tom?"

"Indeed, I do."

"Did she ever hide that money in the well before she died?"

"No. That's an old tale some of the locals spread. She gave it to Elias."

Tom called Larkin's parents to tell them he wouldn't be home. When he hung up, they all just sat at the table pondering what this all meant to them. None of them were to get any sleep that night.

Early the next morning the three of them put together a plan. First, they would catalogue each coin and item in the box. Secondly, they would call the sheriff to tell him of the find. They were curious if there were legal ramifications. Then last of all, they would contact Israel again. They already knew they would sell most of the treasure. Some would be donated to the Brookfield museum, which had just been organized a couple of years before, and some they would keep. It all sounded like a good plan to them.

The catalogue process was a tedious one. There were many coins of the same type. Also, many of the same grade- very fine. But they wanted to know about the coins themselves. Larkin called his dad to have him bring his coin guide from the house. It was one of the few things of his they found after the storm. It contained information concerning coins used in early America that were not minted here. About ten minutes later he arrived with the book. When Lawtin came in the back door with his cane, which he now used all the time, he saw the pile of coins sitting on the table. "Wow! I didn't realize it was such a large amount of coins!"

Larkin said, "Yeah, Dad. So far we have catalogued over five hundred. I just wanted to see if I was right about what they are. Did you bring the book?"

"Sure did. Here you go, Son." Lawtin slapped the book on the table. Picking it up, Larkin knew exactly where to go to find the information he needed.

Lawtin asked Tom, "So this is what kept him here last night? How did he find it?"

"We burned the pile of rubble left over from the barn the storm didn't take away and he was putting out the embers so the fire didn't spread during the night. When the water hit the lid, he knew there was something amiss. It didn't sound right. So, like before, he dug it up! We, Harry and I, think he's inherited his Grandma Mary's gift."

"Maybe so, Tom," Lawtin replied.

"Wow, Dad, this one is a Spanish doubloon. And this one is a British copper. And this one is a Mexican Real. Dad, this is the find of a lifetime and I wasn't even looking!"

"Who's was it? Do you know?"

"We think so. A treasure buried by Percifer Carr about 1775 or so. Don't know how it got on our land though."

"Interesting. What did the sheriff say?"

"There are no legal claims that can be brought against it. It's Larkin's."

63

Correcting him Larkin said, "No Uncle, it's ours. Our- family's!"

Slapping Larkin on the back Lawtin declared, "I'm proud of you, Son."

Smiling and looking up at him he replied, "Thanks, Dad!"

They went back to work. It took them almost a week to finish the job of cataloguing and determining what they would keep, sell, or give away. After it was all said and done there were 5,345 coins. Israel came over when they finished up. He could not believe the sight! "I heard reports it was a large find, but my goodness, this is astounding!"

"Yes," replied Harry, "the Sheriff was amazed as well. He wants us to remove it to his office for safekeeping. He thought we might get robbed!"

Israel laughed and said, "You never know nowadays- even here. So when should I schedule the auction? But I have to tell you, this one will be bigger- much bigger."

"As soon as possible. We don't want to be tempted to keep it. We want to use it with wisdom. I think Percifer would have liked that."

Tom asked, "I hate to put you on the spot Israel, but do you have any idea what it is worth?"

Without hesitation Israel replied, "About, two million dollars, more or less!"

"Oh, my. I'll call the sheriff right now."

"Good idea."

Larkin got to ride into town with the Sherriff and his deputy. For him, it was fun to be in the back seat of a police car. Sherriff Cadwell said, "It's not often we provide security services for our townspeople."

Larkin, not trying to be a wise guy or anything said in response, "It's not often one of them finds two million in treasure either."

The cops roared in laughter. When they arrived at the station, they got out of the car to find a reporter from the newspaper there to greet them. He asked the Sheriff, "Is this the boy who found the treasure?"

"It sure is." The two cops picked up the box and went inside.

The reporter came up to Larkin. "The Sherriff says you're the boy who found the treasure. I'm John Stapleton of the Herald. What's your name?"

"I'm Larkin Palmer."

"Can you tell me about it Larkin?"

"Sure, Mister." Larkin went through the whole story about the fire and hose and Percifer Carr. When he finished he pulled the medallion out of his pocket to show him. "See, it has the initials, "PC" on it".

"That's an amazing story."

"It's the truth."

"What will you do with it?"

"We are going to sell some of it at auction soon. If you want to find out about it call Mr. Israel Waterman the antique dealer who sold my coin last year. He can tell you more."

"Thank you for your time, Larkin, it was nice to meet you." As Stapleton walked away he muttered to himself, "A boy with the gift of finding things. I can make that work. Yes."

"You, too, Sir," Larkin said as the man rudely walked away from him. With that Larkin went in to watch the cops put the treasure in the vault. It was even safer than in the bank now.

After Sheriff Cadwell dropped Larkin back at The Homestead, the boy waved goodbye and went in to see his Uncle Tom. "You know Uncle, I have been thinking about the result of me finding the treasure. It means we will be able to make some changes here that could help The Homestead, but not change it so much that it would hurt it."

Tom was pleased by his maturity. "You don't say? What are your thoughts about it?" Tom motioned for them to go outside. The boy went around the orchard showing Tom his idea for this process or that application. Tom was amazed at what he had learned from him and especially from school about techniques and innovations. Tom listened-nothing more. When Larkin was finished the only thing Tom asked him was, "Anything else, Nephew?"

"Yes, we need to somehow tithe this to the Lord."

"Indeed. Amen."

Israel called the uncles just about dinner time. Larkin could hear Uncle Harry's side of the conversation. "Hello Israel. Yes? Two months? Really? All the way to Albany? You think we need Pinkerton's? We'll do what you think is best, Israel. Thanks. Bye now."

"That was Israel," said Harry. Tom and Larkin looked at each other, smiled, and kept working on dinner. "He's arranged for the auction to be in Albany with Pinkerton's coming here to pick up and transport the treasure there. He thinks it would be safer. Oh, and he wants to sell it in lots; not all together. He thinks we'll get more for it. I told him to use his best judgment."

"Sounds good, Harry," said Tom.

"Yes, Uncle, sounds good."

"Oh by the way, Larkin, this is a bag of coins that we kept out of the treasure for you to keep." Harry placed the bag by Larkin just as they were about to sit down to eat.

"Could I say grace tonight, Uncle?" He nodded yes. Larkin began, "Dear Lord. You give us our daily bread and now as we eat, we give You thanks. But You take away and give to us according to Your will as we have seen this year. Bless us Lord with wisdom that we may use the gifts You give us according to Your wishes. In Jesus name, Amen."

"Amen," said his uncles.

Harry smiled and said, "Dig in boys!"

But, before Larkin put food on his plate, he opened the top of his bag and poured a dozen of the best looking coins in the treasure on it, clanking as they fell. His eyes lit up and he said, "Wow! Thanks, Uncles!"

The news of the find and sale didn't go unnoticed at the local Lodge. The Grand Master and Samuel Enoos, one a doctor and the other a lawyer, tried to find a way to harass the family.

Enoos said, "We both know that it was Edmestons' money. He was a brother in the lodge. And Carr, too. I think we could use some legal methods to scare them. Want me to proceed?"

The Grand Master laughed and said, "I don't think we could take it from them, but we sure could scare them. Sure. Why not? Do it!"

"What about the higher-ups?"

"They won't care, because they told me to do it. Don't really know why." It had been a generation since...

While waiting for the sale in a couple of months, Larkin and Tom finally had time to work in the orchard. By the grace of God, the rains came after the trees had budded and the apples were on them. It may have started out a dry spring, but it ended up a wet one. And the trees were loaded. Larkin took out his pocket watch and looked at the time. It was almost time for his parents to come get him. They were going as a family to Rochester to get the doctors evaluation on his dad's condition. He got up from the table where he had his drawing of the orchard laid out. It showed every tree, its type, and condition. If they knew, it showed its age and the last time it was grafted. Because of the storm, they had put off the grafting project this year, but it would be done next year for sure!

He went into his bedroom and retrieved his coat and shoes. His mom had packed a bag for him from home and they were to be there soon. He could always count on her. They pulled up and honked the horn. Even after getting the money from the sale of Ben's coin, they still had the same old truck. Lawtin thought it was fine. Larkin headed out the door and said to his uncles, "Bye, Uncles, see you in a couple of days."

They replied in unison, "Bye, Larkin. Godspeed."

He piled into the truck next to his dad and slammed the door shut. Shirley was driving. It sometimes hurt his dad's legs to drive now, so rather than try to go it on a long drive like this he abdicated the steering wheel to her. "Hi, Dad. Hi, Mom," said the boy to his parents.

Smiling back at him Lawtin said, "Hi, Son. Ready for a road trip?"

"You bet, Dad."

"I think it will take about two hours to get there," said Shirley.

"That's not too bad," commented the boy. "But Dad, will that be okay for you?"

Lawtin was happy his son was concerned about him and said, "Well if I start to get cramped up or anything, we'll just stop and let me walk around a bit. We'll see."

Shirley drove on toward Rochester and the three commented on the trees and fields. The two adults were as amazed as Tom was about Larkin's knowledge. School seemed to be his priority now and they were pleased.

The doctors didn't keep them waiting when Lawtin arrived. They took him right into X-Ray and took the follow-up pictures of his back. After an hour or so, they called him into the head surgeon's office. All of them went in and waited to hear the findings. "Lawtin, I'm happy to report that it looks like the operation was a success. But, I'd like to caution you that even though you have healed very well, you may never get on the tractor again. The work on the farm is off limits. One more fall like that and either you will be paralyzed for life, or dead."

The other two looked at him. "I've been praying about it doctor; for the Lord to give me understanding and patience. Now I know I need to add acceptance to the list. Okay, but what *can* I do?"

"If you take it easy you can help with the orchard, but that's about all. No lifting over twenty-five pounds. Got it?"

"Yes, Sir. I'm grateful. Thanks."

Patting him on the back the doctor said, "You're welcome. See you in another six months."

The trio got up and made their way to the door not saying a word. When they got out into the hall however, Larkin wanted to know what his dad was thinking. He asked, "Dad, how do you feel about that?"

His dad came over to him and put his arm around him as they walked down the hospital hall and said, "Just fine, Son. God is in control."

"That's right, Dad. That's right."

When they got home from the long day on the road, Larkin put his clothes from the trip away as his mother had asked him to. When he got back downstairs, he picked up the phone and called his uncles. "How's it going over there, Uncle Tom?" he asked.

"Just fine, Larkin. How's your dad?"

"The doctor said he's doing well. He just won't be able to do as much as he used to."

"Can he pick apples?"

"Oh, I think he'd like that!"

"You know I think I can arrange that for him this year. We'll have a bumper crop."

Lawtin overheard Larkin, but wanted to know what Tom had said. "Uncle, my dad would like to hear what you just said." He handed him the phone.

Tom said, "Lawtin, we're going to have a bumper crop this year. Do you think we could count on you to help us pick some apples?"

"You bet, Tom. I'd love to."

A fortnight later the family was getting excited about the auction. It was to be in a couple of days, but there wasn't a car large enough to get everyone in for the trip. Larkin wondered what they were going to do about that. He called Mr. Waterman. "Say, Mr. Waterman, this is Larkin Palmer. We'd all like to be able to go to the auction, but we don't have a car big enough to get us all to Albany. All we have are two pickup trucks."

"Larkin, don't worry about it. I'll take care of it. Expect a car there to pick you up about three hours before the auction."

"Really? Thanks, Mr. Waterman."

Larkin hung up. Waterman didn't, and instead he put his finger on the dial and called the Ford dealer in Hamilton. "Ray, this is Israel. Do you still have that new Lincoln on the lot? Good. I'll take it. No. Not for me, for the Palmers. Yeah, they don't even have a car. Yeah, with this commission it's the least I can do for them. Just send it over to them by ten o'clock on Saturday. Thanks, Ray." Placing the phone on the receiver he said, "There. That takes care of that."

Shirley had the truck up by the door. She was about to call Tom and Harry when two cars pulled into the drive. The lead car blocked her in and she went out to see who it was. A man got out of the Lincoln and came up to her. "Are you Mrs. Palmer?" he asked.

"Why yes," she replied cautiously.

"Please sign here." He handed her a piece of paper on a tablet.

"What's this for?" she asked as she signed the receipt.

"Your new car." The man walked back to the other car waiting for him and got in.

"My new what? But wait!" She looked at the receipt from Nilles Ford. Sure enough, it was all made out to them, but it was stamped, "Paid in full." But in the corner she saw a clue, "Israel". She smiled and went to look at the car.

Larkin ran up with his suitcase and said, "Is this the car Israel sent?"

"So you know about this?"

"Yes, Mom, he said he'd send a car over so we could all go to the auction together. Why?"

"Because he *gave* it to us. That's why."

"Wow!" Larkin put his hands on the new 1974 Lincoln. It was beautiful. Light brown metallic, vinyl roof, with brown leather interior. And it had the works!

Lawtin came out with his bag. "What's this?"

"It's our new car, Dad," said Larkin.

"Is that so?"

"It seems Israel bought it for us," said Shirley.

"Is that so?"

"I better call your brothers and have them wait at their house. We'll go get them."

Enthusiastically Lawtin said, "I guess so!"

"Dad, are you okay?"

"Wow, look at that car. Yeah, I'm sorry, I'm okay. I just can't believe it."

Shirley came back out of the house with her bag. "They're ready, so let's get going."

Lawtin said, "Shirley, I'm driving."

She laughed and said, "I figured."

Lawtin picked up his brothers and headed for Albany. They still had a couple of hours and plenty of time to get there. They talked about Israel and the car, but they also talked about the sale. "I have been wondering how much the auction would bring," said Larkin, "and you know what?"

Everyone in the car said, "What?"

"It doesn't matter. What God gives He gives. We'll use it in the best manner possible and tithe, too."

Everyone in the car said, "Amen!"

When they arrived at the hall, (Israel had rented the VFW Hall because it was large enough to handle the crowd without costing too much) they found Israel right away. Lawtin went up to him and gave him a big hug. "Thank you, Israel. It is one of the nicest things anyone has ever done for us."

Israel wasn't used to "man hugs" but he replied without reaction, "Don't mention it, Lawtin. It was my pleasure. Your seats are up toward the front second row left. Look for the "saved" signs on the seats."

"How long will the auction take?"

"It's set up in 42 lots. There is only one single coin to be sold. All the rest go in lots. Five thousand coins is a lot of coins. So, I figure it will take about three hours, more or less."

"Okay. If we get bored is there a restaurant or something close?"

"Yes, there's an Italian place across the street. Lombardo's. When we finish the auction, I'll find you to give you the official results."

"Thanks for everything, Israel."

"No, please Lawtin, thank *you*. I'll be making a lot of money here today too, all because of Larkin. Oh- and Percifer Carr." They all laughed at that one!

They took a seat and watched the people start to arrive. Larkin was excited! There were people from all over the world coming for the auction. Israel said he had registrations from ten countries and twenty states. Larkin said, "Boy, Dad, I thought the last auction was big, but this one will be something else."

"You've outdone yourself this time, Larkin."

"I guess so. And maybe Grandma Mary had something to do with it, too."

Lawtin winked and looked at the program. Larkin gawked.

They saw a man from India come in the door with a very tall guard with a turban on. Then a girl from South America, he guessed Peru, because of her dress, came up to the front row and sat down in front of them. She turned and asked Larkin, "Are you the boy who found the treasure?"

"Why yes, my name is Larkin."

She held out her hand and introduced herself, "My name is Pilar. Nice to meet you. I am here to try to purchase the Mexican silver the Conquistadors stole from my ancestors."

"I see. I wish you good luck."

"Thank you, Larkin." She turned around as her parents came up to her and sat down. She said something to them in Spanish and they turned around and smiled at him. Larkin figured they didn't speak English and she acted as their interpreter.

He thought to himself, 'Man oh man, I must be famous or something.' Then he saw it- lying on the floor was a flyer for the auction. There on the back page was his picture! He got up and went to the doorman. He asked for a flyer and went back to his seat. Sure enough, Israel had placed the whole story on the back, complete with his picture. *"Aw Mom, look at this!"* He handed her the flyer.

She said, "Larkin you should be honored. This is great."

"But it's so *embarrassing*."

"Sometimes that's life."

"I'm going out to the bathroom."

"Okay, but don't leave the building without telling us."

Larkin got up and made his way to the aisle. When he did, Pilar saw him leaving. She got up and came toward him. He thought, 'Oh great. I've got a groupie.'

"Hello, Larkin. I hope you don't think it to forward of me, but may I ask you to accompany me to the rest rooms?"

"Oh sure, that's where I was going anyway." They walked toward the lobby. He looked at her and found that she was kind of pretty. She saw him looking and blushed.

She said, "This is the first time we come to the United States. It is very different from Peru. Is my English okay?"

Larkin felt a little more at ease and replied, "It is very good and much better than my Spanish." They both chuckled. When they got to the lobby, he pointed toward the Ladies room and he went toward the Men's. While there, he overheard a man with a German accent say he thought this would be a good auction, especially for the seller. He hoped so!

They met back in the lobby and Larkin asked Pilar, "Would you like some popcorn or something to drink?"

"That would be nice. I didn't have time to eat lunch. We came straight from the airport."

Walking up to the concession stand he spied a sno-cone. He asked her, "Would you like to try a sno-cone? They are very good." He pointed at the frozen confection. She nodded her head and he ordered them each one and popcorn. After paying, they went toward the door. Outside they found a bench where they could sit and eat them and be a little messy.

She said, "This is very refreshing. Ice and what flavor is this?"

He said, "It's supposed to be berry. I don't know what flavor it is." They laughed. "I'm getting it all over. I may need to go back to the rest room when we finish and wash up," said Larkin.

She said slurping at the ice, "Me too."

He stuck out his tongue, which had turned dark red and said, "Look!"

She laughed and stuck her tongue back out at him in return.

They talked about her trip and how it was her dream to come to the United States. The fact that Larkin had found an important archeological find was what brought her there. Pilar said, "My father says that you have made an important discovery. He is most anxious to try to buy as much as possible."

Just then the auctioneer called the people to the auditorium. He said, "Five minutes and we will begin the auction. Please take your seats."

Larkin said, "We had better go." Stopping in the rest rooms they washed up and went back in.

"It was nice getting to know you Larkin," said Pilar, "I'd like to see you later if I could. We will be in town for a few days."

"Maybe. Let's talk after the auction with our parents."

"Okay."

Before they went back in they heard the sound of a diesel truck pull up to the front door. Suddenly the doors flew open and two armed guards with guns drawn held them open for two other guards with the treasure in sealed bags. The commotion the guards brought to the hall got everybody excited! Larkin said, "Wow, look at that! Armed guards and everything!"

The Pinkerton Guards, dressed in uniforms and looking very professional, carried the bags up to the front and placed them on the auction table. Israel signed for the shipment while the auctioneer opened it to make sure it was still all ready to be sold. "It's all in order, Israel," he said.

"Good. Let's begin then," said Israel.

They took their seats and Larkin whispered to his mother, "She wants to see me after the auction, Mom."

The auctioneer began. The first item to be sold was a lot of 100 Mexican Silver Reales which the auctioneer held up. "Ladies and gentlemen. This is a roll of 100, Charles and Johanna Mexican Reales, struck in 1542. They are in excellent condition. I'd like to start the bidding at ten thousand dollars." No bids came. "Alright, then, who'll give me five thousand?" The bids started to come. Larkin figured they just had to get warmed up. After a while the two kids got bored. Both sets of parents were quite satisfied with how the auction was going along. Pilar's dad was winning some bids and Lawtin just saw the total go up and up. He wrote the dollar amount of each item sold on his auction sheet. It was going well.

Larkin was restless by the time they were half way through. He knew the Lord was in charge and he figured it was all just fine with him. "Mom, can I go outside?"

"They will be taking a break in a little bit. Wait until then and we'll go out and meet Pilar and her parents."

"Okay, Mom."

When the break came, Larkin was hungry. When everyone stood up Pilar turned around and said, "My parents would like to take your family to eat something when we are finished. They suggested the Italian place across the street."

Shirley overheard the conversation and said, "I'm Larkin's mom, Shirley. I'll speak with Lawtin and let you know. We have a long drive back tonight." Pilar shook her head as if she understood and went to tell her parents.

Larkin hustled out of the hall and was at the concession stand before the rest of the crowd got there. "I'll have two hot dogs and a Coke please."

Uncle Tom came up to him and chuckling, said, "Is one of those for me?"

"Oh, sure Uncle. Help yourself."

Tom took one with a smile and said, "Thanks, Larkin. I don't think I could make it till dinner."

The rest of the group all came together into the front entry. Pilar said to them all, "I'd like to introduce my parents to you all, Manuel and Camille Rojas. We are from Peru."

Larkin said, "This is my Dad and Mom, Lawtin and Shirley Palmer." They all shook hands.

Shirley said to Pilar, "Tell your parents we'd love to have dinner with them." Pilar was excited and told her parents in Spanish. Shirley said to Larkin, "Dad said that we'll stay the night here. It's a long drive and we'll be tired."

Larkin was excited and said, "Alright!"

Pilar walked back over to Larkin and said, "My parents are going back in, but they said I didn't have to. Do you want to go outside and sit?"

Shirley overheard her again. She said to the kids, "Go ahead. When the single coin is sold, I'll come and get you." She started back toward the hall.

Larkin yelled back at her, "Okay, Mom."

They walked out the door.

Pilar asked, "What's the single coin?"

"It's a rare gold piece. They say its worth a lot."

"I hope it brings much for you."

"Thank you Pilar, but the auction is for my family. We will use the money for our farms- for our future."

"That is a wise thing, Larkin."

"I've asked God for wisdom to use this gift wisely. I guess He's already started to help me with that."

"Indeed."

They walked around the property and Lincoln Park with its flags and stage. The clock on the park tower rang four. Larkin took out his watch and checked it. It was four on the dot.

Pilar saw his watch and said, "That is a beautiful watch, and the symbol on the back is interesting. Have I seen it before?"

"Possibly. This pocket watch was my mother's father's. He was a railroad employee and I think it was a gift when he retired."

"May I see it?" He handed it to her.

"This looks like one my father has. I think it is a Mason's cross. He is in a Lodge."

"Hmm. Maybe so." She handed it back to him. He'd have to see about *that* new information.

They sat down on the bench and talked. Pilar told him about the mountains of Peru. He told her about the orchard at The Homestead and the farm. Each of them was enthralled with the others way of life. Larkin asked, "Could I have your address so I can write to you?"

"Oh yes, I would like that."

Just then, his mom came out and yelled, "Larkin, they are about to sell the coin."

"Coming, Mom." He turned to his new friend and said, "Let's go, Pilar. I've got to see this."

When they got back to their seats the bidding had already begun. It was up to five thousand dollars. By the time it was all over, the single gold coin went for twenty thousand dollars. Not as much as the penny last year, for sure, but a pretty nice sum. Lawtin said, "Well that's it, Larkin. It doesn't look like we got what Israel predicted, but it was good enough."

Uncle Harry said, "Let's go celebrate!"

The entire group got up and made their way toward the restaurant. Before they went out of the building, Israel came up to them and showed Lawtin his total, "I'll send the check to the bank as before."

"That's fine, Israel, and thanks again."

"I hope your son keeps on finding things."

"You'll be the first to know, Israel."

They both laughed. But Lawtin had spoken too soon...

Lawtin sat across the table from Mr. Rojas. Pilar sat in between her parents and faced Lawtin and Shirley so she could interpret. Harry and Tom sat on the end by themselves. They all ordered their food and talked trying to get to know each other. Mr. Rojas was in the coffee business and was trying to return the things he bought to the country. He had purchased almost fifty thousand dollars worth of silver coins and was pleased that he was able to do so. He thanked Larkin through Pilar and smiled shaking his head. Larkin could tell he was an aristocrat by his demeanor, grace, and appearance. Pilar was definitely his daughter!

The server brought their food. Pilar had never had spaghetti before. "Really? You've never had spaghetti before, Pilar?" asked Larkin.
"No, Larkin."
"I eat it all the time. It's good."

Just before they all dug in, a song came on over the speaker system above their table. It was a Louis Prima song called, "Angelina". 'Funny', Larkin thought. He could see Pilar smile and tap her foot along with the tune.

The food was the best Italian food around. And tonight, they did a good job on it too! Uncle Tom rubbed his stomach and said, "Well I think that did it. I'm ready to hit the hay."
"Man Uncle Tom, you ate it all?"
"Sure did, Larkin."
"He can eat his weight in spaghetti," said Harry.
Larkin laughed. The server brought their ice cream dessert. Pilar looked at it funny. "They call it Spumoni, Pilar," said Larkin to her, "it's better than it looks."

Pilar finished her ice cream last and sat the dish on the table. The server brought the check and handed it to Lawtin. Pilar saw this and so did her parents, whose eyes lit up and they motioned for Lawtin to give it to them.
Pilar said, "Please, you must allow my father to pay. He would be most insulted if you did not." Out of respect, Lawtin handed the check to Pilar and her father. Manuel smiled and handed the server the money. The families got up, shook hands once again saying their thank you's and goodbyes, and started to walk out of Lombardo's.

Pilar handed Larkin a piece of paper with her address. Larkin said, "Oh, I forgot." Picking up a napkin he asked the server for a pen and he wrote his address down for Pilar. "There," he said handing her the tiny square of paper.
"Thank you, Larkin. I will remember my first trip to America all my life. I will write to you."
Her parents had gone out the door and noticing this she gave Larkin a peck on the cheek and left the building. Blushing, he thought to himself, 'Wow. Maybe I am getting famous.'
Tom came up to him and said, "Better watch out, Casanova!"
Larkin said, "Aw, c'mon Uncle!" and followed his family to the car. They all snickered at that one.

They drove a little ways towards home and found a "Mom and Pop" motel on the highway North- The Family Inn. They got two rooms that adjoined one another. Larkin knew his uncles snored, so he wanted to be in the room with his parents for sure! They took in their travel bags and got ready for bed. It had been an eventful day and they were all tired. It wasn't long that Larkin was in bed that he heard his Uncle Tom snoring in the- next room! 'Oh boy!' thought Larkin, but he went to sleep anyway thinking about his new friend, Pilar, and wondered if he'd ever see her again. The piece of paper fell to the floor and was lost under the bed. Like many friends of youth, this one, too, seemed to vanish as quickly as a breath.

Chapter Six

The Journey

The rest of the summer flew by. School started and the memories of hot days turned to the reality of cool nights. Perfect fall weather for apples! The crop of Macintosh apples was superb. Tom tended to it with organic methods making sure the crop had not been attacked by worms, birds, nor the weather, and making sure Larkin learned everything he could. Tom had such an abundance of apples he sold many to new customers. His business was growing and he contracted with pickers who were friends of Percy's. They expected to begin by the end of September and finish in two weeks. A lot faster than Tom could do it for sure!

Meanwhile, Larkin got back into the swing of things at school. He had missed Ginny. They didn't act like they were boyfriend and girlfriend, but they did talk a lot. The kids all wanted to know about the treasure and everything he had done that summer. However, he couldn't tell them all of it. Could he? He did have fun telling them what he could about the Palmers and most of all Percifer, and how much treasure he had left behind. And of course, show and tell with his coins was cool!

Lawtin was doing much better and used the cane less and less. He wished he could go out and help Percy and Arville with the cows, but he only went out and took a look making sure all was in order. Percy was doing a great job with the farm. Now that they had the money from the second auction, the family was going through the process of redirection for the farm. Larkin had been reading about new innovations and technology for milking machines. He passed on information to his uncle for the orchard and they thanked God for what had been happening in their lives. But just when things seemed to be on a roll, just when things seemed to finally be going good, that's when it happens. With the Eraser, it was always "something." The letter came to The Homestead. It was postmarked from Bavaria, Germany. Addressed to Larkin Palmer, it was from the attorney of the descendants of – Percifer Carr!

Tom called Lawtin. "Lawtin, I hope it was alright, but I went ahead and read the letter from this attorney. It seems ridiculous to me Lawtin, but it could tie up our using the money until we prove that the treasure is ours. They plan on suing to get all of it back. We need to contact an attorney."

"Then go ahead and do so."

"I'll call right away. I don't think they have anything to go on. It sure is aggravating!"

"Indeed! And I'll ask Larkin if he knows anything about the family of Percifer."

"Good idea, Lawtin!"

"Let me know what happens, Tom."

"Will do."

Little did they know it really wasn't the family of Percifer, but a nemesis from the past: The Illuminists and Freemasons.

Tom spoke with their attorney. He asked Tom to forward the letter to him and read it over the phone to him. When he finished, he asked, "What do you think, Mr. Enoos?"

"I doubt very much if they have any claim. It would be difficult to prove a connection to a family after this long. Besides, how would they prove it is Percifer's treasure? I wouldn't worry about it."

"I hope you are right, Samuel. I'll send it on and just let me know how things proceed. Okay?"

"I'll take care of it. Don't worry about a thing. In the meanwhile, I suggest you do not spend any of the proceeds of the sale, just in case."

"Will do, but that doesn't sound very optimistic."

Samuel Enoos laughed and hung up the phone. He put on his coat and headed out his door to the Lodge.

Enoos asked his superior when he sat down in front of the massive desk in the Lodge office, "I had some fun with the Palmers today and I hate to see this wrap up. But to tell you the truth, brother, it spooks me to even do this. I don't want to get rubbed out." He chuckled.

The Grand Master didn't and said, "It's not a laughing matter, Samuel. Only we know about this. It has been secret for a long time and we pass it down to those that need to know. It is- you and me. If we need to bring in anyone else we will. If, that is…"

"What?"

"The higher ups let us."

When Larkin got home from school his dad asked him about Percifer's family. "As far as I know Dad, Mr. Carr had no children and died penniless. And it may have been that the treasure wasn't even his. It may have been Col. Edmestons'!"

"That's interesting. Why do you say that?"

"Because, if he was running the place, the Colonel would have given him money to do so. Without a bank here, he would have buried it. And, seeing as he didn't have anything else, it may not have been his in the first place. But, how would that be proven?"

"It would be difficult. However, as there was the medallion in the box with "PC" on it, it would seem to indicate it was Percifer's. Thanks for the information, Son."

"You bet, Dad. Is Percy out in the barn?"

"Yes, I'm sure he'd like to see you."

"I'd like to go out and help if he needs it. It has been a long time since I was out there."

Larkin went out to the barn to see Percy. Arville was there, too, and he greeted Larkin first. "Well hello, Larkin, how have you been?"

"Just fine, Arville. I've missed coming out here, so I thought I'd say hello."

"It has been a while since you've been out here," said Percy. "How is it going at The Homestead?"

"Great. Uncle Tom is teaching me a lot and its fun, too. Will you be helping with the picking?"

"No, and you might want to tell your dad that he won't have to go either. It seems Mr. Tom contracted with some friends of mine to do it. The crop is so large he didn't want to take chances not getting it all out in time. Soooo- we can watch and "snooper-vise." They all laughed.

"Okay Percy, I'll tell my Dad, but I think he'll be disappointed."

"Yes, that could be."

"Are you done milking?"

"No, want to?"

"I'd like to help again. I miss it sometimes." The two hands looked at each other and laughed.
As Larkin got a stool and a bucket Percy said, "RRRight!"

The Orchard was picked and the harvest was the best in a long, long while. Lawtin wasn't too upset about not getting to help pick, but he went out and got some for the family, so they could can for winter. He was into working on the future of the two farms, as well. Nothing seemed to be happening with the attorney, which placed doubt on spending the money, so he proceeded to call Tom. "Say Tom, have you heard anything from the attorney about the letter we received from Europe?"

"As a matter of fact, I got a letter from him yesterday stating that the people who sent it realized they wouldn't be able to prove anything and have dropped pursuing it. Therefore, we are free and clear."

"Good. I want to start buying the equipment we have been planning on. We have to order yours so you can have it by spring and mine will require a new building. I've called the contractor and he'll be starting now before the snow flies."

"Sounds like a plan, Lawtin."

"Good. Is Larkin still there? It's almost time for supper."

"Yes. He was watching the packaging process. I'll send him home. Bye."

"Thanks. Bye Tom."

Unfortunately, Lawtin didn't know who the family was dealing with and just because "they" couldn't pursue their plan one way, didn't mean they wouldn't pursue it another. But when and how would that be?

And the journey of life went on. The two farms grew ever more technological. The family utilized new methods and became more profitable. Lawtin's new dairy barn now allowed for more cows and the new modern barn at The Homestead allowed for sales of apples and produce there at the orchard. Larkin grew into a wise young man being able to manage either the new dairy at home or the orchard at The Homestead. He and Ginny had become an "item" and had been seriously considering marriage. Both sets of parents approved. Uncle Harry had died when he was a freshman in high school and since then, Tom relied on Larkin even more. What Tom really needed was the company, so Larkin stayed there every other night. Lawtin thought this was a good idea. He didn't want Tom to feel like the family had abandoned him. Besides, Larkin loved being there and helping in the orchard. They had grafted part of it a couple of years ago and it was going well. They had decided to plant blackberries, strawberries, and they were even considering expanding the maples as well, for syrup. Larkin had plenty of time to think about that. What he had not thought of for a long time was The Eraser. He did not want to. There was no need.

When Larkin went to The Homestead Friday after school, he saw Tom putting stakes in the ground by where the old barn had been. "What are you doing, Uncle Tom?"

"I've decided we need to rebuild the old barn."

"How will we do that?"

"We have the ability financially to go forward with it. What we need is the plans. I'm trying to remember where exactly it was and these stakes seem to be close to the old footings."

"I think I can come up with a set of plans Uncle. Is there a barn builder in the county?"

"Yes. There is a crew of Amish builders we can hire. They will be able to handle anything we want."

"Do you want me to get on it right away?" He looked at Tom's reaction when he just stood there looking at him and grinned. "Stupid question, Uncle?"

Tom said, "I'll get on the phone in the morning and see what they recommend to us for materials. I'll place the order as soon as you get me the plans."

Larkin smiled and said, "I'll get on it!"

Chapter Seven

The Cardboard Box

Immediately, Larkin went into the house and to Uncle Harry's old desk. As he took out the supplies he needed to start drawing the plans, he thought about his uncle and that he would be happy to see the old barn back up again. He remembered that Harry had cried when the tornado had swept it away. And then he saw it again- behind the corner of the desk was a cardboard box. It was *the cardboard box!* All the memories came flooding back. He really didn't want to open it up, but something compelled him to. On top was the Journal. A piece of tape held a note to it. He read:

"Dear Nephew, I know it has been a while since you have thought of the contents of this box. I ask you to not delay in reading the Journal. The letter from Germany only solidifies my concern that you know the entire story. Please don't delay. In Love, Uncle Harry."

Larkin laid down the paper he had taken from the desk and picked up the Journal. A tear came to his eye. He knew his uncle had cared for him very much and he missed him. Slowly he opened it, but he just couldn't do it yet. Closing the leather cover, he sat it back down. He rummaged through the box and saw everything he had placed inside it. It was all still there. Every box sat there ominously, and on the bottom, The Eraser Box. What caught his eye was the genealogy. He had not done anything with it even though he had asked his uncles to help to complete it. He unrolled the large paper. Obviously, Harry had done it all. He followed the lines back on both of his parents' sides. Harry had done a great job completing them as far back as 1581 A.D. in England. He was surprised to see how many people in town he was related to: The Buttons, the Halls, the Browns, and the Chases. Indeed, not many people move away from Brookfield and Madison County. He was glad to see this point of reference as he figured he may need it when he read the Journal. Not only would he need that, but a history of the county as well!

Tom came in to find Larkin sitting at the table with the cardboard box. Stunned, Larkin almost jumped out of his chair. "Whew Uncle, you scared me."

"Is that what got you so jumpy?" he said pointing at the box.

"I suppose so."

"Well, I don't blame you. I'm glad I never was given the enormous responsibility, and I'll pray for you every day Larkin."

"Thank you, Uncle. Can you help me if I need it?"

"If I can, you may call on me anytime."

Larkin placed everything back in the box again and shut the lid. Sitting it back in the corner, he figured he'd get to it after he got the plans drawn for his uncle.

Tom began to cook up something for supper and Larkin got going on drawing the plans. He had taken drafting and it was simple enough for him to recall the layout. Having been in the barn so many times, he knew it by heart. The only thing he had to get was the outer wall dimensions.

He asked Tom, "Do you have a hundred foot tape somewhere, Uncle?"

"Yes, its hanging on the north wall of the new barn by the door."

"I'm going out to get a couple of measurements."

"Okay, I'll call you when supper is ready."

"I'll be right back."

The sun was starting to go down, but he could still see well enough to take the measurements. The barn footings were sixty feet wide by one hundred twenty feet long. There was a huge rock on the corner of one end. Larkin lifted up the heavy rock and rolled it out of the way. Then, he went back over and stood on the same spot. He scratched at the spot with his foot. "Thunk." It sounded metallic and hollow. 'Not again,' he thought. He got down on his hands and knees and brushed aside the loose dirt. Indeed, it was another box! This one was significantly larger than any of the others. After dealing with the cardboard box already tonight, he didn't want another one coming into his life. Consequently, he went back over to the rock and rolled it back on top of the lid. Taking the measurements with him, he went in to have supper with his uncle.

After a supper of beef stew and homemade rolls, Larkin finished up his first rendering of the barn. Tom had found a picture of the front and side elevations of it, which helped Larkin considerably. Holding it up Larkin said, "What do you think, Uncle?"

"I think that we will soon have a barn!" said Tom smiling.

Chapter Eight

The Silver Chest

In the morning, Larkin helped Tom with the chores. For food, Tom still kept some chickens, a couple head of beef, and a pig. Plus, he grew a vegetable garden for fresh greens. The Homestead was pretty self sufficient. When they finished, Tom went in to wash up and make a breakfast of eggs and bacon. Larkin stayed behind and went over to the rock. It seemed to call to him. After he saw Tom go in, he rolled the rock out of the way again. From what he could determine, this box was about five feet away from where he had found Percifer's lost treasure box. He was almost afraid to uncover it. He couldn't lift this one, for it was much too heavy. Uncovering the lid, he found the latch on the side and as there was no lock, he flipped the latch open and lifted the lid. He could not believe his eyes! Inside the chest were bars- hundreds of crude silver and gold bars. He almost fainted. He thought the other two discoveries were huge, but this one, this silver chest would be the discovery of the century!

Larkin closed the lid with a quick slap, dust flying about him. What was he going to do? He couldn't leave it there, because the Amish would find it when the building began. He didn't want to make a big deal out of it and let the public know, because there would most certainly be another letter and claim to it. He knew he couldn't keep it a secret, so he went inside to see his uncle. Going in the door, he could smell the bacon cooking and hear the crackling in the fry pan. His uncle asked him, "How would you like your eggs?"

"Over easy, Uncle."

Tom could sense something in Larkin's voice. "What's on your mind, Larkin?"

"I know you won't believe this, because I don't either Uncle, but I just found another treasure out there."

Tom dropped his spatula on the floor and said, "Oh."

Neither one of them said anything after that. After breakfast was cleaned up, the two walked out to where the old barn had stood. Tom followed Larkin over to the corner. Larkin moved the rock aside again. Lifting the lid, Larkin showed Tom its contents. "Yup. I'd say you've found a treasure there Larkin. What you gonna do with it?"

"I think we better move it. But, we need the John Deere for this one."

Tom drove the tractor over to the site and put a chain on the forks. While he was away, Larkin had uncovered the handles and top of the chest with the shovel. They placed the chain through the handles and Larkin signaled Tom to lift. The front of the John Deere began to go down under the weight of the chest. In fact, Larkin was afraid the tractor was going to come off the ground, but as soon as the chest was free from the earth, the rear tires settled back down and the forks came up into the air. The chest was free of its grave, loose dirt dropping all over like siftings of flour.

Maneuvering the John Deer, Tom crept up to the back door of the house, chest swaying to and fro with the chains clanking against the forks the whole way there, announcing to the world what they were doing. Larkin looked around as they made their way to the door, but saw no one. The old outside entrance to the cellar had been nailed shut years ago. Taking a hammer and pry bars each the two men pulled the nails and freed the door. The door creaked open from having rusty hinges. Then, Tom pulled the tractor up to the door and stairs leading to the cellar. Slowly, they let the chest down into the darkness, where Larkin had placed three pieces of steel pipe onto the floor. When the chest rested upon them, Larkin undid the chains and Tom pulled away from the house. He put the tractor back out by the barn and came back to the house, closing the outside cellar door behind him. Larkin tugged on the handle and pulled the chest toward the center of the room. Then he stopped and opened it.

Larkin just stood there looking into the chest. As tempting as it was, he had not even touched one of the bars before Tom came in. Tom took the trouble light by the work bench and placed it above the chest. Larkin said, "I've heard of these kinds of bars before. They would cut off pieces to pay for debts, or just cut them to make hand stamped coins." He picked one up. "It looks Spanish, just like the coins in Percifer's treasure were."

Tom picked up a gold bar and wiped off the dust. He said, "I guess we should count each of them, Larkin."

"That's true Uncle, but my question is, "Who's is this?"".

"Don't know."

Opening the heavy floor door to the kitchen by pushing up, a tether chain catching it before it hit the wall, Larkin went upstairs and retrieved a piece of paper from Harry's desk. He looked out the window and saw a car drive away. As he had not seen it before, he figured someone had come to the orchard and saw they were closed and left. Larkin hoped that was the case. He went back downstairs and the two got to work. Even though the bars were of different materials, they all seemed to be the same size, one and a half inches in diameter and sixteen inches long, and they fit in the chest perfectly. When they were done, there were eight-hundred ninety-eight gold bars and four-hundred silver- twelve-hundred ninety-eight in total. There seemed to be an odd number of gold bars, almost as if two were missing. "Okay, so now we know what we have," said Larkin, "but what do we do with them?"

"Good question," said Tom.

"We don't need the money, so we don't have to sell them."

"No, but think of what good they could do if we gave them away," said Tom.

"Yes, but I think we should consider all the options first." With that statement Larkin closed the lid of the chest, but it slid from his hands and it slammed shut. And then they saw it- a design. The dirt that had compacted into the ornate silver lid had dried and when it slammed the impact knocked the debris loose. There before them on top of the lid was- a Pyramid and the "All-Seeing eye". They looked at each other once, twice, and again a third time. This made all the difference in the world. The treasure would go nowhere! Tom said, "We must tell *no one* about this. The chest can stay here indefinitely. It is time for you to read the Journal, Larkin. You *must* read the Journal."

Larkin heard the fear and immediacy of Toms' statement. They turned off the lights and headed upstairs. They could sense there was something sinister and evil in it, but they needed to know more. Tom did not know, it was only for the Keeper of the family to know. It was up to Larkin.

Chapter Nine

The Journal

Larkin went back to Uncle Harry's desk again. He saw the box still sitting next to it. Picking up the heavy cardboard box, he knew he should study all of its contents very carefully. He thought about his whole situation. Something didn't seem quite right with this. Why would there be a Masonic treasure chest buried on his family's land? The Palmers had never been Masons and in fact, he knew they were somehow against them and their beliefs. Heck, the Masons were good people weren't they? They do good things, don't they?

He sat the box on the dining room table and spread its' contents all out in neat little piles. He figured it was all an amazing puzzle, laid out by his family for him to get to know their history and the dark side of the curse of The Eraser. He had read each item in all the boxes previously, except for the gift letter, and also had never studied the genealogy in depth until today. He figured he'd use that information as he read the Journal- someday. Someday, was now.

He picked the Journal up and held it to his nose. The leather still smelled new. He studied the cover once more and then turned it over. There was nothing on the back except a Bible reference, Leviticus 24:17. He knew it well from Sunday school. It was the "Eye for an Eye" section. 'In these circumstances, good advice, and quite apropos,' he thought. Finally, he opened the pages. He had read the opening page from Lawtin Sr. before, so he turned to page two. On the top it read:

"An account of Lawtin Palmer Sr. to future generations, Sept. 30, 1807"

"My dear children, it is with remorse that I must write this to you. We have fallen victim to a perverse and evil generation of men, who prey upon the weak and control those of easily manipulated minds. I have not, nor will not submit to their plans and will, until my dying breath, expose and lay bare their intentions before the world. In this course, I surmise we Palmers will suffer their shenanigans, and quite possibly death. This story I convey is my account of the cursed eraser, sent as a gift by my friend Nairne.

I received it as a gesture of kindness, but I believe he was duped by his conniving assistant. I say this knowing that he and his superiors wished me to join their ranks before leaving England. Unsure of their supposed Enlightenment, I could not in good conscience oblige them until such time as I could assess their teachings. Having since then learned of their true objectives, I was appalled of it as they, the Illuminists and the Masons, serve none other than the devil. They intend to establish themselves as the masters of the world, infiltrating in the least suspicious of ways, unbeknownst to all. But then, it will be too late, for they will have gained control. Stay away. Do not be duped.

It has since been my objective to refrain from having contact with them or anyone of their persuasion here in Madison County, believing they to have me and my families demise in their thinking, therefore— the curse. It was no accident, but a monstrous trick played upon my good friend Edward.

At first, I was also amused when I received Edward's letter stating that a curse was placed upon an eraser. 'Laughable,' I thought. I even told the family who also shared in the folly. But, after it was taken from my desk drawer and used with such intentions by a jealous youth, I came to consider that it may be true. This is the dark tale, which I plead for your indulgence to never reveal, for if it is, they will realize they have won against us in a most evil way:

My dear son, Lawtin Jr., smitten with a young lass from school named Lois, through the use of The Eraser, caused the teacher Alpheus Hitchcock to commit murder, even his own wife, and thus be put to death this month. All of this was done without Lawtin's knowledge, thinking it to be a mere prank and not giving The Eraser its due. All of it done for naught by my son, who has since repented of his evil and sworn us all to secrecy. Now he believes the curse to be true. As do all we Palmers, who now bear a burden placed on us by the evil of the Illuminati. Beware my family, the curse is real. NEVER USE THE ERASER! If you do the curse will be upon you and you shall bear the result of your work before God. God be with you.

Signed– Lawtin Palmer Sr."

~~~~~~

There it ended. He thought, 'The Illuminati? Wow! They're the most powerful people in the world. But, that name, Alpheus, sure sounds familiar.' He turned to page three and his mind went back in time.

~~~~~~

Jan. 12, 1813

"Today a grievous mistake was made. Erasers are meant to be a help, but this accursed piece of rubber has claimed the life of the son of a dear friend, an infant named Jeremiah Button. And now we know that it works in the hand of anyone with ill will and not merely the owner whose care it is in. The nurse of Mrs. Button, a lady of kind demeanor and of civic mind, came into my study with her list of the many infirm and sick with the epidemic ravaging the county. Her mood was of anger, wishing all to be well and her unable to help, and picking up The Eraser from the drawer of my desk she rubbed the name of poor Jeremiah from the list, thinking he to be well. Alas, this not being the case, the boy took a turn for the worse and met his demise. The woman shall remain nameless here, as she has no idea what has occurred. Only I in horror watched as to what she had done. I felt myself responsible, having left such an accursed thing in view of others. I have since removed it to another place. I shall never forgive myself for my lax care of it and it will never happen this way again. Instead I will pass the curse on to each generation much as Adam did to us."

Signed– Lawtin Palmer Sr.

~~~~~~

Now understanding a little more how serious this was, Larkin went to the table and picked up the obituaries from the Mail Box. Each story he was reading pertained to one of these obituaries placed as "mail", to alert the Keeper of The Eraser. He picked them up and took them over to the Journal. Sitting down, he turned to the next page.

~~~~~~

Sept. 12, 1826–

"My father, Lawtin Sr., placed two previous occurrences in these writings, them being concise and straight to the point. He was most kind to spare detail. As I am now the Keeper, for father has gone to be with the Lord, I will not withhold the grim events, so as to let the reader know just how evil The Eraser can be.

These past years have been a great burden to me. As the only son to remain on The Homestead, I was to be the recipient of it and its curse, so my father showed me the newspaper clippings and the method of his conveyance to future generations. Since his death twelve years ago, I have begun the Journal, in order to ease my conscience and to bring it all to light, so that the evil placed upon us would be known by each new Keeper and by whom it was caused.

As I caused so much heartache in 1807, being unaware it could do such things, I convinced myself of the importance of maintaining The Eraser in new condition, hoping I would never be tempted to use it. However, circumstances have negated that wish, and being a sinner and saint, I have decided that God has placed a weapon meant for evil in my hands, that I may use it for good, which now has been accomplished. This is my story:

Since our Family Palmer has come to these shores of liberty, I have been told by our family of the evil plot designed by those who would take it away. I was not convinced of that at first, being a friend of President Jefferson and Mr. Meriwether Lewis, who at first did not believe it either. Having spent time with Meriwether before his trip out West, I found that in our conversations there was evidence that corroborated the stories my father had told me of Nairne, his associate, and the womanizer, Franklin. Meriwether was later killed one night in Tennessee by them, but I cannot prove it.

The goal of a new world order and the grass roots plan to control us all by the power of the evil one made my blood boil. I could not allow it to happen and told my father that I would continue in his quest to destroy their evil ambitions.

Until his death the local minions continued to try to convince him to join their cause. Many of the rich and powerful have done so and it would seem as if their cause was about to come to fruition. However, I myself now have been involved due to a miss happens at the post office just one month ago. And now it would seem the crisis has been averted– at least for now. This is what occurred:

I went into town to receive the post which I heard was there for me. I tied my horse in front and went up to the door, but when I began to open it, I overheard two men speaking on the other side. It was Dr. Enoos and Wm. Morgan, both Masons who had spoken with my father previously and were men of high authority and stature, although Morgan be a trouble maker. In fact, Morgan had been arrested and bailed out by force by fellow Masons, and they plotted to have him thought dead, allowing for his free movement and escape. Unfortunately, some of these men were tried for his murder and themselves went to the gallows. He had not changed and now they were plotting the receipt of a large shipment of gold and silver to be used for the destruction of our fledgling nation, distributed by means of the many underground Masons. It was to be delivered on the eve of the full moon. I was taken aback and paused a moment before entering. I went in without notice and bid each man good day before going to the postmaster to collect my mail. They watched me as I made my way out and I tipped my hat as I left. I wondered if they thought I had overheard them, but that did not seem to be the case, as they did not follow. However, now that I knew their plan, I felt it up to me to somehow thwart it. And in the days to follow I connived a way to do just that, using the help of two less than honorable bond servants of none other than Dr. Enoos himself! Their reward was to be determined by me.

This was my plan: I expected that the shipment would arrive under the cover of darkness and a contingent of their kind on guard. Therefore, I determined to send the perpetrators while the chest would still be on the wagon. Then, while all still slept, the guards would be overpowered and the wagon removed before help could be procured by them. The two, both Irishmen, were up to the task, and all proceeded as planned. I followed along so that the plan would be followed as closely as possible in order that lives would not be taken.

When we arrived, it was as I expected. Two men slept on the ground near the wagon and two on chairs with guns on the porch of the store. We rode up from behind, while another rode from in front of them. This I did not expect and he woke the four guards as he approached. Our surprise arrival was no longer. The men talked and I recognized the rider to have been Wm. Morgan who proceeded to the door to open it and accept the shipment. Coming back out, he carried an arm full of burlap bags, which I assumed would carry the receipts. They all set their weapons down and began to go to the wagon to unload. As they did, I signaled the Irish to ride in with guns drawn and hold them at bay. While they did that, I made my way behind Morgan and placed a gun at his side. We all wore sacks on our heads that we may not be recognized. I did the talking.

"Don't move or we shall not be kind. This is the plan. My men will take charge of the wagon. Mr. Morgan, you will have all of the guards go to the porch and lay down beside you." They all complied not saying a word except a "humph", from Morgan as he motioned to the men. The bondsmen got onto the wagon and proceeded to drive away, but then Morgan, being the man he was, jumped up to strike me as I turned to mount my horse. I kicked him with my boot in the face, at which he fell back onto the porch. I trained my gun upon him again and said, "Get up and mount behind me you wretch!" He obliged in fear and we rode off toward the wagon making its way to The Homestead. I yelled back, "Don't follow or he shall die!" We rode until we caught the wagon whereupon I stopped and told him to get off. As he began his walk back to town I said after him, "Beware, The Eraser!" I had not taken my head covering off and he replied in surprise, "Palmer!" He knew who I was! How did he know? I quickly urged my horse on and I rode with the wagon upon the old Indian path up from the back of The Homestead. When we arrived, we had by then removed our masks and commented on how easy it was to procure the wagon and its contents, of which we really did not know. I had the men back the wagon into the barn, whereupon we lifted the chest out with a pulley from the rafters and placed it into the ground beneath where the manure pile rested normally in the back corner. I had dug it up the day before, knowing I should hide what we collected.

It had been a long night and the men were glad to be done with it. I opened the chest which was covered with silver and the Illuminati symbol upon its top. There were bars of gold and silver, and a bag of coin, possibly a million dollars worth. I picked up one gold bar for each and handed them their due. They were ecstatic saying they could now purchase their freedom from the tyrant they served, the old Dr. Enoos. I shut the lid and instructed them to unhitch the team and place them on the road upon which we traveled. The wagon I kept in the barn until such time as I could dismantle it. Before I left, I once again told them to never mention the incident to anyone or I would turn them in to Sheriff Whipple. They nodded and rode away. I began the task of covering the chest and as I did I considered the ramifications of letting Morgan report to the Masons' who he had seen. When I completed the task, I went into the house to father's desk. Taking The Eraser Box from the locked drawer, I placed it on the desk. Then writing William Morgan's name upon a piece of paper with a pencil, I took The Eraser from its box and looked at it. As I now felt an obligation to my fellow countrymen to eradicate this menace, I quickly and with malice, erased his name. Afterwards I perceived a foul smell, which I discounted as manly flatulence, as I had eaten beans that evening. I am not so sure what it was. How Morgan would die, I did not know. And now, indeed, he would disappear as they had previously conspired.

As it were, I heard from others in our small community, the events of his death as leaked out by the Masons that were disbanded after this event. When William Morgan returned to his office, Dr. Enoos was waiting for him. The four guards had gone to his home and brought him to Morgan's place. In the meanwhile, Enoos could not find his bondsmen to bring him his horse as they had not yet returned from my home. He was furious that they were not there and consequently knew that they were the accomplices in the wagon. It is unknown what ever happened to the two Irishmen. Enoos charged at Morgan when he came in the door, but he refrained when he saw the boot print on his face, which had swollen significantly since I placed it upon him some hour before! Instead he screamed, "How did this happen? What are we to do now? The Commander will have our hides! But now I shall take care of this myself." With that he placed his weapon in his hand, pointed it at Morgan who said, "Wait! It was Palmer!" and then he pulled the trigger at point blank into his skull. Morgan dropped instantly. Presently, he ordered the Masons to swear on an oath to never reveal what really happened that night. Instead, they concocted a story to place blame for the murder on persons unknown if his body were found. The robbery was never reported! His body reportedly was found in Niagara, but I believe it to be another's. His, I believe, to be buried nearby.

I write this a month afterward, as the newspaper has reported that the Lodge itself has been disbanded and closed by the powers that be. Likewise, many of the Lodges in New York have suffered the same fate and Freemasonry in our country is rife with distrust by many. I can only imagine what they think of me, knowing that we have the chest and that I have turned the tables upon them and have used the cursed eraser that they meant to bring harm upon us, against them, to thwart their prognostications. If anything, they are afraid and rightly so, knowing that I have by their doing– been given the power of life or death over men. They have not come forward against me and I believe they shall never, as long as the Keeper of The Eraser knows the entire story. I pray that each generation reads this Journal as they receive it.

Signed– Lawtin Palmer Jr. 1826

Larkin now knew how the silver chest had gotten there and why there were two bars missing! That Lawtin Palmer Jr. had guts! He took out his watch and realized he had been reading for a couple of hours. The words on the page had come to life, placing him in their contexts and adding unknown complexities to his life. He needed a break. Tom was in the living room and heard him get up. He was waiting to find out what he had learned. Going to the kitchen they drew a glass of water and sat down at the table.

Tom asked, "Well?"

"I know where the chest came from."

"And?"

"Lawtin Jr. stole it."

"What?"

"Yes. He stole it from the local Masonic Lodge and used The Eraser to keep them away. He actually warned them that he *would use it against them!*"

"Ingenious!"

"Yes, but it is still breaking the commandment to use it."

"Did he justify its use somehow?"

"Yes, by saying he was saving the country from their evil."

"I'd say that's a pretty good reason," said Tom.

"Me, too. I guess I had better go back to reading."

"I think so, Larkin."

He sat back down at the table. Taking the Journal again to hand, he turned the page and found this:

"An entry in the Journal of the Palmer men this 8th day of March, 1855".

"I was made the Keeper of the cursed Eraser last year, learning it's' story from my father before he passed. It does not surprise me that some would consider it a curse and others a blessing. An evil man would use it extensively; a righteous man not at all. I have prayed that it would not be necessary to use it as my father did, but much to my chagrin, that was not to be the case. Each generation seems to bring another threat from the dark side, and I am not to be excluded from their plans to dominate us. It would seem that the world has become more tense, the states each one expressing their own sovereignty. What controls this pulling apart is unknown to me, but I suspected that it was a contrivance of the Illuminati. Now, after my experience with the deceased Moses Johnson, I am sure it is. This is my story:

Before my father passed last year, he was concerned for me, that I may be harassed or even killed by those whose plans we have purposed to expose. After having read all of the Journal and letters, I knew that I'd have to keep an eye upon everyone I came into contact with in town, especially strangers. I know who is who in town and Brookfield is my home, and I feel no threat there. But since his funeral, I have felt uneasy. I did not know what it was, but when we went to worship and met the new family, it all came to a head.

The Johnsons moved from the South, purportedly Virginia, and made an impression upon the populace immediately, with their Southern drawl and quaint customs. Some took them to be gentile folks who were very cordial, but in Moses, I saw a side that made me cautious— him to be shifty and waiting to do something. Not knowing him, I took care not to encourage contact with my family. Our wives merely exchanged pleasantries and our sons only greeted one another after services. He came up to me and my friend Elmer Brown, and greeted us. He was curious as to how he could help in the church and informed us he was a carpenter of some experience and would like to add some ornate carvings to the structure. I informed him that he should to speak with the pastor and trustee, in order that it may be done in the proper manner. Elmer excused himself to return home. Seeing his opportunity Moses then asked, "Are you the son of Lawtin Jr.?"

I replied, "Yes, I am. Why?"

"Because Sir, I have been sent to destroy you and your family. We know what you have and it is ours. Beware Sir." Someone walked past and he smiled and tipped his hat to her. Appearing to be happy, he walked away from me as if he had said nothing but pleasantries. I shook where I stood. My wife came up to me to ask what was wrong, but I did not share it with her. I hurriedly gathered my family and we got in the buggy to head home.

I didn't give him opportunity to harm me or my family. I didn't use The Eraser immediately however, giving him a chance to leave town before I had to. He must have also known that I was the Keeper. He must have also known the ramifications of the use of The Eraser. He was either being paid handsomely to do this, or was being pressured to do it under penalty. He contracted with Pastor Clark to begin work on the carpentry for the church and his wife took in laundry. It looked as though he had come to stay. I supposed he had a plan, but I would watch him and his family, for none were to be considered harmless.

I assumed he would limit his assaults upon me to harassment in the public. It was not to be so. Upon returning from a trip to town, I found four of my pigs lying dead in their trough. The next day, my sons sheep were missing, stolen from the fields. I knew who it was, but at this time it was impossible to prove. I set a trap the following day by the barn, placing a rope attached to the door and a snare. When tripped, it would have captured anyone and strung them up to the rafters. It was tripped that day, but the rope was cut the length of a man's leg from the top. It must have produced a tirade of profanity. The pranks however, did not stop. Therefore, after a fortnight next, I lay waiting in the barn, gun in hand. I made sure my family knew I was there and they, too, were also protected by firearms in the house. I waited until four o' clock and began to get tired. Then, the door creaked. I saw no one, but knew there was someone there. I didn't move. The person kicked over the bucket by the front stall. When he did it, he lit a torch. I was afraid he was going to burn down the barn, so I fired upon him. He turned and ran, throwing the torch upon the hay as he exited. It ignited and the blaze flamed up. I jumped down from the loft and grabbed the pitchfork. Pulling the pile away from the building, I saved the barn even though I burned my right arm extensively in the process. In the may- lay I heard the man ride away on his horse heading for town. I knew it was he and he had run me to the end of my patience. I had to protect my family and in effect, the country. I knew what I must do.

The next Sunday he was there at church with his family. After we left the sanctuary I confronted him with a simple statement. "Beware, The Eraser."

He came back with a tirade. "Don't threaten me, Sir. I don't believe any of that superstition anyway. A cursed eraser? Bah! Humbug! Impossible! You shall die, Sir! You shall die!"

The entire congregation heard his outburst and I just shrugged my shoulders as if he were daft. Which indeed, he was. I now knew however, it was time to rub him the wrong way.

After lunch at home, the family and I prayed for the entire Johnson family. They knew what must be done to not only save the family, but again to stop the Illuminati, so they may not retrieve the chest. I dismissed them and went to my desk. I took The Eraser box from the drawer and sat it down. I, too, as my family before, took a piece of paper and wrote down his name. Then I made the decision my father made and his father as well. I took The Eraser from its box and lightly rubbed the name. It came off. I smelled the faint odor of death. I wondered how he would die and prayed for forgiveness. Why, dear Lord, why?

I found out from Mrs. Hoxie this past Sunday. She had taken laundry to Mrs. Johnson each week. It seems the newspaper was correct in that he was murdered in his home. Mrs. Hoxie said the widow Johnson had broken down and confessed the entire story to her, but I surmise she did not know anything about The Eraser. Moses was literally under a deadline. He was given three months to move to New York and complete his mission she said, (although then again, I doubt she knew what that was) and return to Virginia. He was killed by the Masons for not completing the task in due order and she, Mrs. Johnson, along with her family, were to move back to her home state soon.

I am thankful that these, the children, were spared the details of our manly skirmishes. However, I know that these evil men shall return one day, and you my family, will need to use The Eraser once again. I pray for you.

Most Sincerely,
Denton Palmer

While Larkin was reading, Tom was preparing lunch. By now, Larkin was hungry. Young boys are always hungry. Tom brought the grilled cheese sandwiches to the table and sat down. Without hesitation he said grace: "Dear Lord, grant that we may be nourished by these, Your gifts, and that we Your servants may do those things that please You. In Jesus name, Amen."

Larkin said, "Amen."

The two dug in. As they were eating a car drove into the drive. It looked familiar. It was the same car *that had driven out earlier.* Two men got out. Dressed in suits, they were extremely out of place, considering most of the folks around those parts wore blue jeans or coveralls. They came up to the door and knocked. Larkin went to the door and asked, "Can I help you?"

"Are you Larkin Palmer?" asked the older of the two men, who had neatly cut gray hair and looked to be about sixty-five.

"Yes, I am. But who may I ask am I talking to?"

"I'm Grand Master Fitzgerald. May I come in?"

"I'd rather you did not. But, I can come out on the porch." Tom came to the door and the both of them walked out and stood next to the door almost protecting it.

"Fine then," said the Grand Master with a huff. The other man made a move forward and Larkin stepped into a defensive position in front of Tom. Waving his hand back and forth the Grand Master said, "No need for any of that Larkin. We are not here to harm you, but just to reason with you." He motioned for the other man to come forward again. He came forward and opened a leather bag he was carrying. Next to the door was a small table that Tom used as a catch-all. The man pulled two wrapped items out of the bag and sat them on the table. The Grand Master said, "Open them, Larkin."

Larkin cautiously turned toward the table and pulled one of the heavy items from its cover. It was one of the gold bars missing from the chest! Tom and Larkin looked at each other without making a sound. "Do you recognize these, Larkin?" asked the Grand Master.

"And if I did?" replied Larkin.

The other man came at him and said with rage, "Don't get wise, Palmer!"

The Grand Master pushed him back and scolded him saying, "I will have none of that! Come by the tree with me, Larkin, and let's talk."

The other man went towards the car as Tom went into the house and called Lawtin.

They walked slowly toward the "Welcome" tree and Larkin noticed a slight limp to his gate. Larkin asked him, "Why have you come to me now?"

"We want our chest. The Illuminati will not be stopped by some back woods family who thinks they know better than we."

"I'd say we were finally paid for what you have done to us."

"So you admit you have the chest?"

"No, but I know you want it. Only my ancestors know."

"Don't lie to me! Our plans depend on that chest as much today as it did a hundred-seventy years ago! If you don't give it to me you and your family will be sorry."

"On the contrary. Beware, Grand Master Fitzgerald. I know your name."

"Don't threaten me! Your family can't use that forever!"

"Let me ask you, Sir, how long *does* a curse last?"

With that question the Grand Master stormed away from him toward the car. As they left the driver spun the tires on the gravel road throwing rocks well up into the yard and dust high into the air. Larkin just smiled. When he went back into the house, Tom was still on the phone with Lawtin. "Here he is, Lawtin." Tom handed him the phone.

"Are you okay, Son?"

"Yes, Dad. It was just one of "them". I handled it."

"I trust your judgment. Let me know if we need to contact the authorities."

"I will. But tell me, how do we know the authorities aren't one of "them?""

"We never do, Son."

Later on towards supper time, Larkin was drained from a long day. As his Uncle Tom started toward the kitchen, Larkin called out, "Say, Uncle, I'm going to get the bars from the porch and put them in the trunk. Is there a tarp or something I can put over the chest?"

"Yes, Larkin, there is one in the cellar by the paint."

"Thanks."

Larkin went out to the porch. The yard surrounding the farmhouse was very quiet. Even the animals were at peace and calm in the fields. It made him feel better about the day. Even in the midst of the constant threat, he knew that good would prevail over the evil that haunted them. Tom came out on the porch with two plates and two cokes. "I thought we would enjoy a peaceful meal here on the porch."

"I'm with you there, Uncle. I sure hope we aren't interrupted this meal though!" They laughed and sat down in the two chairs facing the barn. The sun was beginning to go down behind it, showing hues of red and gold through the loft. It was becoming cooler and the bugs were coming out too, and they could see them flitting about in dust filled sunshine, but they didn't bother them. They watched God's creation prepare for slumber and Tom yawned out loud. "Oh boy," he said, "I guess it got later than I thought. I'll take in the plates and I'm going to bed."

"I'll take care of this," he said pointing at the gold bars, "and then I'll be hitting the hay too. Good night, Uncle."

"Good night." Tom went in.

Larkin picked up the bars. He thought, 'Well, I guess I know what happened to the two Irishmen that night.' He took them down into the cellar from the access inside the back porch. When he turned on the light, he opened the chest. Placing the two bars inside the trunk made it look complete. He closed it again and placed a tarp over it that he found by the paint. He said out loud, "I sure hope I can do this job." He went up the stairs and let the door down gently so that it didn't slam as it hit the old floors. He placed the rug back on top of it and then the shelf that held some of the laundry stuff his uncle used.

Larkin went into his room and closed the door. A spider ran across his pillow as he sat down on his bed. He took his Bible out of the night stand and clicked on the light by the bed. Lying down, he read from where he had marked it last. It was in Hebrews chapter- ten. He read verses 19-25 which had the heading, "A New and Living Way." What stuck him was verse twenty-two. It said, 'Let us draw near with a sincere heart in full assurance of faith, having our hearts sprinkled clean from an evil conscience and our bodies washed with pure water.' He closed the bible and placed it on the nightstand. He smiled, wondering where the spider had gone, turned off the light, lay back down, closed his eyes and said, "Amen."

In the morning, Tom got up and prepared for church. He woke Larkin. They usually skipped breakfast because they ate in town and only one of them went to do any minor chores beforehand. It was the

Sabbath. It was Larkin's turn to feed the animals, so he hurried along. He thought about the next entry in the Journal he'd probably read today. 'It was from 1901,' he thought. Then he realized it was getting late. As it was out of the way for Lawtin to come over to pick them up, he and his uncle always drove over to his house so they could ride with his parents to church. 'It will be good to see them,' he thought. When he finished, he ran into the house and scrubbed up. Putting on his Sunday best, the two of them grabbed their Bibles and headed out to the car. Since Harry's death, Tom could no longer bear to drive the pickup alone, and so Larkin had bought him a car. It was a '59 Ford. For some reason, Tom always parked it next to the Olde House footing. Larkin always thought that to be strange, because when the driver got out of the car you'd step right on top of the raised lumps under the grass. "Want me to drive, Uncle?" Larkin asked.

"Go ahead Larkin. We'll get there faster."
Larkin chuckled.

When they arrived at the farm, his parents were already in the Lincoln waiting for them. He got in and his dad said, "Sleep late?"
"Not really. It just took too long with the chores."
Tom said, "I think he was daydreaming again."
His parents said in unison, "So what else is new!" They all laughed and rode into town.

When Larkin got out of the car at the Seventh Day Baptist Church, Ginny was there waiting for him. He had missed her this weekend. Usually, he called or saw her every day, but all this commotion had caused him to forget. She didn't seem perturbed. In fact, she smiled and was happy to see him. She came up and took his hand, and they walked into the faded- white church building together. They worshipped and were coming out the door when Larkin saw the car of the Grand Master across the street. When they realized he had seen them, the unwelcome intruders slowly pulled away. Now they knew he had a girlfriend. Larkin was not happy that this occurred. He needed to tell Ginny. He needed to tell her all of it. He said to her, "Ginny, I'd like to talk to you about something and I've been putting it off for a while, even though some of it I just learned of myself. Let's go sit down."

They walked toward the benches out by the picnic area behind the church. Sitting down, he could see the school at the top of the hill. There, he told her all about the curse, while their parents patiently waited for them to come to the cars. She took it very well, accepting it for what it was, and he swore her to secrecy. Larkin was amazed by that, but knew she would have questions. If not now, then soon. They walked back to the cars, got in and headed to the Horned Dorset Inn for their families to eat together.

They all sat down and ordered when they got there. The place was busy, as it was every Sunday after church. It offered breakfast twenty-four hours a day, so that's what Larkin ordered. While they were waiting, Ginny spoke up. "Mom and Dad, Mr. & Mrs. Palmer, Larkin and I, well, we would like your permission to be married after school in the spring." The table became very quiet and Larkin was surprised she had taken the lead in the matter.

Mr. Berry was the first to speak. "I know that you two have been serious for a long time, but we expected you to be going off to college and then be married. I know you'd be well cared for as Larkin has the means, but this is rather sudden."

Larkin spoke up. "Sir, Mom and Dad, I know that is the case, in fact I wondered if that should be the plan as well. But I realized that our families have done it that way for over two-hundred years here. I figured if it was good enough for them, it would be good enough for us."

Lawtin said, "He does have a point. And I know he'd be able to take care of them. But where would you live?"

"Uncle Tom?" Tom suddenly paid attention to them instead of looking out the window.

"Yes, Larkin?"

"Could I build another house on the end of the road on the south twenty acres? We wouldn't have to clear anything and it would fit quite well?"

"I see you've been thinking on this already."

Larkin just looked at him for an answer and said sheepishly, "I already drew the plan."

"Well," he paused and the whole table just sat looking at him in suspense, "I don't see why not."

The whole table and the table next to them cheered and clapped. Lawtin said, "Congratulations. You'll need to speak with Pastor to set it up."

"We will, Dad, and thank you." He shook his dad's hand and reached over and gave him a hug. Just then the food came, so they all just talked about the wedding, their future, and life.

Ginny rode home with the Palmers, because Larkin wanted to show her the Journal, too. He struggled with telling her about the chest in the cellar, but he thought he'd better for her own safety. It was a long process, and he just briefly touched on it all or they would have been there at it all night. He didn't take her to the cellar, but told her about the chest. She asked, "How much do you think it is worth, Larkin?"

"Much more than anything we've found before. Just in precious metals weight I've calculated more than twenty-five million dollars. I'd say double that in a one piece collection, but metals fluctuate with the market."

Ginny's eyes lit up and then reality set in. "But I guess it's' not ours to sell- is it?"

"Yes, actually, it is. But at this point, we need to just keep things as they are. It is a dangerous thing we have here. Very dangerous."

She replied, "I understand. I think."

He pulled out the Journal. Sitting down in the living room, he placed the Eraser on an end table by him. "This Journal is what I wanted to show you. It really explains everything. I've read up to here and I thought we could read this next entry together tonight."He put his finger on the next entry and began to read out loud:

July 20, 1901

"I had hoped that I would be a generation to not be included in the Journal. But, as a Keeper, much to my dismay, I am included. It seems each of us must contend with the evil that haunts us in our own day. For me and my family it has come in the form of Indians. And I know it not to be they who are at fault, even if they have taken on the work from the evil ones.

A few months ago, I went into town for supplies at the Co-Op, and I found that as I loaded up, a couple of Oneida Indians walked up and bumped me, causing me to lose my grip on a bag of feed. The feed fell down the loading dock and spilled all over. I thought nothing of it, even if they didn't say anything to excuse themselves nor offer an apology. They just continued on laughing as they mounted their horses. I just thought it rude and a prank on the white man. I didn't even consider reporting them being the civil individual that I am.

However, the next time I went to town, the same two were at the mercantile. I placed my things in the wagon and went to the post office. They followed me there. I went in and bought some stamps. When I got back to the wagon, all of my groceries were thrown on the ground. Flour, sugar, and coffee were strewn everywhere. I looked around to find them, but they had left. I was now determined to watch for them and anyone they may come into contact with.

I went around town and finally located their horses. They were in front of the bar on Academy. I don't usually go into taverns, much less in the middle of the day, but I did, hoping to see who they had met after their destruction of my goods. Unfortunately, they saw me come in and quit speaking to the man seated next to them. They were all drinking a beer and as I walked up to the bar they asked each other loudly, "Want some sugar in your coffee? How about some bread, too?" They just laughed looking at me for a reaction. I just asked Joe, the bartender, who I knew from school, for a beer. When he brought it I paid, and I asked him if he knew who the white man they were speaking to was. He said quietly, "Some guy from Hamilton named Alfred Frinker. I think he may be related to the people who own Park House, but I'm not sure. You know, I usually don't serve Indians, but the temperance people have been hurting business lately."

I knew the name and they were Masons from Hamilton. When you deal with so many generations of them, you come to know them all. I sat down on the stool and tried to finish my beer and I say tried, because in a moment one of the Indians came over towards me and said, "Would you like to buy some groceries?" He laughed in my face trying to pick a fight. I sat my beer down and started to walk out the door and just ignored him, but he came up behind me and grabbed my shoulder. Turning around I gave him an elbow in the gut and grabbed his head pulling it down and then kicked him in the face with my knee. I had learned of such fighting tactics from a Chinese man I had met previously in Albany. He was rendered unconscious. The other Indian saw this and was afraid, but he yelled at me as I walked out with a smile, "We'll get you!" I knew the harassment would now be on its way— full force. And I knew from whom, and it was not from Indians!

When I got home my wife was upset with me, as she, along with the Mills' our neighbors, were in favor of temperance and I had drunk the evil brew. I told her our new circumstances and she understood why. She now knew that she must pray and that she must trust my leadership in the matter of the Palmer family men. As we slept that night, I heard something in the wood behind our barn. It turned out to be a band of Indians, four or five in number. They actually shot an arrow with a note attached into the wall of my home, which had now stood on our homestead for one hundred seven years. Lawtin Palmer Sr. and his sons had built it in 1794, it being of stately architecture for the time. It had never been struck by an arrow before, as the Oneidas had sold the land to the state in 1791. The note read, "Give us back the chest, or you and your family are dead!" Upon reading it my wife promptly fainted and I, in anger, ripped it to pieces, throwing it into the fire. I wish I had not done so, as it was the only evidence I had of their deed. I had previously read the Journal, so I knew what they were talking about, but I had never seen the chest. I only knew of its' location, having been told by my father.

The next day, I rode into town again, taking the arrow with me. I took it to the bar and throwing open the door, the light struck Frinker in the face and he could not see me at first. I walked up to him before he had a chance to know it was me and I drove the arrow into the bar in front of him with this note. "Beware The Eraser!" I walked out and he did not follow.

Ideally, it would have all ended there. But, it didn't. The next morning, Joe the bartender came to call on us. He was there to warn me of what he had overheard after my arrow trick. "At least that's what he called it," said Joe, "he said that "he wasn't going to be intimidated by some old tale and that he was going to send out those four Indians again to get me." He also mentioned the Indian in charge was named Conagwasa from Hamilton." I thanked him for the information and told him he was a good friend. He shook my hand and left putting his bowler on before he got into his buggy. I didn't wait any longer. I would end this right now.

I went into my grandfather's desk and took out The Eraser box. I placed it on the top of the desk and took out a piece of paper. I wrote down the Indians' name and hoped I spelled it correctly– Conagwasa. Then, for my first and hopefully only time, I erased a man's name. I thought I smelled death, but considered it my imagination. I felt ill, knowing that somehow, a man would die. I did not know how until I read the obituary in the Hamilton Republican this week. The power of The Eraser's curse was greater than I thought in that there was no apparent cause for his death. After reading the newspaper of February 15th, I put The Eraser in my pocket, which I had never done, but I was tired and I went to bed.

It did not end however, and in anger Frinker did send the same Indian band that February night. This time, they used arrows of fire. They struck the West side of the house all at the same time, shot from the cold empty field, which had bales of straw piled there. It didn't take long for the old place to be consumed. Thankfully, we all got out and they did not touch the barn. I didn't know the names of the Indians, but I did know Frinker. The next morning, I went into town a third time to confront them. I saw all of them at the mercantile, but I went to the sheriff's office first to tell him my home had been burned down by persons unknown. He smiled, but he placed his hand in front of his mouth and mustache and said, "Sorry to hear that, Palmer. I'll keep a lookout for the culprits."

I replied, "No need sheriff, God will repay." I went out the door and heard him call out, "What did you say?"

I walked over to the store to find them. The Indians came out on the front steps. Frinker followed. I confronted them right there. "Did you need to replace some arrows boys?" I looked straight at the Indians and said, "Do you want what happened to Conagwasa to happen to you? Don't ever come around me or my family again!" They ran away at high speed. And as for Frinker, I said to him, "Tell your bosses that this is over. I know their names. They know what happened to the greedy Indian. I won't hesitate to use it again. You destroyed my home. I'll destroy you!" His face turned white as a ghost. He dropped his parcel and walked away quickly. I picked up his parcel of coffee and sugar, and yelled after him, "You owe me some flour, too!" I never saw any of them again.

Since then, I dug up the chest. It contained an odd number of pieces of gold bars and an even number of silver bars— as if two gold bars were missing. On top of it all, was a bag of coin, which I procured to build my new house. I felt they owed me that much. If it cost more, I determined I'd dig it up again and use as much as necessary. The house is begun. I hope it suffices for my ancestors."

Signed— Dalton Palmer 1901

"Wow, that's all unbelievable," said Ginny.

He sat the Journal down and said, "So that's how the original house burned down. No one ever told me."

"This is quite the Journal, Larkin. Can we keep reading?"

"One more. Then we need to take you home. Unless Uncle Tom will make us some supper?"

Tom overheard his not-so-hypothetical question and said, "You know I will. I'll call the Berry's and let them know, and we'll take you home afterwards, Ginny."

Laughing he said, "Thanks, Uncle!"

Larkin picked the Journal back up and began reading out loud again. He wondered how much Tom overheard last time. It didn't matter, he was a Palmer too! He began again:

March 18, 1929

"As Keeper of The Eraser, I am angry with myself, and have used it entirely in malice as Lawtin Sr. warned so long ago not to do. It was a mistake. This is the story:

I attended a barn dance tonight. As always, I did my share of enticing the girls to dance with me and some of them did. A man I did not know began to pass a bottle of moonshine around in our corner of the barn. It went past me about three times and it took its affect quite quickly. As the evening passed on, one of my friends, Spencer Button, invited me to a game of cards at the home of a man named Elton Morgan. He was a prominent businessman and was quite wealthy. As I was drunk, I agreed and became an easy mark for all of them playing.

We sat down in the back room of his business and played poker until four o'clock in the morning. The four of us, Morgan, Button, me and Ben Waterman played as men possessed. I lost all of my money as did Spencer. Morgan and Ben played the last hand with great stakes. They bet it all, Ben his home, and Morgan his business. As Morgan dealt the last hand I observed him dealing from the bottom of the deck. The hand went his way and Ben lost it all. I called him on his crookedness and he denied it. Pulling a gun on us, he ordered us all from his store. In fear, we left and he kept it all, including the promissory note for the Waterman house. Ben was devastated for being so foolish. Then I in anger, went to my home, took out The Eraser, wrote the dirty cheats name on a scrap of newspaper and then rubbed it out. The stench it caused gagged me! He must have died instantly for they found him in less than an hour after we left, alone in his bed dead. He was much too young to have died that way, but nothing was ever thought about it. The note was found by the poor widow and placed upon record at the courthouse, she not knowing how Elton came to have it.

I am at a loss as to what else to convey for this entry, except that I shall never use the cursed thing again.

Signed– Harlan Palmer– 1929

Ginny said, "Larkin, that's your parents' house!"

"Yes, I know. That's right. It was passed from the Morgans, to the Buttons, and now us. What do I do?"

"Well, I know you can't give it back to the family, but Israel is the rightful heir. Maybe you should think of something you can do for him and his family."

"Yeah, I guess so. I expect that this cursed thing will place me into many philosophical conundrums." He patted the Eraser which lay on the table.

"Come and get it," yelled Tom from the kitchen. They got up and walked in, sitting down at the table. Their somber look brought an expected question from Tom. "Boy, you two look like you just ran over the family cat."

"We feel like it. There's so much in the Journal, Uncle. It is so sad what has transpired due to that cursed eraser. There's got to be a way out of the curse. There's just got to be."

"What I don't understand is," said Ginny, "these Freemasons. All of them aren't like this are they?"

"I'm sure they are not. But this isn't about individual Masons. It is about the whole and some- corrupted ones. The problem, I think, is that many don't know, but the ones that do. Well…" Larkin was trying to figure out who really the enemy was.

They didn't talk much during or after dinner. The whole process of reading the Journal had been trying and depressing. It made Larkin think about life and those he loved. It made him think about his poor ancestors and their fight against evil. And it made him think that he still had to fight them. As he drove Ginny home, he wondered if he had made a mistake telling her. As he dropped her at her door she said, "Don't worry Larkin, we will do this together. Good night."

"Thanks, Ginny." She got out and came around to his side of the car. She stuck her head in and gave him a kiss. She said, "I love you."

"I love you, too. Goodnight."

She got out of the way and he drove toward home. She went into the house wondering what they would do next. It wouldn't be long before she found out. They watched her go into her room and turn on the light!

"They" were always there. When she turned out the light she looked out the window. There she saw a parked car and someone light a cigarette. She knew *they* were there.

Larkin got home and couldn't sleep. Tom had gone to bed before he got there, so Larkin picked up the Journal and read on.

December 16th, 1962

"I write this entry for the Journal, even though I am not the Keeper. My brother Elias is. I accidentally caused the death of my sister-in-law, Mary. I picked up his eraser and wondered if it worked. It looked too old. I rubbed on a piece of paper on his desk, but it had her name on it. The next day she fell on the ice and died. He said that The Eraser I used wasn't *The Eraser,* but I don't know. He also said The Eraser doesn't work that way. He's just trying to make me feel better. Elias, please forgive me! God forgive me.

Signed– Ethan Palmer– 1962

Larkin thought, 'Oh my goodness. Poor Ethan. He didn't believe my Grandpa. The Eraser doesn't work that way. And he went crazy, too. Oh man.' He kept on reading and as he turned the page he realized he was on the last entry. 'Why is this placed here?' he thought. 'It's out of chronological order.'

Sept. 14, 1944

"After having read all of the information, I find myself to be wise enough to realize that we are in a struggle of good versus evil. To expose the evil of the Illuminati and their quest to dominate the world has been our families' primary concern all of these years. Of course they have moved on, realizing that we had them and we would not give up their property. But, it is still significant and I'm sure has grown in value enough to make them want it back even more. Therefore, I do not expect that I will never have to use it. In fact, the primary reason I write this today is as a preface of perceived things to come.

There has been a bully in the life of my brother and me, a man named John Clinton. He takes advantage of the weak, him being weak himself. He has tormented me, but mostly due to my brother Ethan. Ethan was born "slow". He can read and write, and is quite adept at taking care of himself. But he is no scholar. John has teased and tormented us for years.

But before graduation, he topped them all. He purposely set Ethan up and when it all occurred, it was in front of the whole school body.

We all went to the cafeteria for an assembly for the senior graduates. Many of us knew who would be going off to war. Some of the guys had even signed up after their 17th birthdays and were already gone. But, most of them waited until after graduation. So, the assembly focused on the war, even though some of the families were Quakers. We went in and the honor guard brought the flags in. They placed them and then we all stood up to say the pledge. But when we did, John reached over the chairs, grabbed Ethan's pants and pulled them down to his knees from behind! Ethan was so upset, he ran toward the front without pulling them up, tripping and falling flat on his face! I didn't react quickly, being stunned by what happened and by the time I got up there to help poor Ethan, he was crying and the entire school was laughing. I helped him up and put him back in order and we walked out the side door. I gave John a dirty look and he just smiled that cheesy smile he always got after he had pulled a prank on us.

I was so angry! I went home with Ethan and went straight to the desk. I knew where The Eraser was. Dad had told me all about it, even though he was still the Keeper. I knew I was to be the Keeper and I swore I'd never use it, but when given a choice to be able to, it is sometimes too great a temptation to use it. And I considered it. I had it in my hand and just then dad came into the room. I looked up and he just looked at me. He didn't need to say anything. I placed it back in the box and put it where I had found it. He came over to me and asked, "Ethan again?"
"Yes, Dad."
"Don't worry about boys like that, Son. God has a way with them."
"I understand."

John Clinton was a connected man. His parents had always been wealthy. They were also Masons. They had been, ever since his ancestor William B. Clinton was Governor when Lawtin Sr. was alive. So he knew all of them and he used his connections every way he could. It was no wonder he was a bully. His best buddy was Billy Coone. They were always getting into trouble and John's dad always bailed them out. I thought about that after I almost used The Eraser. There were all those men, both Illuminati and Masons. So I set about to collect names. I came up with lists. Even though the members of the lodges are all supposed to be secret, everyone knows who is and who isn't. First, I got a list of each of the local Lodges. Then I compiled a list of the state when they were at convention, especially all the

Masters, Grand Masters and finally the Commanders. Anyone higher than a 32nd degree Mason of which I was especially interested. They are the Keepers of all the- "true" secrets. They are the ones that know all about the true nature of it all. The lesser men know little and only do what they are told, but to do as they do is still evil. Until I die I will compile as many names of the living as I can, to pass on to the next Keeper to use as he sees fit. You will find it attached to the back page of this Journal.

John went to war just two weeks after graduation. When I read he had been killed in action, it was of no surprise to me. My father's words were true. I included his obit in the Mail Box only because he was merely a perceived victim of the curse, not an actual one.

Elias Palmer-1945

"Wow, a list!" Larkin pulled the back page over and there folded so as not to be seen, were four pages of names and designations. Each list had locations and there had to be over one thousand names. But Larkin knew these names were just the tip of the iceberg. 'I think I'm going to follow up on this,' he said to himself. Larkin had now read the Journal and he still had questions. Especially about how he was chosen instead of his dad and there had to be a reason. But then it dawned on him- the plan of the Illuminati and Freemasonry had been in place since the beginning and his family was to be the only way the world could be saved. But could he? Would he? One thing he did know was- he needed to know more about them. He needed to know- the enemy.

CHAPTER 10

THE MISTAKE

Larkin went to school and saw Ginny the next day. They acted like before and never really talked about any of their new discoveries. They never really said anything about their plans after school to the rest of the friends either. They just lived in the day, remembering the words of Jesus in Mt. 6:34, "Therefore do not be anxious about tomorrow, for tomorrow will be anxious for itself."

When Larkin got to English class, they were studying English literature. Knowing that Larkin had read many of the books in the library before the new one was built, his teacher, Mrs. Solomon, asked which his favorite was. Larkin replied, "I think it is, "Pilgrim's Progress", by John Bunyan."

Mrs. Solomon, being a Quaker said, "That's very interesting. Could you tell us why?"

Larkin took a look around the room. Jim Coone was giving him the evil eye for some reason. Larkin knew Jim didn't like the Quakers, and he guessed that any answer that was good according to his teacher would be something Larkin would have to pay for. But instead of wimping out, Larkin got up and started to walk to the front of the class.

He said, "This may take a while, Mrs. Solomon. May I?"

Inferring he'd like to address the class concerning her question, he walked forward and she, figuring he'd do a good job with it and it wouldn't hurt her lesson plan, said, "Why, yes. Please go ahead."

He began to tell them of the wonderful story line in the book and how he, when reading it, would place himself in a walk or on a certain path. He explained how each of us has a choice to make and which path we would travel in life. He told them of the life of John Bunyan, his conversion, and his time in prison where he probably wrote the book in two portions and how Mr. Bunyan died at an early age due to a cold. He summed up and looked directly at Jim and said, "Each of us must choose to serve good or evil. I guess this was Mr. Bunyan's way of warning us." He watched Jim as he walked back to his seat and the class clapped.

Mrs. Solomon stood back up and said, "Very good, Larkin. Class, please pick up your book and turn to page 45." Coone glared at Larkin for the rest of the period. Larkin somehow knew who the person "they" would use to torment him.

The rest of the school year flew by quickly. By the time April came around, Ginny's family was preparing for the wedding in June. And by now, the school knew all the coming nuptials and the boys were teasing Larkin about it. He was very mature though and dismissed their taunting. The boys sensed it and finally left him alone. He wondered about that. Or was he just being paranoid?

Graduation was scheduled for June 8th at the school auditorium. There were only 25 students graduating that year, with Larkin being Valedictorian for the year 1975. As was customary, he was supposed to address the class but, he had not a single idea of what he would say. This didn't occur too often, for he was always ready to say something to someone!

School let out at noon on graduation day to give everyone a chance to prepare for the event. Ginny had picked out a new dress and was very excited when she left school to go home and get ready. Before leaving she said to Larkin, "I'm so excited! Will I see you before the graduation ceremony or should we catch up to each other afterwards?"

"Why don't we wait until afterwards? I still haven't prepared for the speech and I need some time."

"Okay. I'll see you afterwards, then. Bye, Larkin."

"Bye, Ginny."

They went their separate ways expecting to see each other later on.

Larkin had ridden his bike that day, so he hopped on it and headed towards his house, because his mom had picked up his cap and gown. As he rode along, he passed the Coone place. Of course, Jim saw him pass by and he yelled at him, "Hey Palmer, come here." Larkin acted as if he didn't hear him and kept going, but Coone said, "You better stop Larkin or she's gonna get it!"

"Who's gonna get it?" asked Larkin loudly, stopping with a squeal of his tires to address him.

"You know who. After tonight, you had better be gone or the whole family is dead."

"You don't want to make that mistake, Coone."
"The only mistake there will be is if you don't leave."
"We'll see about that."

Larkin started to ride again and Coone grabbed the bike by the handle bars. He twisted them to the right causing Larkin to crash and fall onto his side. Coone started to pick him up to hit him, but instead, began to kick him. He knocked the wind out of Larkin by kicking him in the ribs. Larkin could only lay there as Coone beat him unmercifully, kicking him in the face and head repeatedly. By the time Coone was done, Larkin was unconscious. The funny thing was- no one saw this occur. No one came out to stop him. No one was a witness. Consequently, Coone just walked back into his house and left Larkin there to bleed to death.

But that didn't happen. Someone drove by and saw Larkin laying there in a pool of blood. It was Mrs. Hoxie and she stopped to help him. She lifted his head and tore pieces of her dress to press into the gaping wound in his forehead. When the next car went by, she screamed for help and they stopped long enough to see what happened and then go for help. Then- the town knew about it! The news traveled almost as fast as the ambulance to the site of the mistake.

By the time the ambulance got there, Larkin had lost a lot of blood. They had no choice but to take him to the hospital in Schenectady. The hospital staff said that if Mrs. Hoxie had not found him, Larkin would have surely died. They called Lawtin and Shirley, and they drove as fast as the Lincoln would take them. They prayed on the way, hoping their son would recover.

When Jim walked into the house, he went into the bathroom and cleaned up, because he was covered with Larkin's blood. He took off his clothes, putting them in the wash and was finishing up as his dad came in and saw all the blood in the sink. Then he knew. Billy hit the ceiling! "Did you do that to Palmer?" Jim cringed as fear gripped him. It wasn't the first time his abusive dad was about to hit him.
"Yes, Sir," he said trembling.
"You don't know what you've done, Boy. You're gonna end up dead! We gotta get you outta here."
Billy picked up the phone. Calling over to the Lodge he explained the situation to whoever he had on the line. "Yeah I know, it might not matter, but we have to try. Yeah, in fact, I think we all had better be careful. Right. Bye." Billy picked up his son by the ear lobe and shoved him in his room and said, "Pack fast. You're going in the Army."

113

"What? The Army? Why Dad? It was just Palmer!"

"Do as I said. NOW! You don't know who you were messing with. You made a BIG MISTAKE BOY!" The boy knew his dad meant business and he packed fast.

In the mean while, Ginny heard about Larkin and was on her way to the hospital with her mother. She had called the school to tell them what happened and to not expect them to be at the graduation. They got onto Highway 20 and were making good time. Suddenly, from out of nowhere a goose flew into their path and Ginny's mom did well to avoid hitting it, but the semi-truck on the other side didn't, and when he veered to miss it, he came over to their side of the highway. The devastation was horrendous and the two died instantly. The car was torn in two and the driver of the truck was taken to the hospital in critical condition- the hospital in Schenectady.

When the Palmers arrived Larkin was already in surgery. They sat in the waiting room with another couple named Liston whose daughter had fallen from a ladder and hit her head. She was unconscious, too. They were talking to them with the TV playing in the background when a local news program came on at 4:00 p.m. Lawtin thought he heard something about an accident on Highway 20 and he looked past Mrs. Liston to see a picture of the truck and car all twisted up. Then he heard it, "The mother and daughter lived in Brookfield. It appears they were traveling to Schenectady to visit someone in the hospital there." He jumped up and cried out, "Ginny!"

He ran, which Lawtin had not done for quite some time, and picked up the pay phone. He called the Berry house. Mike picked up the phone on the third ring. "Hello?" Lawtin could hear the distress in his voice.

"Mike, this is Lawtin. Is it true? Was it them?"

Mike began to cry. "Yes, Lawtin. They were on their way to see Larkin and the truck just..." He dropped the phone and Lawtin could hear him crying in the background. Andy picked it up and said, "I'm sorry Mr. Palmer, but Dad just can't talk right now. Is Larkin going to be okay?"

"Thank you for asking Andy, but we don't know yet. Tell your father I am so sorry. Goodbye."

"Goodbye, Mr. Palmer and thanks."

Lawtin hung up the phone and collapsed into a chair across the room from him. He wept bitterly.

In an hour, Jim Coone was on a bus heading for the South.

He had a one way ticket with instructions to see the recruiter in Ft. Benning, Georgia. He was a Mason and he'd get Jim the best deal he could.

His dad told him he'd take care of as much as he could from his end, but he had better watch out. Billy never told him why, because he didn't want to scare the heck out of Jim.

Billy Coone went straight to see the Grand Master. "Sir, do you know what this means?"

"Yes. If we could only find that Key of Pike's we could just take care of this kid. But, there may be something we can do about it for now."

"What's that?"

"Instead of running, we play hard ball."

"Think he'll fall for that?"

"Maybe. All we can do is try. Here's what you do..." They talked about how Larkin may be so upset at losing Ginny that he may just go away if he thought they caused the deaths. Then they would just say that they would kill his family if he didn't leave. They'd wait until he got out of the hospital and then they'd do it. But then, there was always a chance Larkin *wouldn't* fall for it...

Shirley came down the hall to find Lawtin sitting there in tears. She knew what that meant. She began to cry as well and they held each other and prayed. They prayed for Mike, Andy, and his sister as they dealt with losing a wife, daughter and mother. They prayed for Larkin, that he may recover fully and that the doctors would perform a successful surgery. And they prayed for the truck driver and his family as they dealt with the guilt they would feel after having made such a mistake. And finally, they prayed for whoever it was that beat Larkin, that he may be brought to justice, and most importantly, to faith in the Lord. While they sat there the wife and family of the trucker came in to find him. They had come all the way from Vermont and were worried that he may not make it, too. The doctors seemed to think he had a 50-50 chance of survival. Only the Lord knew for sure.

Just then, Tom came in and saw his brother and sister-in-law sitting there. He didn't let them know he was there and just observed them praying and hugging each other. He prayed as well and went over to them and put his arms around them. He said, "I prayed to the Lord he would be all right. He told me not to worry."

"Thanks, Tom," said Lawtin.

"Thank the Lord!" exclaimed Shirley.

"Amen," said the three.

Larkin was in the hospital for almost three weeks before he came around. He didn't know about the accident. He didn't know that they had already buried Ginny and her mom.

He didn't even remember what had happened to him! He only knew that he hurt. Lawtin and Shirley didn't know what to do about telling him about Ginny. Maybe he wouldn't remember her either. They didn't know. When he did come to, they were standing there with him. He slowly opened his eyes and said softly, "Mom."

She walked over and grabbed his head and began to cry and said, "I'm here, Larkin, and so is Dad."

Lawtin went over and put his hand on his arm. Then Larkin asked, "Where's Ginny?"

Then they knew. Shirley just said, "She isn't here. Just rest right now."He closed his eyes and went back to sleep. She laid his head back down and motioned to Lawtin to go out to the hall. She asked, "How do we tell him and when?"

"Well, I don't think we should wait too long, because it wouldn't be honest. He can take it. He's strong. But let's talk to the doctor about it and see what he says."

They went out for a bite to eat and timed their return so that they would see the doctor on his evening rounds. Dr. Thompson came into the room and took a look at Larkin's chart. He had heard from the nurses that he had regained consciousness. He said, "That all looks good. He should be able to go home in a week or two." They told him the situation about his memory and asked his opinion on whether he could take the shock of Ginny's death this soon after coming around. The doctor said, "Physically he is doing well. If he is a strong individual as you say, I don't see any reason you can't tell him anytime. It won't affect his recovery now."

"Thanks, Doctor," said Lawtin and he shook his hand as he left the room. Lawtin looked at Shirley and she looked at the floor and shook her head.

She said, "I just can't believe it still- Ginny gone."

From the other side of the room Larkin said, "Mom, what do you mean, "Ginny gone?"' He startled them.

Lawtin went over to him and said, "Son, we have some bad news to tell you. Ginny and her mother were in a terrible accident. They have both gone to be with the Lord."

Larkin just starred at them. He bit his lip and tears began to run down his cheeks. Shirley went over to him and gave him a hug. He asked, "How did it happen?"

Shirley told him that he had been attacked and she was driving over to see him when a truck lost control and hit them head on. He just remained silent when she finished. Finally he said, "Can I be alone?"

His dad replied, "Sure, Son. We'll see you tomorrow." They closed the door as they left.

Larkin just lay there trying to remember what had happened to him to put him in the hospital. He traced his thoughts back to school and the graduation. The early dismissal, the speech he had to do, saying goodbye to Ginny, the bike ride home. The bike ride! Jim Coone did it! That jerk. He thought of other things to call him but... He called for the nurse. She came in at a dead run thinking he had a problem. He asked, "Have my parents left the building yet?"

"No, I don't think so. They stopped to use the rest rooms. Do you want me to get them?"

"Yes, please. I've remembered everything."

The nurse ran out and caught Lawtin and Shirley just as they were getting into the car. She yelled to them, "Please come back in. Your son remembers!"

When they got back in he told them how Jim Coone had knocked him off his bike and beat him until he lost consciousness. Lawtin said, "So that explains why he up and joined the Army so fast."

Larkin asked, "He joined the Army?"

"That's right," answered Shirley, "we couldn't figure that one out either."

"Mom?"

"Yes, Honey?"

"Who found me?"

"Mrs. Hoxie."

"Really? She sure has helped me out a lot." He pondered that. "Mom, I want to go home." He started to try to get up, but he fell back into his bed.

Shirley placed her hand on his arm and said, "Not yet. The doctor said a week or two."

"I say a day or two. I'll be up and out of here faster than he thinks."

He was right. In a couple of days he was doing so well the doctor released him. His folks took him home and he went up to his room. He was tired though. He lay down and switched on his clock radio. The Beatles were singing, "She loves you". He thought about Ginny. He cried, but he was in shock from the realization she was dead. He switched it back off.

Looking out of his window, Larkin wondered what he was going to do next. This was much bigger than he ever realized. There were literally thousands of members of the two groups, the Masons and the Illuminati, not to mention all of the sub-groups. All followed Satan to one degree or another. But he needed to know more about them and who *really* was in control. He would get the list his grandpa had started and go from there! Now he was bent on revenge and they had better watch out! Especially Coone! But, deep inside, the Spirit worked within him.

The next morning, Larkin got up and went out to the barn. The cows were just being milked. Percy came up to him and shook his hand. "I'm glad to see you up and about, Larkin."

"Glad to be up and about, Percy!"

"Want to help?"

"No thanks. I just wanted to come out and watch." He walked around and watched how his ideas were working out. He had implemented new cleaning techniques and had the newest milking machines around. The state regularly brought farmers to see the new dairy operations in full swing. He was proud of his work. His dad had eighty-five cows now. They were blessed.

He went outside to see a car drive up to the barn and a man in a suit get out. Larkin knew what and who he was. The man didn't say a word and he handed Larkin an envelope. Turning and walking away, he wasted no time in leaving. Larkin waited until he drove off before he opened it. The note inside didn't say much, just, "Leave now, or we'll kill your parents, too." He thought about it for just a second. Larkin smiled an angry smile and shook the note in a clenched fist above his head. Then he cried out loudly, "Perfect. Just- PERFECT!" Now he knew he must be the Keeper and from this time on, he would do the job to the best of his ability. This move on the part of the Illuminati was another big mistake, because now they had filled him with *passion*.

Chapter 11

The Unexpected

Larkin didn't tell his parents about the threat. He didn't want to worry them with it. He was of a mind to never tell them. He had planned to go to college in Maryland anyway. At least he'd *say* he was going to do that, so that he could research the true nature of his family's nemesis. The new Freedom of Information Act would help him, he thought. And the area around the nation's capital was the ticket! However, he knew he'd have to be almost more cautious there than at home, because there were just so many of "them" in Washington, D.C...

Larkin set it all up. He scheduled his departure and arranged to enroll at the University of Maryland. His parents were thrilled, because it was one of the few colleges that had all the agricultural coursework he wanted and was still close to home. Shirley asked him, "Larkin you'll be coming home for the holidays won't you?"

Trying not to lie he replied, "You know I'll do my best, Mom. I want to make sure I get good grades. That's why I'm going you know."

She looked at him as though she knew he really wasn't answering the question. He went over to her as she sat by the table and leaned over, giving her a kiss on the forehead. She grabbed his hands and said, "I'm going to miss you."

"Me, too," he replied.

Lawtin came into the kitchen and asked, "Are you all packed?"

"Almost, Dad."

"Tom will want to see you before you go, too."

"I know. I plan on going over in the morning before the bus leaves. I have some things I want to say to him, too."

Larkin got up early the next day and started to make a pot of coffee. He took the Folgers can out of the cupboard, put it on the counter and filled the pot with water. Scooping some grounds into the pot, he then placed it on the stove as he had so many times before. He'd miss this place, he thought...

Something moved outside disturbing his daydream. He looked out the window and saw Percy drive over to the barns. It was his turn to sleep at home. Since they had added the second barn, he and Arville took turns sleeping in the quarters there on site. It made it easier for them. Besides, the room was almost nicer than what they had at home!

Larkin put the pot on the stove and sat at the table. He felt much better in the months since Coone had beaten him up, and he got steamed every time he thought about it. He kept himself from the thought of revenge, for that would have been too easy. But he knew he had to go pick up The Eraser and all the information necessary to complete his research. He'd retrieve it when he saw Uncle Tom. Lawtin came in the room and broke Larkin's daydream again. "Smells good in here, but no breakfast?"

"Sorry, Dad. I was just thinking."

"About school?"

"Yeah, school." He lied.

Shirley walked in tying her robe as she made her way across the floor. "Who wants pancakes?"

"Me," both men said in unison. Shirley laughed and made her way to the pantry to get the bisquick.

Larkin said to her, "Don't forget to add the extra sugar."

"Never do."

"Thanks, Mom."

There was little conversation at the table and when they finished, Larkin got up and put the dishes in the sink. He said, "Thanks, Mom. I'm sorry I can't stay to help you do the dishes, but I have to go over and see Uncle before I leave."

"I know." She got up and gave him a hug. "I'll walk out to the car with you."

Larkin picked up his suitcases and went toward the door. He called to his dad, "Dad! Come on! We have to stop at Uncle's before we go to the depot."

Lawtin yelled out from the bathroom, "Coming!"

Larkin heard the toilet flush and he and his mom just looked at each other and smiled. Going out the door the two walked slowly to the Lincoln. Shirley said, "We could have bought you the car you wanted, Larkin."

He replied, "I know, Mom. But, I want to be inconspicuous and use public transportation. If I need a car, I'll buy one."

"Okay. Just let us know what you are up to and how you like school."

"You know I'll call you all the time." He lied again.

Lawtin caught up with them about the time Larkin was about to open the trunk. Larkin thought it was cool to open the glove box and push the trunk release button. (It reminded him of the secret button on the Glory Box.) His dad picked up the suitcase closest to him and wondered why it was so light. Larkin saw the surprise on his face and just said, "You got the light one, Dad." And he did. What he didn't know is that Larkin was taking some of the information from The Homestead with him, and of course, The Eraser.

He got in the car and his dad started it up. Shirley started to cry. She put her hand on Larkin's arm and Lawtin put the car in reverse. She grasped it harder, not wanting to let go. Larkin put his hand on top of it and she released it as he smiled and said, "I love you, Mom."

Running alongside the car, she replied, "I love you, Honey."

They drove toward The Homestead. Larkin saw a car coming toward them at a high rate of speed up Chase road from his uncle's place. He watched it as it whizzed by. He saw the Mason's bumper sticker as it sped past them and then he said out loud, "Hurry, Dad. I think Uncle may be in trouble."

Lawtin hit the gas. When they got in the driveway, Larkin felt better as he saw Tom sitting in his rocker on the porch, shotgun in hand, rubbing the stock as if it were his friend. Larkin pushed the button for the trunk, jumped out, got his empty suitcase and ran to the porch asking Tom, "A little early for bird hunting, isn't it Uncle?"

"Yes. But I thought I'd take some target practice this morning."

"Did you have some trouble?"

"Not really, but some snoopy folks from the big city need to know what its' like here in the country."

"Let me know if you need any help with that," offered Lawtin," I can come over to stay with you any time."

"Thanks, Lawtin, but that won't be necessary." Tom winked at them.

"I hope not, Uncle." Changing the subject he said, "I need to pack a few things before I go."

Tom nodded and Lawtin took a seat in Harry's old chair next to Tom. Larkin went in and pulled the cardboard box from its place. Taking out his grandpa's list, the Journal, the Gift Box and The Eraser, he packed them in the suitcase. He placed the threatening note he received the other day in the box, then he took out his watch and looked at the time. It was ten-thirty. He called out, "Time to go, Dad. The bus will be there at eleven and I still need to buy my ticket."

Lawtin looked at Tom and replied to Larkin, "Okay. But you have to be out here to leave." The older men laughed as Larkin came out the door.

Addressing his uncle, Larkin said, "I left some information on the kitchen table for you, Uncle. Would you read it and do as I suggest?"

Tom looked at him with a bit of wonder on his face and replied, "Why Larkin, I think I could do that."

"Thank you, Uncle." Larkin bent over and gave him a hug. Then, he picked up his suitcase and headed toward the car. He'd left the trunk wide open all this time, so he just went to the back and threw the case in and shut the door. In a matter of seconds, they were out the drive and making their way towards town. Lawtin said to his son, "You know this will be the first time you've really been away from home for very long. Will you be alright?"

"I'll be fine. Don't worry. If I need anything, I'll call." In that statement, Larkin conveyed to his father who he could always count on.

When they arrived, the bus was waiting by the Greyhound Station, which was merely a gas station by the post office. A couple of people had already boarded. Larkin got out of the car and went inside to buy his ticket, while Lawtin took his bags over to the bus. Neither of them noticed that the car that had sped away from The Homestead sat across the street a block down from the station. As Lawtin made his way toward the bus, a man bumped into him, causing Lawtin to drop one of the suitcases. The man picked it up and said, "Oh, excuse me. I'm so sorry. Here's your bag." It was the light one.

Taking back the bag, Lawtin said, "That's okay."

The man just walked on and that was it. But, Lawtin was uneasy about it and looked back to see where the man had gone. He saw nothing! The man had disappeared!

Larkin came out of the station with ticket in hand. He also carried his heart on his sleeve. Lawtin could tell his son was upset. He went to him and gave him a hug. "Don't be sad, we'll see you at Thanksgiving."

Larkin knew the truth however and just agreed with him and said, "That's right. It's only a couple months." But, even though he wanted and expected to be away for a long time, little did he know he would be home sooner than he thought.

Lawtin said, "I think you have someone on your tail, Son. One just bumped into me and he picked up your bag. I don't know what it all means, but just be careful."

Alarmed, but trying to put his dad at ease Larkin asked, "He didn't get anything did he?"

"No, it's here." He patted the suitcase.
"Good. I don't need anything happening to my stuff even before I leave town. But, I guess thieves are everywhere aren't they, Dad?" Larkin looked around to see the car of intruders down the street.

He'd keep an eye on them.

His dad finally said, "Yes, so be careful in the city, too."

"I will Dad, you can count on it." He put his hand on his dad's shoulder and gave him a hug. He turned and started to the door of the bus.

His dad followed him and said as Larkin went up the steps, "Godspeed, Son."

"Thanks, Dad. Be careful and take good care of Mom and Uncle."

"You know I will."

The door to the bus closed and Lawtin backed away as the driver slowly pulled away from the curb. He watched as Larkin sat down by the window and waved goodbye. The car down the street pulled away and went the other direction. Larkin watched and sighed with relief. Maybe they would leave his family alone now. He'd done what "they" had asked.

After dropping of his accomplice, Coone pulled his car into the garage. Then Coone called the Grand Master. "Yeah, I think it worked. We saw him get on the bus to D.C.. Yeah. The word is that he is going to UMD. Should I do anything at The Homestead? Okay. I'll leave them alone. I don't want anything happening to Jim, or me!" He laughed. Then he hung up the phone. It looked to them like their plan had worked. In reality, Larkin was the one who was in control, at least for a while.

After Lawtin and Larkin had left The Homestead, Tom opened the note that Larkin had left for him. It read:

"Dear Uncle, I want you to know I am so grateful to you for everything you have done for me and taught me. I also want you to know that you must never tell Mom and Dad that I plan to not return to Brookfield for a while, as I fear the Illuminati will try to take all of your lives if I do."

Tom stopped there for a moment and sat the note down. Tears began to fall from his eyes, knowing that his nephew had come under the curse of The Eraser and was only trying to find a way to help the family. He loved and admired him so much. He picked up the note again. The rest only contained instructions for him in case Larkin needed money and, of course, to be careful with all of what was in his possession there at The Homestead. He didn't need to be reminded of that. Tom just hoped "they" would leave them alone.

Chapter 12

The Exile

The Smithsonian

As Larkin got off the bus, the enormity of his new environs made him gawk in wonder at, well, almost everything. He had decided to go into the city to stay his first night there. He knew exactly where he wanted to go and where he wanted to be. He hailed a cab because it was just too far for him to walk with two suitcases in tow. When he got in he said, "To the Hay-Adams, driver."

The cabbie looked into the rear view mirror for a second at the young man in blue jeans and a tee shirt. He replied by asking, "Are you sure?"

"You only live once", Larkin said.

"You got that right!" replied the driver and he pulled out and headed toward Lafayette Square.

Pulling up to the entrance, a doorman immediately opened Larkin's door. Expecting something or possibly someone different, he somewhat disappointingly and half-heartedly said, "Welcome to the Hay-Adams, Sir."

Paying the cabbie and laughing as he got out, Larkin answered him, "Don't be so disappointed, um," looking at his name tag, "Chester. I'm going to make you my right hand man for the weekend that I'm here."

He handed him a twenty and pointed at his bags. Looking at the bill, he hopped to attention and said, "YES, SIR!" Chester grabbed Larkin's old suitcases and headed toward the front desk following behind the casually attired young man.

When he got to the counter, the concierge asked Larkin somewhat snidely, "Do you have a reservation, Sir?"

"No I don't, but do you have a room?"

"Yes. But it is two hundred dollars a night, Sir", and looking at Larkin from under his glasses said, "in advance."

Not even flinching, Larkin took out his wallet and placed six hundred dollars on the counter. "I'll be here three nights." The concierge all of a sudden got a different attitude and rang the bell.

"Bellhop, take Mr.?" He looked at Larkin for a name.

"Palmer, Larkin Palmer." He pushed the registration toward Larkin.

"My name is Henry. If you need anything please call us at any time." Again he addressed the bellhop.

"Take Mr. Palmer to room 302. It overlooks the Square and the White House. I hope you find your stay at The Hay-Adams to your liking, Sir!"

As Larkin walked away toward the elevator he called out to Chester, "I'll see you in the morning, Chester."

"Yes Sir, Mr. Palmer." He tipped his hat and smiled saying under his breath, "Nice kid."

Following the bellhop, Larkin was impressed by the Italian Renaissance architecture of the lobby, especially the columns and the woodwork. That was what he really liked. He just gawked at it all.

Once on the elevator, the bellhop asked, "Here for a visit, Mr. Palmer?"

"No, actually, I will be starting at UMD next week."

"UMD, huh? What ya gonna study?"

"History and agriculture."

"That's a strange combination."

"Yeah, but it's what I like."

"Good for you."

The bell on the elevator rang for the third floor. The bellhop got out and headed left down the carpeted hall. Stepping out, Larkin looked up. There in front of him hanging on the wall in a beautiful frame, was an old map of Washington, D.C. The lighting was faint. But for some reason an outline of some of the streets was more distinct than others. Then he saw it. The outline of the square and compass! He thought, 'Why haven't I ever seen that before? I'll have to look into that, too!'

They arrived at his room and the bellhop opened the door for him. When he placed Larkin's bags on the floor by the dressers he asked, "Is there anything else, Sir?"

Larkin replied, "What's your name?"

"Mike, Sir. After Mike Mansfield."

"I'd like to see more of the town from a historical point of view, Mike. I don't have a lot of time to go to all the monuments, so where can I go to find out who built them?"

"That's easy. Go to the National Archives. It has everything."

"Thanks, Mike. Here ya go." Larkin handed him a twenty also and Mike lit up.

He actually thanked Larkin. "Thanks! If you need anything, Sir, just let me know."

"Call me Larkin."

"You got it, Larkin." He tipped his hat and went out the door.

Larkin called his mom as soon as Mike left. He figured he'd be in trouble if he didn't. The phone only rang once and Shirley picked it up. "Hello?"

"Are you sitting next to the phone, Mom?"

"Yes, Larkin, I am! I wanted to know if you made it alright. How's Washington, D.C.?"

"I really don't know yet. All I've had time to do is getting checked into the hotel. I'll see some of the sites in the morning. Tonight, I want to relax."

"We are glad you made it. Make sure you call when you get checked in at the school. Good night, Larkin."

"I'll be fine, Mom. Good night. Tell Dad hello."

"I will. Bye."

Larkin hung up. Then he picked the lighted trimline phone back up. He dialed room service. "Could I get a cheeseburger, some fries, and a Coke?"

"Coming right up, Sir."

Larkin turned on the TV and sat down. He watched the news. President Ford was on talking about President Nixon. He had just granted him a full pardon! Wasn't Ford a Mason? Something sure sounded fishy. Larkin wondered who would be picked for VP and he almost was sure it would be another Mason! Someone knocked at the door. "Room service," came the call from the other side.

Larkin let the man in. He carried the tray above his head and set it down on a folding table set up for food behind the door. "Will that be all, Sir?"

"Yes. Here ya go."

He handed him a tip and the man left the room. It smelled good. In fact, when he opened the tray lid, he beheld the biggest cheeseburger he had ever seen. He picked up the plate and sat back down to watch the rest of the news. A commercial for "The Invisible Man" came on. Larkin said out loud, "A new show. I think I'll watch that." When he finished eating, he sat the plate on the floor. The show came on and as he watched, he began to get tired. Almost dozing off, he got up and switched the TV off. "If that show lasts a year, I'll be surprised," he said as he went off to bed.

Larkin got up early and went down to the lobby. Rather than eat in the restaurant, he decided to walk toward downtown. Chester asked him if he wanted a cab as he went toward the door. Larkin said, "No. But can you tell me where I can get a good home cooked breakfast?"

"The only place you'll find that is at home! But if you go out to 14th and then south to Pennsylvania Avenue, you'll pass more restaurants than you can shake a stick at."

They both laughed and Larkin said, "Thanks, Chester. See you later."

Larkin began his walk toward 14th. It felt good to get out in the crisp, cool, fall Washington air. He wondered how he would feel about his new home after he had been there a while. He knew one thing though, that he loved the thought of the adventure. He loved the thought of his new search for information. He loved Washington!

He turned down 14th. When he got half way down the block he noticed the building facing toward him on the corner of New York. It was one of those "corner-shaped" buildings. He loved the architecture in D.C., too! Some old, some new, but all of it -cool!

When he got to the corner of G Street, he glanced down the block to see what was there. He saw a sign that said "Reeve's" and decided to take the detour and check it out. His stomach was getting the best of him. He was glad he did. When Larkin walked in the door he knew this was gonna be it. It *smelled* good. Not only did it have a great breakfast, but it was a bakery, too! He was excited. Larkin loved baked goods. And it looked like this was the place the locals came, too. He thought he saw Ted Kennedy. This place must have been around for years. When he finished, he thought he'd have to tell Chester that this place offered food that *was* pretty close to home. Purchasing a couple of donuts to go, he went back out toward 13th instead of 14th. Half way down the block there was a news stand, papers plastered all over the walls. Larkin looked through some of the "freebies" for visitors and took a couple of maps of the city. That would help him a bit, so he ventured off toward the National Archives.

By the time he got to Pennsylvania Ave, he had been in one of his daydreams wondering if any of the buildings he was looking at were there when the founding fathers had walked these streets. He imagined tipping his hat to Washington, or saying good morning to Hamilton as he made his way to the bank. Instead of turning toward the Archives, he went toward the Smithsonian by mistake. When he realized it, he thought, 'I really don't want to look for these records yet anyway. I'm going to see some good stuff today!' Larkin changed his plan and made his way to the Castle.

As he arrived, children were wandering around with their teachers and going this way and that. Larkin didn't want to be near them, so he went the other direction off in the corner by himself. Something caught his eye outside the south end of the building. A crane and bulldozer were being moved into the yards. A docent was walking by and pointing toward the window he asked her, "What are they doing out there?"

She replied, "They are going to tear down the shed in back tomorrow."

"Do you think they'll let me go through it?"

"I don't think they let people go in there anymore. But go ask the facilities supervisor, he might let you. His office is by the back door."

"Thanks."

Larkin walked down the corridor and down the stairs. He thought he'd gone too far, but there by the back door was indeed, a small office. He knocked. "Come in, but you don't have to knock." Larkin pushed the door open slowly and it just cleared the edge of a cluttered desk. A short man with glasses sat behind it. He looked up and asked, "How can I help you? I'm Mr. Hall."

"My name is Larkin Palmer. I was told you are going to tear down the shed in the morning. I was also told that it has never really been open to the public. But, I thought I'd ask for permission to see it before it was gone. Would that be possible?"

Mr. Hall changed the subject. "Are you related to the Palmers of the Fortune?" Larkin was surprised by his sudden question.

"Why, yes, I am. My family was the first to have a birth in Madison County, New York."

"Ah-ha! I don't see any reason whatsoever that you couldn't take a look. Follow me."

Larkin was dumbfounded. What did his ancestry have to do with anything? Or maybe here, at the Smithsonian, it had *everything* to do with it. Larkin asked, "Mr. Hall, how do you know my family?"

"Oh, I don't. But I know something about it. It's all on record and I read a lot. My wife died a few years back and I spend a lot of time here. Maybe, too much time. But, I enjoy it. By the way, call me Harry."

"That was my uncle's name. He died a few years back."

They walked toward the shed and Harry opened the door. "We all do. So where do you want to start?"

"Harry, did they do any excavations or look at the site before this time to make sure nothing is lost to history?"

"Yes, they did. But, I didn't think it was good enough. I had an argument with the Secretary about it and almost got fired. I've been tinkering around since then and haven't really come up with anything interesting, so maybe they did do a good job. Why do you ask? Are you an archeologist?" he asked with a laugh.

Ignoring Harry's question he answered, "I've found that if anyone wanted to bury anything in a barn type structure, they'd place it in the corners by the footings. It was an easy point of reference. I assume this used to be the area of the old barns?"

"Very good, Larkin. Yes, it was, and they used the same footings when they built this shed. It used to be a garage and stable, but until 1921 it was a taxidermy shop run by William Palmer. No relation I assume?"

Larkin ignored this question too, and asked, "Where was the manure pile?"

"What?"

Larkin repeated the question, "Where did they put the manure pile?"

"I think it was over there. Why?"

"You'll see."

The floors that used to be in the rooms had already been removed before the structure was to come down. Now there stood an empty shell. Larkin went over to the corner and picked up a shovel left by the archeologists. He went to the corner where the manure pile had been and he *knew* he was guessing, but he started to dig anyway. He dug for a few minutes in about a three foot square. Being down about a foot, he started to get concerned that he would be made the fool and not find anything. Harry just stood there, arms folded, and watched smiling all the while and Larkin thought he would tease him if he didn't find anything. But, the gift, and more importantly, God, was with him and his shovel struck something! Thud! He did it again. Thud! Harry's arms dropped from his chest and he said, "Wait! Let me help you with that." Harry grabbed another shovel and as they dug they unearthed a trunk. It was an old raised top trunk from the mid- 1800's. They made their way around it ever so carefully, trying not to touch the leather or the iron trim that decorated the top and sides. When they got down to the bottom and it was totally uncovered, they stopped and took a break. Larkin looked at Harry. Harry asked, "Who wants to open it?"

"I will. I don't want you to get in trouble with your boss," said Larkin.

"Oh, I think I'm already way past that," said Harry with a laugh.

Larkin reached over and undid the two latches. They moved surprisingly easily. Then, he lifted the lid. Papers. Documents. Harry took one in his hand, looked at it and said, "My gosh! These are about Lincoln and Seward, Lincoln's Secretary of State. Seward must have hidden these. Larkin, if this is what I think it is, you have made the find of a lifetime!"

Larkin smiled slightly and said, "If you only knew Harry. If you only knew," he repeated.

Harry didn't pay attention to what Larkin said, instead, he got out of the hole, pointed a finger at him and said in haste, "Don't move. I'll be right back."

He ran out of the shed and into the Castle. Larkin just stood there wondering what to do next. Soon, Hall came out with one of the archeologists. He didn't take the time for introductions. He just pointed. The man jumped into the hole with Larkin and grabbed one of the documents. With a smile on his face, he almost shouted, "You're right, Harry! But do you know what this could mean? It could re-write history! But wait, we had better think about that. First, we need to get the Secretary. He'll tell us what to do."

With that, they both went back into the Castle without saying anything to Larkin. Larkin picked up the next document in the trunk. It was a letter. In fact, it was a hate letter from someone in Seward's state of New York. He looked at the signature. It was from the Grand Master of the Lodge in New York City! Seward had made many enemies, both in his home state, (even in Brookfield he supposed) and in the South. He was anti-slavery and anti-Masonic. No wonder they wanted him dead the night Lincoln was killed. Maybe there *was* a greater conspiracy. Maybe that was what Harry was talking about! He folded the letter and put it in his pocket, but he didn't know why. Before Harry came back, Larkin got out of the hole and waited. In about ten minutes Harry returned with the other man, the archeologist, and someone else dressed in a suit, which Larkin assumed was the Secretary.

The man in the suit came straight over to Larkin. "You must be Larkin. I'm Dan S. Shipley. I've heard a lot about you already. Harry told me about the manure pile theory. Show me what you've found."

Larkin said, "This way, Sir." They made their way to the corner and the hole. Larkin got down into the hole and Dan followed slowly.

Dan asked, "How did you know this would be here, Son?"

"To tell you the truth, it's previous experience."

"Really? So you've found other things before?"

"Yes, but I always had better clues before."

"Indeed," he said as slowly as his step into the hole. "This find is one we will have to look into. I am a bird man myself, so I'll be giving it over to," he paused to collect his thought as to whom it should be assigned. Looking at the archeologist standing there, who'd previously been in charge of the shed project, Shipley said, "Harry, I think this should be your project, but I'd like to talk with you, Larkin, about you coming on staff here." Harry beamed.

Larkin asked, "On staff? As what?"

"We'll need someone to help catalogue this find. You could help Harry. What do you say?"

"I've done that before. You bet! But I'll have to do it after school. I'm starting at UMD on Monday."

"Done."

Shipley reached out and shook Larkin's hand. Harry smiled again. Looking up at Harry from down in the hole Dan said to him, "Mr. Hall, I sincerely apologize to you about the matter we spoke of last week. This proves you were correct. As I said, I'm giving the entire project over to you. I'll postpone the demolition one month. In the meanwhile, have Larkin help begin with the cataloging. Do not let anyone know what has been found until we see what we have. I don't want to cause a stir." Shipley stuck his hand up and had Harry help him out of the hole. At this the Secretary and the archeologist walked away in a heated discussion.

Larkin scrambled up out of the hole, dirt sliding under his feet, and he picked up his shovel. Harry said to him, "Larkin, we need to seal off the area until we can move the trunk to a room inside. I'll get what we need and be right back."

They had all left him alone in the shed again. He had time to think about this new development. It would take time away from his studies, but it would also give him inroads to his main purpose for being there, to find out about the Illuminati and the Masons. Indeed, this may give him the free access to things the public may never see. He knew that God had placed him at the right place at the right time. He could use it all to his good and maybe even make some spending money, too. Larkin looked around the rest of the room. Could there actually be anything else the archeologists missed? He looked up at the ceiling. The roof above him was tin, but in the center of the room was a lowered ceiling. It extended the entire front to back evenly under the windows that were visible from the street side of the building and was about six feet wide. There was a three foot wide trap door in the middle. However, there was no ladder, nor any way to get up there. 'Surely they must have checked that attic out,' he thought. Harry came back into the room and caught him looking up.

"What do you see, Larkin?" he asked.

"That," he said pointing at the opening.

"It's just an empty attic space. They checked it out."

"Did they look under the floor?"

Harry's eyes opened wide. "No, but *we* will!" They sealed up the building and put the notice on the shed postponing the demolition for a month. They'd get to the attic tomorrow. After they lifted the trunk out of the hole and into his office, Harry asked Larkin, "Hungry? Let's go have lunch. I'm buying."

"You bet, Boss. Lead on."

To say the least, Harry and Larkin had hit it off. While they ate at the cafeteria across the street, they got to know each other a little better. Harry had a tendency to offer lots of information about himself while Larkin just listened. He found out he lived up by U Street in the Adams-Morgan district. He always liked the night life, mostly the Jazz, but not so much of that anymore. He asked Larkin, "Where are you staying? Have you got a place on campus or did you rent a room?"

"Well, I haven't lined up anything quite yet."

"Really? The rooms fill up fast when the colleges start up in the fall. Say, I have a room that is unused. Would you like to stay with me?"

"How much?"

Harry thought a second and said, "Twenty dollars a week. No meals. I never know when I'm going to cook. Besides, I eat out almost all the time since my wife died."

"You got a deal. It's not too far from school either." He stuck out his hand for Harry to shake.

"You may want to get a bike. It's the easiest way around. It's about eight miles to UMD from my house."

"Good idea. Time to go back to work?"

"Yes. Let's go see where Mr. Shipley wants us to set up."

They went back to Harry's office and called Shipley. His secretary, Sally, answered and said, "He just went to lunch, but he said to take the last office used by Smith. He said you'd know what he meant."

"Yes, I do. Thanks."

He hung up. He said to Larkin, "Man that room doesn't even have a window and it's almost as small as mine. We'll just have to make do."
Larkin asked, "Where is it?"
"In the basement- B-102."
"Oh."

They picked up the trunk and placed it on a cart. Wheeling it back to the elevator, Harry pushed the call button. The old Otis service elevator had been there a long time. It rarely was serviced, but it worked like it was new. The door opened and there stood Mrs. Westfall. She was a volunteer that had been around since the Truman era. That's how they kept track of time there, by Presidential terms. "Hello, Mrs. Westfall. This is Larkin, my new assistant."
"Pleased to meet you, Larkin."
"You, too, Mrs. Westfall."

She scooted past the two, briefly looking at the trunk and dismissing it immediately. Harry knew she wouldn't think anything about it, as she thought Harry was insignificant and would never be given an important task. She was wrong this time.

When the door opened downstairs, they pulled the cart out and looking around, Larkin was awestruck. The elevator opened up to an expansive room of – stuff. There was shelf after shelf of catalogued items, each waiting for their time for the world to see them. Larkin was truly amazed at the sight. It was certainly a collective treasure in and of itself. "Man!" he said.
Harry laughed in reply, "That's what I said the first time I saw it, too."

Harry pointed to the hall to the left and they made their way down to B-102. He opened the door and they pushed the cart in. He was right, the room was small, but it had a desk, two chairs, and a small table to set the trunk on. Harry said, "Here, let's move the table next to the desk and we can take each item out to catalogue it. I'll need to get some storage envelopes and other materials for this to happen. They are in supply down the hall. Be right back."
"Okay. I'll put the trunk on the table."

Larkin lifted the trunk up and placed it softly on the table. It didn't weigh half as much as the chests he had found at home, but it was much more fragile. He didn't want it to fall apart in his hands. He opened it again and this time he got a better look at the trunk itself. Considering it had been buried in periodic wet conditions for about 110 years, it was still in pretty fair shape! The handles had almost rotted through, there was evidence of rodent damage, and the outside was still very moist, but was deteriorating. He didn't see any markings and there wasn't even any colorful picture or paper on the inside lid of the trunk, as many of that era displayed. What was important was that all of the documents were protected by a leather cover, thus keeping them from the elements.

Harry came back into the room carrying a load of materials. He sat them on the desk and said, "We are all set. You know, OC, SIA and SLA, and a bunch of others usually does this, but this is our baby. It is not so important that we read each document for its content, but that we describe the persons involved and the dates, etc. Once we have numbered each one, taken a picture record, placed them in the catalogue, and made a copy, then we can go back to fully interpret them. Then we'll know why they are in this trunk and their historical implications. Heck, if we are lucky, we might even get to know why they placed them here in the barn!"

"I've done the same thing with some of my families' documents back home. It's interesting and a fun adventure. I'm sure we'll learn a great deal from this, Harry."

"I hope it is the break I've been waiting for all my life."

"I hope so, too," said Larkin in a soft understanding tone. They both sat down and got to work.

After a couple of hours, they had catalogued about twenty-five percent of the documents. They estimated there to be one hundred, or so. Most of those done were letters. Some were inter-departmental correspondence and some were receipts. But, Larkin was most interested in to whom they were addressed and who they were from. The list of people was exciting: Stanton, Johnson, even some from Confederate soldiers and dignitaries. The rarest was one from President Lincoln to Seward. It was in excellent condition. Both of them were excited about that. How all of the documents fit together was what they would determine later. Harry said to Larkin, "You know that this entire collection will more than likely end up in The National Museum. Especially, especially, if it is what we think it may be. It may finally prove that there was some kind of conspiracy to kill the President. However, it may also be such a find that they may not want to release it, as it may be more than history could accept. If that be the case, it would be a darned shame."

"I agree. It sure would," Larkin replied slowly.

About five o'clock, Harry said, "It's time to call it a day. When I sit slumped over like this my back gets sore. I need to move around. Can you be here in the morning at eight o'clock?"

"Sure can. Do you usually come in on Saturdays?"

"No, but this is too important to let slide. We get paid by the hour no matter when we work, so let's work tomorrow and we can hit it again at your convenience next week. I have all my regular work to do, so we can work on it when you have the time. Okay? Besides, we have to get up into that attic before they tear down the shed."

"Oh. Yeah. In all the excitement I almost forgot about that."

"We can leave all this here. Nobody is going to touch it. That would be work."

They laughed, went out and closed the door. "I'll come to your office in the morning Harry. It has been a very exciting and eventful day. I can't even believe it. It has also been nice getting to know you."

"Thanks, Larkin. You, too."

He patted Larkin on the back as he left and walked out of the Castle. Larkin thought, 'Wait until I tell Chester I have a job at the Smithsonian Institute!'

Instead of walking back to the hotel, he hailed a cab. He was tired from a day of excitement. As he got out of the car at the hotel, he smiled at Chester as he opened the door for him. "Why, Larkin, you seem to be in good cheer. Did you have a good day?"

"Why, yes, Chester, I did. I even got a job at the Smithsonian and I wasn't even looking for one."

"Wow! You don't say? What is your new job title?"

"That's a good question. I'm so new I don't even know what I am!"

They both laughed and Chester closed the door behind him.

Larkin cleaned up and went down to the restaurant for dinner. As he did not have a suit and tie, they didn't want to let him in however, the concierge heard of his dilemma and provided him with a sports coat and tie. He put them on and the maître de allowed him to be seated, even though he raised an eyebrow to this attempt to placate his penchant for the rules. The waiter came and handed him the menu. He announced, "Our special this evening is the pouched salmon. And do not forget the baked Alaska for dessert."

"Thank youuu?" reaching for a name to call him.

"I'm Sam, Sir. I will return in a moment."

Before he had a chance to look at the rest of the menu, someone came up behind him and said, "I've heard the duck is very good here, as well as the lobster." It was Dan and his wife. Larkin started to stand up, but his new boss put his hand on his shoulder and kept him down. "No, don't get up, Larkin. But may we join you? We come here often and it is nice to see a new face."

"Please, yes, Mr. Shipley, I would be glad to have the company."

"This is my wife, Mary."

The waiter helped her to her seat. "Good evening Mr. and Mrs. Shipley. It is nice to have you dine with us again." He left and Larkin had a chance to say, "It is nice to meet you, Mrs. Shipley. I'm Larkin Palmer of New York State."

"Yes, Larkin. I've heard so much about you and your discovery today. How is it you are here at the Hays-Adams?"

"I decided to live it up before I start UMD on Monday. I told the cabbie on the way over that you only live once."

They all laughed at his joke and the waiter came back for their orders. When he had finished his, Mr. Shipley asked the waiter for a bottle of champagne for the table. "I think we have something to celebrate, don't we Larkin?"

"Indeed, Sir. I think we may."

While they waited for their food, the conversation turned to family and roots. Larkin let Mrs. Shipley talk about her four girls, but he really didn't want to disclose too much about his parents or his uncle. The champagne came and the waiter uncorked it with a "pop," without losing too much of the bubbly. Dan raised his glass and said, "To the rewriting of history!"

"To history," they all chimed in, clinking their glasses together. The Shipleys took a sip, but Larkin did not, and sat his glass back down, because he did not drink.

"What did you find in the cataloguing today, Larkin?" asked Dan.

"It has been very exciting. There's lots of correspondence. The best example is a letter from President Lincoln to Secretary of State Seward. It is in great condition. I'm not sure if it will be the document that does the most to establish our case, however."

Mary asked, "And what case would that be, Larkin?" Excitedly, he answered Mary before thinking.

"That Masons of rank, of both the Confederate States and the Union, established a plot to assassinate Lincoln, Seward, and Johnson, thereby throwing the country into turmoil and subject to Masonic takeover and a New World Order."

Larkin noticed the room had become suddenly quiet. Dan leaned forward and said quietly, "Really? That's what you think? How did you come to that conclusion? Perhaps, we should talk about this later?"

The salads arrived just then and Larkin resourcefully changed the subject. He talked as they ate. "Mr. Hall has graciously offered to rent me a room at his home so that I will not be subject to life on campus. I'm kind of a private guy. Besides, we can do things on somewhat the same schedule that way."

"Larkin, I've contacted the President of UMD about you, a Dr. Perkins, a personal friend of mine. He has made arrangements for you to include working at the Institute as part of your course work in History. He said your grades from high school were exceptional and that you were valedictorian. Is that so?"

"Yes, Sir. But, that class was small."

"No matter. I want to do everything I can to support you in your endeavors at UMD. Your contribution to the Institution is already beyond what others have done and you have just begun. I want you around for a long time."

"Thank you, Sir. By the way, what is my title?"

"Assistant to," he hesitated, "Assistant to the Secretary in charge of conspiracies."

Larkin queried, "Conspiracies Assistant? That's gonna bring some laughs." (In fact the man at the table next to him chuckled and placed his napkin in front of his wide grin.)

Dan paused and said, "Maybe so. How about just, 'Junior Assistant to the Secretary'."

"That's good. We can just say I'm working on conspiracies."

"Yes. Hopefully, as this all unfolds, we will know if what you have just proposed is true. If so, we will rewrite history. If not, we will be laughing stocks. This is a big assignment, Larkin. I pray you are up to it." (Still eavesdropping on the conversation, the man at the next table became noticeably irritated and got up to leave.)

"I pray so as well." Larkin hoped the Secretary was speaking from the heart.

The dinner was as good as Dan had said it would be. Larkin had not had lobster before, and he enjoyed it and in fact, it was now his favorite food. What was even better is that his new boss picked up the tab! "Thank you for allowing us to join you tonight, Larkin," said Mary as they stood to leave.

"It was my pleasure Mrs. Shipley, I'm glad you did. And thank you for the wonderful dinner Mr. Shipley. It was nice to get to know you, Sir."

"Good night, Larkin. See you at work."

"Good night, Mr. Shipley."

As Larkin left the restaurant, he said to himself out loud as no one was there to hear, "What a day!" What he didn't know is how many Masons there happened to be in the restaurant with him that night. If he had, his comments to Mary would have been tempered or censored completely.

The phone rang for his wake up call at six o'clock. He answered and said, "Thank you." Fumbling for his shirt, he pulled it over to him from the chair. He felt the pocket and what was in it. The letter! He forgot all about the letter to Seward he had placed in his pocket. He wondered,

'Why did I take that? That was stealing. I guess I'll just put it back. But first I'll make a copy.' Larkin took a tablet of paper from the drawer by the phone and began transcribing the long forgotten letter. The date was March 12, 1865. Unfortunately, he was unable to read the smeared signature. He was only able to read the title of the man who had written it, "Grand Master, Grand Lodge of NYC." That didn't bother Larkin much. What did bother him was this line:

"And Sir, my brother in Washington, the venerable Secretary, will be sure to never let you rest."

'Which Secretary?' he thought, 'was it Stanton?'

It took him too long to copy the letter and it was getting late. He tore off the copy from the notepad, put it in his suitcase, grabbed the original and headed to the door. He waved at Mike as he went past the front desk and Henry just nodded. Larkin had only been there a couple of days and he already liked these guys. When he got to the door Chester stood there waiting. "Good Morning. Would you like me to hail you a cab, Larkin?"

"Yes I would, Chester. I need to be at work in fifteen minutes."

Chester hailed the cab and then pulled him aside. "Sir, may I confide in you?"

As Larkin waited he said, "Why yes, Chester. What is it?"

"Larkin, I believe you are being followed. I've seen a lot in my days and I know a tail when I see one. Watch the man in the blue suit."

Larkin replied, "Thanks, Chester. You're the best."

The cab pulled up and he got in. Looking behind him as he told the cabbie his destination, he saw a dark haired man in a blue suit hail a cab, too. Unfortunately for him, there were none. Larkin just smiled, but he wondered, 'Who knew he was there? Did "they" already know?'

He got out of the cab by the shed and there stood Harry waiting for him. When he saw Larkin get out of the cab and pay, Harry went in the door. Larkin walked in behind him to see that Harry had already placed a ladder up the wall to the trap door. Harry just stood there looking up at it. Larkin asked, "What's' wrong, Harry?"

"I'm afraid of heights."

Larkin laughed and said, "I'll go up first and check it out. If everything is okay, I'll come down, hold the ladder for you, and you can go up. I'll follow you then."

Apprehensively Harry replied, "Well, okay. I'll try it."

"Hold the ladder for me." Larkin got on the first rung and headed up to the trap door. Harry held on as Larkin scrambled up like a monkey on a tree. In fact, Larkin yelled down to him, "This is just like back home at the orchard."

Harry replied sarcastically under his breath, "Good for you."

Larkin pushed on the door. It was stuck shut from the layers of paint and the humidity. He tried again a little harder. This time it let go and the door flew open with a bang as it hit the floor of the attic space. He climbed up into the attic and looked around. There was, like Harry had said before, nothing there. Not even a light. He yelled down to Harry, "Did you bring a flashlight?"

"Oh yeah, I did. It's in the office. Be right back."

"Okay." Larkin just stood in the attic waiting. As he did, his eyes adjusted to the light. Until then it had been a cloudy day, but Larkin noticed that the sun had come out from behind the clouds. It seemed like the sun shone in from three places in the roof. To his surprise, the three points of light all triangulated their light on one place- the trap door of the attic. Just then, Harry returned with the flashlight. "Hey Harry, I think I found something."

Instead of reaching down to get the light, Larkin shut the trap door. Sure enough, there on the back of the door was a pattern in the wood.

Larkin was unable to see what it was in the dark, but the points of light all hinted that this was *the spot.*

Harry called up, "What is it, Larkin?"

"There's a carving on the back of the trap door. If you open it you can't see it because it is face down. If you closed it while you were up here it would be too dark to see it. But there are three holes in the roof and they all shine their light right to this spot. Hand me the flashlight, Harry." Larkin opened the door again and went down toward Harry. When he got within reaching distance Harry gave him the light. Before heading back up he asked, "Do you have a hammer and screwdriver too?"

Harry replied, "Yes. That I do have. And a pry bar."

He picked the tools up and handed them to Larkin. With something in each hand, screwdriver in his mouth, Larkin started back up the ladder. Harry didn't seem to want to come up with him now that he had found something, so Larkin found freedom in this position. So did Harry. Larkin crawled back into the attic and closed the door. Turning on the flashlight, he peered at the backside of the wooden attic access. It was too full of dust to make out, so he got down on his knees, closed his eyes, and blew. Dust flew everywhere and he waited until he felt it had subsided enough for him to look at it again. Before he had a chance to see it Harry yelled up, "What's going on, Larkin? What did you find?"

Larkin responded, "Just a second, Harry. I can't tell."

Larkin took his hands and rubbed. He then traced the outline of the carving with his fingers. First a triangle appeared, then rays from a sun. He knew what he had found. The All Seeing Eye! "It's the Masonic Eye, Harry!" he shouted.

"Oh," Harry replied.

"Why do you say it like that, Harry?"

"I was afraid of something like that."

"I'm going to pry the carving off the back of the door, Harry."

"Do what you think is best, Larkin." Harry already trusted Larkin like he had worked with him for twenty years.

Larkin took the bar and hammer in hand, placed the bar between two boards and hit it. The boards parted quite nicely and one popped out that was about twelve inches long. He placed his hand into the opening and pulled up the next board and then the next. Soon he had a hole about a foot square so he picked up the flashlight to look inside. He paused, took a breath and like so many times before when searching for treasure, he just went for it. Much to his surprise, or dismay, there was- a box! But it was too large to get out of the opening. He sat the flashlight down again and began removing more of the boards. Harry heard all the noise and figured Larkin was still looking, so he just waited for the next report. When Larkin finished his demolition project, he lifted the box out by a leather strap attached to each side of it. It was nothing like any he had found before. It sounded like it contained something glass. He didn't want to open it without Harry, so he lifted the door and stuck his head down saying, "Got it!"

Harry asked, "Got what?"

"A leather box of some kind. I'll be right down."

Larkin made his way down the ladder with the box in one hand, leaving all the tools up in the attic. It seemed like the leather, strap handle was in good condition and would not fall apart if it supported the weight of the box, so Larkin trusted that this was the case. He handed the box to Harry as he got closer to the floor. Larkin asked, "What is it, Harry?"

"I can't say for sure, but it looks like some kind of chemists or druggists kit."

"Why would anyone hide that?"

"I don't know whose it was or why they put it there, but I intend to try to find out, Larkin. What I do know is the group that placed it there."

"Yeah," said Larkin reluctantly, "I know."

Harry headed toward his office with Larkin following along like a puppy. When he got there, he thought twice about opening it there. "Let's go to B-102 with this. It goes along with that case."

"I guess it does, doesn't it?"

They took the elevator downstairs and there didn't seem to be any activity down there. Harry felt good about that, because he didn't want anyone else poking their noses into his case. Besides, Dan had put him in complete control of the shed. When they got to the basement room, Harry opened the metal door with his foot to make sure he had the box under control. Harry didn't wait for Larkin because he was excited! Larkin closed the door behind him and turned on the light. Neither of them said a word. Harry undid the snap that kept the box closed and lifted the lid. There were glass tubes inside! They all seemed to be sealed and they all still contained liquids. The labels on most of them had fallen off and were illegible. One vial seemed to contain a little less than the others. However, on the bottom of the lid he had lifted off, Harry saw another label, and this one identified the owner. It read, "'Brig. Gen. S. Barton, CSA". "What in the world?"', said Harry.

"That's interesting," said Larkin, "I wonder what a Confederate States officer was doing in this shed?"

"And what is in these vials? We need to get them checked. I'll contact our chemist to have them do that right away."

"I'll check into who the General was and I'll meet you back here after while?"

"Good. We will piece it all together then. Good luck!"

"I suspect your assignment will take longer, so I'll wait for you and keep working on the trunk. Good luck, Harry!"

Harry picked up the box, closed the lid, and headed toward the elevator. On the way, he ran into Mrs. Westfall. She saw he had the box and asked suspiciously, "Do we need a voucher for you to remove that from the building?"

"No," Harry replied sarcastically, "I won't be leaving the building. I'm going to see the chemists."

"Oh. Well, be careful." She started to walk away in a huff.

Just then the elevator door opened and Harry got on. Mrs. Westfall, well, she continued walking past the elevator and didn't even say goodbye. As Harry got on, he just shook his head and smiled. Pushing the button, the old elevator door shimmied and shook as it closed. Up it went to the first floor and stopped. He got out and headed toward the left, slipping on a wet spot on the marble floor. His leg went out from under him and he hit his knee. The box went flying out of his hands and across the floor landing on the carpet by the door! He cried out loud, "OH NO!" The people all around him went to his aid. However, he was only interested in the box. Getting up quickly, he went over and grabbed it. To his delight, he picked it up and found nothing broken! In fact, it all had remained the same. He said out loud, "Whew. That was close."

"The guard at the door came over to him, "Are you alright, Harry?"

"Yes, thanks Jim."

"How about your box there?"

"It's okay, too."

"Good."

"Thanks, Jim."

Jim just nodded his head, tipped the bill of his hat, and went back to his post. Harry proceeded to his office where he picked up a form in order to request an analysis from the lab. Then he took it to the lab to drop it off. When he got there the place looked dead. In fact, the lab assistant was behind the counter with her head on the desk asleep! Harry began to laugh audibly. She quickly jerked her head up and being embarrassed said, "Can I help you, Harry?"

"Yes, Sara. I need to get the contents of these vials analyzed as soon as you can."

"That should be no problem," she said as she took the box from Harry as he handed it to her over the desk. "Do you have the form?"

"Yeah, here you go." He handed it to her.

She smiled and said, "I'll have it done by noon. Come back before I go to lunch."

"Okay and thanks, Sara."

Yawning she replied, "Anytime."

Harry smiled and started back to the basement.

In the mean while, Larkin went to the Castle library. He pulled out a set of Civil War reference books that covered CSA armies. Taking them to a table, he sat down and looked in the index of the first one. "Hum, Sam Barton," he whispered to himself, "Here we go, page 415." He thumbed thru a few pages toward the front and he read the description of the General. It didn't say much except that he had mysteriously died after the war there in Washington, D.C.. "Hum, that's odd." He looked at the next book. The index showed, "Biography- Brig. Gen. Sam Barton, CSA, pg. 230." "Now we're getting somewhere," he said out loud. A person next to him at the table looked up at him as if disturbed. "Sorry," he whispered. He read the biography. "Sam Barton went back to his home in Fredericksburg, V.A. after the war, and he entered the trade of chemist. He died on a trip to Washington, D.C. in 1900 while visiting his son." "Aha!" He said loudly. Everyone close to him glared. He picked up his books quickly and mouthed "sorry" as he made his way back to the reference shelves. He was on to something!

When Larkin got back from the library it was almost half-past noon. Harry was not in the basement. He went ahead and got started on the cataloguing again only to be interrupted by a noise coming from down the hall. He looked up and figured it was just a "building noise", but then he thought he saw a shadow. He said, "Hello? Is anyone there?" As there was no response he went back to work. In a couple minutes he could hear someone get out of the elevator and Harry walked into the room. Excitedly he said, "Look at this report! The report shows that its' cyanide in two of them and arsenic in the other two and enough to kill all of Congress!" He handed it to Larkin. "What did you find out, Larkin?"

"Now this is starting to make sense! Sam Barton was a chemist after the war. But that doesn't mean he wasn't one *during the war.* I think we are onto something here, but we can only guess as to why Barton's box was hidden there. Both a Mason and Secretary Seward used the barn to hide something. I wonder why that is?"

Harry replied, "And what was Barton or his accomplices going to do with the poison? There have been many tales of the Masons killing four or five of our presidents using those same methods. I don't know how we'd find out the answer to some of these questions." He stopped speaking. Then he abruptly went over to the trunk and said, "Unless it's in here!" He patted the top of the pile of papers. "I think we had better get to work."

"Let's have lunch first. I didn't have time for breakfast. This time, I'll buy."

"Well then," said Harry, "I know just the place! Follow me."

"Seems like that's all I do, Harry," said Larkin laughing.

When they got out to the sidewalk, Larkin didn't seem to remember many restaurants close by. In fact, he saw none. Looking at Harry quizzically, the older, more experienced man pointed and said, "This way." They headed straight out into the park. It stood under an umbrella, beside a tree. The sign on the side of the vendor's cart said, "Dad's Dogs." Harry said to the obviously Jewish entrepreneur hawking Hebrew Nationals, "I'll have the usual, Hal."

"And what for your friend here?" asked Hal with his New York accent.

Larkin replied, "I'll have a chili dog."

"Good choice! Where did you find this connoisseur of culinary delight, Harry?" asked Hal.

"He's my new assistant, Larkin. Actually, his title is "Junior Assistant to the Secretary." If all being told, Hal, he probably makes more than me and he's only worked here two days!"

"Nice to meet you, Larkin. If what Harry said is true, here's the check." Hal handed it to the boy.

"It was my turn anyway. Harry only suggested your establishment. Nice to meet you, too, Hal." Larkin handed him the money and a tip.

Hal asked, "Keep the change?"

Larkin just smiled and waved it off.

Another customer had come up, so the two of them moved over to a bench on the park mall. They ate and all the while looked at the passersby. There was no need to say anything. They were both comfortable with that and the rapport between them seemed to solidify to an even greater extent. When he finished, Larkin pulled his watch out of his pocket and flipped it open. The cover faced Harry and he noticed the cross on the cover. He asked, "Were some of your kin Masons, Larkin?" The question took him by surprise.

"I don't think so, Harry. Why do you ask?"

"Well, not too many kids your age carry an old watch like that anymore. And it has the Jerusalem Cross on the cover. So, I just assumed you had received it from a relative. I'm a Mason, too."Harry proudly showed Larkin his ring. Indeed, Harry *was a Mason*. "How old is the watch?"

"I really don't know much about it except my Grandpa received it as a gift when he retired from the railroad."

"Somebody from the lodge must have really liked him. That one is only given to Grand Masters or Commanders. It's valuable to the one who has it- no one else."

They got up and headed back to work. Larkin was upset and he thought about this new information the whole way back. This development really threw Larkin into a tailspin. First of all, because the watch had been his grandfather's and secondly, that Harry was a Mason and he'd be moving in with him on Monday! Why didn't Larkin realize that the symbol on the watch was Masonic? Nobody had ever told him. Except Pilar! He remembered that now! He just thought it was a cross! There must be a logical explanation because it had been given to Grandpa Button when he retired. That had to have been it. Maybe the person that gave it to him was a Mason. But did the family have any friends that were Masons? Good question! And as for Harry, maybe this could work to Larkin's benefit. If he had an inside source to Masonic activity, that may be a plus for him. But why didn't Larkin notice the ring before? Was this a trap though? Did Harry know? How was he going to proceed with the investigation of the trunk if the Masons were implicated? Did he already say too much?

When they got back downstairs, Larkin could contain himself no longer. He asked Harry point blank, "Harry, when we discovered that Sam Barton, a Mason, had something to do with this case, you said that

Masons had been implicated in other shenanigans in D.C.. How does your being a Mason affect your objectivity in solving cases such as this?"

Harry looked at Larkin and said very seriously, "Don't worry about that Larkin. I am only a low man on the totem pole, third degree. I don't care if the Grand Master was my brother and he took out the Pope. I'd still report the facts."

"Okay. I just wondered. Let's get back to work then!" Larkin was satisfied with Harry's answer.

By the end of the day, they had almost completed the task of numbering and recording all the documents. They had just a few to go. Harry excused himself to go the rest room, so Larkin took the opportunity to replace the letter to Seward from the Grand Master he had put in his pocket the day before. He was curious to see how Harry would react to it being in the pile. Larkin was finishing up a document when Harry walked back in. Harry took the letter from the top of the pile and sat down. When he saw what it was, he looked at Larkin, sat it down and said, "You need to see this. It's an example of what we were talking about." Larkin looked up and Harry passed him the letter.

Larkin glanced at the letter for a few moments and said, "Looks like hate mail from a lodge in New York. Right, Harry?"

"That's right. I know that happens. Sometimes individual lodge members go too far. That's an example. Wish we could see who it was, but the name seems to be smudged off. So you see Larkin, I can be very objective when I do my research. I must be."

"I'm glad to hear it, Harry. I am as well. It's getting late. Can we call it a day? And I was wondering, do you go to church?"

"Yes, we can call it a day. But I'd like you to come at least three evenings a week after you get into school next week. I think four hour shifts would do so we get this done before Christmas. All good things take time to do properly. And as for church, yes, I do go to church at Foundry United Methodist. Want to come with me?"

"Sure. That would be great. What time?"

"How about if you check out of the hotel, bring your stuff and come to your new room before say, nine-thirty or so. Then we'll go to late service. How's that?"

"Great Harry," Larkin replied, "but what's your address?"

"Oh, yeah. I'll write it down for you." He took a pad out of the drawer and wrote it down. It was 1776 U St. NW. "Can you find it?"

"Oh, I think I can figure it out."

They walked out of B-102 and Harry closed the door. Pausing, he said, "You know, this is getting kind of important, I think I'll lock the door from now on. I'll get you a key, too. Next week we'll take you to human services and get you all squared away as a new employee. You'll need an ID." They talked as they made their way upstairs.

"Okay. Will I have to go through any kind of personnel checks?"

"Why do you ask? Are you a criminal?"

Laughing Larkin said, "No. But I thought I'd ask."

"Well, it looks like Mr. Shipley has checked you out somewhat in order to call the dean at UMD. He's very thorough."

"I suppose so."

"He doesn't hire anyone just off the street you know."

That remark caused them both to laugh out loud so uproariously that Jim, the guard, had to shush them in the hall. They kept it quieter, but you could still hear them as they went towards Harry's office.

Walking into his office, Harry took Larkin aside. He said, "After having worked with you for only two days, Larkin, I feel like I have known you for my entire life. You are like the son I never had. And to be quite honest, you handle yourself like a pro at this job. In fact, you are out of my league. You have a great deal of potential here and I can see you in Dan's job someday. As I have so much to do in my own job, I'm going to ask him to remove me from this project and ask him to assign it to you. I'm going to retire in the next couple of years. You have your whole life ahead of you, Son."

Larkin got all choked up. He replied ever so sincerely, "Harry, I am honored by your words. Your kindness to me is so greatly appreciated. Thank you."

He held out his hand to shake Harry's. Harry not only grabbed it whole heartedly, but he pulled the younger man to him and gave him a manly hug. With that gesture, Harry smiled and released him. He went to his desk to see if there were any messages and finding none, closed up his desk, shutting all the drawers. They went to the door, turned off the lights, and headed out the back. Parting as they got to the corner, Larkin hailed a cab. He got one right away and climbed in waving goodbye to Harry as he waited for his normal bus home.

The cab went up 3rd and took a left onto D. Larkin was sitting behind the driver and noticed a statue between two buildings, hidden somewhat by the trees. It seemed out of place. He asked the cabbie, "Who is that a statue of?"

The black driver said in a huff, "That's a statue of the Mason, Albert Pike. Helped start the KKK. Don't know why it's there."

"I understand. Bad guy huh?"

"Damn right! Here we are," he said changing the subject upon their arrival.

"Thanks for the information."

Larkin arrived at the Hay-Adams just before Chester's shift was over. He opened the door of the cab for him and as he got out Larkin said to him, "Thanks for watching out for me this morning."

"Don't mention it. It's part of my job to be observant- for the customers I like."

"Thanks. Do you work on Sunday, Chester?"

"No, I don't. Will you be leaving in the morning, Larkin?"

"Yes, I will. It was a pleasure meeting you, Chester. As I will be working so close, I'll stop by from time to time. Maybe even come in for a meal."

"It will be good to see you."

Handing him a tip, Larkin said, "God be with you, Chester."

Chester didn't hear that very often from patrons. This time it made him feel good. He replied, "Thank you and the same to you, Larkin."

Larkin went up the elevator by himself. He didn't see Mike. He opened the door to his room. Looking around he saw the maid had come and tidied up the place. He looked for his bags and all were there. He worried about that considering what was in them and the magnitude of the situation, if they were lost or stolen. He was going to miss this place. He looked out at the White House with the lights beginning to come on. It was a beautiful view. And it was the nicest room he had ever had. For that matter, anything beat the only other motel room he had ever had at-The Family Inn!

Larkin took a shower and got ready to go down for dinner. He thought that one of the first things he'd have to buy was a suit. He'd take care of that next week- somehow. It looked like his schedule was already full and beyond his control.

For dinner, Larkin went downstairs and looked for Henry. Finding him behind the counter, Larkin went up to him and asked, "Henry, could you oblige me with the use of your spare suit coat and tie again this evening?"

"I'd be delighted, Sir." He went into the coatroom and appropriated it for him. As he was coming back out, he checked the pockets. Henry stopped walking toward Larkin when he found a twenty dollar bill in the front pocket. He smiled and said to Larkin who had observed this, "You are good luck for me, Larkin."

"Thank you, Henry," replied Larkin as he was handed the coat and tie. Henry helped him put them on and Larkin headed toward the dining room. He smiled, knowing it was he who had left the twenty there for Henry to find.

As he entered the restaurant, Sam approached him. "Good evening, Larkin. Will you be dining alone?"

Before he answered, he looked around the room. As he saw no one he recognized, except Senator Mansfield, he replied, "Tonight, I believe I will be alone, Sam."

Sam motioned for him to follow. He led him to the back of the room by the window. He pulled out the chair by the window so Larkin could see everyone that came in or out of the room. He was pleased with this and said, "Thank you, Sam. This is an excellent choice."

Sam replied, "Gotti likes it, too."

Larkin shook his head and smiled.

After Sam had brought him his salad, he noticed that a family was being seated to his front left. He kept eating so to not to be obvious he was watching them, but, they had a girl with them about his age and she was *gorgeous.* She had long blond hair and an angelic smile. He heard the introductions that Sam made and found out the families' name. It was Jensen. Her name was Ellie. When Sam brought the entree to Larkin he whispered to Sam, "What do the Jensens do, Sam?"

"He is the son of the man that sold Jensen Photograph in 1929. He doesn't "do" anything Larkin."

"I see. Thank you."

As he began his steak, Ellie caught Larkin looking at her and more than once. At first she blushed and looked away. But now when she looked, she kept looking and returned his glances. Now he was blushing. He had not felt this way in a long time. Not since Ginny.

Larkin finished his meal and Sam brought his check. He pulled out the money and left it on the table. As he passed by the Jensen's table Ellie dropped her fork right in front of him. She said, "Oops."

Larkin stopped and picked it up for her and placed it on the edge of the table beside her. Seeing Sam at his table picking up his check, he asked him, "Sam, could you bring," he redirected his speech and asked her, "I'm sorry, I don't know your name."

She answered, "Ellie Jensen."

"Sam, could you bring Miss Jensen a clean fork? She has had a mishap here."

"Right away, Mr. Palmer." Sam went toward the kitchen.

"My name is Larkin. Larkin Palmer."

"Thank you for your help, Larkin."

Her father stood up and came toward Larkin, holding out his hand. "I'm Ellie's father, R.E. Jensen Jr. Thank you for coming to my daughter's aid, Mr. Palmer. I see you have finished your meal. Would you care to join us for desert?"

"I am pleased to meet you both. And yes, I'd like that very much."

Larkin went to the closest chair to Ellie and sat down. He asked her, "Are you here alone or is Mrs. Jensen here as well?"

Ellie answered, "My mother is ill this evening and is indisposed."

"I'm sorry to hear that. I'll include her in my prayers this evening."

"Why thank you, Larkin," said Mr. Jensen. "Are you staying here at the Hay-Adams?"

"Yes I am, Sir. But I will be checking out in the morning."

"Returning home?"

"No Sir, but establishing a residence here in D.C.. I'll be attending UMD and working at the Smithsonian part time."

"Is that so? I know Secretary Shipley. Is he your new boss?"

"Yes Sir, he is. I had dinner with him and his wife here a couple of days ago. I will be one of his junior assistants."

"Very good. What are your duties?"

"I will be working on a new discovery of mine."

"A new discovery of yours, you say?"

"Yes, but I'm not at liberty to say anything about it due to the great historical significance it may convey."

"Really?" chuckling he said, "That sounds quite impressive for a recent hire at the Smithsonian."

Larkin did not appreciate his response and paused before he spoke. Ignoring Mr. Jensens' lack of style, he turned to Ellie and asked, "Will you be attending college this fall?"

Sensing the tension in the air, and shooting darts at her father with her eyes, she responded quickly to Larkin's' question. "Why yes, Larkin, I am. That is the reason Father is here, to drop me off at Gallaudet. I wish to educate the hard of hearing."

"Interesting. Please excuse me if I don't stay for desert. I need to pack. Big day tomorrow; moving into a new place, going to church, you know- Sunday stuff."

"Maybe we will see you again?" she asked.

He stood and answered her. "Sure Ellie. I am glad to have met you both." He turned and addressed Mr. Jensen. "Good evening, Sir."

Mr. Jensen stood and said, "Good evening, Larkin."

Larkin walked toward the door. As he walked away he could hear Ellie say loudly across the table, "Daddy! How could you! That was so inappropriate!"

"But Ellie, I didn't mean anything by it."

Their voices faded away as he made a bee-line to the elevator. He didn't care how good looking or how rich a girl was if she had a father that egotistical- too much trouble. Besides, he wasn't really interested in having a girlfriend for a while anyway.

Mike walked up to him as he got to the elevator. "Hello, Larkin. How are you?"

"Hi, Mike. I guess I'm just fine."

"Are ya leaving in the morning?"

"Sure am. I got a room in a house and I got a job!"

"Already? Where did you apply?"

"I didn't. He just gave it to me."

"Who did? Where?"

"Dan Shipley. The Smithsonian."

"Wow! You are amazing."

"We'll see about that. But, it is incredible. In fact, I haven't even told my family. I'm going up to the room and call them. Thanks for your help while I've been here, Mike."

"No problem, Larkin. See ya."

Larkin got on the elevator and pushed the button. When he got off of the elevator, he walked to the window at the end of the hall. Looking out, he saw a different night time view of Washington. No matter how you looked out of this building you could see something different. What a place! He went to his room and started packing. Not that he had that much, but he wanted to put all of the Palmer items, the Eraser stuff, into one bag and his clothes and other things in the other bag. That way he could just store everything easier. While he was working on it, he thought he heard a noise by the door. Going over to it he listened. Suddenly, someone slipped a piece of paper under the door. He bent down and picked it up. It had Ellie's address and phone number on it. He smiled, but he still thought she would be too much trouble!

In the morning, he got up and went down to talk to Chester, but he wasn't there. Larkin had forgotten that he was off on Sunday. He checked out and said goodbye to Henry. As he made his way to the door with his bags, he saw a limo outside under the entrance. He wondered who's it was. The tinted window came down slowly. Ellie popped her head out and said, "Want to have breakfast?"

"Sure do!"

The chauffer put his bags in the trunk and Larkin got in. The first thing he said when he got in was, "Is your dad coming, too?"

Ellie laughed. "No. I was so embarrassed that he treated you that way last night. He can be so uncouth."

He didn't address it with her, but just asked, "Where are we going?"

"I know a good place over a few blocks from here. It's called Reeve's."

He laughed and said, "That's where I ate the first day I was here. It's fantastic isn't it?"

"I love the doughnuts."

"You're my kind of girl!"

The chauffer let them out and went to park the car. It was obvious that he did not plan on joining them. Ellie went to the door of the restaurant and Larkin opened it for her. He was a gentleman, after all. They found a booth out of the way, sat down and looked at the menu. The waitress came and took their order so all that was left was for them to talk. Ellie asked, "So Larkin, why did you come to D.C.? To go to school?"

He thought about it for a second, because he didn't want to, no, couldn't allow her to know the true reason for his attending UMD. "I found that UMD had all the requirements necessary for what I wanted to accomplish in my life."

The waitress, whose nametag said "Bernice", brought them each a cup of coffee and Ellie raised it to her lips as she asked, "And what would that be?"

"Well, as much as I love history, I also love horticulture. I'm an arborist and my family owns an orchard. I'm trying to accomplish two things, so I can live in the best of both worlds. I know you want to help people, but what are your plans?"

"I don't know quite yet. I had thought about going to Africa when I finish, but Father doesn't like the idea of me being that far away. I guess I'll just see what happens."

"I know how you feel."

"Will you go home when you finish? Or do you think that the job at the Smithsonian will turn into something greater?"

"I don't know. I leave it in the hands of the Lord."

"You seem to be a very religious person."

"I give credit where credit is due."

Just then the breakfast showed up. Bernice sat the pancakes in front of Larkin and a piece of banana cream pie in front of Ellie. They both said at the same time, "Thank you."

Smiling she answered, "You are both welcome." They giggled and dug in.

When Larkin was about finished, he thought of his meeting with Harry at nine-thirty. Quickly, he pulled out his watch and looked at the time. Ellie noticed it and said, "Oh, are you a Mason, Larkin?"

'That's the second person that has asked me that in as many days,' he thought. Ignoring her question he just said, "This was my Grandpa's."

"It's very nice and it looks old, too. My Father has one just like it, only newer."

"So he's a Mason?"

"Oh yes. He's a Commander of the 32nd degree."

Changing the subject Larkin said, "It's after nine. I need to be at Harry's soon. Could I have a ride up there?"

"Sure. I'd be glad to take you."

Larkin took the check and paid the cashier. While he did that, Ellie motioned for the Limo to pick them up. The driver pulled up and got out of the car. They got in and Ellie asked. "What's the destination?"

"Oh. It's, let me see. I put that paper in my pocket here somewhere. Here it is, its 1776 U Street NW."

"Did you hear that, Oscar?"

"Yes, Miss Ellie. We will be there shortly."

As they made their way to Harry's, they talked. Larkin said, "I want to thank you for the company the past two days. It has taken my mind off of other things and made life almost normal again."

"It has been nice getting to know you, Larkin. As I said last night, I hope that we could see each other again and develop our friendship a little more."

"Well, if you don't see me around town, you know where I live now. And, you can always find me at work."

She handed him a piece of paper with her phone number and address at college. She had a private room. "You can call or come see me- *anytime.*"

The limo pulled up to the curb at Harry's and stopped. Larkin said, "Thanks for having breakfast with me, and for the ride."

Ellie leaned over toward him and gave Larkin a peck on the cheek. "You're welcome. See you soon."

Oscar had opened the door for Larkin and he, being a little embarrassed by the kiss, got out of the limo rather quickly. He leaned back in and said, "Good-bye, Ellie."

"Bye, Larkin."

Oscar had placed his bags by the front door. As he walked up the steps to Harry's front door, Ellie rolled down the window. As the limo pulled away, she waved and smiled. Larkin waved back.

Seeing all this out of the front window, Harry came to the door before Larkin rang the bell and opened it. "So when did you get a limo?"

Larkin laughed and said, "Oh. She's just someone I met at the hotel. Her name is Ellie Jensen."

"You mean R.E. Jensen's daughter?"

"Yes. Why?"

"He's got bucks. That's why."

"That may be, but I don't know if I'll be seeing her much anyway." Larkin picked up his bags and went past Harry inside. "This is a nice place you have here, Harry."

"Thanks. Your room is down the stairs in the back. It's set up like a basement apartment. It was used that way during WWII, but I never did anything with it. It's a little dusty down there, but after you get rid of the cobwebs, it won't be bad at all." Larkin walked down the hall and down the stairs. Harry followed.

"I thought you said it was just an extra room? This is a real nice apartment, Harry."

"Well, I lied. I hope you like it. Get settled in and we'll leave for church in about an hour. Come on up when you are ready."

"Okay. Thanks. I won't be long."

Harry went up the stairs. Larkin took a look around the basement. It had a bathroom with a shower, one bedroom, a laundry in a closet by the water heater, a small living room, and a kitchenette! He couldn't believe it! And only twenty dollars a week! He put his clothes in the only dresser in the bedroom. He had plenty of room. He didn't have any hanging clothes, but there was a closet. He'd have to work on getting that suit and some shirts. As for The Eraser, he placed the whole suitcase under the bed by the headboard, next to the wall. He thought he'd have to find a safer place. He'd think on that one.

Larkin went to the bathroom to freshen up. Turning on the cold water tap, it came out in brownish orange ooze. After a bit it cleared up, but, it obviously had not been used in a long, long time. There was one towel on the only shelf, so he placed it on the rack after wiping his hands. He figured he'd have to set up housekeeping and get a few things. That went on his to do list as well. Man; life was getting busy!

Going upstairs, Larkin called out, "Harry, where are ya?"

He heard a call coming from outside the open back door. "Out here on the terrace," came Harry's reply. Opening the screen door, Larkin walked out to the terrace and a different world.

"Wow! This is real nice, Harry. It is a beautiful garden. You would never know something like this existed in someone's back yard in D.C."

"Thank you, Larkin. It is what I do to calm the beast within. I just finished planting the entire wall section by the store there last week."

"It looks like it's starting to come in well. Oh, and look at that maple you have. It is a beautiful tree."

"You know about trees?"

"Yes. In fact, I'm an arborist. My family has an orchard. Didn't I tell you?"

"You are a man of many faces Larkin. You totally amaze me." The clock on the mantle inside chimed on the quarter hour. Harry turned toward the door when he heard it and said, "I think we had better get going or we won't make it in time."

They walked the few blocks faster than Larkin thought they could, at least Harry anyway. They arrived just in time to be seated in the back row. The first hymn had just started to be played. They sat down next to a black woman and two young boys with bow ties; presumably her sons. Larkin didn't sing much that day, but paid attention to the words and those that did sing. He was amazed at the large sanctuary and the collective voice of such a group. It sounded great. He looked around. First of all, to see if he knew anyone and secondly, at the wonderful structure and all the stained glass and finally, to take in all he could about Harry's faith and worship. Already, he could see it was much different than his own.

When the pastor got up to speak, he stood in a pulpit that sat high above the people as if on a precipice looming ever so closely as if to fall on top of them. His words were at first quite quiet. As he went on, his voice became louder. His pace became faster and faster. Finally, as he came to the main point, his voice squeaked and squealed in an uproariously funny climax! Larkin just- giggled. This guy was nothing like his pastor back home. And his message seemed, well, sing-song! It was so funny he would never be able to take this pastor seriously. How was he going to excuse himself from coming back with Harry next Sunday? He just couldn't make himself do this again. He'd have to think on that.

When the service was over, the pastor came to the back door to greet everyone. As they sat in the back row, they were nearly the first ones out. Harry went out first and shook the Pastor's hand. As Larkin came by he asked Harry, "Who did you bring along with you today, Harry?"

"Pastor, this is Larkin Palmer. He works with me, now lives in my basement apartment and will be attending UMD. Larkin, this is Pastor Tomlin."

"It's a pleasure to meet you young man. Welcome to Washington and our church."

"It's a pleasure to meet you too, Pastor. Thank you for your message today."

They began to walk out as the crowd grew behind them. Pastor Tomlin said, "See you next week."

Larkin just smiled as he followed Harry down the stairs. Something caught his eye as he made the final step. A cab roared down the street, as if out of control toward- Harry! Harry had not noticed it, so Larkin ran out and grabbed the old man's coat pulling him back around like a revolving door and out of the path of the cab, just in the nick of time! Harry lost his balance and fell to the sidewalk, but Larkin had saved his life. The cab roared on past and came to its final resting place, smashed into the wall of the office complex next door. The crowd saw it all from the steps. Many of them came down to see if Harry was okay, but the rest of them, started to applaud as if Larkin had saved the day. Which in fact, he had. After having determined that Harry was okay many of the people came up to Larkin and congratulated him on his heroic deed. He just said, "It was nothing that Harry wouldn't have done for me."

When a few of the crowd got out of the way, an older man with a hat, which most men didn't wear anymore, came up to him and said, "I'm Jim Humphreys of the Washington Post. I saw the whole thing. I'd like to quote you as having said that in the paper. What's your name, Son?"

Larkin said, "Aw, you don't have to do that, Mr. Humphreys. It was nothing."

Overhearing them, Harry said, "Oh what you did was more than something, Larkin. You saved my life. I'll be forever grateful. His name is Larkin Palmer of New York State."

Before he could say anything more, the man was gone and it was too late. Larkin said out loud, "OH MAN!" He was not happy. Now he'd be in the paper and he didn't want anyone to even know he was there!

The crowd moved over toward the cab and its occupants. Someone had called the police and the siren was heard a couple blocks away. The driver seemed dazed and was bleeding, but the passenger, a man from India it seemed, because of his dress, was unconscious in the back seat. The people tried to attend to him as they waited for help.

Larkin hailed a cab because he wanted no more attention when the cop got there. He also didn't want Harry to have to walk back home after that incident. They got in and the cabbie asked, "Where to?"

Harry said, "To the best steakhouse you know. This guy just saved my life. We're going to celebrate!"

Larkin said, "You don't have to do that, Harry."

"I insist."

They only went a few blocks past Harry's house and the cabbie said, "Here we are- Bobby Vans'."

Harry said, "I didn't know they were open on Sunday."

"They just started to last month," replied the cabbie, "that'll be ten bucks."

Larkin handed him the money and he hopped out onto the sidewalk. Harry got out a little more slowly. Larkin asked him,

"Feeling a little stiff already, Harry?"

"I guess so. Lets' go in and have a stiff drink, too!"

They both laughed and opened the door to the restaurant. The place was pretty crowded, but there were still tables available. The hostess met them as they walked in. "How many will there be today?"

Larkin answered, "Just us two."

She said, "This way please."

She led them to a table by the window. Harry sat down with his back to the door and Larkin, as he always liked, sat facing it and the window. To him that was the best table in the place. When he looked out into the street however, he wasn't happy with what he saw- it was R.E. Jensen getting out of the limo. He didn't see Ellie. The hostess handed them a pair of menus and said before she left, "Enjoy your meal." They thanked her.

Harry said, "My wife and I used to come here on our anniversary sometimes. It has been here since the 1850's, I think. It's usually real good. Try the rib eye. You won't be disappointed."

Larkin took the menu and placed it right in front of his face hoping that Ellie's father wouldn't see him if he passed by his table. Talking from behind it he said to Harry, "I just might do that Harry. I ate a whole stack of pancakes this morning, but I'm already hungry."

"It has been an eventful day for you hasn't it Larkin? I mean with Ellie, church, saving a life..."

He was interrupted by R.E., "Did I hear someone mention my daughter's name?"

Larkin lowered his menu and saw Mr. Jensen standing right next to their table. "Why hello, Mr. Jensen, how are you today? This is an associate of mine, Harry Hall."

Harry stood and shook his hand. "I'm pleased to meet you, Mr. Jensen. Would you care to join us?"

"No thank you, Harry. I'm meeting the Senator from Vermont to discuss business matters. I'm pleased to meet you." Turning to Larkin he said, "I hoped that I would see you again, Larkin. Little did I know it would be this soon."

"It's a small world, Sir. It's nice to have seen you again as well. Good day."

He left and walked to a table in the back where the senator was already seated. Larkin said, "Man, what are the odds?"

"The odds in what?" asked Harry.

"To run into *him*."

"Oh, well, considering some of the places you've been going to in the past couple of days, I'd say pretty good. You're not exactly slumming-it you know."

"Right! I can easily change that."

"Being a student, you will probably have to." Harry chuckled.

But Harry had no idea that this kid from the farmland of New York wasn't exactly poor, either.

When they finished, Harry paid the check and they started toward the door. Oscar met them there, "R.E. would like me to take you wherever you wish, Mr. Palmer."

Larkin didn't know what to say, nor did he want to appear ungrateful, so he just accepted. "It's been an eventful day Oscar, so if you could just take us back to Harry's place that would be great."

"Yes, Sir."

The ride to Harry's was, in contrast, uneventful. Harry almost fell asleep on the way. When he pulled in to the curb, Larkin said to Oscar, "Just stay there Oscar, we can let ourselves out."

Oscar replied, "As you wish, Sir. And say Larkin, Ellie says, "Hello.'"

"Thank you, Oscar. Tell her the same."

Larkin shut the door to the limo and Oscar pulled away. Larkin thought, 'Well, maybe running into him wasn't altogether bad.'

The two went inside and Harry went directly to a drawer in a desk by the coat closet. He took out a ring of keys and said, "Here's your key to the door. You can go in and out the back most of the time, so you don't feel like you are disturbing me. It looks like we will be on totally different schedules from now on."

"Sounds like it. I may stay at the office after hours just to catch up on my studies." Changing the subject he said to Harry, "Thank you for all your kindness, Harry. I really appreciate it."

"No. Thank you, Larkin. You are truly a fine young man and a life saver. I'll never forget it. I think I'm going to go lie down and take a nap."

"I think I'm going to prepare for tomorrow. I have lots to do."

Harry walked into his room and closed the door. Larkin went down to his room and started a list.

"Let's see," he said to himself out loud, "I need to get to UMD and pick up my class schedule. I'm glad I pre-registered. Then I need to go to the grocery store. Then I want to get some clothes. Then I need to call Uncle Tom to transfer some money to my account. Oh, I forgot! I had better call Mom and tell her what's going on!"

Larkin sat down his list and went to the phone that was on the end table in the living room. He picked up the old black receiver, which seemed heavy to him, but it was hooked up because the dial tone was there. He dialed the number, hoping he could just pay Harry for the calls he made. He'd tell him later and make arrangements. The call went through and the phone at home rang. His mom picked up again like she was waiting for him. "Hello?"

"Hi, Mom! Its' me!"

"Larkin! It is so nice to hear from you! I miss you, Honey."

"Oh, Mom," he said like always, "I have a lot of news for you."

"Already? What happened? Is anything wrong?"

"No, no, not at all and in fact, I have good news. First of all, I have a place to live. Secondly, I have a job. And third, I saved a man's life today so I'm going to be in the Washington Post. Buy a copy and you'll see."

"Wow that *is* a lot of news! I didn't think you'd call me until after tomorrow when you started to go to classes. Tell me all about it."

He told her all that had happened while he was staying at the Hay-Adams, the events at the Smithsonian and his new job, Harry and his new room, and going to church. He never mentioned Ellie or R.E. He said, "So I expect that after tomorrow, I'll have a lot less time."

"I'd say. What's your new address and phone number?"

"Do you have a pencil?"

"Yes, I'm ready."

He gave it to her. Suddenly, Larkin heard the hard-wood floor squeak above him. He looked up. 'Harry must be getting up,' he thought. Then the toilet flushed. He smiled and went back to his conversation with his mom. "Mom, I had better go. This is Harry's phone and I don't want to run up his bill. I still need to call Uncle Tom to transfer some money for me. I need to set up house here. Will you tell Dad and Uncle all the news?"

"Sure will, Son. Call me and let us know how it is going and when you'll be coming home for Thanksgiving."

His heart sunk. He so much wanted to go home, but he knew it would be best to stay away. He had to stick with the plan. "Okay, Mom. I better go now. Talk to you soon. Bye."

"Bye, Larkin." They both hung up. Larkin picked up again and dialed his Uncle. The phone rang on the other end. Tom picked up after the fourth ring.

"Hello, this is Tom."

"Hello Uncle, this is Larkin."

"Why hello, Larkin. How are things going in the big city?"

"It's going great so far, Uncle. But this isn't my phone and I don't want to run up the bill. Call Mom and she'll tell you all the news. The reason I called is to ask you to transfer about five thousand into my account. I need to set up shop and have some money for books and tuition, too."

"Okay, I'll do it tomorrow if you let me know your new account number. Anything else?"

"Yes. Did you read my note?"

"Yes, I did, and I understand. Just don't be a total stranger."

"I won't. Thanks, Uncle Tom. I appreciate it and I'll be in touch tomorrow. Goodbye."

"Goodbye, Larkin."

Larkin went back to the kitchen and added, "Open bank account and call Uncle", to his list. Then, he made a shopping list. He didn't think he'd be eating much at home, but he wanted to have the basics. It would be different not having Mom around. She had done so much for him but, she had taught him well. He would survive. Even if it was on pork and beans!

Larkin didn't hear Harry walking around again, so Larkin figured he had gone back to bed. He sat down in the chair in the living room. It was deep and soft. It gave way to his body, surrounding him in pure, velvety comfort. Larkin was tired, so he closed his eyes for just a second. At six in the morning, Harry knocked on Larkin's door. "Time to get up, Larkin. I know you don't have a clock yet and I didn't hear you moving around. It's six o'clock."

Larkin jerked up straight and looked around in his new surroundings, not really recognizing where he was. Then he replied, "Thanks, Harry. I'm awake."

Harry replied, "I have toast and eggs if you want some."

"Be right up."

Larkin went in and used the bathroom, and combed his hair. Then he went up. He said to Harry, "That chair down there is so comfortable; I just fell asleep in it."

"My wife used to do that, too. It was her chair. Don't expect breakfast like this every morning. I know you don't have anything down there yet."

"I won't. I plan on going to the store after getting my class schedule today." Changing the subject he asked Harry, "Do you think the Secretary will want to see me today?"

"I assume he will after I speak with him. He may loosely set your schedule then, too."

"Okay. I'll come in after I go to the store. It shouldn't be much past noon. I'll report to your office, okay?"

"Sounds good."

Larkin sat down at the table and Harry gave him his breakfast. Larkin smiled as he handed it to him and said laughingly, "Thanks, Harry."

Harry, not being much of a cook, laughed and said, "Don't mention it."

Less than an hour later, Larkin walked into the registrar's office. The line ran all the way to the door, about fifty students deep. 'Oh boy,' he thought, 'this may take longer than I expected.' And it did. When he finally stepped up to the window, it was almost noon. He told the lady his name and she looked up his classes.

She handed him the registration and said, "I have a note here from the President, Dr. Perkins. He'd like to see you in his office."

Taken aback, Larkin just shook his head as he took the paperwork from her. Then he looked quizzically at her for directions. She smiled, pointed, and said, "It's in the Administration Building next door.

"Thanks." He smiled back at her.

Larkin had never been on such a large campus before and it was a little overwhelming to him. He read the names on the glass doors as he went down the hall of the administration building. Finally, when he got to the end of the hall, where the view would be best he assumed, he saw the Presidents' office. Going in, the President's older secretary asked Larkin, "May I help you?"

"Yes. The Registrar's office told me Dr. Perkins would like to see me. My name is Larkin Palmer."

"Oh yes, indeed he would. Let me tell him you are here. Just one moment please."

She picked up the phone and punched one of many extension buttons on it. "Dr. Perkins, young Mr. Larkin Palmer is here to see you. Yes. I'll show him right in."

She hung up, walked over to Larkin and said, "I'm Betty, Dr. Perkins secretary. If you need anything on this campus just call me and I'll take care of it. She walked him over to the door, opened it and said, "Go right on in, Larkin. It was a pleasure meeting you."

"Thank you, Betty. You, too." Larkin was taken by surprise with this red carpet treatment. He was even more surprised when he walked into the President's office. There on the wall was a plaque which had the Masonic compass on it. Dr. Perkins was a Mason, too!

Dr. Perkins stood up and held out his hand to Larkin. "I'm so very pleased to meet you, Mr. Palmer. May I call you Larkin?"

"Oh please do, Dr. Perkins. No need to be so formal."

"Please have a chair, Larkin. I have read your transcripts personally and gone over your proposed course of study here at UMD. It looks like you have a wide variety of interests and skills. I also have heard of your discovery at the Smithsonian and your propensity for all things History. Dan seems to think you'd be a fine archeologist someday. But I think you are one already. Tell me of your discovery, Larkin."

"In my estimation, Dr. Perkins, and if it is what I believe it is, it will rewrite American history. As I have not had the time to fully assess it, I am not at liberty to say what it is."

"That is astounding! I'd like to say that I am impressed. Therefore, I have made arrangements to wave all of your history prerequisites. Based on your grades from high school, you do not need to take any of the 100 level courses as well. They are waved. Consequently, you are now a sophomore. However, you will need to pay for all those credits. Are you able to do that?"

"Yes, Sir. I'll go back down to the registrar and take care of it."

"I'll send them all the necessary information for your totally new schedule for the remainder of your stay at UMD. Secondly, I will arrange for you to be under the supervision of Dan for all of your history classes that are remaining. Therefore, you will not take a single history class here on campus. It will help lighten the load while you do your research. Last of all, the horticulture classes and any other classes necessary to graduate will have to be met here on campus. I don't want to make it too easy for you!"

Larkin said with a smile, "Oh no, you should never do that, Sir."

"Splendid. Do you have any questions?"

"No, Sir, but I am very grateful for this development. I wish to thank you very much."

"Thank Dan Shipley. He has great faith in you and so do I."

Standing up, Larkin pulled his watch from his pocket and looked at the time. He made sure Dr. Perkins saw the cover. Before he shook the doctor's hand he said, "Look at the time. I must be on my way."

Sticking out his hand Dr. Perkins said, "I'm pleased to have finally met you, Larkin. Don't hesitate to stop by and see me anytime. And please, keep me informed as to the progress of your research."

They shook hands and Larkin replied, "Certainly Sir, I'd be happy to do that."

Larkin saw Dr. Perkins' positive reaction to seeing his watch and he now knew that any time he could use it- he would. As he walked down to the registrar's office again, he took a look at his schedule from before. If all that the President had said was true, he would have a very light schedule. However, he didn't know what he would actually be registered-for! He figured he'd just have to wait and see. This was just too good to be true!

As he walked into the office, he hoped there wouldn't be such a long line again. This time, the registrar saw him come in and waved him past all the other students and told him, "I'll have to go over everything the President just sent me, Larkin. Just come back in the morning with your checkbook and we will get it straight. You won't have any classes until next week anyway."

"Thanks. I'll see you in the morning then. Bye." As he stepped out of the building and onto the steps he shouted at the top of his lungs, "YAHOO!" The rest of the kids just kind of looked at him, but after that, he didn't care!

This changed everything. His first stop was at the bank. He opened an account with some of the money he still had left in his wallet. The rest he'd use for groceries. He obtained a few checks and ordered some new ones, too. Before he left the new accounts desk, he told them that they would be receiving a transfer of funds from his bank back home later today. They said that would be fine and he could use his new account right away.

He went out the door and over to a pay phone by the street. The booth was empty, but the door was stuck. He had to kick it with his foot to get it to come open. "Man, people just don't treat other people's stuff with respect anymore," he said out loud laughing. He lifted the receiver, put in a few quarters and called his Uncle Tom. The phone rang a couple times and he picked it up. "Hello?"

"Hello Uncle, this is Larkin again. I have to make a change in plans. Something has happened today you are not going to believe."

"After what your mom told me last night about what's has been happening, I'd believe anything about now, Larkin. The Lord has been blessing you greatly."

"Indeed He has, Uncle. I just spoke with the President of the college and he has already waived some of the classes I was supposed to take. Therefore, I'm now a sophomore. But, I must pay for the credits. I'll need you to send fifteen thousand dollars instead. And get this Uncle-I will have light duty with the rest of my course work. I'll be able to go right into researching my find. This is just too much for me to take in."

"Wait until I tell your mother all of this. She will be so happy for you. And you know she'll want to know how all of this happened. And your dad, he's already been bragging about you at church. This will send him over the edge. And Larkin, I'm proud of you, too, Son."

"Thank you, Uncle. Tell them I'll call next week after I find out everything. And if anything really exciting happens, I'll call right away!"

Tom laughed and said, "Anything really exciting? You're a hoot, Larkin! What's your new account number?"

Larkin told it to him and said that the bank would be expecting it. "I'll drive into town right away and take care of it. Be careful, Larkin."

"Thanks, Uncle. Bye."

He hung up the phone and pulled on the door. It wouldn't budge. He was stuck in the booth! Larkin had a problem. He tried again, juggling the glass doors back and forth with no results. People just kept walking by and didn't pay attention. He started to wave hoping someone would help him. Finally, a man in a blue suit stopped and pushed on the door while Larkin pulled. It opened. As Larkin came out of the booth, he said to him, "Thanks, Mister." The guy just smiled, nodded, and went on. Larkin started on down the street when it hit him. The man in the blue suit! He looked around-nowhere to be seen. 'That's just great,' he thought. He wondered if they had been watching him long. He wondered what they knew. He wondered, 'How long will this surveillance would go on?' He knew one thing though- he'd watch his own tail from now on.

He hailed a cab and one pulled over right away. Of course the cabbie asked, "Where to?"

Larkin responded with a question, "Where would you go to get a suit if you wanted one?"

The black cab driver just chuckled and said, "Well, I guess I'd go to this shop in Foggy Bottom."

"Okay then. Foggy Bottom it is."

The cab ride wasn't long. When he dropped him off he said, "Go down to the basement and ask for Stephen. He's just an apprentice, but he'll fix you up for less money."

"Thanks a lot, Mister." Getting out, Larkin handed him the fare and a tip through the window.

"Good luck, Kid." He drove off and Larkin headed to find a new suit.

He went down to the basement and found the only shop there. It was small, but had its own sense of old world charm. He asked for Stephen. "I'm Stephen. How can I help you?"

Larkin said, "I need a suit, but I have no idea how to start."

The man came out from behind the counter and looked at him. "Follow me," he said. They walked over to a rack on the wall. "What color are you interested in?"

"I thought something in dark grey or blue."

"I think I have just the thing. A man stood me up on this one and I don't think it would take much to make it work for you. Come over here and let me get your measurements."

Stephen took the suit over to the counter and hung it up on a hook above their heads. He told Larkin how to stand and took measurements here and there. Then he said, "Here- take this and go try it on in the dressing room over there." He pointed. Larkin took it out of his hand and went to try it on. The pants were way too long so he just folded up the legs. The coat fit pretty well, so he went back out and showed Stephen. The tailor put his tape around his neck and took a look. Then he pinned up the legs and checked the fit throughout. After his inspection Stephen said, "Not too bad. I'll let you have it for seventy-five dollars after alterations."

"I'll take it. When can I pick it up?"

"Give me until Friday afternoon."

"Do you want me to pay now?"

"Half now and half then."

"You got it." Larkin got out of the suit and went over to the register. It was really old and Stephen had to manually push each button to ring up the transaction. Larkin could tell he was frustrated with it.

"When I take over- this- is the first thing to go!"

"I can see why. It must be seventy-five years old."

"You got that right. Say, what's your name for the ticket?"

"Larkin Palmer. I'll see you on Friday, Stephen."

"Thank you, Larkin. Here's your stub."

Larkin went out the door and headed toward a Woolworths down the street. He looked in to see if they had any clothes at all and sure enough they had men's' shirts and slacks, which was exactly what he needed. He picked out four shirts and two pairs of pants, but he couldn't find a tie he liked. He wasn't picky, (which his presence in a Woolworth's clothing section attested to), but their ties were just awful. He decided to hold off buying ties. He paid for the clothes and went down the street a little further. He didn't see much, so he decided to head back toward Harry's and drop off his purchase. Then he'd go to the small supermarket down the street.

While he was walking, he had the feeling that he was being followed. As he walked he would glance back from time to time, but nothing caught his eye. Then, when he turned the corner, he decided to wait and see if anyone came past. Sure enough, the guy in the blue suit walked right past him and didn't acknowledge him at all. Was it a mere coincidence? He didn't think so. Larkin began to follow *him.* It didn't take much to accomplish it, because he wasn't supposed to have been following Larkin. He'd have to look natural. To Larkin it was funny. To the man in the blue suit it was an annoyance. They walked for a couple of blocks and he could tell the man was getting tired of it. He stopped and bought an ice cream cone from a vendor, turned and walked a couple of store fronts and proceeded to look in the window of a tuxedo shop. It was almost an invitation to Larkin to make a move, which he did. Larkin walked up to him and stood facing the shop as the man licked the Neapolitan ice cream. Neither man looked at each other, but merely their own reflections in the windows as Larkin addressed him. "Tell the Commander that I am no threat here. I intend to merely go to college and have a job. That's it." The man in the blue suit licked his cone one more time, turned the other way and left.

By now, Larkin was only a few blocks away from home, so he decided to walk the rest of the way. He felt relief now that he was alone. He wondered if that would do the trick. Besides, almost everyone he knew in D.C. was a Mason. How hard could it be to find him? He chuckled at that. When he got home, he saw Harry was still at work. He dropped off the clothes he'd just bought and went to the grocery store, and by the time he got back it was almost time to go to work himself. He put it all away and then, put on a new set of clothes. He looked in the bathroom mirror at himself. "Not bad, Larkin," he said. Then up the stairs at a run and out the door he went.

When he got to the Smithsonian, he found Harry in his office. "Hello, Harry. You won't believe what happened today."
Harry looked up at him and pulled off his glasses. "What is that, Larkin?"
Larkin told him the whole story of his meeting with Dr. Perkins. He didn't say anything about his run in with the man in the blue suit.
"I didn't know anyone could do that. But, I guess the President can do whatever he wants. Good for you, Larkin. That will give you much more time to be here.

I talked to Mr. Shipley today and he wants to see you. You know, usually the Under Secretary of American History hires people here and there are a whole bunch of hoops to have to go through. This has become a very large organization with many buildings on the National Mall. We see just a smidge of what happens in it. I have a lot to do and I just run this one building. That's why this project should be yours. So, I think you'll like this news, too."

"Thanks so much, Harry. Uh, where's his office? I'm kinda new here."

Both he and Harry laughed and Harry said, "Go to the second floor."

Larkin went up to the second floor and found Dan's office. He went in to find his secretary under her desk looking for something with a flashlight. "Where did I drop that stupid thing?!" she exclaimed.

Being a wise guy sometimes, he answered, "I don't know, but you'll find it in the last place you look." Startled, she raised her head and bumped it on the bottom of the desk. He went over to help her, and said, "Oh, I'm so sorry." He took her hand and helped her up. To Larkin's surprise it was a very lovely, young woman.

"Oh, that's okay. It was kinda funny," she said straightening herself.

"I'm Larkin Palmer. I heard that Secretary Shipley would like to see me?"

"I'm Sally Britt. I've heard a lot about you. I'll let him know you are here." She walked over to Dan's door and knocked.

He said, "Come in." Sally entered and came back in a flash.

"Go on in, Larkin."

"Thanks, Sally," he said and smiled back at the pretty girl quite intentionally. She returned his smile and watched him all the way in. Larkin was elated.

"Come in and sit down, Larkin. I have something to tell you." He threw some papers on his desk in disgust. Larkin took a seat and looked around the wonderfully built office. Dan went on pointing at the papers he had just thrown, "When Joseph Henry began this institution, he foresaw an agency, untouched by the tentacles of government intervention. When they transferred all the junk from the patents office over here it came with a string attached, government money, and with that, we have been drug into the mud ever since. But, that is not what I called you here to tell you. I thought I'd let you know that my giving you a job on the spot is not the usual way we do things here at the Smithsonian. Many people here go through years of specialized training and education. But when I saw your methods, your intellect and intuition in the field, I knew you had it in you. Now that I have gotten to know you a little, I know that I was right. You say you have practical experience, what would that be?"

Larkin wondered if he should tell him, but figured he could reveal some of it to him. "Back in New York, my family was some of the first settlers in Madison County. In fact, a direct ancestor was the first white man born in that county. The foundation of their original home is still visible by the driveway at The Homestead. Because of this rich history, and the fact that my family still owns the land, I have been led from time to time to find certain things left by the family. One example is the treasure of one, Percifer Carr, caretaker for the Edmeston estate in the late 1700's. I have some of it, but the rest brought around two million dollars at auction."

"Marvelous! That's what I have seen in you here already and is why I have given you the position. Regarding that, I have spoken with Harry today, and he believes the same way as I do. Therefore, I am going to give you full charge of the whole Seward find. Of course, you will report to me directly and I will supervise your progress. If you have questions, ask Harry and he will do his best to help you. But, I don't want you to take him away from his work. He has enough to do. Consequently, your pay scale will be as if you were doing a project. It will have a stipend, so you will have room and board while in D.C. and be based on the amount of twenty-five thousand dollars. It will be a one year project. After that, you will have the option to work as needed. I will write that into the contract and your title is as we discussed at the restaurant the other evening, "Junior Assistant to the Secretary". You may do this project at your convenience, but you must finish in a year! Got it?"

"Yes, Sir!"

"Go down to Human Resources and they will set you all up with an ID and a key to B-102. I don't want that room unlocked at any time."

"Thank you, Sir. I won't let you down. Oh, and by the way, I spoke with Dr. Perkins today and I appreciate your influence with him as well. It will give me much more time for my work here."

"My pleasure and you are quite welcome. Get to work."

"Yes, Sir." Larkin got up and went out the door.

Dan said to himself, "I hope I haven't made a mistake. This is the most important thing that has ever happened during my tenure."

As Larkin went past Sally's desk, she handed him a slip of paper. "Nice to have met you, Larkin," she said.

"Likewise, Sally." He took the paper and walked out into the hall. After the door closed he read it, "Call me any time. 555-456-5656. Sally." He thought, 'Wow, two girls in a week.'

He went down the hall to Human Resources and became an official member of the Institution. Taking his new ID and key, he went down to the basement and room B-102. Turning on the lights, he looked at the pile of work staring him in the face. Someone knocked at the door. "Come in?" said Larkin.

"Hi. I'm James Stoughton. I thought I'd stop by and give you a checklist that we use here so you get this all right. You may know how to do it, but if it doesn't meet all the guidelines, the Secretary will be upset."

Larkin cut to the chase and asked him, "Why would you do this? For the new guy, I mean."

"Let's put it this way- I'm a friend of Harry's and any friend of his is a friend of mine. I don't want to see our friend, Larkin, fail."

"Thanks, James. Take a look at what Harry and I have been doing here and see what you think."

The two men looked it over and James pointed out a couple of procedural problems. Other than that, Larkin was doing quite well. "Looks like you're doing well, Larkin. Just do what I've shown you and you'll complete this project like a pro. By the way, have you found anything good so far?"

"I'm not at liberty to say," Larkin said, playing the game.

"Good job. Never reveal anything to anyone."

"Thanks, Jim. I really appreciate your help and concern. Harry has a good friend."

"So do you, Larkin."

"Glad to know."

"Well, I gotta get back to work. Good luck and welcome aboard."

After James made his visit the process went a lot smoother for Larkin. Sure, he had to go back and redo some things, but it made it all right. Larkin was grateful. The first week went by quickly. He finished recording almost all of the documents, except two. The first was a letter from none other than Ben Franklin. It was to a man named Morgan. "Where did I hear that name? Why is it so familiar? Morgan, Morgan, hum?" Then it hit him. The Mason in the Journal that was from Brookfield! The very same one that was rubbed out by Lawtin Jr.! He recorded the information like all of the rest of the documents, but rather than setting it down, he read it in its entirety:

"My dear Mr. Morgan, upon receipt of the shipment, please be advised that you may use the hidden obverse die when our plans are complete. These will be the first Continental Dollars of the New World Order. It is found in the bottom of the chest under the shipment, encased in a secret compartment. After Gallaudet and I completed the design and die, I myself have prepared it for shipment that it may not become unusable. Remember dear Sir and Brother that you may not proceed unless our plans come to fruition. If they do, we shall then rule our New World!" B. Franklin, July 4, 1786

Larkin thought, 'The Silver Chest! Franklin knew all about it! Heck, he may have even provided it! And it sounded almost like Franklin was conspiring to help overthrow the fledgling government! But it seemed that the shipment didn't take place until 40 years later. Wonder why? And after his family took the chest and Morgan had died, none of their plans were to be. He and his uncle had missed the hidden compartment. It was too dark to see it in the basement. He'd have to call his uncle. If the die was there, that in itself could change history! But wait! If *this* letter was placed next to the bottom, what did the *last* document say?'

He picked it up and began to read. It was dated Oct. 9, 1872 and it was signed by Seward himself. It read:

"To Whom It May Concern:

My fears for my life seem to have come to their completion, as I have had difficulty breathing these past few days after a visit from my dreaded foes of these past 20 years– the Masons. I suspect that when we dined they poisoned my cup, as have many of us who have opposed them. They have come to me in my once trusted friend and doctor, Dr. Verdici, who sat next to me and I suspect placed the poison there.

In preparation and anticipation for my demise these past years, after having failed that dread night, I have compiled documents which I shall place in a trunk, that others may be warned of the plot of conspiracy to overthrow our government since its inception and carried forward even to today. The last act of treason was Lincoln. And even now, I myself, so that their plans against me may be completed. The Black Pope is an evil man and has orchestrated all of it. Our precious revolution and all of our wars are of him, that we may be placed under his control. Even now the cruel death of Abraham, which was perpetrated by Masons under the Jesuits power, no matter which allegiance they subscribed to.

I shall name them here, so there be no misunderstanding or confusion in the matter they being: Sarratts, (the pair), Stanton, Andrew Johnson, Booth, Sarah Gilbert, Dahlgren, Jeff Davis, Judah Benjamin, Gen. Grant, S. Barton, Joseph Palmer, Clotworthy Stevenson, Payne, (the villain) Herold, Azerodt, Arnold, Mudd, Spangler, O' Laughlin, Gen. Hancock, Floyd, Judge Holt, Verdici, the evil Albert Pike, and finally Garrett. These are only those I know of, as the web of the Masonic conspiracy stretches far. All of these are or have been involved with the Masons. Some have already been pardoned or have been made the scapegoat. As for myself, they just loath me for my distaste of them and their pompousness. No one should believe me for my word, but should peruse the enclosed documents. They substantiate all.

I intend to place the trunk in the hands of my son Frederick, who will make sure it will be given to the appropriate people, who someday shall hopefully expose the deeds of these evil men.

Sincerely,

Wm. H. Seward

This was, indeed, the find of a lifetime! He needed to make a copy of this! He took the letter with him, locked the door and headed toward the copy room. After he got off the elevator, he went past Harry's office and yelled at him, "Harry! Call Mr. Shipley and have him meet me in the copy room. NOW!"

Startled by Larkin's demeanor, he knew it had to be important, so he dialed the Secretary's office.

"Sally. Please ask the Secretary if he could come to the copy room? It seems Larkin has made an important find. But don't let anyone else know about it as yet."

"I'll let him know Mr. Hall. But, what about Mrs. Rosenburg?"

"I said no one else, Sally. Not even Hobbins, or Lovejoy!"

"No problem, Sir."

Harry hung up and followed Larkin toward the copy room. When he got there, Larkin had already turned on the machine to warm it up. He placed it on the top and closed the lid. Pressing the button for three copies, he pushed start on the Xerox machine. It started to make the copies when the Secretary arrived. "What seems to be so important that you have called me down here, Larkin?"

Without answering Dan, Larkin pulled the first copy off the machine and handed it to him. He began to read the letter. His eyes opened wide as saucers and he said, "Oh my. What are we going to do with this, Larkin?"

"What do you mean, Sir?"

"This means that we will have to rewrite the all of American history. And the Order," he repeated himself, "the Order, is at fault for contriving to bring about our nations demise."

"I know, Sir. Does that change anything?"

"It shouldn't, but it does. Even though, I am not a Mason. I will have to think on this my colleagues. I will summon you later, Larkin. I need to think."

Disappointed, Larkin looked at him with discerning eyes and said, "I understand, Sir. I'll be waiting for your decision."

Dan went back to his office with his copy in hand. He was obviously upset when he walked past Sally and through his office door. He closed it without saying anything to her at all. He sat behind his desk in deep thought and read Seward's letter one more time. He didn't know the history of each man in Seward's list as well as Larkin did, but he didn't need to in order to understand the significance of the document. It was the largest conspiracy of all time! It explained so many things previously unknown. It would change forever how the world would perceive Freemasonry. It may even cause widespread persecution of its members. It may also cause the Smithsonian to come under the wrath of the Order itself. Not to mention the pressure he would receive from those in both Government and the Order. And what of all the friends he had that were Masons? When he saw Larkin at the Hay-Adams that night for dinner he never dreamed that this young boy would indeed- rewrite history! He had an immense decision to make. What would he do?

Larkin looked at Harry when Mr. Shipley left the room. Harry saw his face and knew at once that Larkin was disappointed in this reaction from the Secretary. He said, "I know what you're thinking, Larkin. You wanted immediate action and the go ahead. But it's a big thing. You don't just make that kind of a call that quickly. Our boss does things right, not quickly. You'll see. Have faith that he'll make the right decision."

Larkin looked at Harry and kind of half smiled, shaking his head "yes". Harry put his arm around his shoulders as they both walked toward the basement to wait. When they unlocked the door and went in Larkin said, "I've made it through all of the documents, Harry. There were fewer than we thought- only a hundred and forty-three. I'm going to go through each of them one at a time now in order to determine how they relate to the last document, Mr. Seward's letter to us. It will take me a long time if I do it right. I think I'll get to know every Mason in town."

Harry laughed. "Well you already know me, so that leaves about ten thousand in my lodge alone. I think there are about three or four million in the world, Larkin. Not to mention all the ones that have already died."

"How many of them are 32nd degree or greater?"This question raised some suspicion in Harry.

"I don't know. Why do you ask?"

Larkin trusted Harry so he said, "Well, it is only logical that those who were in command would know more about the plot. So, why start at the bottom? You start at the top!"

Harry seemed to be satisfied with that answer and even agreed. "I see your point. I'll do some digging for you myself."

Larkin showed a little concern with that and Harry sensed it and said, "Oh don't worry, Larkin. I'll be careful. I'm going to my office. If I hear anything, I'll let you know."

Larkin got up and went to the door with him. "I'll be here until I sort through these in order of importance. I just hope I can determine that. Maybe Seward already had that in mind. I don't know. "

"I'll see you at home, that is, unless we hear something today. But, I doubt if we do." He left and Larkin closed the door. He locked it, because he knew the importance of what he had now. And possibly, so did "they".

By six-thirty, Larkin was getting tired. Harry had not come to get him. That meant Mr. Shipley had not made a decision. Larkin was disappointed, but he had the documents sorted by category and no longer in the order they were found. He had kept track of that, just in case Seward felt that was how they needed to be categorized in order of importance. Larkin didn't think that was the case, but he'd find out. He stretched and looked at his watch. "Time to go home," he said out loud. Just as he was about to get out of his chair, someone tried to open the door. He had not heard them come to the basement. When the person found the door locked they knocked and said, "Larkin, this is Mr. Shipley. May I come in?"

"Sure, Mr. Shipley," he said going to the door, "just a second." Larkin opened it for him and he came in. He could tell he was stressed by the day's events. "Please sit down, Sir," said Larkin to his boss.

Sitting in the chair, Mr. Shipley put his head in his hands. He pushed back his thinning hair, straightened up, and said, "I never anticipated that your appointment would actually mean something of this magnitude to the institution and ultimately, to me. I have struggled with this all of the day and have not completed any other of my work. Larkin, I am at a loss as to how to solve this problem and I came to tell you that you will have to wait, quite possibly for some time for me to make my decision. You must also know that I do not take it lightly. In the mean while, I ask that you trust me and continue on with the rest of this puzzle. I hope, quite possibly, that new information that you find may make my decision easier."

Larkin was touched by the man's forthright attitude and sincerity. He believed Shipley was a man of honor and trustworthiness. Therefore, when he asked for his patience, he did not hesitate to accommodate him and said, "Mr. Shipley, even though I am a young man, my parents and grandparents instilled in me a certain respect for my elders and their ability to make wise decisions. I know the magnitude of this one upon your shoulders and I'm willing to wait for you to make the decision in your time. I'd like you to know that no matter which way you go with it, I will support your decision. Someday, I'll find a way for the information left to us by Seward to be used for the benefit of the people."

Mr. Shipley smiled for the first time that day. He seemed relieved of his burden, at least for the moment. He got up and came over to Larkin and held out his hand. Larkin took hold of it and in that handshake they became fast friends. "Time to go home, Larkin. Mrs. Shipley will wonder what has become of me."

They walked around the desk to the door, locked up and headed upstairs. When they got to the front door Dan asked, "Would you like a ride home?"

"I sure would. I haven't had a chance to buy a bike yet."

"A bike, you say?"

"Yes. I still ride one all the time. It keeps me in shape."

"I must admit to you, Larkin, I have never in my life ridden a bicycle."

"Really?"

"Yes. That's the honest truth. Come. My driver is waiting."

Mr. Shipley dropped Larkin off at Harry's and said, "I didn't know Harry lived in this part of town. But nothing surprises me anymore. Goodnight, Larkin."

"Goodnight, Sir. Thank you."

His car pulled away from the curb and Larkin went in to go to bed. When he got to his room, he pulled one of the three copies of Seward's letter out of his pocket and put it in his suitcase. He knew he had to have one. It was the only real proof he had if the original disappeared. He was so tired he wasn't hungry. Realizing he had a big day ahead of him, he just went to bed. Almost forgetting his prayers, he turned off the light and asked God for help and guidance for his parents, his uncle, himself, and especially Mr. Shipley. He knew His Lord was in control.

The next morning, Larkin called his uncle from the pay phone at the grocers- not that he didn't trust Harry, but he felt that this was too important to risk the lives of his family. Larkin knew that Tom would be back in the house from doing the morning chores already. "Hello?" he said, aggravation in his voice with loud barking in the background, and he added, "Quiet, Sam." Larkin smiled when he realized his dog was with Tom.

"Hello, Uncle, is that Sam I hear in the background?"

"It sure is, Larkin. I suspect he knew somehow that it was you calling. I don't know how he does it."

"Uncanny. Anyway Uncle, I have some news. In my research I found a letter from Franklin to Morgan. In it he talks about the chest.

Supposedly there's a secret compartment in the bottom which holds a die for the minting of coins. If you would, check it out one of these days?"

"One of these days? You bet I'll check it out- today! This is exciting, Larkin. But what does it mean?"

"It means that the prime directive of us Palmer men to keep the Masons from ruling the world is substantiated by the mere fact that we have proof- that being the chest and now this letter. They would never be able to deny we are right."

"It's no longer just our word against theirs."

"Hopefully it never comes to a showdown and we won't need either. But, you never know."

"That's right. Call me on Saturday and I'll let you know what I find. Thanks for the call, Larkin. I pray for you all the time."

"I pray for you all the time, too. Take care of my dog!"

"He's good company. Bye, Larkin."

"Bye, Uncle."

Larkin hung up and looked around. He didn't see anyone. He hoped that his conversation with the man in the blue suit had brought his surveillance to an end. He'd have to keep an eye out. 'You can never be too careful,' he thought.

Larkin had decided to take a cab to a bike shop, but where? He still felt pretty inept about getting around town and knowing where to go. He knew it would take time, so when he got in the cab he just asked, "Where's the best bike shop in town?"

"Bike shop? Let me see," the cabbie said, "there's a new one at the Ace hardware in Dupont Circle. I heard it isn't bad. Want to try that?"

"Sure, why not? Drop me off there would ya?"

"Dupont Circle here we come."

The cab dropped him off and Larkin hoped that it would be one of the last "fair weather" cab rides he'd take for a while. But then again, winter was on its way and he suspected that he'd only be able to ride a bike for a couple of months before the snow flew- if that. He went through the door and a couple of cow bells jingled, ka-clang, and ka-clang. Larkin turned to look at that, the sounds reminding him of home. A guy came out from the area of the paint department, cleaning his hands with a paint rag on the way. Larkin could smell paint thinner as he approached and looked at the man as he said to him, "Had a little spill back there. Sometimes that old paint shaker drives me nuts. What can I do for you?"

"I'm here to buy a bike. If you have one for me."

"If? I have one for every person. Follow me." They walked over to a wall of the building where many bikes were lined up against it. "This one," he said, "I think would work for you. It's one of the new styles, of

European design. If you notice, the handle bars require the rider to bend over while its being ridden. It's what they call, "aerodynamics." It keeps the wind from dragging against the rider. Keeps you from getting tired and makes you faster."

"That's really interesting. Pull it out and let me see how it feels." Larkin saw what care he used to pull it out amidst all the other bikes and figured he must truly care about them and therefore, Larkin surmised he was the owner of the shop.

When he got it out he said to Larkin, "Go ahead and get on. See how it feels to you."

Larkin took the handle bars from him and hopped on. It felt a lot different than his bike with the banana seat and the high handle bars back home, but it felt good. "This *is* different, but I guess after you get used to it, it would feel pretty good."

"For a young guy like you, the transition into something new would be a breeze. Want to take it out for a spin?"

"Really? Outside? You want a deposit or something?"

"I trust you. What's your name, Son?"

"Larkin Palmer, Sir."

"Go ahead, Larkin. Walk it out through the front door and take her around the block. I'll take your money when you come back."

Larkin did as he said and laughed at the man's' confidence in his salesmanship. But it worked, because as he rode down New Hampshire Avenue, he felt like it was almost second nature to him. He zigged and zagged along like he was on a bob sled run, sliding along back and forth in and out of traffic and pedestrians. He loved it! Consequently, he turned around and high tailed it back before the man was to think he'd stolen the bike after all. When he got back to the shop, he sat the bike inside the front door, took his wallet out, and went over to the register. The owner smiled and said to him, "I told you so. That'll be $89.50."

Larkin laughed and pulled out a hundred dollar bill. The man said, "Be careful on the streets. They have laws about how you can ride in the city now." He handed Larkin his change and said, "You have a ninety-day warranty. If you have any trouble with it, I'll fix it free. For that matter, be sure to come in anytime. I'll be glad to help you, Larkin. Are you going to use it to go to school?"

"Yeah and work until winter. I'll be going to UMD."

"That's about nine miles from here. It should go fast if you leave before the traffic rush."

"Wow, that's farther than I thought. I have an early class. What time should I leave?"

"Go before 6:15, or it will be a hassle. Thanks, Larkin."

"Thank you, Sir." Picking up his new bike, he went out the door with a smile and a wave to the owner. He never did get his name, but he sure liked him.

Larkin rode toward home and wondered if he should have bought a lock and chain for it. Just because he didn't steal it from the store, didn't mean that someone wouldn't steal it from *him!* He arrived in less than ten minutes from the circle. He had gotten used to the gears and noticed he'd have to adjust the seat a bit for his height; otherwise, he was happy with his new mode of transportation- at least for now. When winter arrived, he'd think about public transportation.

When he got home, he went in the back door and picked up his check book. He had promised he'd go to see the registrar and pay for his classes. After he put it in his back pocket, he went back outside, but turned around and went back in to see if Harry possibly had anything he could use to lock his bike up with while at school. Going back down to the basement, Larkin looked around the utility closet by the water heater where Harry had a bunch of stuff hanging. Sure enough, there was a cable and lock hanging there, with the key in the lock! He grabbed it off the hook and took a look at it. It hadn't been used in a while and was a little rusty, and he took the key out of the lock to see if it worked. It was stiff, so seeing some spray lubricant on a shelf, he took it and gave it a squirt. PSSST! He moved the key back and forth until it operated freely. He guessed he didn't need to buy one after all, as long as Harry said it was okay first. He'd have to ask him as soon as he saw him for permission. He wrapped the chain around the bike a few times, locked it on it and put the key on with his house key. His watch had a removable ring on the end of the chain for keys. It kept it all together and he liked that. He checked the time. It was almost noon.

Larkin got on his bike and headed toward school and wondered how long it would take under normal conditions, whatever "normal" was in Washington, D.C. He rode up U Street, to Rhode Island, to Baltimore. He figured that was the easiest route until he got to know the town. By the time he got onto Baltimore Avenue, he felt more comfortable with his surroundings, almost like he was out of the city. Nevertheless, he knew very well it was city, at least compared to home.

Upon arriving at the campus of UMD, he pulled up in front of Martin Hall and stopped. It had taken him about twenty minutes. That was with little traffic. He knew he'd have to learn to step up his speed a bit. He'd get the hang of it. He peddled toward the registrar's office. Putting his bike in a rack on the side of the building, he took the lock and secured it. There were about twenty other bikes there and his looked the newest and was one of only two like it. He felt like a trend setter. No matter, it was just transportation.

He walked up the stairs of the Mitchell building to the registrar's office and waved at her as he went into the room. There was no line and she recognized him right away. "Hello, Larkin. How are you? I have your new schedule and a transcript showing the accumulated credits as offered by the university. If it is acceptable to you, all you have to do is sign this and pay the amount on the bottom. If you'd like to take a moment to review it, go ahead and have a seat." She pointed.

"I think I should. I'll bring it right back."

He went over by the door and sat down on one of four chairs there. It rocked from side to side. Larkin hated that, so he moved one over. He read the transcript which showed him having completed each class in the freshman regimen with an "A" in each subject. This news pleased him. The cost seemed to be less than what he expected, in fact, it was much less. He looked at his new schedule and it showed his work at the Smithsonian as an advanced History class and independent study. Wow. This was almost too good to be true. The only classes on campus this semester were his science classes on Mon.-Wed.-Fri. He would not get a free pass on those, which made him feel better. He felt as if he was getting too much of a free ride and that made him uneasy. He took both papers back to the registrar and said, "I appreciate all the President is doing for me, but to be quite honest I feel guilty about it. And as far as the cost for the first year of credits, isn't that too low?"

She said, "I thought you might have misgivings, but don't worry about what the President has done. In certain circumstances with exceptional students he can and does do this in our accelerated program. As far as your costs, there has been an anonymous donor who has paid fifty percent of the first year's tuition for you. The rest is up to you. Don't let them down."

He was flabbergasted. He sat the paperwork down on the counter in somewhat of a daze. Picking up a pen, he signed the document for her. Then he got out his checkbook and paid the balance due for half of his freshman year and all of his sophomore year. He didn't want to have to write another check for tuition until his junior year. Still, he didn't' need all the money that his uncle had placed in the account. He had a lot left over, and he was grateful, but he wondered who had paid. He asked her, "Please tell Dr. Perkins that I am grateful and will not let him or my donor down. By the way, what's your name?"

"I'm Marge. If you ever need anything let me know. It looks like you won't be a traditional student here and the President will be your counselor. Just do well and everything will be fine. I'll tell him what you said. See you next week, Larkin."

"Thanks, Marge. See ya," he said smiling and waving as he left.

She watched him go out the door and she said to herself, "I like that kid. He's not like all these hippies coming here on their parents' dime. He doesn't even talk like them."

On the way out to his bike, he saw a rack of information placed in the entryway for new students. Picking up a few things, he saw coming events on campus. He wondered how much he'd be involved with them seeing as he would be working nights and studying days. As he had never taken a tour of the campus, he took a map and began to walk around and find out where his classes would be held. He saw where fraternity row was, which he knew he'd stay away from, the sports fields and even the golf course! What interested him right away was the campus farm. He knew he'd be there often- unless work got in the way. He went over and said "hello" to a girl pushing a wheel-barrow full of manure toward a pile by the fence. She was wearing chaps and figured she was able to keep a horse there and ride. Now she was in cleanup mode. She smiled, but went on with her duties. He leaned on the fence and just watched for a while, daydreaming about back home. Definitely, he knew he'd be back.

The campus was pretty large and after walking a bit, he wished he had ridden his bike. However, by walking, it made it easier and he did get to go in and see his class rooms this way. He knew he didn't need to skimp on looking around or he'd miss out and possibly be late for his first day! Larkin knew how to be organized. As he walked back towards his bike, he had to stop and look at the map again. A girl sitting on a bench asked him, "Lost?"

He looked up and smiled at her saying, "No, not really, just had to refresh my memory."

"You must be a freshman."

"Kind of. I'm new here, but I am technically a sophomore."

"Oh, a transfer student. Well, I'm Sandy, and I'm a sophomore too."

"Well, I'm not that either. More like non-traditional. My name is Larkin. Nice to meet you, Sandy."

She got a puzzled look on her face, but didn't ask what he meant. She just said, "You look awfully familiar to me. Say, wait a minute, aren't you the guy who saved that man's life out in front of the church the other day? Want to get a Coke?"

He'd forgotten about the newspaper article. "Yeah, that was me. And, gee, I'd like to, but I have to get to work."

"You have a job? Where do you work?"

"At the Smithsonian."

"Really? Are you a volunteer or something?"

"No, I'm a Junior Assistant to the Secretary."

"Secretary?"

"Of the Smithsonian."

"Wow. That's sounds impressive for a guy your age."

"Thanks, Sandy, but I've got to be going now. It was nice to meet you."

"See you around, Larkin?"

"Sure. My classes are Monday, Wednesday, and Friday mornings at the science building."

"Oh. I'm an English major. Well, I hope to see you again. Bye."

"Bye, Sandy."

Larkin walked away smiling and was glad to get away. He had never had this much attention from the girls back home, and he wondered why this was the case here. Was he suddenly that good looking or something? All he knew is that he did not have time for a relationship with anyone right now. He had just too much to do. Besides, he truly was not over Ginny as yet.

Larkin got on his bike and started towards work. It seemed strange to him to be on his first trip from school to work. It was the beginning of a new time for him. It was both exciting and intimidating. He kept track of how long it took for him to get there, which was about forty minutes. That was just way too much time. How was he going to do it in the winter? He didn't want to have to buy a car. He thought he'd check out the bus schedule next. He put his bike in the back by Harry's office and locked it up. Harry came up to him just as he finished and said, "Why don't you just take it down the service elevator with you to the basement. Then you'd know it would be safe."

"Good idea, Harry, and by the way, this is your lock. That Okay?" a thankful Larkin replied.

Larkin walked toward the elevator and Harry said, "No problem. I thought it looked familiar. Nice bike."

Larkin went downstairs to work after unlocking his bike and taking it on the elevator with him. 'Good idea,' he thought again.

Larkin spent the entire afternoon looking at the first document for clues as to how it related to Seward's letter. He didn't see how a letter from a Confederate officer in Tennessee had anything to do with things taking place in Washington. Then, he realized that it may not be directly linked to the assassination, but rather a clue to the entire effort of the Masons. He'd have to change his mind set and be more thorough. The name on the letter struck him though, as one related to Seward's letter and one that had interested him when he read it the other day- Brigadier General Joseph A. Palmer. He needed to see who this possible relative of his was and why Seward thought he had something to do with the conspiracy. Was he a Mason? Was he in D.C.? Maybe he was a friend of the notorious Mason Albert Pike? It was time to go to the Library of Congress!

Chapter 13

The Search

The Library of Congress

Larkin decided that in order to be able to do his research he'd have to make copies of the documents, as necessary, to take with him, so he went to the copy room. As he placed General Palmer's letter onto the lighted machine he noticed something funny about the piece of paper. It had other images on it when it was lit up. He thought, 'What kind of paper was this? And how did they do that?' When he looked at it in the bright light, another letter showed up, but not the one seen without the light. Why would a General in Tennessee write a letter to another CSA officer on this type of paper? What was he trying to hide? The light was so bright he had a hard time reading it while it copied, so he took the copy with him and went back down to his office. He had seen an unused magnifying lamp at the end of the hall downstairs stuffed in a corner. He picked it up on the way and plugged it in by his desk. He turned on the light and instead of placing the document under it he placed it on top and let the light shine up from below. Larkin read these words,

"Brother Barton, This will be my last correspondence as our plans from Brother Pike are almost complete after all these years. I encourage you to deliver your concoction to Dr. Verdici so that the task may be completed. Once the deed is done, you may dispose of it as you will. With God's help the South will rise again. Brig. Gen. Palmer. Oct. 2, 1872"

"Wow. What a discovery," he muttered. The letter he could see was just a letter to a former associate of Palmer's, but this hidden note, this told about how they were to kill Seward! Did Seward know about this hidden message? And if so, why did he see Dr. Verdici? But now he understood why the leather box was hidden in the shed. At least he thought he did. He had to know more about Palmer and Sam Barton. He hoped he wasn't related to the General from Tennessee. Shutting off the lamp, he put the original on the pile, took his copy, locked the door and grabbed his bike. Finally, he was off to the Library of Congress!

When Larkin arrived, he wondered if he'd be able to take any resources out of the Library and what he'd have access to. He was in awe of this building, too. He wondered when this captivation with the architecture in the capital would wear off. He hoped never. It was just so-magnificent. He went to the information booth and he asked what the procedures were. The woman there pointed at a stand with a form. On it was outlined what he had to do, the most important being getting a Reader's ID, which were only available in the Madison Building, except, he was in the Jefferson Building. ARGH! This was the one thing he hated about D.C., all the paperwork and the resultant waiting. Nevertheless, he was thankful that his life here had gone so smoothly- until this point. As quickly as he could, he filled out the form and took it over to the Madison building. Larkin handed it to the woman at the checkout desk with his Smithsonian ID and New York drivers' license. She looked it all over, took a stamp and stamped it, took another stamp and did it again, handed back his Smithsonian ID and drivers license and said, "Your Readers' ID will be mailed to you within two weeks."

He was frustrated and asked, "But what about today? I need to use the library- *today*!"

She looked at him and hesitated a moment. She said, "Have a seat. I'll be right back." She went to an office down a corridor by the rest rooms. She came back with a man in tow and pointed at Larkin who had taken his watch out of his pocket to check the time. As the man approached, Larkin snapped it shut, but the man got a good look at it as he slipped it in his pocket as Larkin stood to greet him. Obviously, he had seen the case and its symbol, and his scowling face instantly received a smile. The man's demeanor changed immediately as he stuck out his hand and greeted Larkin cordially saying, "Hello, I'm the assistant librarian here in the Madison Building, may I help you?" This even took his assistant by surprise as she went back to her stand and she did a double take, obviously expecting that he would react differently.

"I'm Larkin Palmer, Junior assistant to the Secretary of the Smithsonian. I'm new to D.C. and have just applied for my Reader's ID and other identification from the library. I'm working on a special project and I'd like to use the library until I receive my permanent card. Is that possible?"

The Librarian walked away from Larkin toward the stand where his puzzled assistant stood asking her, "May I see his paperwork?" Looking it over he said, "I don't see why not as you fall into the "Special" category of users due to your position at the Smithsonian. I'll tag your ID so you can check out anything from the Library." The assistant at the desk heard all of this and her jaw dropped. He filled out a card and handed it to Larkin saying, "I'm glad to be of service to you, Mr. Palmer. Good luck in your work."

Taking the card from him Larkin said, "Thank you, Sir. It was a pleasure to make your acquaintance."

Larkin smiled as he walked away. The assistant just watched him leave, bumfuzzled.

Larkin went directly to see what kind of classification system they used and where he could find his resources. Classes E & F of American History had huge amounts of materials. He couldn't believe it. He was in the biggest library in the world. Unlike back home, he'd never read all of the books in this library! He found what he thought he wanted and began to read. He found out about both men in relatively little time. Both were Masons. Neither served in the same battles, but both served in Tennessee together, at least for a short time. Both were captured and released. Both went back home after the war. However, there didn't seem to be any real connection between the two men that would draw them to conspire together. What was it? Or, *who* was it? Possibly- Pike?

Larkin remembered something he had read earlier in the library at the Smithsonian, that the chemist Barton had died unexpectedly while on a trip to visit his son in Washington, D.C. How did he die? Did he place the box in the attic then? Who else did he see in D.C. at that time? What or who drew these two men together? 'Wait a minute,' he thought, 'that statue I saw of the Mason Albert Pike. Did he live in D.C. at that time? Or was he already dead?' He decided to find out more about him next. He had a hunch the two were connected somehow, but he'd had a long day and was getting tired. It was almost eight o'clock. It would have to wait.

With that information, Larkin decided to call it a day. Instead of going back to the office, he headed towards home on his bike. The air was cool and he wondered once again how long he'd be able to ride his bike. He was starting to get the hang of this thing. Even when the traffic got slow, he was able to go around it and get there faster than the cars – almost. He saw a Chinese place on the way down H Street and stopped. He realized he had not had anything to eat since morning. Parking his bike out front, he locked it to the light post. He wanted to go past the old Surratt Boarding House which was right down the street, so he craned his neck to see if he could see it. Finally, he went in and the host came up to him and said, "How many?"

"It's just me."

"Dis way."

He followed the man who wore Chinese garb, Larkin thought a Zhiduo, to a booth on the left side. The place was lit dimly, but it gave the eatery a romantic kind of feel. Larkin sat down facing the door, as always. The waiter handed him a menu and went away. Almost immediately the waiter came to take his order. No waiting here. Larkin already knew what he wanted even though he had never been there before, "I'll have Chicken Chow Mein."

"Okay." The waiter grabbed the menu and asked, "What you drinking?"

"I'd like hot tea, please."

"Okay. Bring right back."

The waiter left as quickly as he had appeared. The place wasn't very busy, but it was apparent that it had been. People were starting to leave. Larkin had missed the rush. He looked around the restaurant. It was dimly lit, but he could tell it was an old place with nice Chinese art. As long as it had good food, he didn't care what it looked like. He was hungry and the place smelled good!

The front door opened and a woman came in. It was Sally Britt, Mr. Shipley's secretary. Larkin wondered if she was alone. She hadn't noticed him when she came in, because her eyes had not yet focused in the darkness. The host led her back towards him. He could see it coming- he'd be having dinner with Sally. When she got to the table in front of him, she finally saw him. "Why, Larkin, how are you?" she asked.

"Fine, Sally. Would you care to join me?"

"I'd love to." Turning to the host, she just pointed. The man smiled, bowed, and left her to sit with Larkin.

After she sat down, Larkin asked, "Long day at work?"

"Yes. How about you?"

"For sure. I just finished up doing some research at the Library of Congress."

The waiter came and took her order, and Larkin asked, "Bring mine out at the same time as hers, would you?"

The waiter just bowed and left. The two were now alone. Sally wanted to know more about Larkin.

"Larkin, all I know about you is your work. Tell me a little about yourself. Where are you from?"

"I'm from the farming country of New York. My family owns an orchard there and my dad has a medium sized dairy."

"How about you? Where are you from?"

Sally answered, "I'm from Maury County, Tennessee. And don't say it, I know, I don't have an accent. My dad was in the army and my mom was from Tennessee. We moved all over and when dad retired, they settled there. I'm the youngest, and have a brother and sister. How about you? Have any siblings?"

"Nope. Just me. No cousins either. I have an uncle that's about eighty now, and Mom and Dad. That's it."

"What brought you to go to school at UMD?"

He explained his reasons for picking UMD, but didn't tell her his real reason for wanting to study in D.C. He really didn't want to offer too much more information on himself than what he already had, so he turned the conversation towards her. He got her talking about her brother and sister, and her dog "Sam".

"I can't believe your dog's name is Sam," said Larkin. "My dog's name is Sam, too."

"Really? What breed is he?"

"He's a blue healer. Works well with the cows. What's yours?"

"That's amazing! So is mine. I mean, he's a blue healer, too!"

Just then, the waiter brought their food. Larkin bowed his head to pray. When he finished and looked up she was staring straight at him. Picking up his fork he noticed her stare and asked, "What?"

"Well, I saw you pray. You could have asked me to join you."

"I didn't know. Next time, I will. Do you go to church?"

"Yes, I'm now a Methodist. I go to Foundry United."

Larkin laughed and said, "Pastor Tomlin."

"So you know of Foundry?" she said smiling.

"Yes, I do. I attended there with Harry last Sunday."

"And I can only surmise by your laugh that you feel the same thing about Pastor Tomlin that I do? That he's, well, let's just say, he is not my cup of tea." She picked up her tea cup and smiled.

"I can only say that he's not what I'm used to. I've been thinking I'd look around. Want to come with me and visit some other churches?"

"Where would we go?"

"I don't know. I'll see what's close by. Say, where do you live?"

"I live on Wyoming. I rent from a sweet old woman who has a spare basement apartment. It's only four hundred a month."

"Wow! I guess Harry gave me a real good deal."

"Why? How much is he charging you?"

"Only eighty a month."

"He must really like you."

"Well, he does appreciate the fact I saved his life."

"Oh yeah. I saw the article in the paper. I guess if Pastor Tomlin's sermons don't get ya, maybe the traffic outside the church will."

They laughed, talked, and ate until the waiter came to pick up their plates. He gave Larkin the bill and two fortune cookies. Larkin picked up the bill and a fortune cookie. Twirling the cookie around with his fingers he said, "Did you know that these were invented in San Francisco, not China?"

"Really? What does your say?"

He read it and sat it down not making a comment. She asked again, "What does yours say?"

Not waiting for him to answer she said, "Mine says, 'You will meet a tall, dark, handsome stranger'. Come on, what does yours say?"

"I don't really believe in them anyway." He got up and said, "I'll go and pay the bill. Be right back."

She watched him go up to the register and she reached across the table and picked up his fortune. It said, "Beware of strangers." She looked at him and did a double take on the fortune. Now how could that upset someone that much? He came back and placed a tip on the table. She stood up and he picked up her jacket placing it on her shoulder as they began to walk out. She liked the attention and smiled at him as he opened the door. What he didn't want her to know is that he liked her and didn't want her to be the "stranger" to beware of!

Once outside, he pointed at his bike saying, "I got a new bike."

"It's one of those new European racing bikes isn't it?" she asked.

"I guess so. But they say that it's the trend of the future for bikes. Sooner or later most bikes will be like this."

"Really? Well, I drove my pickup. Want a ride home?"

"Your pickup?"

"Yeah, it's right over there."

She pointed at a blue 1968 Datsun sitting on the other side of the street under the street light. Larkin looked over at it and said, "Cool. I'll throw my bike in the back."

He unlocked it and they walked over to her truck. Picking the bike up over the bed he set it in like it was light as a feather. She noticed he was pretty strong and said, "Do you work out or something?"

"No, never have. Just good old fashioned hard work has kept me in shape. But, I may get all the exercise I need riding this bike every day." They laughed as they got in.

She fired the Datsun up and they took off. Larkin noticed she handled the stick pretty well. Sally asked him, "Where does Harry live, Larkin?"

"Oh, yeah. He lives on U St. NW. Its' number 1776."

"Good patriotic number. Easy to remember, too."

"Yeah, I never thought of that."

Sally pulled up to the front door and she looked over at him and said, "Thanks for a great evening. We'll have to plan a real date next time."

He responded, "Maybe so." There was an awkward look between the two of them. Besides, this was just a friend from work. He opened the door, got out, and shut the door a little too hard, because it was just so light it didn't take much to close it. He got the bike out of the back and stood still while she pulled away waving good-bye. 'Maybe a date next time?' he thought. Well, maybe…

Larkin went in the back gate and sat his bike under the awning of the deck. Even though Harry never had trouble with thieves, he still took out his chain and lock and attached his bike to a four-by-four. If they took it, they'd have to work for it! He went in and heard Harry get up from his chair and come toward him. "Hello, Larkin. I saved some soup for you, if you'd like. I made way too much."

"Oh thanks, Harry, but I stopped and had supper at a Chinese place on H. I ended up eating with Sally, Mr. Shipley's secretary."

"Really? She's nice, Larkin. You couldn't do any better than that."

"Harry. You know I'm not up for that right now. We're just friends that work for the same boss."

"I know, but I'm just saying…."

Larkin cut him off, "Good night, Harry, and thanks for the soup. I'll eat it tomorrow if that's okay?"

Harry chuckled, mostly because of his defensiveness about Sally and said, "That's fine. Good night, Larkin."

Exhausted, Larkin went down the stairs and straight to bed. He was waked by the phone. He looked at the clock, and it was eleven. Groggily, he walked to the hall and answered it, wondering who would call so late. "Hello?"

"Hello, Larkin. This is Uncle. It's there!" He was obviously excited!

"What's there, Uncle?"

"What you asked me to look for. *You know.*"

Finally getting on the same page, Larkin became aware of what Tom was talking about. "It is? Great!"

"Yes. I'll place it back where it was and send you a picture of it. Okay?"

"Sounds good to me, Uncle. Thanks. Bye."

"Bye, Larkin."

He hung up and went back to sleep, a little more reassured than before.

The next few days and weeks went by quickly, Larkin spending a great deal of time at the Library of Congress searching for clues that would connect Generals Palmer and Barton, and also Albert Pike. It seemed to him like an impossible task with the information he had and he wondered if his theory had any legs to stand on. After reading more on Albert Pike, he remembered one of the documents in the Seward collection. Putting all the books back on the shelf, he went back to his basement office, (which he now lovingly called the "dungeon") and went through the document list again. It was only a newspaper clipping attached to a note by Seward that caught his eye. The clipping dated April 16, 1868, was from the Memphis Daily Appeal, of which Pike was owner and editor. It was an editorial, in which Pike called to all "White men opposed to Negro suffrage", to join together into "one great order" to "execute the concentrated will of all".

William Seward's attached note was simple, but explained much. Larkin peered at the faded ink under the light of his desk magnifying lamp. He read:

"That all may understand what Pike has unleashed upon the South, I attach a clipping of his vile ranting in his tabloid, unworthy to be called a newspaper. However, in my travels I have come to discover when this actually all began, that being in April 1867, when many of the Democrats, Masons, and Klansmen came together in Nashville to establish a new direction for their parties. This I found out from Brigadier General Joseph A. Palmer, a reluctant secret Unionist, who spoke to me of those loyal to the Mason's cause, although he being one himself. My friend, Dewitt Senter, later corroborated his claims. Palmer gave me a list of those who followed Pikes' direction in order that sedition and anarchy might reign in the South against Freedmen and Republicans. Those attending were: Nathan B. Forrest, Crowe, Brown, Fussell, Richardson, Pike, Palmer, Bate, Harris, McCallum, Felix Norman and his brother, John. There were also many others who served in the CSA or in state legislatures thereof. After this meeting Palmer determined to stay at arm's length from them and not be seduced to run for office against Senter by them. He was a true patriot led only by his conscience. This I also have found of Forrest, who saw through Pike's ambition and led many of his Masonic brethren out of the KKK and back to civility last year. Although Forrest be a true confederate, he at the least, is a man true to his beliefs of righteousness and justice."

Wm. Seward– March 19, 1870

"Wow," he said out loud, "so my possible ancestor maybe was a good guy after all. But what about his secret letter to Barton? That was two years after this! Did Palmer have a change of heart and then want to kill Seward? Or was he pressured by Pike to continue with an evil plan? And, I still don't know much about Barton. How did Pike have so much control over him?" He walked over to Barton's box and took a look at it again. The vials had been emptied due to the nature of the original contents and the potential hazards involved. He took the fragile glass tubes out and placed the box under the light on his desk. He noticed that the compartments for the vials were shorter than the outside of the box by a good half an inch. "Hum," he muttered, "I wonder." He took hold of the leather on the inside and pulled. It released and pulled straight out of the box as if it were a box inside a box. Larkin got visibly excited and put what was left of the box under his lamp. Inside the bottom of the box was—a trap door! Pulling on a tab, the trap door lifted and there concealed beneath it was a piece of paper. Suddenly, a knock came at his door and a balding man with glasses poked his head in. Larkin almost jumped out of his skin! They both just stood there and looked at each other for a moment. Realizing what he had done, the man said to Larkin, "I'm so sorry to have startled you young man. My name is Bob Applebaum. I'm a historian here and I've heard from my staff at the Library that you are working on the Seward project. What have you got there?" He pointed at the paper Larkin had just pulled out of Barton's box.

Ignoring his question and acting quickly, considering he had just been scared out of his pants, Larkin replied, "It's a pleasure to meet you, Sir. I have heard a great deal about you, your family, and your works. Congratulations on your recent Pulitzer, Sir."

"Why, thank you. But what have you got there, Mr. Palmer?"

"Well, I don't know Sir, I just found it."

"Really? That's exciting! I've never actually "found" much of historical significance before. May I see?" The man of fifty or so came over by Larkin at his desk and peered over the lamp's edge so he could get a look at the paper.

Larkin slowly unfolded the piece of paper carefully so as to not damage it and saw that it was a letter addressed to "Whom it may concern". Hesitantly, not knowing this intruder to his domain, he slowly began to read it out loud, holding it under the lamp:

"To Whom It May Concern; As I have come to be concerned for my well being, I found it prudent to write this record of my dealings with those of whom I felt were my compatriots, but have found to be only my enemies and those that I must fear. But I digress, as it all began after the war, when I was blackmailed by Pike to continue in my evil ways after he used me in the plot against Lincoln, Seward, and so many others up to this day. In all, I have been subject to this evil in the lives of many presidents and their cabinets and am responsible for their deaths in one way or another, these being— Lincoln and Seward, Buchanan, the poison in his tea finally obtaining its inevitability because he knew too much, and Taylor when I was a mere apprentice of the men who killed Harrison. Of them all, I feel the need to tell the story of Lincoln and Seward, whom I also killed at his home in Auburn through Dr. Verdici. The assassination of Lincoln was to have taken place with no gun play, but only with my vials.

This is what happened: The plot was concocted by the Black Pope apart from the Vatican and passed down to each of its participants, and until it all came together, none of us knew each other's role. The actions of each were designed to take place with expediency, with no room for tardiness or lack of execution. Preparations were to be made with care independent of one another as each were assigned tasks which were of each ones' expertise: Stanton allowed for access to Washington D.C. and the correct destinations; Booth was to be the backup if I were to fail in my mission, which I did due to a change in Lincoln's itinerary. The others, Sarrat and her troop, took it upon themselves to band together despite orders to the contrary, and they failed miserably and thus, their executions. It is amazing that the rest of us; Jeff Davis, who was to pay his reward to Booth after he arrived from his flight from Washington; Judah Benjamin, who devised the plot for the Jesuits; Sarah Gilbert who received much intelligence from the other camp; and Johnson who advised us all and really wished the outcome to be different, were never found out. I was least suspect, except for Seward who somehow knew, especially about me. There are many others privy to the plans and to plans of other shenanigans not mentioned here. The whole of it is evil and I wish I could be out, but I'm in too deep and I fear, as I said, that I am to be the next eliminated. The insane madman Pike was too much in control, and he had summoned me to D.C. for some unknown reason before he died almost ten years ago. At that time I stole his property and have placed it in a key place. I shall see my son and place this in a hiding place also, so that at some future time, someone may know the truth of it all.

Beware– The Jesuits control the Masons and the Masons along with the Illuminati are conspiring to control the world."
Sam Barton– Forever CSA! April 5, 1900

"Wow! Where did you find this, Larkin?"

"In the bottom of this chemistry box that I found in the stable."

Not knowing about that, Applebaum replied, "The stable? Do you realize what this is? It confirms that the plot to kill Lincoln was a conspiracy at the highest level and that the Masons in this country did it under order of the Jesuits. This-- is the find of a lifetime!"

"I've had a lot of those lately."

"Huh? Is that so? What will you do with this, Larkin?"

"I'll take it to the Secretary for his opinion and then make a decision."

"Wise idea. In the mean while, I shall not say a word about it."

"I'd appreciate that. IF word got out, our very lives may be in danger."

"Our lives? Oh yes, I see. You're right. My family has been at odds with them for years because we are Jewish."

"Tell me Dr. Applebaum, why did you come to see me?"

"Oh, all this excitement made me forget. I wanted to see if you had anything happening with this project so that I may write a paper on it with you. But, now that you have this, my goodness, you have the works of a book of major proportions in the making!"

"Indeed. Let's follow up and maybe we can collaborate on it. Would that be acceptable to you, Sir?"

"Yes, it would. I'll contact you in a week, after you have had time to speak with Mr. Shipley."

"I'll be in touch. Can you find your way out of the dungeon?"

Applebaum laughed and said, "I think so. It has been a great pleasure to have met you and be present at this momentous occasion, Larkin."

"Same here, Sir." Larkin held out his hand and shook Applebaums'. He turned and walked out, Larkin hearing him get on the elevator. Larkin remembered his fortune cookie from the night before. He hoped it didn't mean Applebaum. He seemed too nice.

Larkin took out his watch and checked the time. It was still early, only 5:30 P.M., but Mr. Shipley usually left at five pm. He put the letters in a folder and headed up to Shipleys' office. When he got off the elevator, Harry was just coming out the door of his office. Larkin grabbed him by the arm as he hurried past and said to him, "Come with me Harry. You've got to see what I'm going to show Mr. Shipley. It substantiates Seward's letter."

"Another find? He may be gone home, Larkin."

"But, if he's not, he should see this."

They walked up the stairs in a hurry. Larkin couldn't wait, so he ran ahead of Harry who couldn't keep up, his shoes echoing on the granite floor and the ceiling above. Just as he arrived, Sally was walking out of the office and locking up. She turned to see Larkin and Harry coming up to her and before she could say anything Larkin spurted out, "Sally, is Mr. Shipley in there?"

Taken aback Sally answered, "Why yes, Larkin. He had to stay late, but I think he's about to leave. Is there something wrong?"

With a big smile as he went by her he said, "Nothing wrong Sally," he replied, "something's RIGHT!"

He went in and knocked on Mr. Shipley's door. Somewhat surprised that someone was there Mr. Shipley answered, "Come in?"

Larkin went in and said, "I'm sorry to interrupt you Mr. Shipley, but I've found something I didn't expect and it seems that it may blow the lid off my whole project."

Before Shipley could answer Larkin handed him Barton's letter. Putting on his glasses that he used only for reading, he read the letter without comment. Harry and Sally walked up behind Larkin and listened. Setting his hand down on his desk, letter resting in it, he took off his glasses and looked up at Larkin. Instead of commenting on it he asked quite frankly, "What would you like from me, Larkin?"

Larkin didn't expect this. He answered, "Your opinion, Sir. What should we do with this new information? It ties it all together."

Standing up, Shipley handed the letter back to Larkin. Before he spoke, he turned and walked toward the window overlooking the lawn and thought for a moment. Harry still didn't know what this was all about and he motioned for Larkin to give him the letter. Larkin swung his hand behind him and let Harry and Sally take the letter to read for themselves. Finally, Shipley turned and looked straight at Larkin and said, "I'd like to think about it. It does substantiate Seward's claims. In the mean while, make three copies of that and hide it. Does anyone besides those in this room know about it?"

"Why yes, Sir. Dr. Applebaum was there when I made the discovery."

"Applebaum?"

"He came to introduce himself to me and ask if I'd like to collaborate on a paper."

Shipley got visibly upset with this news, saying, "He did, did he? Why that..." He stopped and composed himself. "I'll talk to him later. I'll call for you in the next few days. Will you be going home for the Thanksgiving Holiday?"

That question took Larkin aback. Shipley was full of surprises. Because he didn't think he should go home yet, and staying away for the time being was the plan, he answered, "No, Sir. I had not planned on leaving."

"Then you'll be dining with me and my family." Pointing at Sally and Harry he said, "You are included as well. No exceptions. Be there by 1 P.M. sharp. Mrs. Shipley is very prompt with her dining rules. I suspect that's because of Julia Child. I insist you all take the weekend off. When we close on Wednesday I don't want you here until Monday. Got it?" None of them had ever heard him be so direct before. Collectively they paused before they answered, all looking back and forth at each other until they all said in unison, "Yes, Sir", and shaking their heads up and down like bobble heads.

They all turned and headed toward the door. Harry and Sally went first, and as Larkin was about to go out Shipley said to him in a softer tone, "Say, Larkin."

Larkin turned, faced him and replied, "Yes, Mr. Shipley?"

"Good job. I'm going to see to it you are put on staff here for the rest of your life if you want. But finish at UMD first and we'll talk about it." Larkin didn't know what to say. Frozen there for a moment, Shipley came over to the door and put his hand on Larkin's shoulder and said, "You are like the son I never had. I'm proud of you, Son. This is a huge thing, and a huge decision for me to have to make. I'd like to spend more time with you at our home. I'll talk to you later about it all." Larkin went out without saying a word, Shipley closing the door behind him. But Larkin had not forgotten Dan's reaction about Applebaum, even after the invitation to his home.

After all the excitement and the finds of the day, Larkin decided to go home with Harry after he made copies of the letter. He also decided to lock all of the documents up in his office, in his own personal file, and in Sally's file for the Secretary. They suddenly had become very valuable. At least he now knew that Seward had not lied in his letter and this was the proof he needed. The other documents in Seward's trunk were really not necessary now, but would be corroborating evidence. Tonight he might actually sleep, or would he?

Chapter 14

The Test

The National Archives

Larkin had been doing well in his classes at UMD, even though he'd been putting his heart and soul into his work at the Smithsonian. He felt badly that he'd somehow done an end run around the system there and had been hired on a whim by the Secretary. However, the other employees didn't hold it against him, and were amazed at his resourcefulness and ingenuity at work. In fact, it seemed to him like they were silently rooting for him to succeed, somewhat like the self-made hero he was turning into. But, his professors at UMD knew nothing of this part of his life and he had to pass muster with them in his classes.

Larkin was studying for a test in plant science. It was going to be on "woody plants of the Northeast". The funny thing, he thought, was that his professor had come to him asking questions about what he had found in his orchard and woods by The Homestead. He was finding that his experience was held almost in awe by his professors. Few students had as much, and in fact, he even had more than *them.* Larkin expected to fly through the remainder of his classes and was extremely glad he didn't have to take the exempted freshman classes. It would have been such a waste of time.

Larkin wanted to take this test just to prove to his professor he was what he claimed to be. He took his book and went over to the study hall to cram. On the way he saw some familiar faces and he waved at them even though he had not had time to establish any friendships, nor did he want to. But he didn't want to seem unfriendly either, so he smiled and waved.

Larkin consciously sat down by the window facing the ball fields so he could daydream about baseball, if he wanted to. No, he had not forgotten that he wanted to play baseball someday. That childhood dream had almost faded, but was sparked to life from time to time by someone with a ball and glove playing catch. There was no one out there, mostly because it was cold and the fields were covered with leaves. Fortunately, this provided no distractions, so he grabbed his book and got with it. After about two hours, he felt he had it down. Besides, the text, even though written by someone else, was as if he'd written it himself. The only other test he wondered about was chemistry, but he'd done well with that in high school and he wasn't having any problems there either.

Someone walked up and sat down at the table with him. It was a guy he'd never seen before, but he had the same book as he, so he assumed he was in his class. He said to Larkin sticking out his hand across the table, "My name is Marty McKee. I see you must be in my class. Are you ready for the test?"

"I think so. How about you?"

"Maybe. It's not that I don't get it- it's that I just don't really *like* it."

Larkin wondered and had to ask, "Then why are you taking it?"

"I promised my dad. He's a farmer, but I just don't want to take over the farm. I'd rather be a cop."

"Hum. That must be tough. Why not just tell him?"

"I don't want to disappoint him or my family. You know what I mean?"

"I sure do. But instead of making yourself miserable, sometimes it is best to just come out and tell them the truth."

"Yeah, I guess so. Say, what's your name anyway?"

"Oh, I'm Larkin Palmer."

"Larkin Palmer? I've heard about you! You're that whiz kid that the President sent through the accelerated program."

"Oh, I wouldn't say I'm such a whiz, but yeah, that's me."

"Glad to meet you. Are you going home for Thanksgiving? We don't have much time off."

"No, I'm not. Are you?"

"Yeah. But when I get back I hope I can change my major."

"So, are you going to tell them?"

"Yeah. You convinced me. I need to tell them."

"Well, if they come down on you, don't blame me."

"Don't worry. Say, when I get back want to do something? I mean, go hustle some women or something?"

"Well, I'm not in the market for a steady girlfriend or anything, but we could go to a party or two, I guess."

"Great. What's your phone number? I'll call you when I get back."

Larkin wrote down Harry's number and gave it to him. "This is my landlord's number. It rings into my apartment. If I'm not home he'll take a message. Have a good Thanksgiving, Marty."

"You too, Larkin."

Marty picked up his books and headed out the door. Larkin thought, 'That's odd, he didn't even study.' Larkin wondered about that and thought about his fortune cookie again- *"beware of strangers."* Now he thought he was just getting paranoid about it. Or was he? Why did he give him his number? He looked back out the window hoping someone was playing ball, but instead, it had clouded up and was snowing. It was time to head home before he couldn't ride his bike!

By the time Larkin arrived at his apartment, it had snowed a quick, fluffy, four inches. He put his bike on the porch and came in shivering from the sudden change in weather. This was a bad omen for him. He may have to retire his bike for the season and try to figure out the bus schedule for school and work. It was almost Thanksgiving and he felt he'd done well to put the transportation change off this long.

Larkin opened his refrigerator to look for a snack. It was already getting pretty bare in there. He picked up his last apple and sat down on the couch by the light. He snapped it on by its chain pull and picked up the newspaper that Harry had given him, holding onto the apple with his teeth, and shaking the paper with two hands so he could fold it in half. Reading for about half an hour, he drifted off to sleep. He woke to hear Harry walking above him. What time was it? Opening his watch, he found he had been napping for almost two hours. Getting up, he went up the stairs to see Harry, wanting to ask him about a bus schedule.

Harry was sitting at the kitchen table reading the current newspaper as he usually did, before he gave it to Larkin. Larkin asked him about the bus schedule and Harry had one sitting by the telephone. Larkin picked it up and looked at the times for buses to UMD and work. No problem. As he now could work whatever hours he wanted on his project, he decided he would go in on Tuesdays and Thursdays so he could concentrate on his studies the rest of the week. Now that he made that last discovery, Barton's letter, all he had to do was go through the documents one at a time and see if they corroborated those facts. If what Seward said was true, it should all work out well. He didn't see why it would be otherwise. He had confidence in himself and what it seemed God had brought to light. Larkin felt immensely blessed.

It was the second week of November and Larkin was ready for the science test. It was on the Friday before school let out for the Thanksgiving holiday. He went in before the rest of the class arrived, mostly because the bus was the only one scheduled around that time, and walking into the room, he found a place to stand by the heat register. He had not as yet bought a pair of gloves, since the old ones from last year had fallen apart and he threw them away back in Brookfield. All he had was his winter coat, so on the way to school he had stood on the bus with his hands in his pockets. He would buy a new pair on Saturday. Now, he stood and warmed his hands by the radiator, and waited for his professor to show up. Looking out the window, he thought of Ginny and last Christmas with her. He remembered the sleigh ride, and quite remarkably, even Pastor Johnson's sermon. As he felt himself become saddened, suddenly someone came into the classroom and slammed their books down on a desk, bringing him out of his daydream. It was his Professor. Looking at him he asked, "Getting warmed up, Larkin?"

"Yes, Sir. I need a new pair of gloves this winter. I just haven't had time to go get a pair."

The professor held up his to show Larkin and he displayed the ugliest pair of homemade gloves he had ever seen. He said, "Don't ever get married. You'll end up with a pair like this that you can't throw away!"

They both laughed as a couple of other students came in. Larkin took his seat and got ready for the test. The prof announced to the class as he handed out the test, "This is a simple test. No essay questions. I just want to know if *you* know the concepts. There are one hundred multiple-guess questions. I'll have the results posted by the time you get back from Thanksgiving break. Good luck." When he came to Larkin he said softly, "You had better get all of them right, Larkin." He winked, smiled, and gave him the test.

Larkin said under his breath, "I sure had better!"

The test was no problem for him. He breezed through it in less than fifteen minutes, picked it up and walked over to the professor, who obviously expected a question. Instead, Larkin handed it to him and said softly, "Happy Thanksgiving." The professor looked at him in surprise. Larkin turned away and walked out of the hall ready for a break from UMD.

Larkin went out the door into the cold again. The snow crunched under his feet. It had hardened since it fell and now it was packed down as it was walked on by the college's thousands of students. He wondered why it was still even on the sidewalks because the custodians usually had it all removed by this time. Maybe they had already started their break? He chuckled at the thought.

Larkin made his way toward the bus stop. By the time he got there the snow had begun to fall again and he pulled his stocking hat out of his pocket and stretched it around his head. The bus pulled up just as he arrived at the stop. What timing! The driver opened the door and smiled down at him. It was one of the few women drivers employed by the city. Her name was Elvira Jackson and he had already made friends with her. She said, "Come on Larkin, and you, too, miss." A girl was standing behind him waiting to get on, too. He hadn't seen her come up behind him. Trying to get out of the way, he quickly stepped on and sat down on the second seat. She got on and sat in the seat opposite him. She looked familiar, but he couldn't quite place her.

She faced him and asked, "Aren't you going to say "Hi" to me, Larkin?" He looked at her again, this time more closely. It was Pilar!

"Pilar! Is that you?" It had been a few years since he had seen her at the auction and she had changed so much. She had become a beautiful woman. Her long brown hair was curled all the way down to the tips. She had lost all the baby fat she had as a young teen and her curves were more than obvious. She got up out of her seat, came over to him and gave him a hug. They were both glad to see each other. "What are you doing here?" he asked. "Are you going to school here, too?"

"Yes, Larkin. I got here a couple of months ago. I am so glad you are going here, too."

"I can't believe it. Are you done for the holiday? Are you going anywhere? Where are you living?"

"Not so fast, Larkin. I live with a relative who is an employee at our embassy. She is very nice, you will like her. We have no plans for Thanksgiving. We don't celebrate it in my country. And all my classes are done, Si."

"Wow. That is all so cool. Where do you live?"

"We must live close, because we are on the same bus. I live on U Street."

"So do I! I rent from a man that I work with."

"You work? Where, Larkin?"

"At the Smithsonian. A lot has happened since I saw you last. We should get together and catch up. What's your telephone number? I'll call you."

She took out a piece of paper and wrote her address and phone number down for him. She said, "Give me a call and we will set a date. My cousin's name is Celia. She will like you."

The bus came to a stop and someone else got off. They were coming close to her stop. Larkin looked at her address. It was 911 U Street N.W. They lived only a few blocks away from each other. He said, "I'm supposed to go to my boss's house for Thanksgiving Day, but we can do something any other day next week. Think about it and we'll talk."

The bus stopped and she got up. She gave him a peck on the cheek and said, "Bye, Larkin. I'm glad we ran into each other. It is so nice to see you again." She went down the stairs and got off.

Elvira said to Larkin, "Good job, Larkin."

"Oh Elvira, quit that."

When he got off the bus, he walked to his house in another four inches of new fallen snow, and went in the back door. The snow was beginning to come down hard. 'Oh man,' he said to himself, 'we are gonna be snowed in.' He closed the door behind him, snow fluffing up as he did. He hung up his coat by the door and started down the stairs slipping on the top step. He slid down the first three steps and then –

"crack"- he heard it. He broke his ankle! "Ow!" he shouted. The final resting place of his foot was enough to stop his free fall to his room, so he sat up and waited. Because of his position, he couldn't get up to his feet. Logically, he would wait until Harry got home from work. He took out his watch and checked the time. He only had to wait for two more hours- he thought…

Harry got home a little late. It was almost seven. The buses were running slow- extremely slow in the snow. It took him about forty-five minutes extra to get home and the snow was still falling. He came in the door, took off his hat, scarf, and gloves and noticed the door to the basement was open. He went over to close it and looked down the stairs. There asleep, leaning against the wall, was Larkin. How he ever accomplished it while in as much pain as he was, well, he'd never figure that out. Harry called to him, "Larkin? Are you okay?"

"No, Harry. I've broken my ankle. I'm going to need help."

"I'll call an ambulance."

"No, Harry. No need to do that. Call my friend Pilar. She'll come over and help me to the hospital."

"Who?"

"Long story, Harry. She only lives a few blocks from here. Her cousin has to have a car. Her number is in my coat pocket by the door."

Harry found it and said, "Do I call her?"

"Well yes, Harry."

"Oh, yeah. The phone doesn't reach that far."

"Right."

He called the number and it rang a few times. He was about to hang up when someone finally answered. "Hello?"

"Hello, this is Harry Hall, Larkin's friend. Is this Pilar?"

"Yes it is. How can I help you, Mr. Hall?"

"Please call me Harry. He asked me to call you because he has fallen and broken his ankle on the stairs. I can't help him get up or to the hospital. He was wondering if your cousin has a car to take him?"

"Oh no! I'm sorry he has fallen, but my cousin went to her brother's for the night and I'm afraid she won't be able to make it home until the storm is over."

"I see. I guess I'll have to call the ambulance after all. At least he has insurance! It was nice to have talked to you, Pilar. Hope I get to meet you sometime."

"May I come over when he gets home? Will you have him call me?"

"Sure. Thanks, Pilar. Goodbye."

"Goodbye, Harry."

Harry hung up and went back to the stairs. He said, "Sorry, Larkin. No dice. Her cousin is out with the car. I'm going to have to call the ambulance. It's better anyway."

"No. Wait. Call Ellie Jensen. She'll come."

"Now that's good thinking! What's her number?"

"Aw, shoot! It's down here! How am I gonna get it?"

"You're not. I'll call the ambulance."

"Right!"

The ambulance got him to the hospital as quickly as they could-considering the weather. The waiting room was deserted. It seemed like people were staying in and not getting into accidents or hurt at home. The snow had put a damper on everything. They brought him in with a wheel chair. As there was no one there, they took him straight into X-Ray. The Radiologist said, "Yup, you broke your ankle alright." Larkin just looked at him.

"Got to have something to laugh about!" he said in his defense.

"Yeah, right. I have to get to work and school on the bus. This is going to complicate things."

"I'll take you to have it put in a cast. Maybe that will make it easy enough."

The ankle was set in a cast like a big boot on his foot and had a heal pad for support. He could actually walk with it without assistance from crutches. He went a few steps, but decided it would help if he had a cane for support. He said out loud to himself, "Man do I feel stupid."

Someone said, "You ought to."

He turned around to see- Ellie! He smiled and asked, "How did you know?"

"Harry called me after you left in the ambulance."

"I'll get him for that."

"Why? Didn't you want to see me?"

"Oh no, Ellie. That's not it. It's just that when I'm like this, I mean, feeling stupid and defenseless, I get kind of private and withdrawn."

"I see. May I give you a ride home?"

"I'd appreciate it very much. And- thanks for coming."

She smiled when he said that and she grabbed his arm to help him get to the car. Oscar came to the door and took over for her and assisted him to the limo. "Thank you, Oscar."

"You're welcome, Sir."

It was still snowing as Ellie got in next to him and Oscar pulled away from the curb. She said, "I don't know what it is like to go down to your apartment Larkin, but are you going to be able to make it down the stairs?"

"I think so, Ellie. Why do you ask?"

"I was just thinking that you could use our spare bedroom in the loft until you get better. It has an elevator."

Larkin panicked. "I appreciate the offer Ellie, but I think I'll be fine. I have to have this thing on for three months. I had better get used to it."

Oscar pulled up to Harry's house. There waiting for him with Harry was- Pilar!

"Great!" he said out loud when he got out of the car. Ellie helped him to the door and Larkin could feel the tension between the two, even without a word being spoken. Harry took his arm and helped him through the door. Ellie came into the front hall and Larkin introduced the two opponents. "Ellie Jensen, this is Pilar Rojas."

Ellie said, "Pleased to meet you, Pilar is it?"

"Nice to meet you, Ellie. It's, Pilar Rojas."

Turning to Larkin she said, "I need to be going now, Larkin. Think about my offer."

"Thank you for the ride, Ellie. I appreciate the offer as well. Goodbye."

Harry smiled at Larkin as he shut the door behind Ellie. He said, "How are you doing, Larkin? I see you have a cast."

"Yes, and it has to be on for three months. I'm going to have to make some adjustments somehow. The good part is that some of that time I will be on winter break from school. But it still means I won't be able to get as much done at work."

"Maybe we can copy all of the documents and bring them to you. You can use the phone and on nice days go to the places you need to go. You'll just have to prioritize," offered Harry.

"That may work." Larkin frowned at Harry for saying anything about his work.

"I can help too," chimed in Pilar.

Trying to talk her out of it in order to minimize her involvement he said, "That's nice of you, Pilar, but it would be too much of an imposition for me to ask you to help me that much."

"I can get research information for you!"

"Really? I had planned to go to the National Archives on Monday. You'd do that for me?"

"Yes. Just tell me what you want and I'll find it for you."

"Thanks so much, Pilar," he said half-heartedly. He and Harry looked at each other in resignation to the fact that she was now involved in something she should not have been.

After Pilar left, Larkin decided he had better call his parents. He dialed the number and waited for someone to answer. It was his dad. "Hello?"

"Hi Dad, it's Larkin."

"Well hello, Son. How are you?"

"Well to tell you the truth, I've been better. I fell and broke my ankle today. Considering that and the fact that we are having a huge snow storm, I don't think I'll be able to make it home for Thanksgiving."

"How did you do that?"

"I came in from the snow and slipped on the top stair. I went down a couple steps at the wrong angle. I found out those bones don't bend that direction."

"I'm sorry. How's it doing now?"

"Okay. The doctor says the cast will be on for at least three months. I can do my work from here and with the winter-Christmas break, I can stay here and recuperate."

"Your mother will not only be disappointed about Thanksgiving, but also Christmas, I guess."

"Yes, I'm sorry. It is going to be a hassle to be down like this."

"I truly understand, you know."

"I know you do. How are you doing, Dad? Is it snowing there?"

"I'm doing fine. Hardly need the cane anymore. Yes, it started to snow, but I think you got a lot more than us."

"They say it won't let up for a while either."

"Well, I hope you get better soon, Son. I'll tell your mother. God bless."

"Love you, Dad. Bye."

By the time Monday rolled around, Larkin already hated his cast. Not to mention the ramifications of his lack of mobility. Harry told him before he left for work that he'd have Sally find someone to make copies of all of the documents for him and he'd bring them home with him. Pilar was on his doorstep before Harry left. Harry opened the door and let her downstairs. "Thank you, Harry. It's cold out there."

The storm had almost brought the city to a standstill. The buses and snowplows were the only things on the road, only because they were big enough to traverse the snow drifts, which were now almost two feet tall. Harry said, "I think I'll be the only person there today, Larkin, if I even make it!"

"If they can't find anyone to make the copies don't worry about it, Harry."

Harry replied, "If it is this slow, I won't have much to do anyway. I'll have the time to do it!"

"Thanks, Harry. See you later."

Harry went out the door and Pilar said, "He's such a nice man. What do you have for me to do?" She came over to him and got a little closer to him than he was comfortable with. He tried to move away, but he was sitting in his chair and was sunk deeply into it. He was trapped. Instead, she sat on his lap!

Answering her question he said, "I put the list of documents I'd like to see on the table over there." He pointed at the kitchen table.

She said rather half-heartedly, "Oh." Forced to get up, she got off his lap and went to the table and picked up the list. "You want pardon records of confederate soldiers?"

"Yes. I have a hunch."

"Okay." She went over to the refrigerator and looked inside. Seeing that all he had was a bottle of Coke, she remarked, "You don't have much food, Larkin. Would you like me to pick up a few things on the way by the store?"

Wanting her to leave he said, "Sure, here's some money." He started to take his wallet out of his pocket and she said, "Don't worry. We'll settle up when I get back."

"Okay. Thanks, Pilar."

She asked, "What do you want me to buy?"

"Oh! The list is by the phone. When I run out of something, I write it down."

She went over to the phone, picked up the list and started up the stairs. Scanning it quickly she said, "This is a big list. I'll be back as soon as I can."

He yelled up after her, "Bye, Pilar, and thanks."

"Bye, Larkin."

After she left, he sighed a big sigh of relief. He started to feel a little trapped by her attention. He thought, 'What is it with all these girls? Am I the only single guy around?'

He got up slowly, walked over and turned on the radio in the corner. The cabinet-style receiver looked like it had been there since the 1930's. It crackled and popped as it warmed up. When it finally quit wheezing, he heard the reports that the city was socked in. In fact, they announced that all government workers were supposed to stay home. The bad part was that the storm was stalled and was not supposed to clear out all week! The phone rang and startled him. Hobbling over, he picked it up and answered. "Hello. This is Larkin."

"Hello, Larkin, this is Ellie. How are you today? I thought I'd check up on you."

He rolled his eyes like he couldn't believe it and answered, "I'm doing fine, Ellie. I just need to keep off of it and wait for the cast to come off. I'm fine." Stretching out the cord of the phone, he took a sip of coffee that was setting on the table.

"Is there anything I can do for you?"

He just about spit out his coffee when she asked that question. Setting his cup back down he said, "Oh no. I'm in good shape here.

Harry is even bringing my work home for me. I'm just going to rest today. Besides, this weather is awful! I'm glad I don't have to get out in it."

Sounding disappointed she replied, "Well, okay. But if there is anything you need or just want some company, give me a call. And don't forget my offer!"

He tried to close the conversation. "Thank you Ellie, I haven't forgotten. You are so nice. I'll talk to you later then. Bye."

"Bye, Larkin."

"Whew," he said out loud, hanging up the phone.

Larkin had been taking some pretty powerful medication and the pills made him sleepy. Sitting in his comfy chair, he dosed off. He awoke to someone knocking at the back door. He expected it to be Pilar returning from her errands so he just called out, "Come in. The door is open!" He heard a female voice, but it wasn't Pilar.

It was Sally! "Larkin, it's Sally. Can I come down?"

He panicked, but said, "Yeah, sure Sally, come on down." Why was she here? She clomped down the stairs in her boots making a squish, thud, squish, thud sound as she descended.

"Hi, Larkin! I was already at work by the time they told us to stay home and so was Harry. He told me you got hurt and needed help, so I copied all the materials you needed and told the Secretary you'd be out for a few weeks. He wondered if you'd still be attending on Thanksgiving though."

"Thanks, Sally. I hadn't really thought about it. I think I can make it as long as we get a ride."

"I can come by in the truck and pick you both up. I put 400 pounds of Kitty litter in the back for traction."

That was one thing he liked about Sally; she had it together, was always prepared, and didn't care what other people thought about it. "That would be great, Sally. I accept your invitation. Tell our boss I'll be there would you?"

"I'll call and leave a message with his butler. I doubt if we will be going to work anymore this week. They expect this mess to last a while."

"Yeah, I heard, but it reminds me of back home. I kinda like it."

"I suppose you would, you- Yankee." She gave him a push on his shoulders.

He just laughed and said, "Thanks again for bringing my work to me. I won't get so bored just sitting here and I can get something accomplished to boot. No pun intended."

Just then Larkin heard the back door open. It was Pilar! 'Man!' he thought to himself. She started down the steps and Sally asked him, "Are you expecting company?"

Larkin didn't know what to say, so he just told the truth. Pilar walked in with her arms full of groceries and papers. She went to set them on the kitchen table and smiled at Sally as Larkin said, "Sally, this is my old friend Pilar, and Pilar, this is a friend of mine from work, Sally."

After setting everything down, Pilar came up to Sally, held out her hand, and said with her Spanish accent, "Nice to meet you Sally, as Larkin said, I am Pilar."

"Same here, Pilar. How do you know Larkin?" Sally wasn't playing around, she wanted some information!

"I meet him years ago at an auction his family had in New York."

"Oh?"

What she really wanted to know was why she was there now, but she didn't ask. Larkin offered the rest of the story. "I just happened to see her on the bus from school the other day. We are both going to UMD now. Isn't that something?"

"Yeesss. Well, I better get going, Larkin. I'll call to tell you and Harry what time I'll pick you up Thursday. Okay?"

Nervously, Larkin replied, "Okay. Got it. And thanks again, Sally."

Sensing his uneasiness, Sally winked at Larkin, turned, and went up the stairs saying, "Bye, everyone."

Pilar and Larkin both called out, "Bye."

Larkin thought about what had just transpired. Sally was obviously not put-off by Pilar. Now Pilar knew there were two other girls in his life, but she didn't seem to react in a jealous manner at all. He wondered about that. She went over to the table and started to take the groceries out of the bags. She asked him, "Larkin, where do you want me to put these things?"

"Let me help you, Pilar." He got up out of the chair and hobbled toward the kitchen table. Before sitting down he said, "I forgot to ask, how much did it come to?"

"Just sit down and you can tell me how it goes. Oh, it was only twenty-four dollars."

"You did a good job. Thanks." He took out his wallet, gave her the money and asked, "Where's the cookies?" Spying them on the table, he opened the bag of Oreos and took one. She did too, but watched how he ate his taking the cookie apart and licking the icing.

She asked, "Why do you eat your cookie like that?"

"I don't know. You can eat these many different ways. With milk, dipping them in milk, eating off the icing first, you name it!" Finally, he sat down.

She just shrugged her shoulders and kept eating hers the way she had begun-whole.

After putting the groceries away, with little help from Larkin, Pilar got out the file from the National Archives. "These are the papers you wanted. They are just a bunch of service records, Larkin. I think they call them "Pardons."'

"Exactly. I want to see if President Johnson gave special treatment to any of the officers that were Masons from the South. I just have a feeling about it." He looked to see if Pilar would react to his statement as he knew her father was a Mason, too. She didn't blink an eye and just looked over his shoulder as he read the first few lines. He dropped the document from the bottom of the pile and it flew to the other side of the table. She put her hand on his shoulder and leaned forward over him to retrieve it brushing her breast across the side of his face. She placed the document on the table next to him and just stood in the same place as before. Larkin at first blushed, but continued to read without a noticeable reaction. After a long, but pregnant pause, he said to her, "Pilar you don't have to stay around while I work. I don't want to impose on you. You have been so helpful already."

"Oh? I don't have anything to do Larkin. My cousin is stuck at her brother's and I, as you know, am out of school, too. May I stay and keep you company?"

Larkin didn't know what to say. He wondered if God was testing him somehow. There were three girls all on the prowl for him and this one was becoming more aggressive by the minute. Just then, someone walked in the back door followed by Harry calling down to him, "Hello, Larkin! Are you alright?" Larkin felt saved.

"Yes, Harry, I'm fine. I'm down here with Pilar and she just brought me some groceries and paperwork. Want to come see what I'm working on?"

"I'll be down in a minute. I just want to freshen up. I had to walk home. The buses aren't running anymore."

From this, Pilar took the hint that Larkin didn't want the kind of company she was thinking about, and yet, she was not offended. Maybe, she was testing him to see how he felt about her? Was he a friend? Or was it to be more? She didn't know or really care. He definitely did! She backed off and said. "Maybe you have more work to do here than I thought. Can I come back to check on you tomorrow?"

Feeling a sense of relief he let down his guard a bit. "Sure Pilar. Come over any time. You're the best friend I have from Peru!"

She laughed and started toward the door. On the way up she said, "See you tomorrow, Larkin."

"Bye, Pilar."

She went out the door as Harry came from upstairs. He called down to him, "Hey, Larkin, want a beer?"

'Beer?' he thought, 'I don't think I've ever had a beer.' He yelled out an answer, "Sure, Harry. Why not?"

Harry came down the stairs with two bottles of beer in his hand. "Why did you answer that way, Larkin?"

"To tell you the truth Harry, I've never had a beer before. My parents don't drink and I've never been in a bar. Besides, years ago my grandparents were in the Temperance League. But after the day I've had today, I need one. I think."

"Wow!" exclaimed Harry, "Really? Never had a beer?"

"Yup. So let's see how this goes."

Harry had opened them upstairs and he handed the frosty bottle to the young man. He said, "Bottoms up!" and took a swig.

After smelling the top of the bottle, Larkin did the same. He didn't know what to think of the taste. He didn't think it was bad, but it was "hoppy" enough he didn't know if he liked it. But to be polite, he figured he should try to finish it with Harry. He motioned for him to sit at the table with him. "Pilar brought this pardon list home from the National Archives. I have a hunch that President Johnson treated the Mason CSA officers with more leniency than others. Do you think that may be a good hypothesis?"

"It's possible, but it may be hard to prove. Even if the records show some favoritism, you may have a hard time proving anything."

"I expect that, but I'm going to be as thorough as possible. It will give me an idea on how it would relate to the two letters we have. I'll also see if there are any of these men in the Seward letters as well."

"That may be an angle to come at it from."

"Say, this beer is starting to taste better."

"That's the problem for a lot of people."

"I can understand that. I think I'll stop at one." Harry and Larkin laughed at that one.

"Say Harry, I think I may have a problem with all these girls that are trying to get into my life. I just don't want that right now. I still think about Ginny and I'm not over her. Can you run interference for me? Like maybe say, I can't come to the phone, or I'm sleeping, or *something*?"

"I understand Larkin. I'll do the best I can."

"What about Pilar?"

"Don't worry. I'll take care of it."

"Thanks, Harry."

Harry got up to go to bed. "I'm tired Larkin. That was a long walk home and after one beer, I'm ready for bed. It has that affect, too. But only for us old guys."

Larkin laughed and said, "You know, I think I'm tired too. Good night Harry. Thanks for the beer."

Harry waved back at him as he went up the stairs and muttered half to himself, "Man, his first beer. Isn't that something?"

Larkin thought about what had happened that day. If all of this was a test from God, He sure was not making his life easy! In fact, he wished if he had to take tests, they would all be as easy as the one he took last week in school! He prayed God would help him and his family. Then he went to bed.

The next couple of days were made a little easier with Harry at home. He helped Larkin if he needed it, but most importantly, he kept the "hounds" at bay. All three of them had called at least once and Pilar had come over, but Harry had come up with an excuse each time. It allowed Larkin time to look at the Presidential Pardons and the stack of documents from Seward. Larkin appreciated the respite. He had to laugh when he looked in the refrigerator the next day. When he opened the door, he saw a flat package of something on the shelf. He picked it up and read the label- Tortillas made of corn. He didn't think he had ever had one before, nor did he think he had ever seen them sold like this. Maybe, just maybe, she thought she would be making diner there for him? Or she bought them for herself and forgot to take them? He'd just have to ask her the next time he saw her.

The phone rang and Harry answered it. Larkin could hear every other word. He knew it was Sally and Larkin assumed she was calling to tell them when she'd be there to pick them up tomorrow. He was right. Harry yelled down, "Hey, Larkin. Sally is going to pick us up at about noon. She doesn't know how bad the snow will be and doesn't want to be late."

"I don't blame her, Harry. I'll be ready."

"Okay. Want to have a sandwich with me?"

"Sure, but let me come up there. I'm getting tired of being down here all the time. I'll be right up."

Larkin went up the stairs rather well, he thought. When he got the landing, the first thing he did was look outside at the blowing, falling snow. He thought it was beautiful. The yard was completely covered in the white winter splendor, about two feet deep. The tree branches hung low under its weight and the powdery precipitation swirled as summer dust devils as it raced across from one side of the yard to the other in the wind. The sun shone through it, each flake reflecting in a dazzling radiance. It was an awesome sight to behold, but only for Larkin. Harry came up to him and said, "Man what a mess. I hate that stuff." Turning, he walked back to the kitchen and Larkin just smiled, shook his head, and followed him. "I made us a couple of peanut butter and jelly sandwiches. I figured we will have plenty of turkey tomorrow."

"You got that right, Harry. I like these, but I toss a piece of bologna in between the two."

"Hum. I never thought of that. That might be good."

"It is. And sometimes I grill it, like a grilled cheese."

"That's pretty creative. I should call you, "The Simple Chef." But I doubt Julia Childs would make something like that. By the way, she may be there in the morning. I heard she is a friend of the Shipleys."

"Well if that's the case, we should have a great meal!"

They sat eating their sandwiches and looking out at the cold, early winter storm. It was kind of like a purposeful silence-created by God to give them an ear to hear how He is in control and that they should be thankful. Thankful for all His blessings- even the snow.

After a good night's sleep, the two bachelors sharing 1776 U Street NW, got up refreshed and looking forward to getting out of the house this Thanksgiving Day. The snow had let up a bit, but it was still coming down. They wondered if Sally would really be able to come and get them. They'd wait for her call and in the mean while, just get ready. Larkin wondered how they were supposed to dress. "Say Harry, how formal is this dinner going to be?"

"Well, knowing the class of people we are going to *dine* with, I think we had better be dressed in our suits Larkin."

"That's what I was afraid of. It will be hard to get my new suit pants over my cast."

"OH! I never thought of that. What are you going to do?"

"Well, I cut the leg out of my blue jeans, and they go over my cast. So, I'll wear them with a dress shirt and sports coat. It's the best I can do."

Just then the phone rang. Larkin answered. "Hello?"

"Hello, Larkin, this is Sally. I hate to tell you this, but the Secretary just called me to say he has cancelled his dinner today because of the storm. He doesn't want any of us risking our lives for, in his words, a "turkey leg". He hopes you and Harry will accept his apologies and offers a rain check for Christmas, perhaps."

"I understand, Sally, and I'm sure Harry will as well. What are you going to do, Sally?"

She answered, "I don't know, Larkin. I didn't buy a turkey or anything, but the way this weather is, I just feel like a bowl of soup, or chili, or something. I know one thing- I'm going to just stay put. This is too much snow for me!"

"Yeah, me too. Well, thanks for the call and everything, Sally. Happy Thanksgiving."

"Happy Thanksgiving, Larkin."

They both hung up. She sounded disappointed to him. In reality he was, too. Of the three women, Ellie, Pilar, and Sally, he really thought of Sally as the best. He didn't know why. Maybe it was because she was the most like him. Maybe it was that she was the most, well, personality wise, average, plain Jane, or down to earth and more importantly, beautiful. He'd have to think on it.

Larkin told Harry what Sally had conveyed. He was disappointed too, just because he wasn't going to put his mouth around the turkey leg that the Secretary said wasn't worth the trip. Obviously, he disagreed with his boss again! "Well, I guess let's see what we have in the cupboards and turn on the TV. The Detroit-Dallas football game will be on around noon. Who do you think will win it this year, Larkin?"

Larkin really didn't know, because he didn't follow football, so to humor him he said, "I think Dallas will take it this year, Harry."

"Really? I'll bet you a case of beer Detroit wins."

Smiling Larkin said, "You're on!"

"You want a beer?"

"Sure. But these pills may not go too well with it!"

"Oh yeah. Well, I'll bring you a Coke."

"Thanks, Harry."

When Harry sat down he turned on the game. It wasn't on yet, just the pre-game show, so they sat and watched that. The game finally came on and Howard Cosell was doing the announcing. Harry said, "I don't know how this guy ever got his job, but I think I could do much better."

Larkin laughed and said, "Let's see how he does this game."

"No need."

By the time the first half was over, the score was tied. Harry got up to use the rest room and walked toward the back of the house. As he did the door bell rang. Larkin got up and answered the door, finding a man with a large box in his arms. He asked," Is this the Hall residence?"

"Yes it is. Can I help you?"

"Yes, you could take this box out of my arms!"

Larkin smiled when he got that answer and took the heavy box from the delivery man at the door. He could smell food in it. Larkin sat it down and asked him. "Do I need to sign anything for this?"

"No. It's from Julia Childs, courtesy of Mr. Shipley. Have a nice Thanksgiving!"

"Thanks! You too." The guy just turned around and left.

Harry came out of the bathroom and asked, "What's that?"

"It looks like it is the Thanksgiving dinner you thought you were going to miss."

Harry looked at the box. It said on the side, "From the kitchen of Julia Childs." He said, "Wow! This is going to be great! Did the boss send it?"

"He sure did. Let's go eat!"

Harry went to get the plates and Larkin sat two TV trays out in front of their chairs. Larkin asked Harry when he returned, "May I say the grace, Harry?"

"Why of course, please do, Larkin."

Larkin bowed his head and said, "Dear Lord. The lives you touch change as much as the weather. But in it all, you are in control and in it all you provide. Although this has been a tough year, I have seen you in my life and for that I am grateful. For all of your blessings we thank you and for this food which we truly did not expect. In the name of Jesus we pray. Amen."

"Amen," said Harry, who now wondered more than ever about his new young friend.

As they ate, they turned the game down low and talked, looking from time to time at the score whenever Cosell would go ballistic. They talked about Larkin and his uncles, his parents, and life on the farms. Harry shared how much he missed his wife, the traditions they had for the holidays and what it was like to live in the Nation's capital all these years. The two were getting to know each other, but Larkin withheld as much as he could so that Harry would not learn the truth about the

Family Palmer and the secret they held. Just about the time they were dishing up a piece of pie, Cosell blew a cork and said, "Ladies and gentleman, you are not going to believe this, but they have done it, the Dallas Cowboys have beaten the Detroit Lions!"

"Larkin, you were right. How did you know? I never would have picked them. Now I owe you a case of beer!"

"Aw, it was just a guess. I'm going to pick this mess up, Harry. I need to work up some room for that pie. And forget the beer, I'll just drink yours!"

"You already do. And besides, you know my house is your house, Larkin."

Smiling at him, Larkin got up and started toward the kitchen with the plates. Harry took down the TV tray by his chair and took out a pipe from a stand next to his chair. Larkin went back into the room to clean up the rest of the food and he smelled the cherry flavored tobacco wafting from the living room. Surprised, Larkin said, "I didn't know you smoked, Harry."

"This is my one vice. I smoke my pipe after "good" meals in the evening. Which I don't have much anymore, so I don't smoke much do I? The misses even put up with it. I guess she figured one vice is better than two."

Larkin didn't comment, but just went back to the kitchen to finish the cleanup. As he washed and dried the dishes, he thought of the many times he helped his mom, talking and looking out the window at the snow. He missed his mom and her perpetual smile. He missed his dad and his soft reassuring manner. He missed Uncle Tom and his always optimistic, upbeat attitude. He wished he could have gone home. He wished so many things - damn that eraser!

When he finished he looked back into the living room to find Harry fast asleep in his chair, pipe snuffed out and sitting in the ash tray. Turning quietly, he tip-toed with his cast as best as he could toward the back door, and closed the swinging door that led to the kitchen. When he got to the stair he looked out the window. What was that? Was it a man looking at the house from across the street? No; couldn't be. He looked again. No- it wasn't a man- it was a woman! But who was it? He tried to make her out, but it was still snowing enough to obstruct his view. Then- she was gone. He shrugged and went down to his room to do an impression of Harry, falling fast asleep in his chair for the rest of the afternoon.

Larkin awoke to the sound of Harry getting up out of his chair to go to bed. Larkin could hear his footsteps as he made his way to the other side of the house. That was his cue to do the same. As Larkin got in bed, he thought of his parents again, and the reason he was even in Washington, D.C. It wasn't really an education, and not really to find information, it was really to combat the Masons and finally, it was really-The Eraser. He hadn't thought of it much lately, being too immersed in his job, his women, and his new life. He leaned over the side of his bed, pulled up the covers, and looked underneath. The case was there gathering dust. In the morning, he'd get it out. Besides, he wanted to see something he didn't think he remembered ever reading before.

Larkin slept well after the turkey and all the trimmings. He ate breakfast rather quickly, listening to the radio as he wolfed down his cereal. They had begun to play Christmas music already. He loved it and now an Italian song called "Gesu Bambino" was playing. He drifted off into another of his daydreams about past Christmases, but awoke from it in his last bite of cornflakes. He got up to take the bowl to the sink and tried to find a place to set it, as the chores, especially the dishes, were starting to pile up with him being "gimped-up". He found a place for it and turned his attention to the task at hand. He was determined to look in the case today.

He hobbled into his bedroom, got on his knees, and reached under his bed to pull out his suitcase. He pulled it out quicker than he probably should have and sent dust bunnies running around his legs. Brushing some of them aside and standing up, he placed the case on his bed, which bounced up and down making the springs squeak. He opened the case with reservation. Not because of fear, or even hate, but because he didn't really like the task of being the "Keeper." There in the open case lay the life he was destined to follow. He had left some of the boxes at home. They were just too large to bring along. But the small ones and pertinent items, he had brought with him. On top was the Journal, which he sat aside. Under it, he saw The Eraser box, but he took out "the" Gift Box instead. Opening it, he took out the letter from Nairne to Lawtin Senior. The other day he had realized he had never read it. It was the original letter that had accompanied The Eraser. He unfolded it carefully. It was in surprisingly great condition and was like the day Nairne had penned it. He read,

---

"My dear friend Lawtin, It is with great excitement that I send this gift to you. I surmise you shall be the only person in the colonies to posses one. And if not, for I hear of others who have tried to formulate one, this one I guarantee is of better quality than any other. I pray you do not let your children have it, for it is meant for you in your work. The Eraser will remove marks of any lead pencil leaving no sign of its former appearance. Therefore, new writing may then be done in its place. It is amazing! Use it as you may need, for I have many more for sale at three schillings! I ask you to consider investing in my new endeavor, as I expect to sell many of them. Our first run is of 100 and I have orders for most. Best wishes to you and yours this Christmas, Edward. Sept. 1770."

"Hum," Larkin said out loud to himself. In this piece of history, he now saw how Lawtin Sr. got the idea to keep the Eraser to himself and was glad that Nairne had suggested it in this note. The fact that an eraser actually removed marks seemed so natural and simple to Larkin, but for the inventor and his ancestors, it was truly an amazing thing. My how far technology had come! He folded the letter up and put it back in the Gift Box. It really had not given him any more information, except to cement in one of the pieces of the puzzle called, "The Family Palmer."

He refreshed his memory as to what he had packed in the suitcase and placed it all on the bed one at a time: the Journal, the Gift Box, The Eraser, the contents of the Mail Box and the Barn Box, and last of all, the family tree. He had brought these along for a purpose and that was to explore all of the "loose ends", especially the information in the Mail Box and the Barn Box. Heck, he had only read two of the fifteen documents he saw in the barn box! He looked at his genealogy once again. Considering he had found so many things these past few years, he began to wonder if he *had* inherited genes from his Grandma Mary, who was always finding things for people. Anything else he would find was only there for him to find out.

Someone knocked at the back door. He looked up to the ceiling in his room as if at the door. "Shoot!" he said to himself. He had really wanted no interruptions today. Harry went to answer the door remembering his promise to ward off the "triple threat" of Larkin's' life. It was Pilar. She had not been around since before Thanksgiving. Harry greeted her warmly but said, "Hello, Pilar. I hate to tell you this, but Larkin has not been feeling well. Would you mind if I let him rest today and have you come back later?" Harry did not specify a return date and Larkin smiled as he overheard from his room this tactical maneuver. Larkin could sense her disappointment by the tone of her voice when she said, "I'm so sorry to hear that, Harry. Why, yes. I will come back some other time. Tell him I said, "Hello"."
Shutting the door he said to her, "I will, Pilar. Goodbye."

For the moment, Larkin was free and clear. Harry came to the stair and called down, "Did you hear that, Larkin?"
"I did Harry, and thanks!
"You okay down there?"

"Yes, just doing some work. Or should I say- research."

"Need any input?"

"No thanks, Harry. But if I come onto anything I'll let you know."

"Okay." Harry had learned to give the boy space. He knew he did good work that way and if he wanted help he'd ask for it, so he left the landing and went back into his kitchen.

Larkin picked up the genealogy again. He looked at his mother's side and noticed the familiar names from town and almost instinctively asked his mom, as if she were there, "Mom, who was Mariah Button?" But, she wasn't there and he knew he missed her. Looking back farther on the chart he saw a couple names scribbled to the side of Elizabeth Palmer- John Hall and Marcy Hall. Who were they? It must have been an addition by his uncle, Harry, before he died. It sure looked like his writing anyway. He thought, 'Hey, I wonder if I'm related to Harry Hall? Naw!' Going on in his thoughts, he saw a name that might give him a clue- Major R. Button. Was he the one who passed down the watch? Was he the lone Mason in the family? And, by marriage at that? He took the watch out of his pocket. He knew nothing about it except that his Grandpa had received it as a gift at his retirement. He could see the obvious things about it, it was old, it was fashioned for a Mason, and it was in good shape. Once again, he looked at the outside, turning it over and over again to see if there was an inscription or anything else. Nothing. Sally had brought nim his magnifying glass from work, so he picked it up and looked again on both sides of the watch. Nothing was to be found, except the Masonic Cross symbol. 'Well,' he thought, 'I guess I'll try the inside.' Opening the case, he saw- nothing, just a watch's dial and a blank inside cover. Sadly, he was about to close it when an idea came to him. 'Wait a minute,' he chuckled at the irony of the statement, 'what about under the timepiece?' Carefully, he separated the movement from the case. He laid it on the table and looked at the back side of the case. At the top was the name of the watchmaker and the date of its manufacture: 1820. On the bottom, were the initials: R.B. "AHA!" Larkin said out loud. He realized he had said that rather loudly and listened to hear if Harry would react to it. Thankfully, he did not. Just as carefully, or even more so, he placed the movement back into the case and snapped it together. It still worked! Larkin had done a good job on that, but more importantly, he had found out who the original owner of the watch was- Major R. Button! And his was the name circled on the genealogy that he used to find the button and press it to discover the "Glory Box". Were these just a bunch of random facts or coincidences? And, what did they prove? And who gave the watch to his Grandpa Button? Did the Freemasons via the Buttons try to infiltrate the Palmer family by marriage? Was his grandpa Button a *spy*? Did his mother know? Was it all an evil scheme?

After all of these questions flying around his head, Larkin was ready for a break. He left all of the things lying out on his bed and started upstairs, but he took his genealogy with him, so he could ask Harry about the Hall names. He walked into Harry's kitchen with the genealogy in hand. As he sat at the table, Harry looked up from his paper and asked peering over his glasses, "What have you got there, Larkin?"

"It's my family genealogy."

"Oh, that's interesting. Mine's in the other room."

"Really? I have a question for you then. Look at this." Larkin pointed to the two names of Marcy and John Hall. "Do these two names look familiar, Harry?"

Harry's eyes lit up. He put his paper down and said, "Hum, sounds familiar. I think they do, Larkin. Just a minute!"

Harry got up and went to his desk. Picking up the desk pad, he pulled a large folded piece of paper from underneath. The pad slapped back down as he turned to come back to the kitchen and he unfolded the document on the way. He pulled his glasses back in front of his eyes and said with surprise, "Yes, yes, here they are. They were from Rhode Island! We are related, Larkin!" He sat it down on top of Larkin's and pointed. They compared the two and indeed they were related. Harry said, "I knew there was something the first day I saw you at the Smithsonian! I just knew it, Larkin!"

"This is amazing! I'm living in D.C. with a long lost relative! Mom and Dad won't believe it."

"And as far as I know Larkin, you, and your family alone, are the only relatives I have. I thought I was all alone."

Harry began to cry. It was a special moment for both of them. Larkin put his arm around the old man. "Be happy, Harry. I am."

"So am I, Larkin. Thank you so much for bringing this to me. It means a lot. More than you will ever know." Harry turned to face him and gave him a hug. Just then, someone else knocked on the back door. Unfortunately for Larkin, Sally had seen them through the window of the kitchen and was smiling as Larkin went to answer the door.

She said smiling snidely as she walked in, "That was very touching, Larkin."

He laughed and answered her jest saying, "Oh, we just found out I am Harry's only living relative."

"Really? How did you find this out?"

Walking into the kitchen, Larkin directed her to the two charts. Sally knew instantly what it meant and she was thrilled. Her face beamed as much as Harry's. She had seen what the death of Harry's wife had meant to him and the affect of it on his life. This, well, this meant new life for Harry; a purpose; a tie to another of his kind; a kinship that he always felt was there. Indeed, Larkin was like the son he never had. "Wow, this is amazing! But how?"she asked.

"Oh, I just saw it and questioned Harry. That's all."

"Well, it's truly a miracle that God has placed you here at this time, Larkin, at this place," she said.

Larkin thought about her statement. She was right. And she placed the credit where it should be-with God. He was beginning to really like this girl.

They all sat down and talked, mostly about the weather, which Sally said was still bad, and that only trucks with four wheel drive and emergency vehicles were able to get anywhere, except hers, of course. The time passed and after about two hours Larkin had to pee. He stood up and said, "Excuse me, but I have to go to the rest room. Be right back."

He started toward the basement and realized he had left all of his things out of the case on the bed. He panicked hoping he would not be followed down to his room. He went there first, threw all the stuff into the suitcase, closed it, and slid it under the bed. Just in time too, because as he made his way to the privy, Sally was on her way down the steps.

She saw him go in and asked as she passed the bathroom door, "Can I get a drink of water, Larkin?"

He stood there smiling and said, "Sure, Sally. Help yourself."

He hurried and as he completed the task at hand, zipped up quickly. As he came out of the bathroom, Sally had the glass to her lips and was pointing at all the dishes in the sink. "What's all this?"

"Dishes," said Larkin with a grin.

Sally looked at him and said, "Smart butt!" She rolled up her sleeves, bent over and got the soap out from under the sink. Turning on the water, she plugged the sink, squirted some soap in it and started to sort the dishes. Bubbles popped up over the edge of the sink as the water ran in.

Larkin said to her, "Sally, you don't have to do that."

"I know, but you have a seat and talk to me while I do them. Besides, I like bubbles!"

He went over to the table, pulled out the chair and sat down. He said so seriously that she turned when he started to speak, "You know Sally, um, I mean, I really enjoy being around you. Thanks for coming over today."

She smiled, and with a grateful yet pleased look said, "I'm glad to be here with you. I feel the same way. Look! I'll even do your dishes!" He laughed and they continued to talk until she finished up. They all fit in the dish rack so she just let them air dry and she sat down across from Larkin at the table. She asked him in a somber tone, "I heard from Harry that you lost your girlfriend to an awful car accident earlier this year. I'm sorry, Larkin. It must be hard for you."

He hung his head and replied, "Yeah. Her name was Ginny. I was in the hospital and she was coming to see me. A truck came over the ridge in the wrong lane. She and her mother were killed instantly."

He began to cry and pushed back a tear to the side of his face. Sally got up out of her chair, came over to him and stood by the side of his chair. Moving her long red hair out of the way, she took his head and hugged it by her side and said, "That sounds terrible. But why were you in the hospital?"

He raised his head and placed his hands on her hips shoving her back a bit so he could look her in the eyes. Not wanting her to know what the entire situation was all about he just said, "Let me put it this way Sally, if God doesn't get the guy that put me there first, I'll get him."

That statement really shook her as she had never seen him act with hostility toward anyone before. He was always nice, kind, and pleasant towards everyone, even if they had disturbed him. In fact, he was the most patient man she had ever met. She didn't know what to make of it. She did know one thing though- he meant it.

Larkin got up out of his chair and grabbed her firmly by the waist. Placing his hand softly on her cheek, he bent down and placed his lips on hers ever so softly. She responded in kind and looked into his eyes after that first kiss, and she pressed him for another, which he now was glad to do. After the second though, he stopped and said, "I'm sorry. I shouldn't have done that. I guess I got caught up in something I shouldn't have. I just can't make any kind of commitment right now." He fell back into his chair placing his elbows on his knees with his head in his hands.

Sally understood. She kindly and softly said as she bent down towards him, "Larkin, I understand. I don't expect anything. Let's give it time. I like you and we are friends. Don't worry."

He looked back up at her with a smile and shook his head in affirmation. Then he said, "Thanks for doing my dishes."

It broke the tone and she just slapped him on the back of his head as he tried to avoid the half-hearted blow. She laughed and straightened up asking, "Want to get something to eat with me? I'll drive us to the best pizza place in town and I can guarantee there won't be a crowd! Not with this weather."

"Think we can make it?"

"I can get that truck anywhere. Sure we can make it!"

"Then let's go. I haven't been out of here since I got the cast." He grabbed his coat from the rack and they headed up the stairs.

Harry heard them coming and said, "I was wondering where you two disappeared to. Are you headed out?"

Sally grabbed her coat from Harry's kitchen as Larkin responded in the affirmative. "Yup. Going out for a while. I have a bit of cabin-fever here, Harry," Larkin said.

Winking at him he said, "I don't blame you, Larkin. Be careful out there." Yelling after them as they made their way to the truck Harry said, "Don't get stuck. I have no way to help you guys!"

Sally yelled back at him, "Don't worry, Harry. I can handle it!" And she could and much more.

Chapter 15

The Third Degree

The Masonic Temple

Sally and Larkin made their way to Luigi's. At least that's where Sally thought they were going. But she was wrong. As they made their way toward L Street, suddenly a snow plow appeared behind them. It was like the driver didn't see them- or did he? The plow came up behind them about 20 MPH faster than Sally, picked up the rear of the little blue Datsun and catapulted it up in the air! It flew like so many snowflakes, flittering in the wind. Sally didn't have time to react and the truck up-ended. Fortunately, it hit a huge pile of snow on the corner of 18th and just stuck straight up, nose down to the ground. The two passengers were belted in, and the only thing that flew around the cab was her purse and, of course, the kitty litter in the back! It billowed into the air, creating a giant plume of grey bentonite ash that covered her truck and the sidewalk beneath it. It was a mess. Larkin saw the face of the plow driver as he made the turn and drove away. Yes, that's right. He drove away. He had no intention of slowing down or helping them. He had done it on purpose!

"Sally! Are you alright?" Larkin yelled to her, as the noise from the revved up engine was deafening.
"Yes! Just a sec."

She pushed her body back from the wheel and reached forward, turning the key to the off position. It stopped. They looked at each other in shock. Each was covered with chunks of litter and they looked like ghosts of grey. Sally began to laugh. Larkin brushed some of it from his hair and began to laugh too, as they hung there like bats strapped to a wire.
He said, "Let me help you out of that belt." He reached down past her waist and unsnapped the belt holding her in. He lifted himself up and did the same. Somehow, he got the door to open on his side. But he was afraid to open it lest the whole truck flip back upright from its perch against the snow.

He looked at Sally and asked before he tried it, "What do you think?"
Without missing a beat she said, "Go for it."

He opened the door and – nothing happened, no problem. He slid out head first and landed in the mixture of snow and litter. Taking the time to brush off a bit first, he then proceeded to go around and let Sally out of her side. He opened the door slowly. As he did, out she slid. The truck didn't move. He helped her brush off too, and they both went around and faced the truck from the street. It looked funny sitting there with both doors open nose down in the snow. A car drove up behind them and they realized they had been the only people there while this all occurred. The driver rolled down the window and asked, "Are you two okay?"

"Yes, Sir," answered Larkin.

"What the hell happened?"

"Snowplow hit us."

"And he didn't stop? What an asshole!" He started to drive away, but slowed and asked, "Want me to call a tow truck?"

"Yes, please," answered Sally.

"Where's a cop when you need one?" said the driver closing his window and leaving them alone.

Sally came over to Larkin, put her arm around him and asked, "What do you make of this? He was trying to do that, wasn't he?"

Even though he knew better, he answered, "I don't know, Sally. I don't know."

A cop showed up about the same time the tow truck arrived and they told him what happened. But, then he questioned them as if Sally had done something wrong. "Did you have anything to drink tonight, Miss?"

Larkin didn't like his methods and said, "Officer, we just told you that a city snowplow came up from behind us and ran right over us. And no, neither of us has had anything to drink."

He looked at Larkin and said, "Shut up, Kid. I wasn't asking you. If you don't, I'll run you in. Now Miss, I'd like you to come over here and walk a straight line for me."

Larkin threw up his hands in disgust and walked toward the back side of the truck. The cop asked him, "Hey, where are you going?"

Sassing the cop back he said, "I thought you didn't want to talk to me? I'm going to show you the marks on the truck from our yellow snowplows, Officer."

Intrigued by what Larkin had said, the cop dropped his misinformed interrogation of Sally and came over to where Larkin was standing. Sure enough, on the whole undercarriage and the back bumper were yellow paint marks- from a city snow plow. Pointing at it Larkin said, "See?"

The cop just said, "Well, I'll be. I didn't believe you. Be right back." He went over to his black and white and called the station on the radio.

"Hey, Sarge. I got a hit and run over on L and 18th. Looks like one of the city plows hit a car and just took off." The two kids couldn't hear what the reply was because the cop jumped in and shut the door. At least the cop wouldn't give *them* the ticket. He came back to the truck in a minute. "The Sarge says there were no city plows in this area. He doesn't know who hit you. Sorry, but you'll have to get out of this mess yourself."

The two just looked at each other in disbelief. Larkin followed him to his car and said to him, "What? I suppose we did this as a prank?"

The cop ignored him, got in his car and drove away. Sally couldn't believe her eyes and ears. "Why did he just leave, Larkin? Why didn't he help us?"

"Because it *was* a city plow and they're covering it up. But why?"

Larkin walked back over by the truck. Closing both the doors he said to Sally, "Get on the other side up about half way on the snow bank. I'll do the same." She saw what he had in mind and climbed up the hill of snow. Larkin stuck out his good foot onto the mid-section of the truck bed. Sally did the same. He said, "On the count of three, push with all you've got- one, two, and three." They pushed and it didn't take much effort as the light, little Datsun began its decent back to the street. The front end teetered on the weight of the whole vehicle and it fell straight back on its tires bouncing once as it hit- "whump, bump." Perfect. The tow truck driver had watched them do all of this without saying a word. He got in his truck and drove away as silently as the cop had.

They got back into the truck and Sally turned the key. It started and she asked, "Are you still in the mood for Pizza?"

"Not really."

"Wanna go home?"

"I think so."

"Okay." She put the truck in gear, let go of the clutch and headed back toward Larkin's.

They didn't say much on the way home. Both of them watched the operation of the truck, curious if it was road worthy. It seemed to be. Thinking about what just had occurred, each one of them was more in shock than anything else. Each of them didn't want to be alone. When they got there, Larkin wondered what to say so that Sally would come in with him. She wondered what to say to get an invitation. In unison they each asked, "Do you want to..." They laughed and Larkin asked, "Want to come in?"

"Yes. I don't want to go home."

Larkin got out and went to the back fence facing the sidewalk. It opened to the sidewalk and had one small space in which she could park her truck.

Fortunately, the snow wasn't too deep there for him to pull the fence open enough for her to drive in. Harry observed all of this from the kitchen window and wondered why. They hadn't been gone long enough to have had a pizza. She parked and Larkin closed the fence. He took her hand and they walked in together. Harry's curiosity got the best of him and he met them at the door. Instantly, he knew something was wrong by their demeanor. Looking shaken, they came in and stomped their feet and tried to brush off the remainder of the kitty litter. Harry smiled a bit at this, but saw the seriousness on their faces. Sally spoke first. "Harry, we were attacked by a snowplow."

"What? How were you "attacked" by a snowplow?"

"Let's sit down," said Larkin, "my leg is killing me."

They made their way to Harry's kitchen table and sat down. Larkin resumed the story. "We were going to Luigi's and suddenly a city plow came up behind us. He lifted the truck right up into the air and just threw it into a snow bank. You should have seen it Harry! It was standing there right on its nose, doors wide open. Anyway, the cops came and didn't do a thing. In fact, he claimed there were no city plows in that area! He even blamed Sally!"

"What? That sounds almost- suspicious."

Sally looked at Larkin. Larkin had not said anything about his suspicions, figuring he had to keep his mouth shut about that. Harry continued when he said nothing, "Do you want me to do some "private investigating" Larkin?"

"It does sound like something is up, but, what? Why would someone in the city pick on us? It doesn't make sense. I don't think you need to do anything, Harry. I'd say some city driver got careless and they are just trying to cover up for him."

"Yeah, that's probably the case."

Knowing differently, Larkin agreed with him to close the conversation. "Yeah, so don't waste your time, Harry."

"Okay." He turned to Sally and said, "Never a dull moment with Larkin as a boyfriend is there, Sally?"

She looked at Larkin. He blushed. Sally asked Larkin softly, "Is that what we are?"

"Harry, are you jumping the gun a bit there?" asked Larkin.

"Well from what I see, I'd call it that."

Harry got up and went to the stove. Picking up the tea pot he poured himself another cup. Larkin didn't say anything about it, avoided the statement, and said to Sally, "Let's go down to the basement, Sally. I guess we need to talk." She got up first and headed to the stairs. Larkin said to Harry. "Sorry about the mess, Harry."

He pointed to the melted snow and litter mixture. Harry said, "I meant to ask you about that."

Larkin said laughing, "I'll tell you about it later."

They got downstairs and Sally said to him, "Larkin, I need to clean up and I don't see that happening unless I get in the shower and change these clothes. Do you have anything I can put on?"   Larkin thought a second and answered, "Yeah, Mom gave me some flannel PJ's you can wear."

She headed toward the bathroom. Larkin said, "There's a new towel in there and I'll get you the PJ's."

She went in and closed the door. The water came on and Larkin heard her get in. He knocked and she called out over the noise of the shower, "Just lay them on the sink, Larkin. The door's open."

Larkin didn't really want to go in, because he was just too shy, but he did and he just had to look because, well, he was a man, but he didn't see anything except the outline of her auburn hair against the shower curtain. He sat the PJ's on the sink and said. "There you go, Sally."

"Thanks!"

He left the room and went out to the kitchen. He was really flustered after that. He hadn't felt like that since Ginny. He put on a pot of coffee. Sally came out drying her hair as she walked toward him. "That felt good. I had to get that mud out of my hair. I guess kitty litter makes a mess when used in trucks for traction."

They laughed and then the pot of coffee started to perk. They sat down and just looked at each other waiting for the other to say something, just like minutes before when they had come into the house. This time Larkin said, "A lot has happened today, Sally. It seems like God throws things at us as if He wants us to be together for some reason. Like I said before, I don't know if I'm ready for it. Maybe He thinks I am and I need to move on. To be honest Sally, I'll have to think on it."

She stuck her hands across the little table and took Larkin's. With tenderness he had not seen or felt since Ginny she said, "I understand and I really don't know where I am in this either. I do know that I care for you and I'll pray about it."

Larkin smiled. Here was a woman of faith that was spunky, caring, resilient, hard working, and so many other things that he liked, and best of all, simply beautiful. She leaned across the table and gave him another kiss, this time more tender, more like she loved him. The pot began to boil on the stove which broke the spell for the moment and Larkin got up and grabbed it off the burner. She got up and went to the cupboard and got two cups. They didn't say anything. She looked at him and he at her. They poured the coffee and went into the living room. Larkin turned on the old radio. She sat on the sofa and put her cup on the coffee table. He did the same. Sitting next to her, he nervously reached for his cup again and took another sip and then sat his cup back down next to hers. Leaning back, it only seemed natural for him to put his arm around her, which he did. She snuggled into him and they just sat there not saying a word, just listening to the music. Finally, they fell asleep.

Larkin awoke first as the announcer came on with the first broadcast of the day. It was still dark in the room as the sun had not yet come through the small basement windows in his room. He laid Sally down with her head on the arm rest and made his way to the bathroom. He was still a mess. He jumped in the shower and got cleaned up. He forgot his clean clothes and when he finished had to put a towel around himself as he went to his room to retrieve some. Sally was awake with her head still down and saw him sneak down the hall. She peeked and smiled as he went past. He didn't notice.

While he went into his room to dress, she went into the kitchen and began to make breakfast. Someone knocked at his back door. Larkin didn't hear it and Harry was still asleep in his room. Sally sat down the spoon she was using to fix gravy on the stove, turned down the heat, and went to the door. It was Pilar. She was stunned when Sally came to the door in Larkin's PJ's and said to her, "Good morning, Pilar. Can I help you?"

Pilar handed her a newspaper and said, "Good morning, Sally. No. I just brought Larkin his paper and was going to see if he wanted to have breakfast. But as I see he already has company, please just tell him I was here."

Sally smiled taking the paper from her and said, "Thanks, Pilar. I will." She shut the door and skipped down the stairs. Pilar walked away, unhappy, but she wasn't going to give up.

Larkin came out of his room as she came back down the stairs and asked, "Where'd you go?"

"Pilar brought this for you."

She handed him the paper as she passed him in the hall and went into the kitchen. Larkin just rolled his eyes and said, "Well, that was nice of her." He changed the subject. "We need to get you some clothes. I have some old blue jeans that might fit, but we'll have to cut off the legs. I have a tee shirt and sweater that will work too, I think."

He sat down at the table. She brought biscuits and gravy over to him and sat down with him to eat. He got up and filled their coffee cups with reheated coffee from the night before. She was eating and smiling coyly at him as he sat back down. "What?" he asked.

"You know what," she replied.

"What do you mean?"

"Pilar."

"Oh. Well, I know she likes me. And she has been so helpful. But, I have never led her on, and I want to be honest with you Sally, there's another girl named Ellie that comes around too."

"Oh yeah, I remember her. They are no problem, Larkin. I know where I stand, and I know you. Besides, I'm not the jealous type."

"Good, I mean, you have nothing to be jealous of or about."

She got up with her empty plate and said slapping him on the arm, "I better not. Now, where are those clothes?"

Larkin got up and sat his plate next to hers on the counter. She stopped by the sink. They looked into each other's eyes and couldn't help it; they kissed. He wanted to pick her up and carry her off to his bedroom. And she wanted him to. But instead, he said, "I'll, um, I'll put your dirty clothes in the washer if you go into my room and get out the pair of pants in the bottom drawer. I'll bring the scissors."

"Okay."

Sally ran into his room and he picked her clothes up off the bathroom floor. Placing them in the washer, he pulled the dial and it began to fill. She came out with the jeans in her hand and said, "You think these are going to fit? You have such a skinny waist. My butt will never fit in these."

Larkin laughed and said, "You'll see." Taking them from her he held them up in front of her. Marking the legs first, he took the scissor and cut them off to her length. He handed them back and said, "Go try them."

She went back into his room and put them on. She was surprised, because they did fit. He called out, "They fit, didn't they?"

"Yes! Where's the shirt and sweater?"

"Oh, just a sec, can I come in?"

She was standing there with no top, braless and half- naked. "Sure," she said.

When he entered the room she was facing him. He blushed and turned around saying, "Sally, I thought you said I could come in?"

"I did." Coming up to him, she put her arms around him from the back and said, "I didn't say I was decent."

He turned, and grasping her by her arms, pulled her towards him.

They kissed, moved toward the bed and forgot all about the shirt and sweater for a brief moment. She fell onto the bed, but Larkin stopped short. "Sally, you know we can't do this. As much as we want to, we must wait. I want to be a virgin the day I get married. Are you? I mean, don't you?"

She stopped, sat up and thought about it for a moment, amazed at what he had revealed and wondering if she should trust him with that much information. She was afraid he'd laugh, but she said, "Yes. I am and I do."

She got back up covering herself with her arms saying, "Where's my shirt?"

Turning away, he went to the drawers and opened up the middle, and getting out a tee, he shook it out to show her what it said, and said, "It's one of my favorite places, "Baseball Hall of Fame, Cooperstown, NY.""He threw it to her as she stood there shivering in the cool basement bedroom, hunched over with her arms folded down in front of her. She smiled and grabbed it, having to expose herself to him again as she caught it. She looked at him, slid it over her head and pulled her long hair out from inside it. He said laughing, "Sorry. I couldn't resist doing that."

She went over to him as he went to the closet, and he took out the sweatshirt he had in mind. She saw it was another baseball souvenir. This blue and white one said, "New York Yankees". Larkin looked at her. "That looks good, but you need socks." He went through the drawer and found a pair and made her sit on the bed. She objected, but he took each foot and placed the big socks on her little feet, rolling up the tops several times to make it work. Seeing his tenderness in this, she got up hugged him and gave him another kiss. They separated, looked at each other and smiled. Larkin was lost in the moment, but was about to be awakened from this daydream, brought back into the reality of the Family Palmer and into the reality of- The Eraser!

Someone was pounding on the back door. "Open up. This is the police!"

Harry went to the door first and opened it. Larkin came up as soon as he could with Sally following. "Is this the home of the owner of that pickup parked on the property?"

Harry answered, "No, Sir. It does not belong to me. It is owned by the friend of my renter."

Larkin came to the top of the stairs and addressed the cop. "What seems to be the problem, Officer?"

"I have a warrant for the arrest of Sally Britt for failure to report an accident and leaving the scene."

"WHAT?" shouted Larkin.

Harry tried to calm him down by saying, "Those charges are incorrect officer. There was an officer present at the scene."

"Well, she's going to have to tell it to the judge. Are you Sally?" he asked seeing her behind Larkin.

"Yes, Officer, but this is a trumped up charge, and who levied it?"

"Ask the Sergeant. He knows, but you'll have to come with me, Miss Britt."

She stepped forward and looked at Larkin. He said to her, "I'll call Mr. Shipley. We'll be there soon."

He addressed the cop, "Which station are you taking her to, Officer?"

"Thirteenth precinct," he replied.

Sally angrily went with the cop and they headed to his car. Larkin ran down the stairs and got his coat. Then he stopped at the phone and called Mr. Shipley. He spoke with his maid and told her all about the situation. She told him she'd convey the information and have him call right back. Larkin sat down. He was irate. Harry came down the stairs and asked him, "Is there anything we should talk about, Larkin?"

"What do you mean, Harry?"

"Why would anyone target Sally like this? She is innocent of all of it. And like you said yesterday, why would anyone attack you with a snowplow unless they wanted you dead? Is it *you* someone is after, Larkin?"

Larkin went silent. After a pause he said to him, "I'm sorry, Harry, but I can't tell you. They would come after you too. In fact, you may be on their list already. Remember the incident at church?"

"On *whose* list, Larkin? *Who* is after you?"

"The Illuminati. And the Masons, too, of course."

Harry's face dropped as he said, "Oh. Them." Harry sat down with a thud. "You know, I can't help with that."

"I know. It is too big for you and you don't need to know the particulars. It goes all the way back to our ancestors; the ones we were talking about the other day. And that's all you need to know, Harry, but I'll take care of it and put a stop to it. I always do."

"But, *how*?"

"It's not for you to know. Just trust me."

"Okay. If you say so, Larkin. I trust you."

The phone rang and Larkin picked up. "Hello? Mr. Shipley?"

"Yes, Larkin, it's me. I don't know what has happened here, but I'll have my chauffer take us down to the station. I'll pick you up at Harry's in a few minutes."

"Thank you, Sir."

They hung up and Larkin said to Harry, "Mr. Shipley is coming to pick me up. If he doesn't pull enough strings, I will."

Larkin got up and went up toward Harry's front door. Harry followed him up and they both just sat there and waited. While they did, Harry asked him, "Are things getting serious with you two kids?"

Larkin looked at him and said, "Much more than I ever intended, Harry, but she is perfect for me and I think I just may love her. I don't know why God sent her to me, but He has and I need to deal with the timing."

"Oh."

"Don't worry about us, Harry. We have it under control."

"Okay. I'll trust you in that, too."

The limo pulled up in front of the door. As Larkin went out the door he said to Harry, "Don't worry. It will be fine."

Harry just nodded his head. Larkin held onto the rail as he limped down to the driver who was waiting to open the door. When Larkin got there, the driver tipped the brim of his hat at him and opened the door. Larkin got in next to Mr. Shipley. Shipley asked, "What does this all seem to be about, Larkin? I'm sure Sally did nothing to deserve this charge."

"You're right, Sir. And I can take care of it. I know what it is and who's behind it. If you will allow me to speak with the Sergeant alone when we get there, we will be out in less than five minutes. You'll have to trust me, Sir."

"As always, I do trust you and I will do as you wish. But if you should need me..." The Secretary stopped short as if to offer his service to Larkin.

Larkin said, "Thank you, Sir."

The station was not far away, the snow was manageable for his driver, and it didn't take long to get there. The two men got out and went toward the door. The steps were slippery and Larkin almost fell on them due to his cast, but slowly, he made it in. He went straight to the front desk. "I'm Larkin Palmer. I'd like to see the Sergeant about Sally Britt."

The desk cop just smiled, pointed and said, "Have a seat."

Rather than sit, the two men withdrew to a spot by the elevator and stood talking about the storm and the canceled dinner. Larkin thanked Mr. Shipley again for the wonderful dinner that was delivered. "You are most welcome. I would like to extend an invitation to you and Harry again for Christmas if you will be around, and of course Sally, if she gets out of jail," he said smiling.

Larkin nodded and just then the front desk cop said, "Palmer. Go to the second door on the right."

"Be right back," Larkin said confidently to his boss.

He left Mr. Shipley and proceeded to go down the hall and into the door. The Sergeant's name on the door was Ben Steiner. When he went in, Steiner told him, "Sit down, Palmer, and let's talk."

"Okay Sergeant, but I already know what this is all about. No need for the third degree. I've had a lifetime of this. Let's not play games. You'll release Sally and drop all the charges. And this will be the last time you harass me or anyone I come into contact with while I live in D.C. Let law enforcement in the area know it, too. Got that Sergeant?"

The cop laughed at him and replied, "Do you know who you are dealing with here, Boy?"

Larkin smiled and said, "Do you know *what* you are dealing with here Sergeant?"

"What do you mean?" The sergeant got a little nervous.

"I know your name, Sergeant Steiner."

Suddenly, the Sergeants' tone got much better and realizing that what he was doing wasn't worth his life, the man picked up the phone. He dialed the front desk, "Martin, release the Britt girl and drop all charges. I don't want to ever see her in here again."

He hung up the phone and said to Larkin, "And the same for you, Palmer. I won't be seeing you again."

"Thank you, Sergeant Steiner."

The young man got up, kept his eye on the cop and left the room. The Sergeant just went back to work and ignored him. Behind him was the Masonic square and compass on a plaque. Larkin was always right. He felt like he was becoming world renowned.

Larkin went out to the lobby and Mr. Shipley saying, "Sally will be out in a minute, Sir."

"No problems, Larkin?"

"No, Sir. Just a misunderstanding."

The cop at the desk overheard the two men and just smiled. In a minute, Sally was coming out to greet them. She asked Larkin, "What took you so long?"

Larkin laughed, put his arm around her and they began to walk out down the hall. The Secretary paused as he didn't know what to make of this development in their relationship. He had to catch up to them and asked, "Can I assume you two have been spending some time together?"

They laughed and said in unison, "Yes, Mr. Shipley."

"Good. Good," he said as he placed his hat upon his head.

They got into the Limo and started back towards Harry's house. That was when they got the third degree. Mr. Shipley asked, "This seems sudden, Miss Britt; Larkin. I hope you will keep the tone at the Smithsonian purely professional?"

"Don't worry, Sir," answered Larkin first, "we shall."

"Yes, Sir," said Sally.

"Good. Good."

He addressed Sally, "I have invited you all to my home for Christmas dinner. I hope that this time the weather cooperates with my plans. Will you be available, Sally?"

"I had no other plans, Sir."

"Good then."

The driver pulled up to the curb at Harry's. Larkin said to Mr. Shipley as the two got out, "Thank you for your assistance Mr. Shipley, and for the ride. We don't know what we would have done without you."

"You are quite welcome, Larkin. Please feel free to call upon me at any time."

"Thank you, Sir." He shut the door to the limo and off it went.

Larkin and Sally went up the steps and Harry opened the door. He said, "Well, that didn't take long."

"I told you so. You just have to trust me."

"I do. I mean, I will," said Harry.

"So do I," said Sally, "but Larkin, there's more to this than you are telling me, right?"

Harry and Larkin looked at each other. He didn't answer at first, but delayed and finally said, "Come on in and sit down."

They walked into Harry's living room and all took a seat, but Larkin got back up. He said to them both, "I have never divulged the information I am about to tell you to anyone out of the family, except for Ginny. I expected to marry her and my family thought it best when things began to get scary, as they have here the past couple of days. I figured I'd have to do this again someday if I ever got involved with someone, (he paused and looked at Sally), and rather than have you two give me the third degree, I had better tell you. For the safety of us all, and I can't stress this any greater, you must never, ever, tell anyone what I am about to tell you. Understand?"

They didn't answer, but just nodded in the affirmative. They knew it was a command. He began the long story and briefly hit the high points about the family, The Eraser and its curse, and that he was now the "Keeper" in charge of the mission forced upon the Palmer men. The two listeners in the room never budged nor asked a question, but sat spellbound by the entire story. Larkin finally finished and asked, "Any questions?"

"I thought the Freemasons were just a club of guys getting together for fun and do charitable work. Can you tell me more about them?" asked Sally.

"Sure, but I want it to come from a Mason, not from me. Harry, can you tell her a little about the background of Freemasonry?"

"Well, we *are* a secret society. People blame lots of things on us that aren't true at all, but since I've met Larkin, I have thought a bit about our order. We aren't blameless. It goes all the way back to Egypt and along the way we have brought in many pagan ideas and beliefs. We accept anyone that believes in a god into membership.

It can even be the devil and I have to admit, I don't know all of it either. We only learn as we become of a higher degree. There have been evil men in the organization in the past and I have to admit, we are not a Christian organization. Therefore, we must be anti-Christ, I guess."

"Does that tell you I'm not just some Christian zealot out to spread rumors about Freemasonry? Heck, even Seward knew and so did the anti-Freemason movement of his day that it was evil in its beginnings and also in what it has become. Any other questions?"

Then Sally asked, "Where is it?"

"The Eraser? Oh, it's downstairs."

"Downstairs? Really? Can I see it?"

"Yes, but you must promise me, both of you, to never touch it while alone. Someday I'll let you read the Journal and show you the Mail Box obits. Then you will understand its power."

"We promise," said Sally.

"Me too, Larkin," said Harry.

"Well, come on downstairs then."

"I have a question Larkin," said Harry.

"Yes, Harry?"

"This fits very nicely into all of your research, doesn't it?"

"I'll have to tell you much more than I wish to really answer that question Harry, but yes, it does."

"I figured."

They went into his room and he pulled out the suitcase from under the bed. Opening the top, he pulled The Eraser out and placed the box into Sally's hands. "Open it," he said.

She opened The Eraser box and took a look at it. She said, "It's just a regular old eraser."

"Read the note Lawtin Sr. wrote. It's folded up on the bottom." She handed The Eraser to Larkin and carefully took the note out of the box. Harry picked up the box to examine it. Sally read the note out loud for Harry's benefit;

"Dear Sons,

In the course of a lifetime are many mistakes,

To remove the mark, *this* is all it takes.

With malice it never take away,

For with consequences you must pay.

Use it sparingly, strive for perfection,

If you do, you shall receive God's election.

Destroy it not, for you all shall be,

the object of its hostility."

Lawtin Palmer Esq. −1770 A.D.

"Wow! That's pretty cryptic. What does it mean?" she asked.

Larkin laughed and said, "That's exactly how I described it the first time I read it. It means *this:* The Eraser can kill. All that needs to be done is erase someone's name with malice and they shall die. If the Keeper destroys it, he will die. And if it is not passed down to the next generation, the entire family shall die. Now, you see why this is nothing to make light of and in no way is this a regular- old- eraser."

The two understood the gravity of it all. "Yes, we see, Larkin," said Sally slowly.

Harry handed The Eraser box back to him. "One last question, Larkin," asked Harry. "Does it work and have you ever used it?"

"Yes, very effectively. And no, I have not. But, I have been very tempted. Up to this point all I have had to do is threaten to use it and it is just as effective. But, someday I suppose, I will have to."

"Is that how I got out of jail so fast today?"

"The Sergeant is a Mason. He knows, and I told him in so many words that I knew his name. Oh, and Harry, we need to talk about that."

"No we don't, Larkin. From now on, I am no longer a Mason. But, I will use it to our advantage, if need be."

"Thank you, Harry." He gave him a hug. Sally came over and joined them in a group hug.

"One day, I will try to bring you both up to speed on all of it, but there's a lot to know. For now, this is all you need to know and as far as I'm concerned, much too much. I don't want either of you hurt, and that's why I told you. But, now you will need to be careful as well, because if they think you know they may try to get more out of you. So please, keep me informed of anything you may think weird or out of place. And together, we may be able to stop them from harassing us."

Larkin put everything back in its place and slid the suitcase back under the bed. Harry and Sally waited and the three of them started back upstairs. Harry said, "Let's celebrate Sally getting out of jail!" They all laughed and went up the stairs.

Sally said, "Those are words I never thought I'd hear!"

They had a great dinner and laughed and talked all night long. It was getting late and Sally wanted to go home. She asked Larkin, "Will you go out and see if the truck starts?"

He replied, "You saw what the roads are like and it's cold. I don't want you going home tonight." He turned to Harry and asked, "Harry, I know you didn't expect to have two renters in your basement and it is more of an imposition on you in your home. But from time to time Sally may want or need to stay the night. Would that be okay with you?"

He replied, "You are both my family. She can be here any time."

Sally started to cry, got up, and gave Harry a big kiss on the cheek. "Thanks, Harry", they both said.

Larkin got up and started downstairs. On the way he said to Harry, "I think I'm going over to the Temple to do some snooping around tomorrow. I want to see the Albert Pike collection."

"The House of the Temple?"

"Yup."

"On R & 16th?"

"Yup."

"Geez, Larkin. You got balls."

"So I've been told."

The two went down the stairs. Larkin put Sally's clothes that had been sitting in the washer all day long into the dryer. Getting ready for bed, she put on the same PJ's that she had the night before. Changing in the same room as Larkin, she had no shame with him and yet, she didn't try to tempt him any. She knew the bounds of their relationship and she respected it and Larkin. He was getting used to it already but, he still diverted his eyes. He made a bed for her on the couch, which was really pretty comfy. "We could do this like half the kids over at UMD, but like I said, I want it to be right and we'll just have to wait."

"So do I," she said. "Can I tell my mom about us, Larkin?"

"Oh yeah, I forgot about our parents. So much has happened so fast. Let's do it on Christmas as a surprise for them all. Okay?"

"Okay. Oh, Larkin," she came over by him and gave him a kiss good night and said, "I love you."

It floored him. But he knew. And she knew he loved her too. He replied, "I love you, too, Sally. Would you pray with me? We need to take this to the Lord."

She bowed her head as Larkin began. "Lord, we thank you for your loving kindness for us, and for your mercy, your care and protection. For your lasting forgiveness in Jesus, we thank you and because of Him, beg your love. As we journey through our lives we ask you to be with us. And we thank you that you have sent us each other. Let us always remember you in our love and give you the glory for it all. We especially ask your protection for us, Harry, my family and all those under the curse. May you give us wisdom each day and the strength to serve you in truth and love. In Jesus name. Amen."

He kissed her again and she happily jumped onto her makeshift bed. He said good night and went into his room. After he got in his cold bed, he heard Harry walking above him and then stop. It was as if Harry was trying to listen for them, wondering what was going on. He'd have to set him straight about the situation.

The next morning he woke before Sally. He had lost track of the days. He thought it was Wednesday. Larkin went up and found Harry sitting at the kitchen table with a cup of coffee in his hand and, as always, the newspaper beneath his eyes. He looked up and said, "Good morning, Larkin. Sleep well?"

Larkin took a seat and answered him, "Harry, I want to set something straight before there are any wrong assumptions about Sally and I. We both said we loved each other last night. We have decided to tell our parents on Christmas. But, I want you to know something. We have decided to remain pure until our wedding night, as we are both still chaste. It is very important to us both. I don't know when we'll get married, but God will help us with that."

"I'm glad you told me, Larkin. I think that is a very wonderful thing and to say the least, one that most kids don't abide by anymore. I applaud your wise decision."

"Thanks, Harry. Can I have a cup of Joe?"

"Sure, help yourself. Where did you learn to call it that?"

"Oh, I think my Uncle Harry taught me that."

"Smart man."

Sally had come up the steps and said to Larkin, "Hey, don't put that pot down. Pour me a cup, too." She came over to Larkin and he handed her his cup. She took a sip and put her other arm around him as he poured himself a cup. He placed it on the table and took hers out of her hand, placing it on the table too. Then he bent down to her mouth with his and gave her a sweet, soft, prolonged kiss. Harry looked up twice from his paper and smiled, happy for the two of them. Larkin broke from her lips and asked, "Harry, what day is it?"

"Wednesday."

Sally went over to the window and cried out, "Look! It's sunny outside and it has quit snowing!" She ran for the back door. Larkin went after her and they both burst out of the door into the back yard. Sally picked up a handful of snow and patted it into a ball. As soon as she could, she let fly at Larkin, hitting him in the side.

"Oh no you don't," he said, "I have to warn you. I was the pitcher on our state championship team." She stuck out her tongue and went "pfffffp" at him.

"You're going to get it now!" he shouted playfully.

Larkin picked up some snow, took aim and threw it at her. It struck her in the back as she ran away from him. He noticed she didn't have any shoes on. He said, "Hey! You don't have any shoes on!"

"So?" She threw another snowball right at him and it hit him in the head.

"Hey! You're a good shot. Where did you learn to throw like that?"

"On the boys' summer league- I was the pitcher!" She laughed.

"What?" He ran after her and caught up as she was about to reach the deck. He tackled her in a bank of snow piled up by the wind. It exploded from the momentum, and flew like kitty litter in the back of a truck! They got covered in the white puffy snow and they laughed the whole time. Harry watched them from the window. "Ah, to be young and in love again," he said.

They came in laughing and wiping the snow from their bedclothes. "Whoa. That's colder than I thought," said Sally. "I'm going down to take a shower and change Larkin. I've got to call about work."

"Your clean clothes are in the dryer."

"Okay. Thanks." She went down the stairs fast as a rabbit.

"I see you're getting around pretty well in that cast now." Harry pointed to the back yard referring to the escapade he had just witnessed.

"Yeah. I am. Isn't she great, Harry?"

"I told you so."

"What do you mean, "I told you so?""

"Don't you remember? At work one day when you first started. I told you that she was the best of the three."

"That's right, you did."

"I'm glad you found each other, Larkin."

"Thanks, Harry. I'm going to change, too. Then I have to get going."

Sally finished up and Larkin took his turn. She went to get dressed and call to see if she should go into work. It was a chore for him to stick his foot with the cast out of the shower door and take a shower. Sally peeked into the bathroom and saw the cast hanging out there and laughed at him asking, "What are you doing, Larkin?"

"Trying to keep it dry. Why?"

"For a smart guy, you sure are dumb. Why don't you just put a plastic bag around it?"

"Oh. That would be too simple, I guess." He began to laugh at himself and she just joined in and they laughed so hard they almost cried.

He got out and she handed him his towel. He covered up quickly. "Sally, now quit it," he scolded her. She wasn't really looking and was faced the other way, but she was playful and liked to tease him. He blushed, just as he always had. Even with the girl he had now come to love, he still would blush the rest of his life. When he finished dressing he asked her, "What did you find out about work?"

"The Secretary told everyone to stay home today and come in tomorrow."

Larkin asked, "Want to go over to the Temple library with me?"

She answered, "From now on, Honey, we are inseparable."

It was the first time she had called him that. He kind of liked it. They put on their coats and headed up the stairs. Calling out when they got to the top Larkin said, "We're going to the library at the Temple, Harry. See you in a few hours."

He called back from his room, "Okay. See ya."

They went out the door and made their way to the truck. The snow had piled in behind it, so Larkin took the shovel by the back door and moved it all to the side. Pushing the fence doors open he looked out into the street and said, "Looks like the traffic is starting to move again, Sally. The road doesn't look too bad either!" Sally had been looking her truck over as this was the first time she had seen it in the sunlight since the time of the accident. It was in good shape except for part of the grill, which had a slight curl in it. She came over to the driver's door.

She said, "Good. I'll start her up."

She got in and turned the key. It started up right away and she backed it out as Larkin directed her into the street holding back the traffic for her. He hopped in and off they went. On the way, they listened to the radio. The radio was tuned to a station that had Christmas carols playing. Larkin said, "It seems like they play carols earlier every year."

"Yeah, but I like them. I could listen to Christmas music all year round."

"Me, too." He smiled, even though in the back of his mind was their destination.

She pulled into a parking space in front of the Temple. Getting out, Larkin looked up the flights of stairs and at the sphinx-like statues, one on each side of the stairs at the entrance. The date on the front of the building said 1733. The sign at the street said two hour parking, so they'd have to watch the time.

When they entered the doors, he looked up at the beauty of the building and all of the granite, but Larkin didn't come for that and he knew just where to go. Going up the stairs, he went into the room with the Pike Collection first. Sally followed along behind him, realizing he was all pumped up and in his element. She watched him carefully and he handed her his notebook as he read each description of the historical artifacts he perused. Finally, standing prominently in the center of the collection, was a full size replica of the statue of Pike that was in the park. Then at last, sitting down, they began to read some of the works Pike had compiled. It was tedious reading and they would comment to each other if they came upon anything worth discussing. Sally finally said, "I didn't realize the Scottish rite was so connected to the occult. Pike was certainly an evil man."

"Yes, indeed. Worst thing is that most Masons have no idea. I'm sure Pike helped make the order for the assassination of Lincoln. At least that is what the other letters say and I wanted to find out more about the guy."

"What other letters?"

"Oh. Many of them that I have found. You may not have seen them all, but just copied them for me. I need to show you all of the documents. You won't believe it. It substantiates my hypothesis that the Masons took Lincoln out. I've told the Secretary, and he has a huge decision to make, basically, whether to rewrite history."

"Wow, Larkin. I didn't know that what you were doing was so important. You could become famous."

"I'm already famous. The world just doesn't know about it yet, but the Masons sure do. Oh, and by the way, I may have the gift of finding things."

"What?"

"Yeah. My grandmother, Mary Chase Palmer, could find things for people. I'm convinced that I have inherited that gene from her. I've found a lot of things in the past decade. I'd say, even more than she ever did."

"Interesting. You'll have to tell me more about that!"

"I will. I'll show you some of the Journal tonight."

A man came up to them. He said, "I'm sorry, but we are about to close. May I help you return the documents, Larkin?"

Sally was startled by his question and use of Larkin's name. Larkin just smiled and replied, "Why thank you, Sir. You may have all of them. But if I may ask, could I see some of the private collection?"

Larkin figured if they knew about him, he should have the guts to get into the collection of works reserved for Masonic scholars. The Mason replied, "I don't know why not. I'll arrange for a private showing on Friday and come in to assist you myself. Is there a certain document you'd like to see?"

"If I could, I would like to see Pike's personal copy of Morals and Dogma?"

The man was taken aback by Larkin's request. He thought a minute and said, "I don't know if we have that in our collection, Larkin. But I'll find out and call you. Are you still living with Mr. Hall?"

"Yes. Call anytime. Ah, I'm sorry, but I don't know your name, Sir."

Laughing he said, "Let's keep it that way, Larkin."

Larkin laughed and said, "I understand. Let me know."

"I will."

Sally and Larkin went out toward the truck and checked the time, they arrived just in time as a cop was checking chalk marks on the tires he had marked just about two hours ago. They beat a parking ticket! When they got into the truck Sally said, "This is bigger than I thought, Larkin. They know you. I'm starting to get to understand it all."

"You will tonight when you see the Journal and the Mail Box obits." Actually, Larkin was hoping he would not scare her when he told her the whole story and what he'd seen since he was the Keeper.

They got home and went down to his room, not wanting to disturb Harry. They figured as they didn't hear him walking about that he was asleep. Sally made dinner and they ate quickly. She was looking forward to seeing the documents. When they finished, Larkin went into the bedroom and brought out the suitcase. He took out the Journal and the Mail Box obits. Larkin said to Sally, "In order for you to understand the Journal, we need to read the obits first, and then bring them out again as we read the Journal. It makes more sense that way."

Sally nodded her head and asked, "Will you read them to me? I think it will mean more that way."

"Sure. You may be right."

They sat down on the couch and Sally snuggled into Larkin's side. Before he began, he told her how he had found all of the boxes and treasures and the context of the finds at the time. Then, he picked up the first of the obits and began to read. By the time he had finished the entire lot, it was late. He remembered how long it had taken him and Ginny to get through them and this was the same. It was almost two in the morning when he finished, but Sally had not missed a lick of it. He sat the Journal down and asked, "Do you have any questions, Sally?"

"No, Larkin. I now understand the enormity of it all: Your family's curse, the sadness and loss, the duty to not only your country, but to the world. What will you do, Larkin?"

"My Grandpa Elias started a list of all the Masons in the state. With all of their names, he hoped to ward off the enemy and for it to somehow be a deterrent. But there are too many-almost 4 million. I cannot kill four million men, nor do I want to. The Eraser would be gone. I have come to realize that I must go to the top and compile a list of the 32nd degree Masons and above only; those that may really know the truth. Even at that, I wonder how many of those *really* know. When I do have the list compiled, they dare not come after us. In the mean while, I'm going to set the history of the USA on its head with my discoveries."

"I'll do what I can to help you, Honey."

"My mom calls me that."

"She does?"

"Yes, and I scolded her every time. It embarrassed me."

"Do you want me to stop?"

"No. With you, I kind of like it."

She smiled, leaned up and gave him a kiss. They fell asleep on the couch in one another's arms again.

They awoke to the phone ringing. It was only six a.m. and Larkin ran to it after he dislodged himself from Sally's arms. "Hello?"

"Is this, Larkin?"

"Yes."

"This is the man from the Temple. We have the document you wished to see. I will be here at nine Friday morning. We are not open to the public that day. Do not be late as I will meet you at the front door to let you in promptly at that hour."

"Thank you, Sir."

The line went dead. Larkin heard the line click again. Harry was listening. He hung up and went over to Sally as she began to stir. She asked as she stretched, "Who was that?"

"The man from the Temple. He said I could see the document. I'm amazed at that."

"Why?"

"Because, I'm not one of them. There must be something else going on here. Maybe I should go alone, in case it's a trap. I don't want anyone at risk. Regardless, they usually just personally attack anyone that lays claims to conspiracies involving them. They merely try to destroy their characters. Still, I don't think they'd do me harm."

"I don't want you to go."

"I have to. I saw something in one of his other works the other day I want to follow up on. And that, Morals and Dogma, is his most famous of books. I've got to see it. You get up and get ready for work."

They decided to go out for breakfast, and Larkin would drop off Sally, so they started to get ready to leave. In the mean while, Harry heard them and decided to call, "the man from the Temple", himself. He knew who the man was and he wanted to tell him to leave Larkin alone. He placed the call as he heard them talking in the basement. "Dean, this is Hall. Say, I know you are going to let Larkin look at one of Pike's books, but I wondered if there was anything other than that on the agenda for Friday?"

"Stay out of it, Hall. It's too big for you."

"You don't have any orders from above do you?"

"I said- stay out of it!"

Dean hung up on him. Harry sat the receiver down slowly and thought about what just happened. He had never felt so threatened in his life.

Larkin and Sally got in her truck and headed downtown. They wanted to stay away from the hustle and bustle of holiday shoppers, so they went to Larkin's favorite place- Reeve's. In fact, Sally loved the place, too. She found a place to park and they walked in the cold air, their breath visible as rising plumes by the customers sitting at tables on the other side of the glass. They came in the door and the hostess greeted them. "Hi, Sally! Usual table?"

"Yes, Mabel."

She showed them the way to a table in the corner facing out. It was a couple tables from where Larkin and Ellie had sat previously. They sat down and Sally said, "Thanks", as Mabel handed them the menus. They took off their hats, gloves, and coats and settled in. Sally asked Larkin, "What are you in the mood for?"

"I think I'd like to have French toast and ham. I haven't had that for a long time."

"I think I'm going to have crepes with Swedish lingonberries."

"Sounds pretty dainty to me."

"They are, but they are good."

When Mabel came back with two glasses of water they gave her the order. That gave them time to talk. They talked about the invitation to Mr. Shipley's house for Christmas. They thought it odd he would include three employees into his private life and family traditions. Then Larkin saw her- Ellie walked in the door! When she took off her coat, she made a bee line straight to them! Larkin said, "Here comes Ellie, Sally. Get ready."

"Why Larkin, I'm so glad to see you! And Sally, how are you?"

"We are just fine, Ellie, and how are you?" offered Sally.

Ellie ignored Sally's question and commented on the use of the plural in her response. ""We" are fine? Does that suggest a new couple in D.C.?"

"As a matter of fact, Ellie, it does. You could say we are "committed"," replied Larkin.

"I see," said Ellie in an unhappy to disappointed tone. "Are you going home for Christmas, Larkin?"

"As matter of fact, we were just talking about that. We will be attending the celebration of Christmas at the Secretaries' home this year."

"Oh, how nice. I've heard they decorate their home very nicely-with the four girls and all. I'm going to the Riviera with Daddy. I plan on coming back with a tan this year."

"Oh bravo, Ellie," replied Sally sarcastically.

Ellie got the hint and said, "Well, Happy Christmas to you both, if I don't see you. Ta-ta." She walked over to her table and sat down.

Mabel brought their food just then, saving them from having to continue to talk with Ellie in earshot of their table. They commented on the food and Sally asked him what he would do for the rest of the day. Larkin said uncommitted, "I'd like to go by the school and see if my grade from the test is posted. Although we do start back on Monday and I guess I could get it then."

"Whatever you want, Honey."

Larkin looked over at Ellie and it was apparent she had overheard Sally call him "Honey." She just huffed and slammed down her fork. She obviously was not taking the news of their commitment very well. In fact, Larkin wondered, 'Just what was their commitment?'

Mabel brought the check and Larkin handed her the cash right away. They wanted out of there, only because they felt their space had been invaded. Indeed, it had.

They got up and walked out as fast as they could. When they went out the door Sally began to laugh and said, "Well, it looks like I've wiped out all of the competition!"

Larkin came up and gave her a hug saying, "They didn't have a chance!"

Instead of going past UMD, they decided to go to Sally's place and get her some fresh clothes for work. Besides, Larkin had never been there and he wanted to see where she lived. More importantly, *how* she lived. He had wondered if she was a slob or anything and going over when she had been gone for this long was a good test, he thought. However, the rules there were quite different than at Harry's. Her landlord did not allow men to come in without permission. Sally knocked at the door to her back entrance. The place was set up much like Larkin's, but Sally had a separate entrance on the side as well. The old lady answered and asked, "Yes, Sally?"

"Mrs. Heidelmann, this is Larkin Palmer, the boy I told you about from work. I'd like to show him my apartment if you don't mind? We only plan on being here for about an hour."

She was reading something and was preoccupied. Finally, she said, "Oh yes, I remember you saying he was cute. Sure, but let me know when you leave. Nice to meet you, Larkin."

She started to shut the door and go back in but, Larkin stopped her. "Is that a church bulletin you are reading there, Mrs. Heidelmann?"

"Why yes, Larkin, it is. I attend Mount Olivet Lutheran Church. Are you looking for a church, Larkin?"

"As a matter of fact, Sally and I *are* looking for a church. Would you mind if we attended with you next Sunday?"

"I would be thrilled for you two to come with me, Larkin. I usually attend the early service at eight-thirty. Is that okay?"

"It is just fine. We will make arrangements to meet you there or Sally and I will pick you up."

She got a puzzled look on her face. Larkin saw it and he said, "Sally and I are spending a great deal of time together and we may be coming from my house that morning." The octogenarian frowned at that.

"Oh, and don't worry, there is absolutely no funny business going on!"

With that she smiled and shook her head saying, "See you Sunday, then."

Sally looked at Larkin and smiled as she put the key in her door. When the woman had closed her door and could no longer hear them, they looked at each other and laughed- hard!

When they entered, Larkin got his first look at Sally's place. He could tell a lot about her. The place was clean and well kept. She had all the "girl" things around the room. And she actually had curtains. She said, "Come on. I want to show you my room." She went to the closet and opened the door saying, "Take a look at this. When I first got the job at the Smithsonian, I went nuts and bought all these fancy clothes. Some of them are four years old and are almost out of style. But, I wear them anyway."

That led Larkin to ask the question, "Say Sally, I never asked you this before, but how old are you anyway?"

"Why? Does it make a difference?"

"No. But, I'd like to know."

"I'm twenty-four. I have an associate's degree and plan on going back to get my bachelors. I just have to find the time. Besides, I make plenty at my job already."

"You know I'm only eighteen, don't you?"

"Yeah. I'm robbing the cradle." Going up to him and giving him a hug she said, "But you're such a hunk I can't resist." She gave him a kiss.

He smiled and said, "Yeah, I guess I am aren't I?"

She slapped him on the butt and went toward the bathroom. I'm going to get cleaned up and change. You can turn on the TV if you want." She feigned unbuttoning her shirt and he said, "Sally, quit that!"

She laughed, went in the bathroom and turned on the water. He went into the living room and turned on the TV. It had been a long time since he had watched TV just for the heck of it. There had always been a purpose, like a game or some special event. So, he flipped through the channels to see what was on. The Today Show was just coming on. A rerun of "Car 54 Where are you?" was on, too. But, he turned on the news to see what was happening. He sat and listened to the morning news and weather. Not much very newsworthy was happening. The blizzard was all anyone had talked about for days and today's news was no exception. The weather man didn't expect any more snow for a while, but he said that there may be more before Christmas.

Sally came out in a towel and said, "Let's just stay in tonight at your place for dinner. We can go to the store and pick up some stuff. Then we can *really* talk and get to know more about each other, like, how old we are."

"And stuff like that?"

"And stuff like that."

She gave him a hug and in so doing, lost her towel on the floor. She bent over to get it and Larkin turned, looking the other way. He blushed once more and shook his head as she walked into her room to dress. He said out loud to himself, "I guess I'll just have to put up with that until we get married." Then, alarmed by his statement he said, "What did I just say?" He stood there in a daze.

In less than a minute, Sally came back out of her room and said, "You said, and I quote, "until we get married." Are you proposing to me, Larkin? Because if you are; this isn't very romantic."

"No, Sally, I'm not. Not yet. But obviously my subconscious believes it is the next step for us to take. And if I do, I promise it will be romantic."

He took her by the hips and pulled her to him and planted a big kiss on her. She didn't resist and said when he was through, "Thanks." When they did separate, she went towards the TV and asked, "What's on?"

He was surprised by her lack of pursuit of the subject of marriage, but was actually happy that that was the case. He was not ready for it and wouldn't be until after college unless, something happened, of course. After thinking about all of this, he finally answered her question. "Oh, I had the news on, but it's over. I don't want to watch TV anyway. Let's go do something."

"Like you go to the store while I go to work?"

"Oh yeah. Like go to the store."

The phone rang. "Hello?" answered Sally. Larkin overheard her side of the conversation. "Yes, Sir. I can do that. Thank you, Sir. Goodbye."

"Well, well, well," she said. Coming up to him, she put her arms around him and said coyly, "It looks like I get to go and see what you like to eat. That was Mr. Shipley. He said take off the next two days, help you with your research, and then come in on Monday. Remember, I brought you your work?"

Larkin rolled his eyes and then thought about what he had just considered a minute ago. Maybe she did actually already have them married! At least in *her* mind! Obviously, this *was* to be their commitment! Sally said, "Just a minute. I'm getting out of these work clothes and into some blue jeans."

She ran into her bedroom and in less than a minute she was back. They went upstairs and told Mrs. Heidelmann that they were leaving and she happily waved at them as they left. Sally asked as they walked, "Do you shop anywhere in particular?"

"To tell you the truth, I have only gone one place since I have been here and it was right by the house. Just a "Mom and Pop" kind of place. Do you go to a "real" grocery store?"

"Sure do. And it has the best meat section. I like a good steak!"

They went out to the truck, but before they got in Sally said, "Hey Honey, come here a second." He walked around to the driver's side. "Get in," she said. Larkin looked at her. She had never asked him to drive before. She said it again. "Get in."Larkin got in. Or at least he tried to. When he drug his cast into the driver's seat, he could not get it past the foot pedals. She said, "Thought so. Get out." She motioned for him to get out. They both just laughed and she said, "Just thought I'd check. What were we thinking? You can't drive this thing!" They both got in their former, respective seats and off she drove.

She drove to the Super Value, Sally parked and they got a cart on the way in. Larkin drove it, feeling like he had to drive "something" and said right away, "So, it looks like you want steak tonight. What kind?"

"I like a good rib eye, about an inch and a half thick, without too much marbling."

"And a salad?"

"Yes."

"And a baked potato?"

"How did you know?"

"Just a guess. I need some other stuff, so we may as well get it all. And if you're going to be around, I might as well stock up and get some stuff you like, too."

"Why thank you, Honey."

They walked around and she did most of the shopping, but he told her all of the foodstuffs he needed and some he didn't. While they shopped, he noticed a little girl with her mom that had a balloon tied to the cart handle, which she pulled on back and forth, up and down, much to the chagrin of her mom. But, she was cute, he thought. Sally noticed him watching this all happen and thought to herself, 'Well, it looks like he likes kids.'

They filled the cart and went to check out. When the checker was done the bill was a hundred and nine dollars. They had gotten more than they figured. Larkin didn't think anything of it, but for Sally, that was a lot to spend at the store. He took the checkbook out of his back pocket. She asked, "Have you got enough?"

Larkin laughed and said, "Oh, I guess I should tell you about that too. I have plenty of money. See?"He showed her the balance of his check book. It still said $4,600.00. Sally was amazed- actually, shocked.

"But you don't live like that, Larkin," she said.

"No. Don't need to. I live life like the steward I think God wants me to be. I share. He shares."

"Can I quit my job?"

Larkin just looked at her and raised an eyebrow.

"I'm just teasing. I like my job."

"So do I."

"But why didn't you tell me?"

"Would it have made a difference?"

"I might have started coming around sooner!" She laughed and said, "But I think I would have come to the same conclusion. I still would have loved you." The girl cashier looked at him as he handed her the check and smiled as if affirming Sally's statement. He felt good about it.

They piled all of the food into the back of the truck and got in. Sally leaned across and said, "Come here." She kissed him and said, "Thanks, Honey."

When they arrived at Larkin's, he got out and opened the gate to the parking spot. Sally pulled in and stopped. Shutting the gate, Larkin picked up a couple of sacks to carry in and Sally did, too. Smiling at each other, no words were said. Going inside, they wondered where Harry was, because he wasn't home. He had not left a note either, which was unusual for him. They put it all away and looking on the shelf of the refrigerator Sally spied the tortillas and asked, "Where did you get these, Larkin?"

He chuckled and answered, "I guess Pilar thought she was going to spend a lot of time here."

"Well, I guess Pilar was wrong." Sally picked up the tortillas and threw them in the trash like a Frisbee.

They walked into the living room and Larkin turned on the radio. Sally said, "We need to get you a TV."

"I've thought about that, but I have never really watched TV too much. We listened to the radio a lot and only watched special things on TV. There's a lot of garbage on TV and I just don't need it. And, it's easier to talk this way. Besides, I think we do need to talk and get to know each other much better. I want to know all about you."

"Okay. Let's talk."

She sat down on the couch and patted the seat next to her. Larkin came over, sat down and she did the same snuggle that she had become accustomed to. "Where do we begin?" Larkin asked.

"Why don't you tell me about Ginny? I'd like to know what I'm up against."

"Actually, you're not up against anything, not anymore. She was part of my life and now she is gone to be with the Lord. We were to be married in June. We only kissed. I've *seen* more of you than I ever did of her! She was my high school sweetheart, the proverbial, "girl-next-door". I loved her and I shall never forget her."

"I understand. I had a boyfriend in high school, but we never got serious. Since then, I have dated a couple of guys, but they were jerks and all they were after is my body. I saw through them all. And I'm glad I did. I love you." She leaned back from him and pointed at her body and said, "And by the way, you are the only one to have seen *this*."

He smiled. "Ah- that!" He said more loudly and with emphasis.

"What do you mean?"

"Well, I have to admit the first time I met you I thought you were beautiful and I was flattered when you gave me your phone number. But when you did, the shy side of me came forward and I thought I shouldn't ever call you, because you were too, I guess, pushy or forward. Actually, I was scared. I usually don't go after girls at all, much less that type."

"What do you mean, "That type"?" Things were getting tense and Larkin had to express what he thought a little better.

"Oh, don't get me wrong, I never thought anything but the best of you, but I never had a girl give me her number before unless I asked for it. If it weren't for you coming into the Chinese place that night, I just never would have called you. God was in control to have us meet that night and get to know each other. He took my fears away, but there's one more thing."

"What?"

"Well, you do embarrass me. With- that." He pointed at her body.

"Oh. I just feel so comfortable with you. I'm just not embarrassed when I do that. And to be totally honest, that very first day I met you, I fell in love with you. I knew you were the one when I came up from under the desk after hitting my head. It was love at first sight. Do you want me to be more modest? I can *try* to contain myself. I don't do it to tempt you at all. I totally *trust* you."

"If you *could*? As I said before, I love you enough to wait for you *and* I'm a man. I know what I'd like to do sometimes, but why even take the chance? Can you try?"

"I'll try to make a conscious effort to stay clothed in front of you." He laughed. She giggled. She kissed him and he began again.

"Where was I? Oh yeah, when Ginny and I were little, I'd go over and play with her younger brother, Andy. He was really hurt by the loss of his sister. That reminds me, I should call them or something for Christmas. Last Christmas Ginny and I did a lot. She came over for Christmas Eve and my family spent Christmas day with her family after church. We all went to the same church together. I made her a bracelet for her present. I don't know whatever happened to it. I never got to go to her funeral because I was still in the hospital. It was a bad deal and made it harder for me to accept. I still wonder sometimes if it's true." He paused and sighed, knowing he was jumping all over the place and then went on, "She gave me a sleigh ride for my present. It had just snowed and it was cold. We snuggled up on the ride and just watched the world go by as Ginny drove us to church and to my house for my families' gathering. She was romantic, but much different than you."

"She sounds like she was a very nice person."

"She was. Everyone loved her. And I mean it- everyone. She didn't have an enemy in the world."

"Do you think your parents will like me?"

"I think- I think, they'll love you as much as I do."

That put Sally over the edge and she began to cry. Larkin didn't know what to do or say, so he turned her face toward him and he brushed the tears aside. He said, "God sent you to me to heal me. I thank Him every day for you." He kissed her again, which led to a very long make-out session.

They were interrupted by Harry coming in the back door. They wondered why he never used the front door anymore. They guessed he just wanted to let them know of his presence. "Anybody home?" he yelled.

"Yeah, we're down here!"

"Can I come down?"

"Sure, Harry," yelled Larkin.

"I went to stock up on a few things, but forgot my list, so I just went for a walk. It's so nice out today."

He sat down in his wife's chair. "What have you two been doing?"

"We went over to Sally's today. I got to meet her landlord. She's nicer than mine." Larkin laughed.

Harry said, "Right!"

"She even invited us to her church."

"Church? Where does she go? Are you going?"

" She's Lutheran. We can't disappoint her now. We said we would."

"Well, it will get you out to see another denomination. Maybe it's a good thing."

"I'll let you know what I think of Lutheran doctrine after I hear the Pastor."

Harry nodded. "What did you think of Sally's place?"

"Well, it's fixed up nicer than mine, but she pays a lot more. I guess you get what you pay for."

Sally and Larkin broke out laughing and Harry even had a hard time holding it in. He stood up and said, kidding them, "Well! I don't have to sit here and take this kind of abuse. I'm going up to my place."

Larkin jumped up with him and came over to tell him something. He whispered, "We are trying to talk and get to know each other. I'm going to eat down here with her tonight."

Whispering back loud enough for anyone to hear he replied, "Okay."

Larkin went back and sat down. "Are you hungry yet?"

"Not yet. I'll cook later. Just let me know when you get hungry, Honey."

"Okay. Where were we?"

"We were kissing. But before that, we were talking about your family and Ginny."

"Well then, tell me about your family. You said you are the youngest?"

"Yes. My brother, Drew, is the oldest and is over in Korea in the Army. My sister, Cassie, is home in Tennessee and works at the Durango boot factory in Franklin. Mom just sits at home and works on stuff for the church because she's' pretty involved at the Fourth Avenue Church of Christ. Daddy likes to go out on the lake fishing and he is into old cars. He fixes them up."

"No one into baseball?"

"Well, Drew liked to go to watch our high school games, but he was only hustling the cheerleaders."

"Oh. Well, I like old cars. In fact, all we ever had is old trucks until a couple of years ago when we got the new Lincoln."

"Lincoln?"

"Yeah. Israel Waterman gave it to us as a gift."

"A gift?"

"Yeah. He sold some of the treasure I found and felt compelled to give us the car. His commission on the sale was huge."

"Oh. I see. Is that how you got so much money?"

"Partially. We put a lot of the money back into the farms, and God has blessed that, so we have been doing very well on them. Everything we put into it, we have gotten back two times over, and this is only the fourth year."

"Wow. Sounds like you are good businessmen."

"And, good farmers. My uncle and dad really know what they are doing. My contribution was to bring it all into the 20th century with innovations. Of course the money really helped with that. Oh, I did bring along my bag of coins from the treasure box of Percifer Carr. Want to see them?"

"Yeah, that sounds neat."

Larkin chuckled.

"What are you laughing about?" She asked hotly.

"I'm glad to hear that I'm not the only one that still says "neat."

"Oh. I always say that."

"Glad to hear it." She wasn't like many of the other kids either, with "far-outs" or "grovies". He was very glad to hear it.

Larkin went into the bedroom and pulled the suitcase out from under the bed. He opened it and unzipped the top pocket under the lid. It held the bag of coins his uncles had given him. He handed it to her. Opening it, Sally poured the twelve coins onto the bed. She couldn't believe their condition. "These are beautiful Larkin. How much are they worth?"

"Oh, I don't know, maybe, a couple thousand dollars. We sorted through the treasure pretty quickly and I didn't look to see what my uncles gave me. I really don't know, Sally."

"Want me to find out?"

"How?"

"Mr. Higgins at the Smithsonian. It's his specialty. He'd be so excited, he'd do it for free."

"I'll think about it. I really don't need the money and they are my last part of the treasure."

"Well, if you ever want to know what they are worth, I'll find out for you, Honey."

"Okay." He picked them up, put them back in the bag and placed it back where it came from.

He thought about the rest of the things in the suitcase and if this was really the place to keep it. What if "they" broke in and stole it while he was at work? Maybe he should take it to work and hide it at the Smithsonian. No one would ever find it in all the storage in the basement. He would have to think on it. They went back out into the living room. Sally said, "Let's take a nap. I'm tired."

"Yeah? Well, I just might be able to do that."

They snuggled up next to each other on the couch and went to sleep. The radio's crackling and popping woke them up. It sounded weird, and it began to smoke so Larkin got up fast! He ran over and pulled the cord from its socket. Then, he pushed it out away from the wall and took a look into the back. No fire, but it sure stunk! Sally got up went over to it and asked, "Do we need to call the fire department?"

"No, but I need to tell Harry!"

He went up the steps and knocked on Harry's door. "Come in, Larkin," came Harry's call.

"Say Harry, the radio just blew up. It was smoking pretty badly, so I unplugged it."

"I've been expecting that for a long time. Those old tubes haven't been replaced in years. Don't worry about it. I'll get it fixed someday. In the mean while, it is to be considered a piece of old furniture. Okay?"

"Okay. Do you mind if I get a TV?"

"Oh no. Not at all. I wondered why you hadn't already."

"Thanks, Harry."

Larkin started back downstairs and he noticed how fast he was able to do so with the cast on his foot. He didn't like the fact he had to wear one pair of jeans all the time though. In fact, he thought it time to take them off and wash them. He had other clothes he had to wash anyway. Therefore, he went down and took a detour to his bedroom before going back in with Sally. He took off his pants and put on his PJ bottoms, which were big enough to absorb the cast. He took his hamper to the laundry room. Sally wondered what he was doing and came in by him. "Let me do that for you, Larkin." She shoved him out of the way and started to sort his clothes into piles- colors, whites and other.

Larkin asked, "What ya doing with the piles?"

"You don't sort them before you wash?"

"I haven't done much wash before this fall. Why do you sort?"

"Ever have pink underwear?"

"Oh. That's why! No, but I don't want them to be." He laughed.

She smiled and said, "Are you hungry yet? We can eat while these are washing."

"Sure sounds good. But we won't have any radio or music to listen to."

"We'll make our own music."

She stood on her tip toes and gave him a kiss. He watched this and said, "Say Sally, I've never asked you before, but how tall are you?"

"Oh, I'm five foot two. And you?"

"I'm six foot one. Opposites attract, I guess."

She walked toward the kitchen and she told him to sit while she made their dinner. He thought that was a good idea. He said to her, "Now that you know what I like to eat, let's see if you can cook it!"

"Ha! Wise guy. I'm a pretty good cook. You just wait and see."

He read the paper while she began the feast. He commented on current events and she would just agree with him and his analysis of the situations. She really thought he was a genius. She had never met an eighteen year old with this much knowledge. She asked him. "Do you read a lot?"

"I read every book in the Brookfield library. Not to mention the school library. Why?"

"I figured. You know too much. I mean, a lot."

"I'll take that as a compliment."

"Oh, it is. I think you are the smartest guy I know, including much older people at work. Seriously."

"Thank you. I don't know what my IQ is, but I'd like to find out."

"I can arrange that, you know."

"I've come to find out you can arrange almost anything, Dear."

"Dear? I didn't know you could be so demonstrative."

She sat her spoon down, went over and gave him a kiss. He just kept on reading the paper pretending to ignore her. She slapped him on the shoulder and went back to work. She had the meal done in a little while and placed it all carefully on the table. Sitting down, she bowed her head. Larkin took the cue and began to pray. "Lord for these your gifts which we are about to receive, we give You thanks. And for the hands that prepared it. Amen."

Sally looked up, smiled, and said as she unfolded her napkin, "Amen".

Larkin took a bite of the steak and said," This is good. How did you learn to cook?"

"I learned while my dad was stationed in Germany. The cook on base was one of the family's friends, so in the summer time, I'd do KP for minimum wage. I learned to cook and he got help. It worked out."

"Did you learn any German cooking?"

"Yeah. Sauerbraten is one of my specialties. Do you like it?"

"Yes. Some of the German ladies in church would invite us over. I especially like bratkartofflen and spatzle."

"Do you speak German too, Larkin?"

"Yes. Do you?"

"Naturlich!"

"Ach du liebe!"

"Well, I guess we have something more in common don't we?"

"We do. We do."

Larkin shoved another bite of baked potato into his mouth and just smiled. Good looking and she could cook too! They finished up and he helped by drying the dishes. It also helped to fill the time and to bring about the same kind of conversation he and his mother had experienced back home. Larkin said, "You know, I used to dry for Mom all the time. Dad never liked the job and it gave us time to talk. My mom knew everything about me. And we shared so much this way. I feel guilty not calling her every day to tell her what's going on with my life. It seems strange."

"I know how you feel. I used to call home all the time when I first came here. It seems like you get going in your own little world and nothing can stop it. It doesn't take long at all to lose touch with everyone you love. I try to call once a week now."

"My parents never were the type to spend a lot of time on the phone anyway, so it makes it even harder."

They finished up the KP duty and Larkin pulled out his watch. It was already 9:15 p.m. Just then, he heard the dryer stop. "Just in time," he said.

He started towards the laundry and Sally said, "No you don't! I'll get it. Besides, I want to fold your underwear!"

"Sally!" said Larkin in jest.

She laughed at him as she went down the hall. He went in and sat down on the couch. He took a book that he had started a week before and began to read, but when Sally came in, he sat it down. She said, "You can keep reading, Honey."

"Are you sure?" he asked.

"Yes, completely. I'll be happy to just sit here beside you."

Larkin picked the book back up and continued to read as she took her position next to him, snuggled in under his arm. She was very comfortable and so was he. He kept reading for an hour or two and realized she had fallen asleep. He laid her down and covered her with the comforter that his mom had given him. He got up and went to the bathroom. When he came out she was standing in the hall waiting and she said, "My turn".

She walked past him and he went into the bedroom to put on his PJ top and climb in bed. She came in and took "her" same pair of PJ's out of his drawer and turned away from him to put them on. 'Well,' he thought, 'at least she turned away.' But, he could still see and he just closed his eyes. She asked, "I know I shouldn't ask this, because it was not our deal, but could I sleep in here with you? You know I won't do anything."

"No. You're right, it's not our deal. So, you just head to the couch, Dear."

"Okay. Man, you're too good for my own good. Just checking."

"Good night, Sally."

"Good night, Honey," she said as she made her way to the couch.

He woke up at seven and went out to the kitchen. Taking out a plastic bag, he duct taped it to his cast. He went in and got into the shower for the first time with the make-shift cover suggested by Sally. She sure was a smart girl. It worked well and even though he had not taken many showers in the past couple of weeks, at least this was the first comfortable one! He got out and started to dry off. Taking the bag off his cast, he checked to see if it was wet- not a drop! Good idea she had. He got dressed in his "one pair" of jeans and a sweat shirt and he went into the living room to see if she was awake, but she wasn't there. He turned to find her in the kitchen making breakfast. He said, "Good morning!"

"Good morning, Honey! Will you watch this while I go pee?"

"Oh sure." He shook his head.

He walked into the kitchen and she handed him a spatula. She ran to the bathroom and said, "Be right back." The eggs were almost done and he could smell toast in the toaster. She came back and said, "Thanks. You sure took a long time in there. I almost peed my PJ'S."

He laughed and said, "Sorry, but it felt so good to finally have a real shower without my leg sticking out! Your idea really worked."

"I told you so. I ain't so dumb, you know."She winked at him.

He gave her a hug and went over to pour them a cup of coffee. By the time he had done that and sat down, she brought him his plate. "Hope you like yours sunny side up."

"I do."

They said grace and started eating. Larkin asked Sally, "I have about a half hour to get over to my appointment. Will you drive me?"

"Yes. I'll come back and clean this up and you can call me when you want me to come and get you."

"Great. Thank you."

"Just put your plate in the sink. I'll go brush my hair and we can go."

She retrieved her purse, and pulled her brush out. By the time he had their dishes in the sink she was ready to go, so they got in the truck and left. She pulled up to the front of Temple and he got out. Leaning in he said, "I'll call. Thanks."

"Bye, Honey."

She drove off. It was five minutes until nine. He was early, so he walked up the steps to wait, but when he got to the door the man came and let him in. "Good morning, Larkin. How are you?"

"Just fine, Sir. May I call you by your first name at least? This is awkward."

"Yes, you may. My name is Dean. Follow me. I'll take you to the viewing area."

They went up a flight of stairs and proceeded down the hall to the private library. Dean took out a key shaped like an ankh and opened the heavy brass door to the locked room. Holding the door for Larkin he said, "In on your the left is the table with the document. I know you know how to handle it with care."

"I do. Thank you, Dean."

"You have one hour."

Larkin went in and sat down at the long wood table where the book had been placed. He opened it. He was only interested in the peripherals, and not the text. There was a scratch pad and pencil next to him. Thumbing through the book one page at a time, he noticed some of the pages had Pikes handwritten notes. Finally, he found what he was looking for- an apparent repetition. A code! On the last page of each odd numbered chapter was written just one word. He wrote each word down on the pad and tore it off. That was all he needed. It said, "The key is in the book." But- what book? What did the key open? To what was it a clue? Actually, he had no clue! He was good at treasure hunts and this was an important one! He was excited! For the first time- he was baffled.

He placed the book back on the table as he found it. Then, he got up and tried to open the door. It was locked from the outside and he could not leave. Their security system made sure all the documents in this room stayed there! He knocked on the door. Dean opened it for him asking curiously, "Only staying for 20 minutes, Larkin?"

"That was all the time I needed, Dean."

Larkin walked out past him and Dean shrugged as he locked the door behind them. As they walked down the hall to the front door Larkin asked, "Will you call Sally for me, Dean, and have her come to pick me up?"

Dean smiled and said, "Sure Larkin, I'd be happy to." He let Larkin out and said, "See you again sometime?"

"I don't know, Dean. Maybe."

"Goodbye, Larkin." Dean closed the door and it snapped shut with an eerie metal clank like the door of a jail cell. Larkin saw the similarity and didn't like it.

Larkin carefully trod down the steps one at a time and sat on the last step at the entrance of the Temple. He thought about the clue left by Pike. He didn't know what it meant, but he'd figure it out someday! Sally pulled up in about ten minutes and he made his way to the truck. He pulled the door open and she asked, "Well? I just about crapped when I got a call from "them.""

He got in saying, "I'll tell you in a minute. Drive."

She put it in gear and off they went. He tried to make her squirm for a second by not saying anything. It worked, too, because she said to him roughly, "Larkin Palmer, if you don't tell me what happened, I'm going to clobber you!"

He laughed and said, "Nothing happened. Dean was as nice as could be, if that was his real name. But, I did find a clue."

"What kind of clue?"

"It was written in code on the last page of every odd numbered chapter in a book by none other than Pike himself."

"Well, what did it say, for crying out loud? You're driving me crazy!"

He laughed at her again. "It said, "The key is in the book". Now what that means, I just don't know."

"What book do we look for? What kind of key did he mean? There are so many questions. And what does it open? Man, that's going to be hard to find out."

"I'm good at treasure hunts!"

"Oh yeah, I forgot."

They drove home, but not to stay.

Having accomplished what he wanted for the day, he sat at the kitchen table and took out the newspaper to look at the ads. He looked at Sears, Wards, and JC Penny first. Sally came up to him and asked, "Hey, what ya looking for?"

"Want to go buy a TV?" he asked her.

"Yeah! But do you know what you want?"

"No. But, I think there is a couple in the Sears ad that looks good. I want to stay with the American name brands, like maybe, Philco, or Motorola."

"Well let's go! We can look at them all in person!" When it came to shopping, Sally was the best; an expert with no rivals.

They went to Wards first, because it was the closest. There were about fifty TV's all turned on the same channel for them to compare the pictures. They began to look at them moving back and forth and forth and back between them. They started to get confused and after a bit they all started to look the same. Finally, a salesman came up to them and said, "I've been watching you two do the same thing everyone else does when they first come in. Just trust me, because the Hitachi here is the best. It has the best picture, clarity, and is 80% transistor. It also has the best warranty. I watch them every single day for eight hours. I know what I'm talking about."

"Larkin would like to stay with a known American brand," said Sally to the salesman.

"Well little lady, the Americans are falling behind on TV's. The Asians are running laps around us in the innovation field. Won't be long and all TV's will be made overseas and be 100% transistor."

Larkin said, "I've read about that. What does Consumer Reports say about it?"

"Same as me. You won't go wrong."

"How much?"

"It's the same price as the Philco of the same size; $349.00"

"Does it come in a box?"

"Yup. And I'll throw in rabbit ears."

"You're a good salesman. Write it up."

After Larkin paid, the salesman went to the back room and put one on a cart. He picked up a rabbit ear from the shelf and asked Larkin, "Where's your vehicle?"

"Follow me," said Sally. She walked ahead of both of them and went out the front door to the parking lot. "Wait here and I'll go get the truck." She ran away while they waited.

The guy said to him, "Must be hard to drive with that cast?"

"Yeah, but I have a chauffeur this way."

The guy chuckled.

He smiled at the salesman.

Sally drove up and stayed in the Datsun. The two men let down the tailgate and lifted the TV into the back. After that, Larkin closed the tailgate the guy shook Larkin's hand and said, "Thanks. It has a one year local warranty also. So, if you have any trouble, bring it back here. We'll fix you up."

"Thanks. Merry Christmas."

"Merry Christmas."

Larkin got in and they started towards home. Sally began to laugh. Larkin seemed puzzled at that and asked, "What?"

"You bought the first one the guy showed you. You didn't even stay with an American TV like you said you wanted to. Man, are you ever a shopping wimp."

He hung his head and said, "Yeah, I know. But it did look good."

Sally laughed and said, "It did. I guess the proof is in the pudding. We'll see."

She drove to the gate and Larkin repeated the procedure of opening it for her, only this time she had to back in because there wasn't enough room to get the TV out if she drove in forward, because of the gate. Larkin waited and when she shut the truck off and got out, she came over by him. He had the tailgate open and said, "I wish I had a dolly. It would be easier to get it into the house."

"I can help you. It has handles. You take one side and I'll take the other."

He opened his eyes a little wide as if she were thinking big. Larkin pulled it to the edge of the tailgate and positioned it so they could each pick up a side. As he slid his side down, he wondered if she would be able to handle the weight. He was surprised, because she kept up to him all the way to the deck and up the steps to the back door. When they got that far, they had to set it down. She said, "Lets' take a rest."

"Okay, Dear." He smiled.

"I'll open the door," she said, but Harry had seen them and came to the rescue.

"I'll hold that for you two."

"Thanks, Harry," they chimed in unison. They looked at each other and smiled. Picking it up, they started down the stairs. Larkin went first so he could absorb the weight as it came down. In fact, after she got to the second step, she sat her end down and said, "Why don't you just let it slide all the way down, Larkin?"

"Good idea." The box was wide enough it went from stair to stair without as much as a bump. When he got down to the last one he said to Sally, "Go get the rabbit ears while I unpack this. I left it in the front seat."

"Okay."

She scrambled back up the stairs and told Harry (who was waiting at the top to go down) to go and see the new TV. When she got to the truck, Sally thought she saw someone looking through the fence at her from the other side. The street lights shone behind whoever was there, revealing a ghost like figure. She called out loudly, "Who's there?" No one answered, but the image moved away. She quickly grabbed the rabbit ears, locked the doors to the truck and ran back in, and with purpose, locked the back door behind her.

When she finally got to the basement, Larkin had the TV out of the box. She came up to him and said, "There was someone out there spying on me."

"You mean on "us?""

"Yeah, you're probably right- on *us*. Does that happen often?"

"More often than I'd like. I've had to warn them to stay away more than once before."

Harry overheard all of this. He didn't say a thing. He just wished they would leave Larkin alone. So did Larkin.

Harry and Sally looked at the instructions to the Hitachi. Larkin took the packaging and put it back in the box. The Styrofoam made it sturdy like a table. It was the first time he had ever seen anything packaged in Styrofoam before. He then went into the kitchen for the duct tape. Wrapping the box all back up again, he placed it across from the sofa. Then, carefully, he sat the TV on it. Sally said, "I was wondering what you were going to set that on. Not too pretty, but good thinking, Honey."

"Thank you, Dear." They all laughed at his makeshift table.

Sally unpackaged the rabbit ears and sat it on top of the new TV. Larkin found the two screws the ears attached to on the back and placed the leads in them. Then he plugged in the TV and gave it a minute to warm up on the vacation mode per the instructions before turning on the TV itself. Sally said, "Can I do it?"

Larkin looked at Harry smiled and then said, "Sure, Dear."She pulled the knob out. It came on immediately and the three looked at each other in amazement.

"Hey, it came on fast. No warming up and great picture," said Harry.

"Told you so," said Larkin.

"No you didn't," retorted Sally.

They both just laughed at each other and gave each other a kiss. Harry said, "Just in time for the news." Harry sat down in his wife's chair and began to watch. Larkin and Sally just looked at each other with fear as if to say, "Oh no! How often will he be here watching TV now?" Were they about to lose their privacy? They worried needlessly. When the news was over Harry got up and said, "I think I'll go upstairs. I can watch TV anytime. It's time for bed." He winked at Sally. "Good night, Kids."

"Good night, Harry," replied Sally.

Larkin picked up the instruction manual and began to read. He found out it had a UHF dial too. He didn't know if any of the channels in D.C. broadcast in UHF so he had to find that out.

When he finished he said, "I gotta admit, it is a nice set."

"Yeah it is. You did good." She patted him on the head.

She wasn't going to hold his shopping faux pas against him forever.

They sat and watched TV until the channels signed off at midnight. Then they fell asleep with the test pattern on the screen. Larkin woke to the sound of something at the back door. By then the TV screen was broadcasting snow, but gave off enough light for him to see to walk to the stairs. He looked up and saw the silhouette of a man at the door. It looked familiar. It wasn't a man. It was a woman! The same woman who had been looking at him in the snowstorm! He ran up the stairs as fast as he could, but to no avail. When he looked out, she was gone! Sally came to the bottom of steps wondering what all the commotion was about. "What are you doing, Larkin?"

"There was a woman at the door looking down the stairs. I know I've seen her before, but I couldn't make out who it was again."

"A woman, huh? Think it was Pilar or Ellie?"

"Ellie wouldn't do anything like that, but Pilar; that is a possibility. Wait a minute-her dad is a Mason, too. I wonder?"

"You never know. I think we should get a dead bolt put on the door and a curtain. What do you think?"

"We can get the curtain tomorrow and call a locksmith, too. Let's go to bed. She won't be back tonight."

They took their respective places, he in his bed and she on the couch. He hated making her do that, but it was the right thing to do, even if their human natures wanted otherwise.

In the morning, Larkin went upstairs and told Harry what had occurred the night before. He apologized to him saying, "Harry, I am so sorry that I have brought this evil upon you.

I never knew they would be this disturbed by my actions here. I guess I'm getting close to something and somehow they have found out about my project and success at the Smithsonian. But, who is it?"

Harry and Larkin looked at each other and at the same time said, "Applebaum!"

"Do you think so, Harry?"

"I don't know Larkin, but he seems the logical choice."

"But his family hates the Masons and KKK."

"I know, because he's Jewish. But, who else? How about Stoughton?"

"No, he's my friend."

Larkin paused, thought of another name but didn't say it, and finally said, "I'd like to get a dead bolt put on your door, Harry. Would that be okay?"

"Do it, Larkin."

"I'll call today. And I think Sally and I will get some type of shade for the window, too."

"Okay."

"I'll try to make this place as safe as I can for us, Harry. In fact, we may even stay somewhere else if it gets too dangerous here. Know what I mean?"

"I do. Whatever you think is necessary, Larkin. I don't want anything to happen to any of us."

"Me either. I'm going to wake Sally up. Talk to you later, Harry."

Larkin went back down to the basement. Going in by the sofa, he sat down next to Sally. She opened her eyes and smiled. He bent over, gave her a kiss and said, "Wake up sleepy head. Let's go shopping. Only this time, you're in charge!"

"Glad to see you woke up on the right side of the bed, Honey!"

She got dressed in front of him as usual and went to the bathroom to spruce up. He didn't think anything was ever going to change with that. Unfortunately, he was starting to get used to it and it didn't bother him as much. It seemed to never bother her. He got dressed in his room and when she was ready they headed out the door. He said as they left, "I called a locksmith that Harry recommended and he said he'd come over today. Harry's going to let him in and get us each a key."

"Good. Last night gave me the willies, even if it was a woman."

They got in the truck and headed over to Sears. She thought they had the best curtains. At least that was where she had bought hers. On the way Larkin asked her a question, "Say Sally, I have something to ask you."

"You're not going to propose to me in my truck, are you? It's not too romantic and you promised it would be romantic."

"NO. No. I'm not going to propose. But, I do want to know if you'd like to stay in the Hay-Adams over the Christmas Holiday with me?"

"*Really? The Hay-Adams?*"

"Yes. If you do, I'll arrange it."

"I do and *I'll* arrange it."

"Oh that's right. You'll arrange it. We'll both try to take a week off of work. That won't be a problem for you will it?"

"No. I usually just sit there anyway, because Mr. Shipley takes the last two weeks of the year off to use up his vacation time."

"Then there should be no problem for you to do the same. Let's try to book it from Christmas to New Years. Oh, and- two beds! And, Merry Christmas."

She looked over at him, started to cry and said, "I was wrong, Larkin. You can be romantic in a truck." He laughed at her and reached over to give her a peck on the cheek. She said wiping her eyes, "Thank you, Honey."

Chapter 16

The Theft

Sally bought the shade for the door window and all of the downstairs windows. Sears had it all. Larkin was amazed at how quickly she accomplished this, especially her knowing what would be needed for the hardware to hang them. Unfortunately, he found out *he'd* have to hang them, with Sally's assistance of course! They went home with their purchase to find that they were locked out, because the locksmith had already completed the job. They knocked on the door and Harry came to let them in with a smile. They noticed that he had to open the lock with a key on the inside. Larkin thought that was smart. "Thanks for letting us in, Harry. That was smart of him to install it so that you have to have a key to open the dead bolt from the inside."

"Yes. That way if it is locked, they can't just smash the window and come in. Of course, that only works if you remove the key." He took the key out of the lock and handed it to Larkin.

They came in with the sacks from Sears and Sally opened one of them to show Harry. "Do you like the color, Harry?" she asked. It was a light brown.

"Pretty safe, I'd say. Yes, its fine, Sally."

"I stayed with a man's color."

"Good thinking."

Spending the rest of the day borrowing tools from Harry and putting up the shades, the two saw how easy it was for them to work as a team. They got along well and the job turned out great. Larkin was pleased with the results. More importantly, so was Sally.

They sat down at the table to take a coffee break. Sally remarked, "I've been off of work for so long, I'm not looking forward to going back on Monday. You still have an out," she said pointing at his cast.

"But, I still have to go to school. It won't be easy on the bus."

"You'll make do. You get around pretty well on that thing."

"Oh yeah, I do. You know, I'm going to need to have a suit made to fit it for Christmas. I better call that tailor I used. What the heck was his name? I'll have to look."

"Wasn't he down in Foggy Bottom?"

"Yeah, but how did you know that?"

"I looked in your closet. The tag is still on one of the sport coats, which you still haven't worn."

"You looked in my closet?"

"Girls *always* look in guys' closets."

"Oh. Then go see what his name is so I can call him!" He pointed at the bedroom.

"Okay. Okay!" Sally got up and ran to the bedroom. In a flash she was back with the tag.

She handed it to Larkin and he read the red tag. Stephen was his name.

"Oh yeah, Stephen. I'll call him right now. I have a feeling he'll be there." Sure enough, Stephen was there. Larkin explained the situation and asked if he remembered him.

Stephen said, "Sure I remember you; 38 tall-slim with a 30 waist and 32 inseam. Yeah."

"Do you have anything that would work?"

"Sure do. Can I ask how big the cast is?"

"About ten inches in diameter. Right leg. Up about eight inches from the bottom."

"I can have one ready by Monday afternoon. It'll be a hundred bucks though. It's a pretty nice suit."

"You got it. I'll come over after school. Thanks."

"See ya, Larkin."

They hung up. "That was easy. He's a pretty good man."

"At least you'll be ready with a suit for Christmas at Shipley's."

"Speaking of which, I want to go all out while we are at the Hay-Adams. Let's dress up the whole time we are there. Okay?"

"Sounds good, Honey. I better call and get a room first don't you think?"

"Oh, yeah. Call then." He pointed at the phone.

She ran over to the phone, looked in the phone book and dialed. Someone answered and said, "The Hay-Adams. May I help you?"

"Yes. I'd like to book a room for the week of Christmas through New Years."

"Have you ever stayed with us before, Madam?"

"No."

"Well, I'm sorry, but we are all full for that week."

She got an unhappy look and mouthed, "They're full," at Larkin. He motioned for her to give him the phone. "Hello Henry, is that you?"

"Sir? With whom am I speaking?"

"This is Larkin Palmer. You say there are no rooms available for the holidays?"

"As a matter of fact, Sir, there is one, but it has two queen beds. Would that be sufficient, Sir?"

"Two beds. Indeed Henry, it would be perfect. Book the days for us would you?"

"Yes, Sir. Will you be having a guest sir?"

"Yes, Henry, my fiancé."

"It will be good to see you again, Sir."

"You as well." Larkin hung up.

She lit up and said, "Your fiancé?"

"I only said that to be more proper. They don't put up with shenanigans at the Hay-Adams. I'm not going to propose today. It's just not romantic in my basement apartment you know."

Sally changed the subject and said, "So you know the people at the Hay-Adams, huh?"

Feeling pretty cocky and showing that she wasn't the only one who could pull strings he said, "Yup."

Larkin turned and walked back toward the kitchen asking, "Want another cup of coffee?"

"Yes, Honey," was all that she replied.

They watched the new TV that afternoon and into the evening. Before it got too late, she called Mrs. Heidelmann to arrange meeting her at her church. She said to Sally, "I was afraid you had forgotten and weren't going to go with me, Sally."

"Oh, we had not forgotten. We just got busy with some housekeeping things for Larkin. I had to whip his place into shape. You know these men."

"Yes, I do. My dear, Herman, was just as bad. So, I'll see you before the service begins?"

"Yes. We'll meet you in the narthex about fifteen minutes before. Is that okay?"

"Yes, that is perfect. See you there, Dear."

"Goodnight, Mrs. Heidelmann."

After hanging up, she went over to see what Larkin was reading. Larkin had the habit to read the Word before he went to bed on Saturday night. He wished he'd remember to read it all of the rest of the week, like his pastor urged the people to do, but he at least always prayed every day and he'd read the Bible in the mornings; sometimes. Sitting down next to him Sally asked, "What are you reading?"

"It's the passage where Jesus asks Peter if he loves him. Do you know which one I mean?"

"I think so. Is it where he uses a different Greek word each time for love?"

Larkin was pleased with her knowledge and answered, "Yes. It made me think. How do you "love" me Sally? Is it more than just our desire for each other or do you truly, which word did He use, oh yeah, "Agape", do you "Agape" me?"

Not even trying to tease him or make a joke, she became very serious and said, "Honey, I truly Agape you."

"I Agape you too, Dear." He set his Bible down and she snuggled into him. They again fell asleep on the couch, not really knowing what they had just said to one another, but it didn't matter, because they meant it.

They met Mrs. Heidelmann in the narthex just as they had planned. She was very happy to see them and introduced them to her friends along the way as they took their seat in the fourth row from the front. Sally was a little uncomfortable with that seat, but it didn't matter to Larkin. His family always sat toward the front. The pastor came from the sacristy and bowed in front of the altar. He greeted the congregation by saying, "Peace be with you."

The congregation replied, "And also with you."

"I would like to welcome you all this morning, especially our visitors. May you be blessed by our worship today. Our service begins on page one hundred fifty-eight of our hymnal."

The service began and Larkin found it to be much more formal than what he was used to. That didn't bother him and in fact the theological meaning of each portion of it made the whole thing refreshing to him. He could see how it all came together as it was explained with quotations in the hymnal as they went along. The pastor's message was doctrinally sound, he thought, with both the law and the gospel being presented in a way that left him feeling up and not beat up like his church at home. It was like he had discovered, "grace." He was very happy; relieved, comforted, and reassured. The congregation did not celebrate communion that day. The final hymn was "How Great Thou Art". Larkin whispered to Sally, "This is my favorite hymn."

When it was all over, they were ushered out from the front. Larkin liked that because they were some of the first to get out and shake the pastor's hand. He said to them, "I'm glad to see two young people with you today, Mrs. Heidelmann. Who might they be?" She introduced them and he asked, "Are there to be plans for a wedding?"

Larkin blushed and said, "Not yet Pastor Olsen. But, do you offer pre-marital counseling?"

The pastor was happy when he asked this and said, "Why, yes. If you ever want to know more about us, our beliefs and how we practice marriage, just call me at the office. I'd be happy to talk to you."

"Oh Pastor, I do have one question for you now. How does your Lutheran Church feel about Freemasonry?"

"It is not usually condoned. They are secret society und das ist verboten."

"Gut. Ich versteh." That meant there were probably no Masons in the church.

Pastor Olsen winked and said, "If you'd like to talk about that subject I have a good tract the LCMS put out called, "What to say to the Freemasons", from CPH.

"Thanks, Pastor." Larkin smiled at that one. If Pastor Olsen only knew...

Sally smiled and took his arm at this point and they said goodbyes to Pastor Olsen. Larkin helped Mrs. Heidelmann down the many stairs to the church and said to her, "Thank you for allowing us to worship with you today. It was very nice and the pastor's message spoke to me."

She corrected him and said, "God spoke to you today, Larkin. Thank you for coming and please come with me again. Maybe on, say, Christmas Eve?"

Sally knew she had no family so Sally said, "We will, Mrs. Heidelmann."

"Goodbye, Sally and Larkin." She walked toward her 1949 Buick parked by the curb.

They watched her leave, standing arm in arm. Larkin said, "It was nice of you to say we would go with her on Christmas Eve. I thought you'd want to reserve that for us."

"She has no family and I have always liked candle-light services. Don't you?"

"I do. The one here must be spectacular."

"I have heard they go all out. The children's choir is the best around."

"Well, we will have to get up early to prepare for lunch at the bosses'."

"I know. It will be no problem. It won't be that late."

The next morning Sally got up real early to go home and get ready for work. She told Larkin she would probably be spending more time at home during the week now that she had to be back at "the grind stone" once again. But, she said she was grateful for the opportunity to do what she had during the storm. In fact, she said if it weren't for the storm, they probably wouldn't be together. She said she'd always call it, "The Love Storm."

Larkin said, "You're goofy."

"Are you leaving for school soon?"

"Yeah, the bus leaves in a half hour, so I had better get going."

She gave him a kiss and left. He got dressed and went out to the bus stop. He was getting used to public transportation. Heck, Harry had done it for years. It was good enough for him! However, Harry did complain from time to time. It was, "The bus was late. The bus was early, or cold, or too full." Maybe Larkin should think about his assessment of the bus a little more?

After the bus dropped him off at UMD, he went over to check his grade first. He was right about the test because he *had* aced it. Smiling, he walked toward the class room. His professor looked up and waved at him. As no one else was there, Larkin sat down and the professor came over to him. He asked, "How did you weather the storm?"
Larkin pointed to his ankle cast and said, "Not very well I'm afraid."
"What did you break, Larkin?"
"My ankle. It still has to stay on a couple more months."
"Well, at least you'll have the Christmas break to relax."
"That's what I have been thinking and the cancellation of school after Thanksgiving for the weather helped a bit, too."
Some students began to file in, so the Professor said, "I'll catch up to you later."

The class lecture was on material he had already read and it was nothing new for him. He had started to daydream a while before the bell rang. As it was his only class for the day, he decided to take the bus over to work and surprise Sally. He also wanted to see something at his office.

When he arrived at the Castle, he was welcomed by Jim, the guard, who was always friendly. Larkin decided to stop in and see Harry first. Harry was unusually busy due to the effects of the storm, but was "digging out" of it, so to speak. Larkin waved "Hi" to him and Harry put his hand over the receiver of the phone and whispered, "I thought you weren't going to come in? Can't stay away, huh?" Harry resumed his conversation and Larkin just nodded "yes" as he waved and walked over to the elevator. Getting on, he went down to B-102.

Unlocking the door, he turned on the light and walked to his desk. Everything seemed the same just as he'd left it. Or was it? Somehow, someway, he could tell that something *was* different. Like, someone had gone through his "stuff." He couldn't place it though and he sat down. He wanted to see one of the other documents that he had; one that pertained to Pike; one that Seward had placed in the file; one that might just give him a clue to, well, a clue to the key. He looked through the pile once. He thought he must have missed it. Then, he looked again. No, it wasn't there. Then he looked one more time and still found nothing! Now he knew what was missing! The document about Pike! Someone had been in his office and stolen the original document! Thank goodness that Sally had made copies of it. One set for the Secretary and one set for Larkin at home. Thank goodness! Why he didn't just look at his copy at home, he didn't know. But now he knew someone didn't want him to know about the clue. Who? Was it the person he didn't suggest to Harry at the house? *Was it- Mrs. Westfall?* He got up from his desk, locked the door and went to see Harry again. This time he was off the phone. He said to him, "Harry, someone has stolen one of the Seward documents off of my desk."

"How do you know, Larkin?"

"I know. It had to do with Pike. Thank goodness Sally made a copy. I'll just have to look at it again. But, we have another problem then don't we, Harry?"

"Yes- security. I'll have to contact the Secretary and see if he wants to place the collection under guard."

"I think that would be wise. I'll get it all together. Just let me know where to take it, okay?"

"Will do."

Harry picked up the phone and called the Secretary's office. "Sally, is Mr. Shipley available?"

"No, Harry, I'm sorry, he is in a meeting. Can I give him a message?"

"Yes. There has been a breach in security. Someone has stolen one of the Seward documents from Larkin's office."

"Is Larkin here?"

"Yes. Have the Secretary call me about it, would you? I'll call the head of security in the mean time."

"Will do, Harry." Sally smiled when she heard that Larkin had come into work. She went to the Seward file that she had copied for Larkin and removed it from the file cabinet. She wondered which document was missing. If she had to guess- anything to do with Pike!

Larkin cleaned up his desk and put everything into files. It took him almost an hour, but it was something he should have been doing anyway. Then he put all of the documents in numerical order into a pocket file with draw strings so nothing could fall out. His desk was now void of anything. In fact it looked like he didn't work there. He sat back down and looked at the list of documents to see which one was missing. It was number 37, named- Pike! Larkin's phone rang. It was the Secretary. "Hello, Larkin. I'm glad to hear you were able to come into work today, but I don't want you to do anything that would be difficult while you have the cast on your foot. Understand?"

"Yes, Sir."

"I hear from Sally that we have had a breach of security and a document has been stolen. If that is the case, I want the rest of the collection under lock and key with security. I'm glad you insisted that copies of all of them were made right away. What concerns me is: why would someone want just *one* of the documents? Are you onto something that you have not told me about?"

Larkin had not planned on telling him about what he had found at the Temple, but he knew he must. When, was another matter. "No sir, nothing that would cause a theft. And what makes you think that anything I do here would cause someone to steal?"

That question caught Mr. Shipley off guard. He didn't know what to say except, "I think we need to speak in person. Please come to my office and bring the file with you, Larkin."

"Yes, Sir." Larkin wondered what had brought this on and what it meant.

He got in the elevator and went up. Harry had obviously not spoken with Mr. Shipley because as Larkin walked by he saw the file and said, "Where are you going with the file, Larkin?"

"I just spoke with Mr. Shipley. He wants it in his office."

When he got to the Secretary's office, Sally eyes lit up and she said to him, "Hello. Why did you come in today, Larkin?"

"Just to see you, Sally," he replied smiling.

"Liar. I know you came in to work."

Smiling, laughing, and walking toward Mr. Shipley's door he said, "Caught me!"

"Go ahead on in. He's waiting for you."

Larkin opened the door file in hand, and went in. Shipley said, "Have a seat, Son. Larkin, the reasons I have not released the information that you have revealed are very complex. Many deal with current events and politics in our day. To not consider them when making a decision of this magnitude would be an error. I wanted to wait until Christmas to tell you of my decision, as a gift. I was going to tell you that we were going to go all out and release your findings to the world. But now, after this development, I know that would have been a mistake." Larkin started to say something in protest but Shipley waved his hand and said, "Hear me out Larkin, please."

Shipley got up and walked around and sat on the corner of his desk. "I know, yes, I know where the document has disappeared to. No, not its exact location, but I surmise that those it pertained to were the ones who have it. Yes, I know it's the Masons. And I know how they play the game. Sometimes they use slander. I also know that your life may be in danger. Not to mention Sally as your companion. So, for the time being, I suggest we go underground on this project. The originals shall be under lock and key with security. You will work off your copies. I shall keep my set here in my office under lock and key. I'll have Sally make a copy of the missing document to place in the originals file until such time as it is found and returned. Any questions?"

"When you say "underground", what do you mean?"

"You will work only at home and it will be perceived that you have completed the research. I will make an announcement to that effect at the next directors meeting. When you have everything completely wrapped up, no matter how long it takes you, I'll then make the announcement to the world that Lincoln was killed in a conspiracy by the Freemasons of both the North and the South."

"Will I still be paid?"

"Yes, by me personally."

"I can't ask you to do that, Sir. I have means."

"I was not aware of that, Larkin. Regardless, I *want* to do that."

"Thank you, Sir."

"Any other questions?"

"Just one, Sir." Mr. Shipley didn't respond, but just waited.

"Did you pay half of my tuition for the year?"

"Yes, Son."

Larkin got up and said, "It has been nice working with you, Sir!" He winked.

"Same here, Larkin. See you on Christmas Day."

Larkin went out of Shipley's office and Larkin sat across from Sally. She was waiting for him to say something- and waiting. Her eyes grew larger and larger. Finally, Larkin burst out laughing. She said, "If you don't tell me what Mr. Shipley said I'm going to hit you, Larkin Palmer!"

"He fired me."

"What!?"

"Well, in effect he did. I'm never to come back. I'm going to work underground."

"You mean at home?"

"That's what I mean. Did you get the time off for Christmas?"

"Yup. No problem."

The door to Shipley's office started to open. Larkin got up and mouthed to her, "I'll talk to you later."He made his way out of the room and down the stairs. Then he went out the front door to the bus stop.

Chapter 17

The Warning

When he had returned home, Larkin tried out the new key Harry had given him. He couldn't believe he had not tried it already. It worked just fine. Going downstairs, he took out his home file and looked for document number thirty-seven. That's when it hit him. That same eerie feeling he had when he went into B-102- like someone had been in his stuff. He thought, 'Oh no. "They" couldn't have been here too!' He opened the file. Sure enough- it was gone! He went for the phone, but stopped. There placed by the phone was an envelope addressed to him. He opened it and read, "We know what you know. Don't try to go any farther. If you do- she will die." He thought, 'How could they know what I know? They must have watched me. No, the pad! I wrote it down. How stupid! They know exactly what I know! And that's why they let me read Pikes' Morals and Dogma. But wait a minute! How did they know that this particular document, number thirty-seven, had that information? Because, they had *all of them! Someone had given them everything I had!* Who could be the traitor? Who could be the leak in security? Was it Harry? Was it Shipley? Or even worse, was it Stoughton? Or, like I suspected, was it Mrs. Westfall?' He really didn't know who he could trust in this vast maze of Masonic activity! He called Sally. "Sally, open the file of copied documents and see if number thirty-seven is there."

"Why, Larkin?"

"Just do it!"

"Okay," she said, startled at his tone with her. She came back and said, "Yes, Larkin it's here. But, why?"

"Someone got into my apartment and stole my copy, too."

"But, how? You just got the new locks!"

"Make two copies and bring me one after work would you? And from now on, you are staying with me. I don't want you to be alone."

"What do I do with the other one?"

"Put one in the original file for Mr. Shipley."

"Okay. See you after work."

Larkin wondered what to do with this new letter. Should he destroy it so Sally would not see? Would it scare her? She didn't need to see it, but he needed it for another confrontation.

He thought the one with the sergeant would be the last while he lived in D.C. This one would take care of them all! Suddenly, he panicked and went to the bedroom to look for the suitcase. It was still there. Pulling it out from under the bed he opened it faster than he ever had. It had not been touched. But that didn't change a thing; it was time to see the Commander...

He went up the steps and looked outside. There she was, the ever present shadow, standing beside the same trees. Larkin made sure she saw him and he took his finger and motioned for her to come to him. At first, the figure hid behind the trees. Then seeing that Larkin knew she was there, she came forward. He somehow recognized the walk and the stature of the woman. Then he knew who it was- Pilar! Before she got there, he could tell she was hesitant to continue. She began to chicken out stopping and starting up several times. He thought she might run, so he just yelled out, "Tell him we need to meet." She stopped in her tracks. She nodded, turned, and walked away. Within five minutes the phone rang. He answered, "Hello?"

"The Commander will see you at the Temple at nine tomorrow morning. Be there."

He was not intimidated by the tone and Larkin recognized the voice and replied, "I will, Dean."

Sally got home about an hour after Larkin got the call. She knocked and Larkin came to let her in. She was terribly upset and as soon as she got inside she started to cry. He took her in his arms and hugged hard. Before she could say anything he said, "I have a meeting with the Commander at nine."

"Really? What will that accomplish?"

"It will put all this game-playing to rest. Now that I am the Keeper, I go through this harassment all the time. There may be more of "them" here, and "they" may not all know me, but the buck stops at the top. So, if I tell him to make it stop, it *will* stop."

"I saw the name of the Commander on a picture in the Temple. It's McPherson."

"Thanks. I might need that. Let's go downstairs and have some coffee."

They walked down the steps and into the kitchen where he had just made a fresh pot. She sat down in her chair with a thud. She said, "This "Eraser" stuff can really be draining, can't it?"

"You can never really imagine until you have lived it. I'm sorry to have pulled you into it."

"I guess I'm in it for life then. No matter how long that is."

Larkin felt his pocket to see if the warning letter was still there. He picked up their coffee cups and sat hers down in front of her. "Thanks," she said.

"Did you bring the document?"

"Yes, I did everything you told me to. Here is yours."

She unfolded it and placed it on the table. He read it and said, "This doesn't make any sense. All it talks about are things I already know about Pike. I'll have to read it a few more times." He sat it back down and asked, "Are you hungry?"

"I'm starving."

"How about a pizza? I'll order out."

"Yes. Pepperoni!"

"Pepperoni it is!"

The delivery boy knocked on the back door and Larkin went up to let him in. It took a few seconds and Larkin finally got it open because of the new key. The key didn't work as well this time. The boy seemed nervous and Larkin could sense it. He asked him, "Is there something wrong?"

"Well, there's some guy in a blue suit watching the place from across the street. There, over by the trees."

"Oh, him. Well, don't worry about him. Here's a twenty. Keep the change."

The boy got a funny look on his face, but then said, "Wow. Thanks!"

Larkin went down with the pizza after locking up and said to Sally, "The guy in the blue suit is back."

"What guy in the blue suit?"

"Oh yeah, you don't know about him. When I first got to town, he followed me for a while. Then one day, I got behind him and followed him. You should have seen it. It was so funny. When we finally spoke, I told him to tell the Commander that I was just here to go to school and work. Obviously, my work is getting to them and they are getting scared."

"Obviously."

He picked up the document again and read it as he took a slice of pizza from the box. He asked Sally, "How do they keep it this hot in the cold weather?"

She just looked at him and smiled as she picked up a piece for herself, and didn't respond as he began to read it again.

By the time he was done with the slice he had gone over it a couple more times. It was just a description of Pike himself from a member of the Masons. Then, his eyes lit up. "Sally! I think this is it! Listen, "Pike was known, not only for his expertise in the occultist art, for which he wrote many volumes of incantations, retractions, and other works, but also as a Satanist and possessed a ring in which he could summon the devil himself.""
"What?"
"It's not a key to a door. It's a key to a book; a book of retractions; that removes spells and curses! That's the key!"
"Oh, my goodness. If they find the key to remove the curse, they could kill you with no fear!"
"Exactly. I have to find out where it is- first!"

Sally began to cry. Larkin got up and pulled her from her seat, giving her a hug. "Don't worry. We're the best team out there. We'll find it first and they will have nothing over us. Besides, I have the "gift". " Losing their appetites, they didn't finish their pizza, but instead, went to sit on the sofa. He clicked on the TV first and sat down holding her in his arms. He thought about Pilar and Ellie. It really bothered him. They were obvious plants to work "undercover" so to speak. He was disappointed in Pilar, who seemed the ultimate Judas to him, trying to tempt him with her body. And Ellie, she was sent to tempt him with her wealth and all things worldly. "They" thought they had it covered didn't they? But God had different ideas. He had sent Sally. They watched TV for a while and that was where they fell asleep.

Larkin woke and got up to go to the bathroom. He washed up, put on his clothes, got something out of his suitcase, went into the living room, and turned up the TV to see what the temperature was. It had been a cold beginning to winter in Washington, D.C.. Sally sat up, rubbed her eyes, and asked, "What time is it?"
"It's almost time for me to go."
"Do you need to take The Eraser?"
"Oh no. You *never* do that. They could take it from me and that would be that. It always has to remain behind with someone you can trust to protect you in case they take the Keeper hostage. In fact, my Dear," he handed her a slip of paper, "here is a list of the people I think will be with me. I'm glad you spotted McPherson's name."

"Does this mean what I think it means?"

"Yes, it does. You will be home with this list and The Eraser."

"That's what I thought it meant. I don't know if I can do that, Larkin."

He took her face into his hands. "Didn't know what you were getting into by falling in love with a Palmer did you?"

"Sure didn't."

"Second thoughts?"

"No. I'm just worried about *you.*"

He laughed and said, "You sound like my mom. But, she knows, like all of the wives before, we do what we have to do. It's, well, just part of us. But I'd sure like to change it. With the key there might just be a way. But first, we have to find it. They must not have it at their libraries, or they would not be after me. So, where could it be?"

"Excuse me Honey, nature calls."

Sally got up and went to the bathroom while Larkin picked up the mess on the kitchen table. The pizza was cold and hard as a rock, so he just threw it out. He looked at his watch- time to leave. Sally came back into the kitchen with him. She had been looking at the list while in the bathroom. She sat it on the table. Larkin took The Eraser out of his pocket and sat it beside her and the list. He said, "If I'm not home in two hours, start with the name on the top and proceed in order. If I'm not here, presume I'm dead."

She sat down and shook her head. Looking up at him she said, "Come home to me, Honey."

"I will; God willing."

"I'll pray. All this other stuff is of the devil. We can't let them win."

He smiled, patted her on the head and said, "That's my girl. You already have the Palmer spirit!"

"I'll pray the whole time you are gone, Honey. I'll do what needs to be done."

He gave her a kiss and said, "Thanks."He walked toward the door and then on to the bus stop.

After Larkin left, Harry called down to Sally, "Sally, where did Larkin go?"

She yelled up, "To see the Commander!"

"Oh. Why?"

"They got in here somehow and stole his copy of document number thirty-seven. He says he has to put a stop to it.
 Will you pray, Harry?"

"I will. Let me know when he gets back."

"I pray he *does!*"

As always, the bus was on time. Larkin was glad, because the outside temperature was only 10 degrees Fahrenheit. Just as he got on, the man in the blue suit got on in the back. He looked cold. Larkin turned in his seat and waved. The man just looked straight ahead and rubbed his hands together in the warmth of the bus, which really wasn't very warm. They arrived at the Temple in less than ten minutes. On the way he wondered what he'd have to do and how he'd use his arsenal of Palmer weapons in their conversation. After he arrived, he walked up the steps to the to the door, one by one, with his cast following the good foot all the way, up, slide, up, slide, but he found he was 10 minutes early. The man in the blue suit went toward the back of the Temple to another entrance. Dean came to the door to let him in. When he opened it, billows of steam formed as the inside air mixed with the frigid air coming in with him. It gave Larkin the impression he was walking into the gates of Hell. Indeed, he was.

Dean wasted no time taking him to the Commander. Rather than to an office, he took him into the main entrance of the meeting hall or if it were a church, the narthex. Dean bowed when McPherson met them and left the two alone. The Commander, dressed in his Masonic robe, spoke first. "Larkin Palmer, "the Keeper". I have heard of you and your family for years. I never thought I'd be the one to finally rid us of your menacing presence."

Larkin smiled and said, "Nice to meet you, too. Before you get too confident, Commander McPherson, I know what you know," he pulled out his first weapon, his words, and said, "Let's not play games any longer. I thought you'd get the message from the man in the blue suit and the sergeant. Obviously you think document thirty-seven changes everything. But only for the person that finds it first. You know I have the Chase- Palmer gift. So guess who's *going* to find the Key? Oh- I'll leave you with one last thing to think about, if you have the power in D.C. you think you have, call them ALL OFF until I'm finished with school. Then, I will be out of your hair."

Larkin started to walk away, but McPherson stopped him, "You saw our letter yesterday, Palmer. She will die."

Larkin stopped and slowly turned around. His blood began to boil as he pulled out the weapon he knew he needed and as he became angry, he shoved his clenched fist out in front of him and shouted, his voice echoing throughout the grand hall, "No more threats. What did I just tell you? At this very moment *she holds your life in her hands! She is at home with a list and The Eraser!"*

McPherson turned as white as a ghost. Slowly he said with clenched teeth, "You have until you graduate, because that is the day when all our fury will be unleashed."

Larkin turned and quickly walked out of the Temple. He said out loud smiling as he hit the cold winter air outside, "So, I *am* famous!" He shivered. He had won another battle, for a time, but he knew he had to find the key!

He didn't want to wait for the bus right in front of the Temple, so he walked down a block to the next stop. He sat down and shivered again, not so much from the cold, but from the realization that God had been with him in his hour of need. Being inside the house of his adversaries, in the midst of evil, he felt the prayers of Sally and Harry. He said out loud, "Thank you, Lord!"

The Key was all he could think about on the bus ride back to Harry's.

Under his breath he said slowly out loud, "The key is in the book." Where was the Key? What was it called? Was it a book? Or was it maybe a pamphlet? Was it in a library someplace? Where would Masons hide such a thing? Or did they hide it? So many questions! He took out his watch to check the time. He had just been gone an hour and the only thing that had really kept him from getting home earlier was the bus schedule. They really needed more buses in D.C..

Watching out the window of the bus, he began to daydream again. He closed his eyes. They traveled past all of the row houses of the same size, each one allowing the sun through in flashes as it rose slowly in the east, making his eyes see the blood in his eyelids as it went by. It reminded him of what he had just gone through at the Temple- seeing red that is!

Looking at the row houses again, he thought it was a good idea the city planners had excluded high rises from D.C.. It gave the place character, and high prices. But it didn't matter, because he didn't think he'd make it his permanent home anyway. Not at this rate! He wanted away from this evil. He wished he were back home. He missed his family and the orchard, too. Even the cows! He did have one thought though, 'Sally and I need to get out and learn more about this town, and now that we'll have a little more freedom to move around, we can do that'. He was so glad God had sent her to him. They arrived at his stop and he pulled the cord. Getting out, he took a step onto the sidewalk smiling, because he knew God was in control!

He went to the back door and took out his key. Sticking it in, he started to open it and he could hear Sally running up the steps to the door. He pulled it open and she burst through the door jumping into his arms, legs flying around his waist. She gave him a big kiss and said, "Oh Larkin, I'm so glad you're home."

"I told you I'd be back. We have nothing to worry about until…"he stopped in mid-sentence.

"Until what?" Sally asked, still hanging by his waist.

"Until I graduate. We have until then to find the key. And, or maybe, get out of D.C.".

She hopped down to the landing. He pulled her toward him and held her by her waist. "I could feel the Lord's power as I confronted him in the hall. I'm sure your prayers helped. As I walked to the bus stop I could only think of Romans chapter eight, verse thirty-one, "If God be for us, who can be against us?" He is always with us, Dear." She nodded, gave him a kiss, and they walked down the stairs.

Sitting upstairs in his living room, Harry wondered what had happened. He just had to know. He went to the back door and yelled down, "Larkin, can I come down?"

"Yes, Harry, I wish you would."

Harry came downstairs and asked, "Well, how did it go?"

"I called his bluff. They won't bother us again until graduation. Then I have to leave D.C.".

"Graduation? You know it won't matter whether you are in D.C. or not. They will come after you anywhere you are."

"The only thing I know for sure is that we have some free time. And the Secretary has given me freedom, too. To continue to work on my project and for me to do what I must. In the meanwhile, Sally and I can take a breather. I think, although they have never kept their word before."

"I know. I'm worried about you. I prayed the whole time you were gone."

"Don't be worried; my God is greater than theirs."

"I know. But I'm just a man."

"Say, Harry. I was thinking, that locksmith, is he by chance a friend in the Masons?"

"Oh yeah. I think I better call another one. We can get a different key made."

"I think that would be the safe bet. I just got a new TV!"

The rest of the day was a good time to just keep out of the cold and rest. Harry invited them up and they made a pot of chili and listened to the TV in the background. Sally went to the fridge and asked Harry, "What have you got to drink, Harry? Larkin doesn't have any beer, and I love beer."

"You love beer, Sally?" replied Harry.

She found some on the shelf, took one out and said, "Good deal. Yes, I love beer. When we lived in Germany, we'd go to all the local Rathauses. Best beer in the world. And the Oktoberfest was the greatest! I loved it. And nothing goes better with chili than beer."

Larkin and Harry looked at each other and smiled. Laughing Larkin said, "Well, next time we go to the store we'll get some for you."

"I gave him his first beer a couple of weeks ago. Can you believe it? His first beer?"

Sally smiled came over by Larkin and put her hand on his shoulder as he sat at the table and said, "Yes, I can believe it. He is so innocent in some ways. And yet, he has done so much I would never have dreamed of." Looking at him in the eyes she said to him, "You are such a complex man, Larkin Palmer."

"Thank you, Sally Britt."

She walked over to the stove, tested the pot of chili and said, "Soups on!"

Larkin smiled and thought of his mom and said, "God truly did send you to me."He got up and walked over to get the bowls from the cabinet. Harry just watched the two as they interacted with each other. It reminded him of himself and his late wife. It was good to see love in his home again, he thought. How he had missed it.

"Say Harry," Larkin said, "I have been meaning to ask you this and I didn't know how to, because it goes against what I have asked you before and what you agreed to." Harry listened intently to his words as he crafted them. "But, last week I asked you if Sally could stay here from time to time. I know it's not the deal you agreed to, and I can pay you more rent if you wish, but, I'd like her to be able to move in with me. Not for reasons others would want, but only for her safety. I just don't trust "them" even now. Would you consider it, Harry?"

This surprised both Harry and Sally. They looked at each other in shock. Harry just said, "I would really like that. You are made for each other and I would love to have you both here. The rent is totally waived. You are like my son."

Larkin almost began to cry. Sally did cry. For two reasons: Harry's statement and Larkin's concern for her. She knew he loved her and this just substantiated it. Larkin said, "Thank you, Harry. We'll give Mrs. Heidelmann notice and move her in the first of the year. But I don't know where we'll put all those fancy clothes!"

Larkin went over and gave Harry a pat on the back and handed him his bowl. Sally went to the fridge and got another two beers out and said, "We need to celebrate!"

Harry said, "Amen!"

As they ate, Larkin and Sally told Harry of their plans to stay at the Hay-Adams for the week of Christmas and New Years. He was also surprised about that and Larkin noticed his eyebrow raise a bit when they told him. So, Larkin reaffirmed what he had told him the morning before, "Remember what I told you about, about Sally and me, Harry? How we have decided to remain pure until our wedding night? Well, this still stands, here, and no matter where we are. I know it's tempting, but with the help of God we will remain strong. We'll have two separate beds there and here, well, we can switch back and forth; maybe one night on the couch and one night in the bed. That way my back won't go out!" They chuckled. Nothing need be said about it anymore. Sally knew Larkin was serious about it and now Harry did, too.

Larkin got up for another bowl of chili and asked, "Anyone else want seconds?"

"I do," replied Sally.

"Not me," said Harry, "I'm ready for a nap. See what I told you about beer and guys over sixty, Larkin?" They all laughed as Harry got up, put his bowl in the sink and said, "Wake me up if I sleep until 5 o'clock. If I sleep more than that, I won't sleep all night."

"Okay, Harry," replied Sally.

Larkin sat her bowl back in front of her. As they began to eat their second bowl, Sally asked him, "Are you sure you want me to move in? I know that will take away a lot of your privacy. I know how important that is to you."

"I've considered it all, Dear. But I know what's more important and that is- you. I couldn't live with myself if anything happened to you. I need you near me. I want you near me."

Sally began to cry again. She wiped the tears from her face after having taken a spoonful of chili to her mouth and she drooled all over herself. It was a messy sight! Larkin laughed and took his napkin to wipe it off her face.

"Schmultzgesicht," he said.

"Ya. Naturlich

Harry's phone rang. Larkin raced over to pick it up. "Hello?"

"Larkin, this is your Dad."Larkin could tell from the tone of his voice that something was wrong, "You need to come home Larkin. It's your Uncle. He's not expected to make it much longer."

"What is it, Dad?"

"It's his heart."

"I'll be there as soon as I can."

"I'll tell your Mom. Bye."

"Bye."

Sally could see there was a problem. "What is it?"

"My Uncle Tom. He's dying. We have to go right away."

"I'll call Mr. Shipley and your counselor at UMD. They will understand I'm sure."

"I'll call the airline and get packed. Then we'll take you over to your place and get some clothes. You are coming with me, aren't you?"

"Why yes, Honey! Why do you ask?"

"I just couldn't tell from your statement about Shipley and Dr. Perkins."

"Oh. Well I was going to include myself, too. But you know this does pose a small problem, don't you?"

"What's that?"

"We will have to tell them about *us*."

"Oh. Yeah. Well, God has His reasons. We just go along for the ride."

He knew his words were true. But what was to come of his trip back home to Brookfield? "They" didn't want him there and their threat was very real. In going home to help place his uncle to rest, to introduce his new love, and telling his parents about his excursions into becoming the Keeper of the cursed Eraser, he knew his life was about to change forever…he just didn't know how much.

----------- To Be Continued -----------

ABOUT THE AUTHOR

C. A. Fiebiger, is a native of Roseville, Minnesota, attended Eastern Montana College in Billings, Montana, now MSU-Billings, receiving his BA in History, with a minor in Philosophy in 1987. He released his first book, The Baker and Malachi, in the summer of 2013.

He currently resides in the Nashville, Tennessee area with his wife Shirreen and daughter Tara. He has two older children, Gary and Candace, and four grandchildren.

Watch for the release of the second book of the series, "The Keeper", soon.

Made in the USA
San Bernardino, CA
24 February 2014